My Side of the World

World

and

Other Tales of Death

A Collection

by

Beka Wueste

Fox Island Press

Praise for Beka Wueste's Writing

<u>"My Side of the World and Other Tales of Death"</u>

"**5 Stars** | Lyrical and thoughtful... a moving, imaginative, and unforgettable exploration."
- Readers' Favorite Book Reviews

"**5 Stars** | An extraordinary collection that redefines how we view mortality... fans of Le Guin, Alice Sebold, or Ray Bradbury will find much to love here."
-San Francisco Book Review

"**5 Stars** | Graceful and empathetic...Wueste's ability to move seamlessly between realism and the fantastical recalls writers like Isabel Allende and Alice Hoffman."
- Manhattan Book Review

"**5 Stars** | Excellent, well-written, and woven together so well... surprising, suspenseful, and chilling stories that are sure to keep readers engrossed from beginning to end."
- Reader Views Book Reviews

"The eight short stories comprising "My Side of the World and Other Tales of Death" clearly showcase author Beka Wueste as an exceptionally talented, impressively imaginative, and engagingly original storyteller. An inherently fascinating and memorable read from cover to cover."
- Midwest Book Review

"Death has never been more alive than in the words of Beka Wueste... whether loved or feared, Wueste's manifestations of death have the power to shape the deeds of the living."
- FH Rexroad, author of The Wizard Realm Saga

<u>"The Unsent Letters of Lucy Prior"</u>

"Wueste's prose seamlessly balances sharp wit, aching nostalgia, and raw honesty. A deeply introspective and emotionally resonant novel."
- Kirkus Reviews

"**5 Stars** | Beka Wueste pens an explosive fictional debut as she captures grief and death in an uncanny way. *The Unsent Letters of Lucy Prior* is an emotional rollercoaster as readers are left changed by the life of Mrs. Prior and the letters she's left in her wake. "
- Reader Views Book Reviews

"A captivating novel that explores a lifetime of love and emotional trauma... a poignant, heartfelt, and provocative read."
-BlueInk Review

"**5 Stars** | Author Beka Wueste weaves an intricate and colorful tapestry of Lucy's life, using an unconventional narrative that invites readers to delve into her most profound feelings and emotions. Lucy's story feels incredibly vivid and authentic, as if it belongs to someone living in the real world."
- Readers' Favorite Book Reviews

<u>"Fireflies in a Jar"</u>
"Original, deftly crafted, emotionally engaging, 'Fireflies in a Jar' showcases author Beka Wueste's genuine flair for the kind of narrative driven storytelling style that raises her novel to an impressive level of literary excellence."
- Midwest Book Review

"**4 Stars** | "A warm, funny, and quietly heartbreaking look at one woman's struggle to see herself as worthy. The beauty of 'Fireflies in a Jar' is how it balances these heavier moments with humor and hope.
- Manhattan Book Review

"**4 Stars** | A true testament to the fact that you can't love others unless you first love yourself... If you love gritty books that prompt transformation, you don't want to miss out on this one."
-Reader Views Book Review

To Dan

I will follow you into the dark

“Life, it is thanks to death that you are precious in
my eyes.”
-Seneca

“What is death? A ‘tragic mask.’ Turn it and examine it.
See, it does not bite.”
-Epictetus

“No, the journey does not end here. Death is just another
path, one that we all must take.”
-Gandalf

An Introduction from the Author

—

"The way to see how beautiful earth is, is to see it from the moon. The way to see how beautiful life is, is from the vantage point of death."

- Ursula K. Le Guin

"I'm not here to change your mind, I'm here to open it." I heard this refrain many times during a two-week, seven-country World War II trip through Europe. Our tour historian, who hailed from Ireland and taught in England, frequently reminded a bus full of (nearly all) Americans that sometimes what we think we know as undisputed truth might not be the full picture. He didn't want to persuade us to agree with him, but he wanted us to be willing to consider new information, from new perspectives.

So it is with this collection of stories inspired by death. If you are someone for whom death is a forbidden or daunting topic, I understand that it is already a leap for you to pick up this book in the first place. You might expect my Tales of Death to be spooky or macabre, but that is not the intention here. I don't believe death is inherently spooky. But I do think it's worth acknowledging.

Haruki Murakami wrote, "Death is not the opposite of life, but part of it. By living our lives, we nurture death." Death has been part of my life as long as I can remember. Culturally, it was never hidden from us. I grew up in a family that not only encouraged children to attend funerals, but in fact, some of my fondest childhood family memories are the big parties we threw after. We left our tears in the churches and the graveyards, and once we were at the party, we flipped an emotional switch. We'd tell fun stories and celebrate the life of the departed. There would be food, and music, and laughter.

All of this made sense to me, and made death understandable. It was nothing to be afraid of. When you die, people will be glad they knew you, and you will live on in the memories they hold and share. This understanding has been especially helpful in instances of the unexpected deaths of loved ones.

As I grew older, I realized that my experience was not universal. I discovered a number of my friends had grown up in families that didn't talk about death. Their elderly relatives died at a distance, in the confines of a nursing home or hospital. Whether it was fear, superstition, or propriety, the adults in their lives had shielded them from death, keeping them away from funerals and keeping the topic off-limits. To speak of death was taboo, as if it would invite misfortune. I saw how people who had always avoided death had a hard time facing it, and wondered if it really needed to be that way.

For me, death is always present, something I think about almost every day. Not in a morose way, but in a framing of my own existence, a reminder that every moment of life is precious and without guarantee, and also that the departed are not so distant from the living.

I believe this acceptance of death as a natural part of life was crucial during autumn 2024, when my mother Rachel received a diagnosis of late-stage, terminal pancreatic cancer. Her prognosis was only weeks to live. For her, death was just the next step in existence. She opted for home hospice, which allowed us to maximize time with her. She also asked us to throw her a going away party with her children and grandchildren so she could actually enjoy it while she was still alive and alert enough to appreciate it, which we did.

My mother's calm in facing the end of her life was both inspiring and instructive. This book was written before my mother became ill, but we did talk about it during her hospice days, and she strongly encouraged me to publish it. During those final weeks, I once asked her, "Are you scared of dying?" She answered, "No, I'm only sad I don't have more time to tell people how much I love them."

I had not set out with the intention of writing this collection. The stories within were created at random over a period of several years between drafts and revisions of my novels, "The Unsent Letters of Lucy Prior," and "Fireflies in a Jar." At one point, I realized I had eight stories, and none of them were long enough to be published on their own. As I evaluated them for a potential collection, I realized they were tied together by the theme of death.

In this collection you will find stories about people who experience the loss of a loved one, people who fear the potential loss of a loved one, and some people who don't fear death at all. There are stories of how grief can shape us, for better or worse. These stories also hop genres a bit, including sci-fi and magical realism. I don't restrict myself to one genre as a reader, and I feel no reason to do so as a writer.

So now, read on, and remember: I'm not here to change your mind about death, but I am here to open it.

Happy Reading,

Beka

My Life with Death

—

"To live in this world

you must be able
to do three things:
to love what is mortal;
to hold it

against your bones knowing
your own life depends on it;
and, when the time comes to let it go,
to let it go"

-Mary Oliver

8

I am in the midst of my third and final deal with Death; and I fear, however poorly the most recent went, that this will be the deal I regret. I write this journal in the event that I ever look for the information contained within. Tonight I will get into bed, and I will fall asleep, at which point all of the knowledge I am about to document will be forever gone from my mind.

Death and Their dogs have been with me from the moment I drew my first breath. Yes, Death has dogs. A massive pack of hounds who assist Death by escorting the newly-departed spirits to their first stop in the afterlife, as they transition into immortality. Sometimes they even keep a dying human company in their final hours, days, or weeks.

Before I continue, I need to clear something up: Death doesn't look like you expect Them to. I say, "Them," because Death, while a being, is neither male nor female, but Death is most certainly not an "It." I've never seen an accurate depiction of Death in art or culture, and They are difficult to describe.

Death doesn't look like the Grim Reaper, or the Ghost of Christmas Yet to Come. Death's hand isn't bony, because Death doesn't have hands. Not like you think.

They have diaphanous, ever-undulating appendages that would best be described as tentacles or cilia.

Neither is Death terrifying in appearance, as some traditions would depict. Death is neither some imposing woman nor a frightening demon. Death is gorgeous, with a soft, glowing aura, shimmering, iridescent. Their voice is like a soothing harmony of indistinguishable voices. Death is quite attractive; you can understand why some people become obsessed.

As I said, Death has been with me from the beginning. Sometimes, Death's hounds get confused by their instructions, and Death has to call off Their dogs after they've already moved to retrieve a soul. Such was the case with me. I entered the world slowly, following a long and complicated delivery. As I emerged, one of Death's hounds attempted to grab my soul through the nape of my neck.

People sometimes claim to have memories going back to their in-utero days, but I can tell you with absolute certainty that I recall every detail of those moments where I nearly wasn't born alive. I felt the hound's teeth tugging, burning as if my flesh was being singed with hot iron needles, creating what would later be classified as a birthmark I carry with me to this day.

The hound nearly succeeded, until I heard Death's chorale voice. "No, wait. Not her. Not yet. She needs to stay. Only the mother is coming with us today. That's right, leave the baby. She doesn't have an appointment scheduled." And then Death smiled at me, well, as close to smiling as Death can achieve without a human mouth. As much as my gunk-covered newborn eyes could perceive, anyway.

The hound released its grip, blasting me back into full mortality. I shrieked at the pain of my soul slamming back into my little body. The doctor and nurses took no note; babies are supposed to cry, after all. Besides, they were too busy trying to save my mother.

"They're taking her, don't let them, I need her!" I tried to scream, but they didn't listen. They couldn't understand me, since to the medical staff I sounded no different than any other infant they'd delivered.

"Shhhh, don't fret little one." Death reassured me, petting the hound who'd attacked me, as another hound circled my mother's bed. In an instant, Death threw Their voice, turning a nearby nurse into a ventriloquist dummy. The nurse's mouth moved, delivering Death's promise. "Here, now you have a friendly face to help you understand. We won't hurt your mother. We're just here to take her where she's supposed to be. It's time for her to move on."

The nurse didn't realize she'd been possessed, used. No one could see the hound, nor did they seem to notice that they passed through its body as they frantically fought to keep my mother alive on this earth.

At last the hound jumped onto my mother's gurney, in the same way a loving dog might jump up to cuddle with a family member. The dog curled up on her chest, its slowing sighs matching her waning breaths.

Finally, I saw the essence of her soul exit her corporeal form. My mother, who I would never get to meet in life. For a moment, I could tell she saw me, before the dog began to trot away. My mother followed behind, fading as she receded.

I looked for Death to demand an explanation, but both They and my hound were gone. I was alone, my wails of mourning drowned out by the sounds of machines emphasizing that my mother had not survived.

That was the first time I saw Death, but it wasn't long before I saw Them again. With my mother gone, my dad had to take care of my five-year old sister, Kiersten, and me. He never recovered from the loss of our mother, though. Daddy was hardly able to take care of himself, let alone us, and we were increasingly in the care of his parents, who loved us intensely and tried to shield us from his sorrow.

The hound came around our home sporadically at first, staring from a distance. Startled, I tried to draw Kirsten's attention, but to my shock she couldn't see him. She couldn't even see him when he walked right up toward us, sniffing the air as if trying to find his prey.

Only a toddler, I was too young to have the full vocabulary to express what I'd witnessed upon entering life, and what the hound's presence signified. One of us would be leaving soon. I wasn't concerned for myself, because I knew I'd follow the hound to my mother. What terrified me was not having my sister with me while I was still alive, nor not having our dad with us when he was the only parent we had left.

It soon became clear the hound was in fact coming for Daddy. Night after night, that hound circled our dinner table, always settling at Daddy's feet. As Daddy became inactive, staying inside, collapsing more and more into himself, the hound drew closer to him, his constant, invisible companion.

Desperate, I convinced myself that if only we could make Daddy laugh, make him happy, he'd want to stay, and the hound would have to go away. I did everything I could to entertain him, and from time to time it worked, I earned a smile, but still the hound remained. It grew clear that there was nothing any of us could do to change his mind. He was determined to move on, and the hound was there to accompany him.

Late one night, after Kirsten and I were supposed to be asleep, we heard a noise from Daddy's room. We ran to check, my chubby little legs struggling to keep up with Kiersten's lengthy bounds down the hallway. She got to him first, screaming, trying to lift him, to snap the cord, anything. I knew it was no use. I saw the final flickering of my father's spirit, already far away, fading in unison with the tip of his hound's tail.

All I remember from the next few days was trying to cheer up Kiersten, but it was no use. The more I tried, the more she resented me, finally lashing out. "Leave me alone! Everything was fine before you! You killed my mom... and because you killed her, Daddy killed himself. I hate you!"

Horrified, I shrunk into myself, and wished I could disappear. Sitting alone on a bench near Daddy's burial plot, the thought crossed my mind, "I wish I was dead." Instantly, as if summoned, Death appeared, this time possessing an old man, with my birth hound, across the graveyard. The elderly man sat next to me, and began to deliver Death's words, just as the delivery nurse had done.

"She doesn't mean it, little one." Even through a stranger's voice, Death's words were calming. "Your sister needs time to work through it, all people do. But don't take other's grief onto yourself. You can't absorb it, and you can't let it make you think these things. It's not your time."

"When is it my time?"

"I don't know, but it's not now, or else I'd have received your discharge notice, and you and your hound would be on your way." The hound nodded solemnly in agreement. I touched my hand to the back of my neck, understanding the hound hadn't meant to hurt me in the delivery room. Looking at the old man, I sought clarification.

"So you don't get to choose?" I'd assumed Death was in charge of departures.

"No, there are a great many wiser beings than I who work on the eternal calculus of the whens and whys, to keep a cosmic balance. I don't know the reasons, I just know who I'm to send my hounds to, to carry out our tasks as assigned."

"Then you don't know why my mom died, or my Daddy?"

"I'm afraid not."

"Can you ask someone?"

"It's not my place. Nor is it yours. There's a system. Whether it is logical, or fair, that's not for me to judge. I have a role to serve."

"Were you ever alive?"

"Not the way you think of, but I'm alive right now." DeathAsElderlyMan placed a kindly hand on my shoulder. "Now, I have to go, but remember what I said. Other people's grief is not your burden to bear, or you'll break. Forgive your sister, and be good for your grandparents."

"Can I ask you one more thing?"

"Yes, little one, but then I must be on my way."

"Will I see you... soon? Can you promise to stay away? It's not that I don't like you, but I want my family to stay for a while. Please."

"That's not a promise I can make. I don't know when someone is leaving until I get my assignment. At that point, it's fixed. Sometimes if someone is very ill for a long time, I have advance notice, but otherwise, it's often as surprising to me as it is to you all."

"Please leave my family alone."

"I'm your family, too. I will see you when the next appointed time comes. Until then, be good, and stop wishing for me."

The man snapped back to himself, seemingly unaware that we'd been talking, and unsure why he had a reassuring hand on my shoulder. He shook himself back to his senses, stood up, and walked away, leaving me on the bench, alone.

Due to the nature of my dad's death, and how it made everyone feel, my grandparents opted to forego a wake, and instead took us straight home from the burial. I remember my sister seething silently in the car until she fell asleep. I tried to stay awake, but only woke when we pulled into the driveway and my grandfather scooped me up into his arms. He squeezed me with such affection, whispering "You're home now, you're safe with us."

As we got into our pajamas, I remained silent, afraid of causing my sister to yell at me again. I didn't know how to make amends with her when she was right. Before me, she had two parents, a happy family. I broke it, I broke it all. Despite Death's instructions not to internalize her feelings, the guilt was so strong, I couldn't even raise my eyes in her direction. She didn't acknowledge me, either.

Quietly I got into bed, accepting forehead kisses from Grandma and Grandpa. I stared at the ceiling, futilely willing myself to sleep. At some point, Kristen left her bedroom, because my door creaked open, letting the smallest bit of light fall across the floor. Without saying a word, she shut the door behind her and crawled into my bed. She began to cry, so I hugged her, and she hugged me back. We fell asleep like that, consoling each other in a sisterly embrace.

For the next few years, I saw no hounds. No sign of Death. I wondered if my cemetery pleas had actually worked, if we could all just be good and happy and healthy together for decades to come. Kiersten thrived at my grandparents' home, and over time came back to herself, full of cheer and love. We had the usual spats sisters have, but she never again accused me of harming our family with my existence.

Our grandparents lived in a somewhat rural area of Carroll County, MD, not too far of a drive from the small, old Main Street in Taneytown, but still slightly isolated, surrounded by woods and a big pond. We spent lots of time outside with our grandparents, who tried to teach us basic survival skills, and how to respect wildlife and protect the land. We became a solid family unit, healing together.

One year for Christmas, Grandpa surprised us with our very own dog, an Irish wolfhound we named Sadie. She was our shadow, accompanying us on our adventures, whimpering when she had to stay home while we were at school. Sadie used to take turns sleeping at the foot of our beds, alternating between my room and Kirsten's. I preferred the nights Sadie stayed with me, since she was like a little heater, keeping me toasty warm.

Life reached a point that was fulfilling and content. Grandpa had told me I was safe, and he was right. I felt so assured in my situation, that I almost forgot about Death. Until I received a horrific reminder that Death will always follow.

Sadie was sleeping soundly on my bed when she snapped up at attention, running to my window. "Sadie, come back to bed! Silly girl, what do you think you see? Is it the buck again?" I followed her gaze and saw a pack of dogs. Hounds. Death's hounds, in a silent line, holding vigil at the edge of the river downhill from our house. I tried to convince myself it was just a dream while simultaneously knowing it was real. I raced from my room, down the stairs, and without pausing to put on a coat or even shoes, I sprinted out of the house into the snow wearing only socks and flannel pajamas.

Sadie followed me the whole way toward the river where the hounds were gathered, snapping at them and running in a circle around me as if to protect me. But they weren't there for me, and they sauntered past us, as though we were invisible.

Slowly, deliberately, they stalked up the hill toward the house. My house. My home these past seven years with the only family I had left—my sister and my grandparents. I counted the hounds. There were three. The awful math played out in my head: one for each person still in the house. The hounds walked silently in lockstep, never moving their gaze from the house, intent on arriving punctually for their appointment.

The slushy snow quickly permeated my pajamas, and cold overtook my flesh. My mind no longer controlled my body, my head unable to communicate with my quickly-freezing limbs. I saw the hounds continue to move, in no hurry as they were exactly on time, and I knew I still had a chance to stop them, to head them off. I just had to get up.

Why couldn't I just get up? Why couldn't I make myself stand? I tried desperately to lift myself up with my tiny arms, but they couldn't gain the momentum to prop up my weight. My iced-over body felt too heavy to stand.

"Sadie!" I tried to yell but managed only to whisper urgently. "Go! Go, stop them!" I hoped she could slow them long enough until I could convince my body to obey my brain.

But Sadie wouldn't go, she wouldn't leave me. Whimpering, she instead moved to help me off the ground. She burrowed her snout under me, into the snow, wedging me. All the while, I never took my mind off the hounds, desperate to believe that despite their progress, I could somehow overtake them. She finally managed to lever me up from the ground, steadying me as I gazed up.

I turned to run away from the river and up the hill, back to the house as quickly as I could. I had to get back and warn them. I had to stop those hounds and save my family. Kiersten, my sister, I had to save her. Our grandparents. I had to save them all.

Realizing my intent, Sadie tried to hold me back, her jaw locked onto my pajamas. I tore away, pulled loose and tried to get up the hill, but by now my frozen feet could hardly obey. I attempted to scream, "Fire!" That would surely wake them all up, but instead all I could manage was a non-verbal mix between a shriek of terror and a battle cry.

It was then that I saw the flames spreading and forced my feet to move forward back up toward the house. As we approached, the sharp sting of smoke struck my frosted throat and lungs, making it difficult to breathe as I labored up the hill.

The hounds were still outside, and I reached out my hand to grab one, as if I could force it to leave. My hand made contact with one of them who turned and snarled at me. My frost-bitten flesh now burned where I'd touched its fur, and the hound knocked me back down the hill, sliding along the slick, frozen top layer of snow. Sadie charged at one of the other hounds, and for her trouble got pushed down alongside me, both of us tumbling and slipping with our limbs intertwined and our bodies stinging from where the hounds had touched us.

Time moved slowly, I could see the house consumed by flames as I heard sirens and alarmed shouts. A neighbor found us there, at the bottom of the hill, wrapped in a sad bundle of flesh that was both burned and frozen. He pulled me close to his chest, cradling me to him while shouting.

"Thank God, you're alive! I found her! I found the little one, she's down here, she's alive!" Sadie and I were quickly mobbed by first responders and neighbors, getting us to an ambulance to administer first aid.

One of the rescue workers, trying to catch his breath, asked me urgently, "Miss, who else was inside the house? How many people are inside the house?"

I looked at the house and saw the fading outline of three hounds. Everyone was already gone, and I didn't even get to see them walk away.

"Grandma, Grandpa, Kiersten." I whispered, knowing it didn't matter. There would be no saving them. The worker's face fell, but then he tried to recover and give me a reassuring look. "Ok. Thank you. You let these people take care of you now, we're going to keep working to get your family out," he lied. He knew there was no one left to save.

"Can Sadie stay with me?"

"She needs to get looked at, too, but we'll try to make sure she gets to see you as soon as possible."

That night in the hospital room, an orderly stopped by my bed on her usual rounds. At first, she was startled to see me awake but then asked how I was feeling. "I wish I was dead." Her face twitched and when she opened her mouth, Death spoke to me again.

"I thought I warned you about that kind of talk."

"You don't *want* to be wanted?"

"No, I want to do my job. I don't like being summoned. Besides, you don't really wish that."

"Yes I do. I want to be with my family. I want to be with them now. I wasn't supposed to see you again, not for a long time."

"You asked not to see me, and I told you I made no promises."

"I'm alone, again. I have no one."

"You have Sadie."

"Your dogs hurt her. They hurt me, too!" I gestured emphatically with my hand, covered in ointment and bandages.

"I'm sorry, but you know not to touch them. They only hurt Sadie because you tried to stop them from doing..."

"...Their job. I know, it's all you ever say. It's not fair. Why do you all keep picking on my family? Why do you hate me? Why do you want me to be alone?"

"I don't want you to be alone."

"Then why do you keep killing everyone I love?"

"I don't choose who, I don't know why. I just know when it's someone's time, and then I make sure they keep their appointments."

"I don't believe you. You must hate me. What did I do to you?"

"Dear one, I don't hate you. I'm actually rather fond of you. There aren't many people I can talk to, you know. And not many who've seen the real me. I feel like I can be myself around you, no pretense."

"Will Sadie live?" I feared the answer but needed to know.

"I've received no instruction to retrieve her, so it looks like she'll be staying with you once you're both recovered."

"You really don't want me to be alone?"

"Of course not. I have no motive in the deaths I execute."

"Then will you stay with me?"

Death used the orderly's plump arms to motion toward her soft figure. "I think this body has other tasks to complete tonight. I don't want to get this human in trouble by keeping her with you too long."

"No, I mean, will **you** stay with me? The real you. The squiggly, sparkly silver-blue version of you."

"If I do that, you'll appear ill to other people, they'll think you're slow to recover. And they won't be able to see me, so if they catch you talking to me, they'll think you are mentally troubled."

"I don't care."

"Of course you do. Plus," Death added, using the orderly's pudgy hand to take mine, "When I'm the 'squiggly' me, I can't touch you. Isn't this nicer? Now rest, so you can heal. The sooner you heal, the sooner you get to be with your Sadie. I will stay a little longer with you in this body, and then you need to sleep."

"What's going to happen to me?"

"I can't know that. I only know it isn't your time."

"Will you be at the funeral?"

"I will, little one."

"And will you stay away after that?"

"You know I can't promise that. Sleep now." And with that, Death was gone. The orderly woke from her occupied trance, dazed.

"Thank you for staying with me." I smiled at her as best as I could in my exhausted state. "I think I can fall back asleep now." She squeezed my hand obligingly, promised to check in on me the next day, and continued her rounds.

Death hadn't known what would become of me, but even if They had, I wouldn't have understood. I learned that I wasn't bereft of family, not entirely. I had a Great Aunt Helen, Grandpa's long-estranged older sister. I didn't recognize her when I saw her at the graveside, but then there were so many people there that I didn't recognize.

A number of mourners stayed away from me, anyway. A rumor went around my school that I was cursed, and that I caused everyone in my family to die. That maybe I even started the fire. After all, wasn't it suspicious that I was the only one not in the house, that I'd taken the dog outside with me?

Even well-meaning people who felt sorry for me didn't know what to say, and I quickly grew tired of entertaining their awkward attempts at finding a silver lining, telling me it was all part of a plan, at least they were in a better place now. One mourner turned out to be a reporter in disguise, and when he started to ask me questions, Aunt Helen swept in. She swiftly excused him from the cemetery, and she was commanding enough that he didn't try to argue with her.

She turned to me, tall and striking with her white hair pulled up into a severe chignon. "What a parade of utter bullshit this day has been. That asshole was the cherry on top of a shit sundae, if you ask me."

I was unused to hearing adults speak this way— my grandparents had never cursed in my presence. For a moment, I wondered if this was actually Death, but the cadence was wrong.

The giantess leaned over me, assessing me with a skeptical gaze. "You know who I am?"

"No," I responded, shaking my head and hugging Sadie tighter to me.

"Well, it's you and me now. I'm Helen, and we're the only family either of us has left, so I hope we can get along. But that's more up to you than it is to me."

"Can Sadie come?"

"Of course. What kind of monster would keep a child from their dog? Besides, I think Sadie is going to like your new home just fine." She packed us up into her station wagon and we drove north, further into New England until I lost track of which state we were in.

Aunt Helen was right about Sadie liking our new setup, and I liked it too. Seeing how everyone in my grandparents' town was either sorry for me or suspicious of me, the total change of scene was exactly what I needed.

Decades before she took me in, Aunt Helen had come into money and used it to buy a defunct summer camp. She converted it into "Louisa's Refuge," a home for an odd assortment of people. The resort residents included recovering addicts trying to stick to their sobriety, terminally ill individuals who were out of treatment options, lonely oldsters who didn't want to waste away in elder care facilities, and various people who wanted to take care of the aforementioned guests.

I was told that Louisa's Refuge was named after Aunt Helen's best friend who experienced an unfortunate, isolated death before Aunt Helen was able to see her one final time. Despite the sweet nature of the homage, neither the residents nor staff called it Louisa's Refuge, calling it instead the "Last Resort."

When we pulled into the campgrounds, Aunt Helen escorted us to the main lodge, where she had set up a spartan room for me. "Look kiddo, I believe in being honest. I never had kids, and I don't know anything about being a mom, but you never had a mom and don't know much about being a normal kid, so I think we can get through this together. If you give me grace to make mistakes and trust that I'm trying my best, I'll do the same for you. Fair?" It seemed perfectly fair to me.

For a weird little girl who had burn scars to match her dog, it was a perfect place. I got to meet people who knew nothing about me, and who didn't have the energy to *want* to learn about me. I was allowed to be as anonymous as I wanted. I attended a local school that was primarily filled with farmers' kids who didn't care about me. They neither bullied me nor embraced me—an arrangement with which I was quite content.

As soon as I got back to camp each day, I made rounds to greet some of the residents and staff with whom I formed relationships, then ran around in the woods with Sadie. Everyone at the resort took care of each other—a true community. Wanting to earn my keep, I offered to help in the kitchen, but everyone thought I was too young, and they also worried about my feeling unsafe around the stoves and other hot surfaces.

It wasn't long after my arrival that the first hound showed up. I was expecting them, knowing that some people came to Louisa's to die in the peace of nature. At first, I flinched and pulled my burned hand to myself, drawing my breath sharply.

Sadie's snarl brought me back to attention. I calmly reassured her and slowly approached the hound. "I know why you're here, and we won't get in your way." At my promise, the hound nodded and slowly walked toward one of the palliative cabins.

Thus began a new period of my life. I learned to accept the hounds, so much that they no longer unsettled me when they arrived. Eventually, they made it clear I was welcome to accompany them to specific cabins. Understanding these were people who had the least time left, I realized I could earn my keep by acting as their companion in their final hours and days. Whatever they needed, I provided. If they wanted me to read to them, talk to them, sing to them, even just sit with them, I did. (As best I could, I was still in elementary school and hadn't mastered novels yet, and I didn't know all the songs they requested.)

At first Aunt Helen seemed unsure of my new role. Initially her concern was that I would upset the guests, and then she wondered if they weren't going to upset me. "You're becoming a little death doula, then?"

"No one should die sad or alone. Sadie and I make sure they don't."

"Understood, but I don't know if my brother would like me having you spend so much time dealing with death."

"Aunt Helen, I'm not scared of Death. I know Death. I've known Death my whole life. Since I'm comfortable with Death, I can help other people feel more comfortable, too. If I ever mess up, I'll stop, but I promise you it's good for everyone."

She relented, and for the next seven or so years we achieved a kind of harmony. I got to know the Last Resort's employees and volunteers, and I split my time between school, the woods, and my duties as a "death doula." I took my responsibility seriously, feeling honored that I got to help people approach death with acceptance and even find some final moments of peace. I listened to confessions, I prayed with people according to their individual faiths, and perhaps most importantly, I held hands as they slipped away.

Once, early in my tenure, I learned that not all death-bed confessions are ones I'd want to hear. An older woman spilled a horrible secret: a grisly crime she'd committed, repeatedly, over a series of years, against multiple victims. She began crying, grabbing my hand and repeating, "Forgive me, forgive me!" I was unprepared for the revelation and ripped my hand away from her. Before I even knew what I was saying, I began to condemn her.

"How dare you come here and try to die in peace?!" I felt a blazing flame of righteous anger rising in me. "You don't deserve to die in peace, and you don't deserve to die with anyone by your side. I DON'T FORGIVE YOU. I hope you suffer now, and I hope you suffer forever after you're gone."

During my rant, her hound stood up and placed themself between us, trying to discourage my rage. I couldn't stop. I began to unleash a level of vitriol I didn't even know I had within me, until suddenly, the woman shuddered and began to speak. It was the voice of Death, possessing this monstrous human.

"ENOUGH, CHILD," DeathAsTheDyingCriminal bellowed. Then, more softly, "This human is aware she is bad, that she has done wrong. She will be dealt with, but it is not your place as a mere human to judge anyone."

"But she..."

"I know what she did. And make no mistakes, consequences will follow."

"What kind of consequences? Like, Hell?"

"The human concept of Hell is absurd and insufficient. In many ways you are all limited beings, incapable of understanding that which isn't literal or analogous to your earthly experiences. Regardless, her consequences are not your concern. You are here to help people pass peacefully."

"I know, and I..."

"If you cannot do so with maturity and grace, perhaps you shouldn't retain the gift you possess. Not everyone has the privilege to speak with me, to have a relationship with me, to see my companions and interact with them. Mistreat a dying person again, and it will be the last time you ever see me in this life."

"You'd take it away? You'd... shun me?"

DeathAsTheDyingCriminal sighed. "No little one, I would miss you too much. I do need you to understand your role, and remember your place, though. Can you promise me you will?"

I solemnly promised, and when Death exited the dying woman, I took back her hand and spoke softly to her. She died later that night, and I stayed with her until her final breath. No one came to her funeral, but I didn't tell Aunt Helen that I knew why. I understood my place.

From then on, I restrained myself from reacting to, or from criticizing, anyone for what they told me, serving only the mission of being at their side during their hour of death. Aunt Helen and the rest of the staff mused that I had a knack for knowing everyone's departure time.

Of course, I could never explain to Aunt Helen that I had inside knowledge thanks to the network of hounds, who always alerted me when someone's time grew close. She once said she thought I had a sixth sense of some kind, so I tested the waters, teasing her that I could in fact see people's souls departing, but she was too no-nonsense to really believe any supernatural explanation.

The First Deal

We continued on in our harmonious existence into my teenage years. Death once said They were fond of me, and I was growing fond of Death. Saying goodbye became the norm for me, and I didn't question it, until Death took Sadie from me. You could argue she lived a good long life for a dog, despite the early trauma from the fire that killed our family. Sadie was old, and she didn't have any kind of violent or gruesome death. She slipped away quietly, in a death for which most people would be grateful.

But I was not grateful.

I summoned Death. I knew how to do it, and I was too angry to contain the impulse. I walked into the woods ready for a fight. The occupied body of one of the Last Resorters, Glenn, followed, with Death as puppeteer.

As soon as we reached an isolated clearing, I turned around and let loose. "Bring her back, you sonofabitch." Aunt Helen's salty language had rubbed off on me over the years we spent together.

"Done is done."

"Fuck you. Bring her back."

"Can't say I care for how your vocabulary has evolved since the last time we spoke like this."

"Bring. Her. Back."

"I only do what I'm assigned. It was her time. You know this, and yet you keep making me tell you. I don't make the timelines, I don't set the appointments."

"You know what she means to me. You know I need her. Bring her back." I balled my fists in anger, and as the scar tissue stretched across my hand—the marks from the burn I'd gotten when Sadie fought to save me—I felt unspeakable dread at the loss of my companion.

"I have neither the ability nor authority to do that."

"Then let me talk to someone who can."

"You would have me treat the ancient and timeless beings who keep our entire universe in balance as if they were a customer service team? Yours is not the only planet that concerns them. There are countless planets in countless galaxies they have to keep in order."

"Why don't you at least face me in your real form, instead of treating Glenn like he's your marionette? Show yourself."

"If I do that, I won't have a face to express myself, and you won't understand how very disappointed I am in your attitude." DeathAsGlenn made an exaggerated frown.

I don't know why I even tried negotiating since my past experience showed Death couldn't be moved, but my desperation drove me to bargain, and I proposed what would become the first of my three deals with Death. "Don't do this to me. At least...let me see her one more time. She still exists, right? Like, one of your dogs?"

"Not exactly, but yes, her essence still exists beyond the mortal veil. She's with the other companions in a—for lack of a better term—vestibule to permanent existence, waiting to be reunited with their people before moving on completely."

"Ok, how about this? Let's make a deal. Don't bring her back, just take me to her. Let me see her spirit, just for a little while. In return, I'll accept that it was her time and I'll let her go, and I won't hold a grudge against you."

To my surprise, DeathAsGlenn considered this, thoughtfully holding his chin with his freckled hand.

"A deal? Yes, I believe I can do that. *However*, you have to understand a few things before we make a deal."

I nodded, ready to hear Their terms.

"First: You get 24 hours exactly. No more, no less."

"Got it."

"Second: Your 24 hours starts the second you fall asleep tonight."

"Perfect. Anything else?" These terms didn't seem altogether unreasonable if it meant getting to see my dearest companion for even a tiny fraction of the time I wished.

DeathAsGlenn continued, "Finally: during this time, you will seem near-dead to everyone else. They won't be able to rouse you, at all, until exactly 24 hours after you fall asleep."

"That's fine, I don't care. Is that all?"

"Yes, that is all. Understand as well that she won't look the way you remember her. She's not a corporeal canine anymore."

"How will I know it's her?"

"As I said, she'll be waiting for you."

"Thank you. Truly. You should probably let Glenn go now."

Poor, confused Glenn didn't recall following me into the woods, but realized he must have been trying to comfort me, and I allowed him to escort me back to camp.

That night, we had a memorial ceremony for Sadie. Last Resorters took turns sharing their favorite stories of my amazing girl. I cried and laughed with my fellow campers, basking in the warmth of their remembrance. I was, admittedly, distracted by the knowledge that I would get to see her again, and so soon. After the party dwindled, I excused myself, allowing everyone to give me hugs of comfort and condolence. No longer able to wait, I got into bed and tried to force myself to sleep.

Of course, whenever you try to fall asleep quickly, your body has other ideas. I stared and stared, until finally, I was no longer in my bed.

Death was right to be vague. I cannot describe what the place was like where I arrived, as it was some sort of location where human physics don't apply. All my life I've tried to think of how to describe what I experienced, but our language is too limited. In short, no sooner had my spirit entered this other plane than a fuchsia flash of energy came swirling up to me, knocking me over with an enthusiastic welcome. It was my Sadie.

Time moves differently when you aren't in your body. I savored every last microsecond with my girl. We were both ephemeral, but in our way, we ran, embraced, exchanging the intense affection that pets engender from us.

Although I knew our time was limited, it filled me with great relief to see that she was happy, and frankly, that she *was*, at all. I'd once fought with a friend about whether animals have souls, and while I strongly argued that they do, I'd be lying to say some part of me wasn't afraid that Sadie's earthly death was the end of my beloved friend. I was overcome with gratitude for this gift from Death and wasn't even bitter when it was time to return to life.

This was my first deal with Death, and I didn't fully appreciate that Death's bargain's always came with a catch. I realized the gravity of my actions as soon as I came back to consciousness. Aunt Helen sat, weeping, holding my hand, silently mumbling what sounded like a prayer despite her ardent dislike of religion.

It hadn't even occurred to me what my supernatural shore-leave would do to my guardian, my only family. Not only had she lost a dog she'd come to care for as her own, but within less than a day, she discovered the unconscious body of her niece, seemingly comatose without cause. I was in a hospital, surrounded by the buzzing, beeping, and whirring of machines.

In my grief and desperation, I had acted incredibly selfish. I didn't give any thought to how my absence would affect this woman who had come to cherish me as if I was her child.

"I'm sorry." I struggled to speak with everything hooked up to me, but it was enough to alert her to my willingness to talk. Medical staff ran into the room, examining me repeatedly, confounded that they were unable to discern what had been wrong with me, and how I was instantly healed. They made vague suggestions that the Last Resort stuff had misdiagnosed me from the start due to their loose licensing.

Aunt Helen didn't care. She took me home immediately. I was very sorry for how I'd hurt her, for the stress I'd caused. From that moment, I promised myself I was going to be a model child, on my best behavior, and would do everything I could to make sure this wonderful woman knew how much I loved and appreciated her.

When I started college, it was a difficult adjustment to live with people my age. There was a clear expectation among my peers that we all had shared cultural experiences that we could reference with conversational shorthand, but I'd missed out. I had been too immersed with dying people to have much of a life.

Two of my suite-mates turned out to be very kind people, though, and we got along very well. The third was a rather superficial and difficult girl. One of our suite-mates had to go home for a funeral after her grandmother finally succumbed to mesothelioma.

While two of us tried to comfort her and help her pack, promising to pick up any assignments from her professors, our inwardly-focused suite-mate couldn't contain her curiosity. "I've never known anyone who died before. Like, what happens? Do you get her stuff?"

I wondered if there's a connection between people who've never experienced tragedy and the lack of empathy they generally exhibit.

Anyway, college was overall good for me. I wasn't far from home, so I was able to visit Aunt Helen fairly easily. I took classes to help me in my quest to become a professional death counselor, including psychology, anthropology, world religions, and more. I had never been a great student, but my professors liked my insights, and I did very well.

Aunt Helen was so proud at my graduation. I returned to the Last Resort, now as a full-time member of the staff. For a few years all was peaceful. Eventually, though, Aunt Helen slowed down, and one day her hound showed up. I asked if she still had time, and the hound nodded in affirmation.

For once, I wasn't angry at Death for taking someone from me. I could see for myself that Aunt Helen was tired and nearing her own point of being ready to let go of life. During those final months, we grew even closer than we ever had been. She finally told me about Louisa, the love of her life. It turned out Louisa's family had forced her to marry a very wealthy man who would bring them status in their conservative town. They also forbade her from ever speaking to Helen again.

This agreement crushed Aunt Helen, understandably. Louisa's husband died in some sort of embarrassing circumstances, leaving Louisa a wealthy widow. Unfortunately, before she could enjoy her newfound financial freedom, she became terminally ill. She wrote to Aunt Helen, begging forgiveness and asking her to come visit before it was too late.

Aunt Helen's deepest regret in life was that she refused her dying lover's last request. At the moment, she couldn't bring herself to do it, and Louisa passed within a short time. She left everything in her considerable estate to Aunt Helen, who of course felt unworthy of the gift. As penance, Aunt Helen put every bit of it, and herself, into establishing Louisa's Refuge.

I asked Aunt Helen if she wouldn't mind very much if I didn't stick around after she was gone. The Last

Resort wouldn't feel the same without her. "I've never believed in people guilting their children into carrying on a family business. Everyone gets one life to live, just one, and you can't live it on behalf of your ancestor's wishes. Go, find somewhere new, different, maybe somewhere sunny. Go live your life."

When at last Aunt Helen's soul departed her body, I smiled at her spirit, and she was shocked to realize I could interact with her. "I told you I could see them leaving," I shrugged playfully. She blew me a kiss with her long, thin hand, before turning to accompany her hound. I wondered if she'd be reunited with Sadie. I wondered if she'd get to see Louisa. She had helped so many people into the afterlife, I could only hope she'd get the welcome she deserved.

Following Aunt Helen's advice, I moved to a place where there was both plenty of warm sunshine and plenty of dying people. I loved Florida from the moment I arrived. It was a wild departure from everything I knew, and each day brought new people into my life. I had been able to get a job at a retirement complex with multiple tiers of care, from assisted living to nurse-supervision to hospice care.

I'd never really had a normal social life anyway, and this continued in Florida, so I was available to come to the community whenever I was needed. Of course, I always knew when I'd be needed before the rest of the staff did and planned accordingly. Eventually I was there so often and was so well-liked by the rest of the staff, that I was offered one of the dorm-style apartments at the facility. I had missed my old campground community, so I took them up on the offer.

In addition to helping people pass, I also enjoyed getting to know some of the livelier, healthy residents in the cafeteria. Some of them were so full of vigor and personality, and I liked hearing their stories. Often, they would get visits from family, bringing them proudly to the cafeteria, showing off this nephew or that granddaughter like they were a prize pony.

That's how I met Miguel. He arrived like clockwork to visit his mother, Magda, every day that he could. His schedule was erratic, as he worked in corporate technology sales. He wanted her to come home and live with him, but she insisted he wasn't as good a nurse as the professionals that she needed. "Besides, he travels too much for work, I didn't like being alone."

His job had him flying all over the country for new business pitches and in-person demonstrations. More than once he offered to take a pay cut and a position which would allow him to stay home, but Magda wanted him to keep doing what he was good at and seemed to enjoy.

As I became friendly with her, one day she invited me to join her and Miguel for lunch, excited to finally introduce us.

"This is the girl I was telling you about, the one who helped Ruth last week. She never left Ruth's side, not once. It was a blessing." Grabbing my face with her hand, she emphasized, "YOU are a blessing. Come, sit with us!"

"Well, how can I refuse an invitation like that?" I accepted, and shook hands with her son, who immediately distracted me with how attractive he was. I'd never had any kind of romantic relationship before, never even considered it, but the moment his hand touched mine I felt a shock and couldn't stop staring at his smile. I was smitten.

Our meals together became a regular occurrence. He and Magda would sometimes make takeout containers for me when I was holding vigil with a resident getting close to death, and didn't want to leave them alone. With his work demands, Miguel didn't have much of an active dating life either, so our lunch dates became important for both of us.

We fell in love quickly, and my life changed. I actually used some of my vacation time to join him on some of his work trips, seeing parts of the country I'd never even thought about before. He was lovely and generous and funny and everything I would have wanted if I'd ever imagined a partner. Magda urged us to keep up this frenetic pace, with a constant refrain, "Get married, have babies, let me enjoy my grandchildren!" Before I knew it we were engaged. When we left for our long honeymoon, Magda teased, "Don't worry, I'll tell everyone they can't die until you get back. Now forget all about us and have a good time!"

We did have a good time. An amazing time, actually. We settled into our happy little home life. I moved into his house, but his work trips took him away, so often it allowed me to maintain my bedside vigils without feeling like I was missing out on time with him.

The Second Deal

I never should have let my guard down. I should have known, I'm not allowed to be happy. Not in this life. One day at work I received an urgent message. Miguel collapsed at the airport while waiting for his flight. I shoved Magda into my car and broke every traffic law in a race to the hospital. By the time we arrived he was in a coma. Doctors explained he had no brain activity, that he wasn't breathing on his own, but I couldn't focus on what they said because I was too distracted by the hound.

It rocked back onto its hind legs and began to climb up onto Miguel's bed, just as I'd seen with my mother on my birth day. "No! No! Stop!" I screamed, trying to shoo the invisible creature away. Hospital employees tried to restrain me, and I understood I must have looked like a hysterical wife. I needed to talk to Death immediately, but there were too many people in the room. The only idea that popped into my brain was the chapel, so I sprinted down the halls until I made it. I dropped to my knees in front of the altar, squeezed my eyes shut, and feverishly begged Death to appear.

The chaplain walked up behind me, placing her tiny hand on my shoulder. I pivoted my head to see a tiny, elegant woman. When she spoke, her husky voice seemed incongruous with her petite frame.

"I fear I know why you want to see me, but I must remind you, I don't make the schedules, I only make sure people move on when it's their time."

Without standing, I threw my arms around her legs, pleading, "You can't you can't. Please don't! Let him stay. Please!"

"I'm sorry little one, but that's not possible. Surely you knew that before you even asked."

"We were just getting started! It's not his time, it can't be!"

"I assure you, we wouldn't be here if it wasn't his time."

"You can't take him! Magda and I, we can't live without him! She'll die, I'll die. You'll be killing us!"

Tilting her head, she looked lost in thought for a moment, then adjusting her posture corrected me. "I have checked, and neither you nor Magda are scheduled to depart within this year. You will not die if he leaves."

"Then... I'll kill myself."

DeathAsTheTinyChaplain recoiled, pulling free from my arms. "That is not something to threaten. Taking your own life is a serious matter."

"Then understand how serious I am. I will not live without him."

"You aren't going to do it though. You aren't scheduled for departure."

"Well, I'm moving up my appointment."

"You can't do that."

"Yes I can, and then you'll miss me. And then I'll get to be with him."

"Are you sure you'll be with him? I've told you before, your human understanding of immortal existence is confused and inaccurate."

"It's worth a try, if it means even a small chance of being in his presence."

"Why would you make these threats? You know how this works."

"I don't want to be apart from him. Can't you understand that?" I wept uncontrollably as I pleaded.

"That's not for us to decide. I have a job to do, and so do you. Go sit with him, while he's still here."

Desperation poured from my mouth. "I would do anything, anything for him to stay. Please help me, you have to at least try to help me! Talk to the decision makers, change their minds!"

Death shook the small woman's head. "I've indulged you too much already. Or have you already forgotten when I enabled your reunion with Sadie?"

"I do remember, I do! That's why I know I can be satisfied with just a little more time, you'll see!"

"That was very different; I allowed your soul to pass, no one else died because of it. If he stays here, on this planet, past his due date, it would upset the balance and someone else has to go. You don't know who that would be...what if it's an innocent child who has to go in his place? Could you really live with yourself if you allowed that? Do you believe he would be able to live with himself?"

They were right, he would hate knowing someone else died because of him. "Fine, but just...not yet. Give me a little more time. Give me...give me one year. Just one more year. That's nothing!"

"You make it seem like a simple task. There are infinite variables that go into planning each arrival and departure."

"You said I was your family. Well, that makes Miguel your family, too, so you have to help him if you can!"

"Very well. Please wait." Again, the vacant look took over the chaplain's face. "I have received their response. There is precedent, on other worlds. Therefore, they will allow this exception for you."

Thus, I struck my second deal with Death. It was more than I could have hoped. "Thank you, thank you!" Once again, I wrapped my arms around the little legs.

"There are points we need to discuss."

"Of course," I assented as I wiped my face. "Terms of the deal."

"Pay attention. First: you get exactly one year. Not one second more."

"Understood."

"Second: Your year begins the moment you fall asleep tonight.

"Got it. Yes. Ok."

"Finally, his hound stays."

"What? Why? We know he's leaving; it's not like he's going to make an escape. We don't need him hovering around as a constant reminder for the next year."

"It's not that. I mentioned precedent. I am told that in every other instance, no one stayed the full time of their reprieve."

"What?" I couldn't follow this line of conversation. I just wanted to get out of there and get to bed so I could have Miguel back with me.

"There is a 99% likelihood that before the year is out, you will ask me to come back and take him. He will not be quite himself. He will not... relish existence. Blessings are relative, based on perspective. He may find it a curse, a burden. You will find this unnerving and wish to end the arrangement early."

"Not me. Never. I'm going to make the most of every last minute you'll let me keep him. Can I go now?"

"It feels as if you are not understanding."

"I understand. There's a risk, but anything in life worth having is worth a risk. Please, can I go now?" I stood, slowly rising until I was taller than Death's petite avatar.

DeathAsTheTinyChaplain sighed. "You may go."

I decided not to go home, opting to stay in the room with Miguel and fall asleep there, so I wouldn't miss one moment with him. Magda insisted on staying, too, though that was because she thought he had only hours or days left.

True to Their promise, Death released Miguel just as I nodded off. Just as when I'd miraculously awoken in my adolescence, his full, instant recovery confounded the doctors. Magda declared it a miracle, crossing herself and uttering prayers of thanks in at least three different languages.

After a period of monitoring, my husband was fully discharged and I was allowed to take him home, his cursed hound following us closely. As I was about to exit through the sliding doors of the hospital, a janitor grabbed my hand, squeezing my burn scars as he warned, "Borrowed time is not standard time."

In all the times Death had spoken to me, this was the first time I felt scared.

I couldn't waste time thinking about that, though. I only had one year and had to figure out how to fill it with every adventure Miguel ever wanted to experience. His office granted him an extended leave, and I planned to fill it with every kind of excursion and outing imaginable.

Right away though, it was clear something was wrong. He didn't seem fully himself. He was like a desaturated version of the Miguel I knew, washed out. He was more like an echo of the man he'd been before the coma. He didn't show interest in any of the activities about which he'd been passionate. I took him out for his favorite meals, but he had no appetite. He complained that the food had no flavor. He was listless, and absolutely nothing sparked any enthusiasm.

My attempts to reassure him were futile. He withdrew more and more, turning into a shell of the vibrant person he'd been. Always, his hound curled at his feet, faithfully keeping watch. The rest of his family tried to engage him, too, but nothing worked.

Magda became discouraged and then grew suspicious. "Those doctors, they did something to my boy! I knew something was wrong when they couldn't explain how they healed him!" She was convinced they'd illegally experimented on him and wanted to sue. I did my best to keep her calm and focused on keeping him company.

Sometimes he would just sit and stare, as if he was trying to figure something out. He constantly complained of feeling cold. At first, I thought it was just a hangover from the coma, but it kept going on. He frequently looked distracted, and when I asked him about it, he grew upset. "I feel like I'm missing something. Like, you know those dreams where you miss a math test you never even knew you had, so you can't graduate...or like the dreams where you accidentally sleep through a job interview and miss the appointment? I feel like that all the time, like I'm missing a deadline or an appointment, like I'm not where I'm meant to be."

He put his face to his hands and began to cry. "I just... I don't feel like me. I don't feel like I'm supposed to even be here, to be alive. Is this... am I depressed? I don't know, I don't know. I just feel wrong. I haven't felt right since I woke up."

The temptation entered my head to confess everything to him, but even if he did believe me, how would it make him less upset to know his wife had hidden such a massive secret from him?

Sighing, buckling into me, he whispered through tears. "I know you're trying to help me, and I love you for it. I love you so much. I just can't shake this feeling that I'm trespassing in my own life." I helped him draw a hot bath and gestured for his hound to follow me.

In the hallway, I whispered into the hound's ear. "Go, fetch your master for me." The hound nodded, plodding away. Moments later, the doorbell rang. I opened it to see my neighbor, Roger, holding the casserole he'd promised to bring by earlier in the week. It wasn't him, of course.

"May I come in?" DeathAsRoger asked, in a tone that was far kinder than I expected.

"You know why I asked you here?" I couldn't look at him, it was breaking me to ask for his help.

"I anticipated the request." He was still holding the casserole and was using it to gesture.

"Are you going to make me literally ask you?"

"I need to know you mean it. There is no going back, so you need to be sure."

"Please, don't make me say it out loud."

"All you have to do is ask, and it will all be over."

All the air dropped from my lungs, my stomach clenched. I felt a weight on my tongue, as if my heart was physically pulling it back into my mouth so I couldn't utter the words. Finally, I mustered, "Please, help him move on. Take him. Take him with you. Please."

"Consider it done."

"How will it happen?"

"When he falls asleep tonight."

"So, I can put him to bed, I can be with him still?"

"Yes. And then it will be done."

I can't write about it. I can't write about how it felt to pull him out of the tub. How it felt to dry him off, help him into his pajamas. I encouraged him to call his mom. I can't yet think about how it was, to hear them talk, knowing it was the last time. How casually he said "good night." Not "goodbye," but "good night." How it felt to stroke his hair, to trace my fingers along the outline of his face, to commit him to physical memory. How it felt for him to smile at me.

There aren't words to describe how it felt to watch him close his eyes. How it felt to see his hound curl up on our bed next to him, resting its head on my husband's chest, as it stopped rising. How it felt when his hand let go of mine. I couldn't bring myself to watch him walk away. I've watched hundreds of people leave, but when I saw his last breath, I rolled on my side and turned away.

I pretended to sleep, rather than reveal to him that I had any kind of relationship with Death.

The Third and Final Deal

Magda is the strongest person I have ever known. Over the past few days, she has pushed aside her own grief to prioritize mine. She lost her son, whom she has known his whole life, yet she has carried me through this experience, I who only knew him for such a brief time.

The funeral was this afternoon. My husband is officially gone. I said my goodbyes to everyone and was about to leave when a groundskeeper caught my attention.

"Guess it's just you and me again. Like old times."

And then, DeathAsGroundskeeper winked at me, as if we were friends, as if They hadn't, once again, taken my happiness from me. So, I made my third, and final deal with Death.

"I need a favor."

"So soon?"

"Grant me this one, and I'll never ask another one again."

"I'm listening."

Without a pause, I replied. "Here is the deal. I want to forget you."

"Forget me? You're human. Knowledge of death is baked into your very being. "

"No, I don't mean the abstract concept of death. Of course I'll know I'm going to die some day. It's **you**, specifically, Death yourself, I want to forget."

They looked wounded. "You don't mean that. You can't. I'm your oldest companion. I've been with you from the beginning."

"Exactly, and you've authored every misery I've suffered. So I want to forget you. I want to forget your hounds. I want to forget every moment I've ever spent with you. To forget that you exist at all."

"No, please."

"I don't want to hear you, I don't want to see you, I don't want to know anything about you. Not until it's time for me to leave."

"I don't think you've thought this through. We've been through too much together."

"You told me you could do it. You threatened me once, remember? The woman who hurt kids? I told her to die miserably, and you said you could take away my gift. Go ahead, take it. I'm returning it to you. I don't want it."

"You'll miss me."

"No one could ever miss you. I've never understood whether you are a supernatural spirit or an extraterrestrial alien, but what I do understand is that it is YOU who are a limited being. You can't comprehend the depths of human emotion. You never could."

"If you're sure..."

"I am."

"There are conditions."

"Naturally."

"First, it will be for the rest of your mortal life. No going back."

"Good. Next?"

"It will start the moment you fall asleep."

"Fabulous, I feel pretty tired. What else."

"You will have to relearn how to interact with dying people."

"It's about time for a new profession, anyway. If that's all, I've got a nap to get to."

"You really mean it?"

"With all my heart. If you had one, you'd understand how much that means."

"Very well... goodbye, little one. If you change your mind before you fall asleep..."

"Goodbye."

And so now I am documenting this. I am going to hide it in an old box of junk in the attic that I have no reason to go through, and I've prepared an envelope for this with a note to myself. "Place in safety deposit box. Do not open until you are 99 years old, or on your death bed."

I wonder if I'll take myself seriously. Even if I open this up and take a peek, will I believe it? We'll see. But given how Death always pulls some trick, I want this as a fail safe.

Truly, I am mad at Death, but They are right. This is an awfully big part of my life story to erase, an enormous portion of my very identity to give up. I'm so tired now, and I don't know if that's to blame for my current nervous state, but I am starting to have doubts. When I wake up tomorrow, I will be me. Just me. No supernatural conversations with human conduits, no invisible dogs, no gift for knowing someone is about to leave. It's over.

There's always a catch with Death, so what will it be this time? Will I be tormented wondering where the scars I have came from? Will Death take more than just their own memories? I suppose I'll have to lose my time with Sadie in the afterworld. Will I remember losing my mother? I only saw her in the brief moment that Death allowed. What about the peace of mind that came from seeing Aunt Helen depart? What torments will Death design to play out for the rest of my life in exchange for this deal?

Yet as anxious as I am about losing part of myself, I am excited, too. It will be nice not to live waiting for something tragic to happen every time I find even a little happiness. I wonder who I'll be, without the influence of Death. Tomorrow begins the first day of my life, my true life, without Death.

The Patron Saint of Pianos

—

"While they were stoning him, Stephen prayed,
'Lord Jesus, receive my spirit.' Then he fell on
his knees and cried out, 'Lord, do not hold this
sin against them.' When he had said this, he fell
asleep."

-Acts 7:59 - 60 (NIV)

Within minutes of arriving at his new job, Eric met the woman he was going to marry. Neither of them knew it at the time, of course, and it took over two years of dating and another year of engagement before their big day. Eric was new in town and had taken a job at the police station there looking for a change of scene after years spent working a grim city beat near the border of Arizona and Mexico. He'd had enough of dead bodies and desert heat and headed as far north as he could for the freezing weather and friendly locals of Minnesota.

Kalyna Thiebaud, affectionately known to most people as "Lyn" or "Lynnie," was a local, born and bred, and worked as a municipal dispatch operator for local police, fire, and rescue services. Everyone knew her and held a special affection for her, which they gladly cast on Eric, once he and Lynnie started dating. Her family—two loving parents and a mischievous older sister, Beatrice—welcomed him as one of their own. Eric had never been close with his own family and was swept away by their love and acceptance. They started to call him "Rick" or "Ricky," nicknames no one had ever used for him, but which he embraced because, to him, it was a sign that he belonged.

In no time at all he was a regular at restaurants and bars, had an extensive group of friends, and found himself invited to join everything from the bowling league to the baseball team. It was everything he'd been looking for. He'd traded in sunshine and the benefits of city life for the cold (it seemed as if there was always snow) and a community where the local second grade play passed for culture. He didn't miss his old life for a second.

As a couple, Eric and Kalyna, "Rick and Lyn," became an institution in the town. Their colleagues sometimes teased them about how annoyingly cute it was that the two ate lunch together every day during work, but they also encouraged the pair to "hurry up and get married." One afternoon, Eric managed to get Mr. Thiebaud alone and informed him that he'd very much like to marry Kalyna.

"Will you get married in the church?" Mr. Thiebaud eyed him, knowing Eric didn't have a faith of his own.

"Of course, whatever makes her happy."

"Good answer, but will you keep going to church after?"

"Mr. Thiebaud, sir, you know I haven't been to church regularly since I was a kid, but if it makes her happy, then yes, I will go."

"You've never explained why."

"Why? Why I want to marry her?"

"No, why you stopped going to church."

"Oh, I guess that's my grandmother's fault." Seeing his would-be-father-in-law raise an eyebrow in surprise, Eric quickly continued. "No, not her fault, but... let me start again. I was staying at my grandmother's house, and she had all these icons of saints everywhere. I asked why the one was holding potatoes, and she explained it was St. Stephen holding the rocks that were used to kill him."

Mr. Thiebaud stared, waiting for a point.

"So she's telling me his story and mentions that it was St. Paul who killed him, or rather, had him killed, and in a method Jesus had strictly told people *not* to use. She told me St. Stephen was considered the first martyr, and was a saint because his death was unjust. So, if killing Stephen was wrong, and Paul was behind it, I just couldn't understand any thinking that would worship one saint who put out a hit on another."

"Put out a hit?!"

"Well, I know Paul himself didn't throw a rock, but that didn't really make it better, did it? Pilate didn't actually nail Christ to the cross, right? But we didn't make him a saint! And then, not only does Paul get away with it, and with using his influence to persecute a bunch of other innocent civilians, too, but he gets to write half the New Testament, telling everyone else how to live their lives, and he gets called a saint with churches built in his honor and cities named after him. It just... I couldn't go along with that. Paul shouldn't be a saint, when he's really just a mid-tier gangster."

"Boy, you are talking a lot of nonsense right here in this moment."

"Look, you have to understand, I used to encounter people like him all the time on my old beat. Criminals who avoided justice because they didn't personally pull the trigger, because they had the right lawyers who could bend the law. Men who could call a hit on Friday and go to confession Sunday, with a priest who let them by because of all the donations the criminals made to the parish in an attempt to buy back their salvation."

"Rick, son, St. Paul was not a mafioso or cartel king or whatever you want to accuse him of. He was an apostle! Yes, he did something bad, but the Bible is full of good people who do bad things and go on to do good. Just look at Moses! He killed the Egyptian overseer!"

"True, but the overseer was a criminal who was in the act of trying to murder someone, and Moses stepped in, like a modern day 'good guy with a gun,' right?"

"Still, the overseer was killed, and dead is dead, isn't it?"

"No, not really. In my professional experience, there are degrees of terrible ways to die, and not all murders are committed equally. Killing a man to stop a murder, in an unforeseen moment of passion, is slightly different than a premeditated execution of an innocent person, carried out in the most painful way possible, like Paul having sad little St. Stephen stoned."

"So, killing is ok as long as it's in the heat of the moment?"

"No, I mean, it's never ok, which is why Moses was rightly punished. Remember he had to journey alone in the desert, suffering without adequate supplies, had to leave his people and his homeland for decades. I think that was a pretty major consequence, like serving his time."

"Then, you think he was rehabilitated from his murderous ways?"

"Well… I don't know about that. He didn't seem to mind when all those Egyptians got killed, painfully, in so many ways, what with the plagues, and the drowning in their chariots…I do think deep down once you have a taste for killing it never really leaves your system, and he probably always had the itch for blood, deep down. Sir. Ahem."

"Young man, I have to tell you, when we started this conversation, I was sure I'd give you my blessing, but now I'm frankly terrified that lightning will strike me if I keep standing next to you, blaspheming against all the saints *and* the prophets."

"That's really not my intention at all; I'm not trying to disrespect your belief. But you asked what turned me away from church, and honestly, it's the hypocrisy that says Paul is holy, but Judas is evil, when they basically did the same thing, facilitating the death of an innocent man through legal methods by mobilizing the authorities."

"Now Paul is Judas?!"

"No, because at least Judas had the decency to hang himself."

In spite of himself, Mr. Thiebaud erupted into a bellowing laughter. "Ricky, you've got a twisted misunderstanding of Scripture, but a strong sense of right and wrong, and that's a start. I do believe you mean well, even if you are misguided. Who knows, maybe marrying my daughter will be your salvation, and she can bring you back to light."

"If anyone can help me be a better man, it's your daughter. So, I have your blessing?"

"Mine is not the blessing you should be worried about, but yes, you have my...let's call it an endorsement."

The theological debate behind him, Eric was free to ask Kalyna to marry him, and she accepted. Nearly the whole town was invited to, and showed up for, their wedding. It was a big affair, as the fire department banquet hall was filled to capacity and beyond, with revelers spilling outside into the parking lot.

Eric adored Kalyna, and she adored him. They fell more in love with each other every passing day. She was clever, hardworking, honest, fun, and an incredible mother to their twin girls, Ashley and Dana. He didn't understand how he'd been so lucky to meet her just when he did, so for a while he waited for the other shoe to drop. It never did; life was just... good. From time-to-time people would kid her about her "wild child" days back in college, but for the most part she was seen as a model citizen.

He knew he was fortunate. Every Sunday after church they had dinner at his in-laws', along with Beatrice and her husband, a local named Jack. Eric and Jack became best friends, joking about the burden of being married to sisters who were so close to each other.

To Eric, the consistency of his family routine gave him the calm he'd sought after the trauma of witnessing so much violence in his early career. Each night as a family, they'd clean up after dinner, then he and Kalyna would tuck in the kids, reading to them from their favorite books. He and Kalyna took turns making silly or scary voices for the characters.

His favorite part was when Kalyna would end story time with a song, often one made up on the spot for their girls. Kalyna hated singing in public, it was something she shared only with her husband and their daughters. She had a pretty voice, nothing spectacular, but nice to listen to. He once asked her why she never sang at karaoke nights or in the church choir. "Because," she explained. "It's just for you. I sing for you all because I *love-love* you." This was her term she used often with Eric to emphasize that her love-love for him was distinct and surpassed her love for other people.

Life was idyllic. His career as a police officer was so predictable it bordered on boring. Crime rarely ever happened, and when it did it was usually harmless pranks by local teens with too much time (and toilet paper) on their hands. More often than not, instead of a crime, he was called on to help an elderly person start their car, or some other mundane task.

After starting out his career dealing with kidnappings gone wrong, drug dealers, sexual assaults, domestic violence, missing and exploited children, and even cartel vendettas carried over from the old country, his new routine was exactly what he had needed. He'd nearly quit police work entirely, exhausted from seeing the worst of humanity, from the endless nightmares and horrific flashbacks that plagued him.

Before he became a cop, he thought death was a simple state of being. Seeing the variety of mutilated corpses in his first year, he understood that some deaths are absolutely worse than others. In his nightmares, he was always a bird, flying over the scene of the crime, watching himself responding, taking in the grisly display.

It seemed unreal to him now that he could have found the town, the job, and the wife of his dreams. Over time, the nightmares faded, he slept better, felt happier, as if everything violent was a world away and a lifetime ago. He allowed himself to become so secure in his new life that he expected things would always continue just as they were. No drama, no surprises, no wrinkles.

Eric's mistake was letting down his guard—actually believing life could be calm and consistent. He tricked himself into believing the events of his life were entirely under his control, so when the piano teacher arrived in town, it rocked him more than it should.

The old high school had been crumbling for decades, and the town had finally secured funding to build a new one. For years, nearly every fundraiser had been dedicated to this cause, and finally the state agreed to send some money after an inspector gave them a report that the building was "an absolute hellhole of asbestos and black mold, better suited as low-rent apartments for struggling rats than as classrooms for human students."

With the new high school nearing completion, it was time to clear out the old building of any contents worth keeping, before it was demolished. Kalyna, Beatrice, and Jack were nostalgic over Sunday dinner, remembering good times in a bad building.

"That gym was a wreck for ages even before our time." Kalyna recalled. "It was already falling apart by the time of my senior prom, remember? We begged the PTA to let us host the dance anywhere else. They didn't let us, and ugh, the gym smelled so bad, and no one wanted to have to hang decorations in the mildewed rafters, so it was plain as could be."

"THAT'S what you remember from your senior prom?" Joked an unbelieving Jack.

Kalyna had never mentioned prom before, so Eric asked, "Who did you go with?"

"Not who she wanted to, that's for sure!" Beatrice teased.

"Beatrice, be nice to your sister." Mrs. Thiebaud chided her elder daughter.

"And please, let's not talk about this anymore." Mr. Thiebaud supported his wife in redirecting the conversation. "We're here for a nice, family dinner. No need for inappropriate stories, especially not in front of my grand-babies, got it?" Eric was confused, but knew better than to go against Mr. Thiebaud, so he let it rest.

Plans were made for a goodbye party to the old alma mater, taking place of the annual winter dance, complete with an auction and a concert, to be held in the new school's state-of-the art event space. The hope was that the new facility could also serve as a community center for town functions, as the local municipal buildings were of a limited capacity.

To mark the end of the era, alumni and faculty from the school's history, which was essentially the entire population of the town, were invited to attend the winter dance concert. A few people had moved away over the decades, naturally, so they made their way back for the occasion.

Among them was Pete LaSalle, the former music teacher from Kalyna's era. His arrival raised eyebrows and caused a ruffle of remarks delivered in the snarky, subtle way of a people who are too familiar with each other's history, and who assume everyone else is equally in the know. The innuendos swirled, and Eric heard the surprise as he was out and about on his daily patrols.

"Never thought we'd see LaSalle again!"

"Can't believe Pete showed, after everything that happened."

"Uh oh, look out ladies, he's back."

"Look out gentlemen, you mean. All the women in town are about to only have eyes for Pete. Maybe he's aged poorly!"

"LaSalle's back?! Man, I haven't seen him since his dad died."

"I wonder if Jared and Derick know he's back yet."

"I hope this dance turns out better for LaSalle than the last one!"

Some of these were directed at Eric. "Ooooh, I bet Lynnie sure is glad to hear the news. Maybe time she picked back up on those *private* piano lessons!" This was delivered with a knowing wink that left Eric unsettled.

Eric had never heard of this teacher, and suddenly Mr. LaSalle was the talk of the town. No one seemed to remember that Eric was not a lifelong townie, and he found himself feeling in the dark. For the first time since moving there, he felt like an outsider. He particularly didn't like the insinuation that there was something between his wife and this teacher. Yes, he knew she'd had some fun during college, but by every account she'd been nothing short of an angel ever since.

The idea that something inappropriate took place between Kalyna and the teacher ate away at Eric quickly. It took up residence in his mind and was all he could think about. "No," he decided. "There's no way anything happened between them." After all, she had been a minor, LaSalle had been an adult. The town wouldn't be so wink-wink nudge-nudge about a serious crime.

For a moment Eric considered simply asking Kalyna what happened, but he knew she'd chide him for being gullible enough to fall for small-town gossip. Even deeper down, he didn't want to ask her because he was afraid that she might confirm the rumors, and he didn't think he could bear that. She was his refuge from all the darkness he'd witnessed, and he needed her to continue being the woman he'd placed up on a pedestal. So he decided to try and move past the whispers, but his attempts to convince himself were unsuccessful at easing his mind.

He hadn't even met this Mr. LaSalle, yet already found that he hated him. Now, hate was not a sensation Eric was used to feeling. He didn't even know what this guy looked like, but imagined punching him the moment they met. When his made-up image of LaSalle's visage floated into his mind's eye, Eric would ball his fist up, anticipating the satisfaction of landing a blow on that smug face.

The imaginary confrontation consumed him. Driven to see the man for himself, and unable to wait the two more weeks until the winter dance concert, he got home from work and ran to his wife's bookshelves, and, finding her old yearbooks, pulled out one from her senior year, the class of 1984.

Opening to the faculty section, there he was. "Peter LaSalle, Music" read the caption. To Eric's dismay, LaSalle was handsome. The rest of the page dropped out of focus, blurred, with only this one portrait standing out in relief. Classically good looking. A winning smile with perfect teeth. The kind of man that other men wanted to look like, Even the most macho man wouldn't hesitate to affirm LaSalle was undeniably attractive.

Flipping back to the student section, he found Kalyna's picture. There she was, cute as could be, innocent. Eric's yearbook endeavor only served to ramp up his obsession, and his desire for a violent man-to-man match. He remembered some of the disfigured corpses he'd seen in his old precinct, the handiwork of rival gangs. In his mind he began to paste LaSalle's face over that of various victims. Putting the yearbook away, he grabbed a beer from the fridge, quickly followed by a second, nursing his feelings of torment.

He had to know what happened. When Kalyna got home from shopping with her sister, Eric didn't even let them close the front door before launching into his questions. "Who is Mr. LaSalle? Were you close? Did he hit on you? What happened?!" He knew he sounded crazed, and he didn't like it, but it was out of his control. She looked at him like he was speaking in tongues.

"Mr. LaSalle? My old piano teacher? What about him?"

"He's back in town!" Gesturing at her with his third bottle of beer, he questioned, "Or are you somehow the only person that doesn't know?"

A hint of a smile pulled the corner of her mouth and her eyes drifted away, but in an instant she shook it off and put on a mask of indifference. "Oh, did he come back for the winter dance concert? I didn't even know anyone had invited him. I wouldn't have thought he'd come back anyway, now with his folks having passed and all."

"I didn't even know you played piano, but everyone else seems to know he was your private tutor. What happened?"

Beatrice stepped in the door, loaded down with even more sacks of gifts. "Here, my car's still running and I gotta get home. I'll catch up with you tomorrow."

"Did *you* know Mr. LaSalle?" Eric asked, desperate.

"HAH! Do I? Not as well as your wife!"

"Grow up!" Kalyna, exasperated, was trying to make order of the disorganized shopping haul, while also removing her mittens, scarf, hat, and boots.

Kalyna's annoyed dismissal just encouraged Bea, who began performing an imitation of her sister. "Oh, do you think Mr. LaSalle will dance with me at prom? Oh Bea, he's so handsome, he's so talented. Do you think he likes me? I love him, Bea. I *love-love* him!" Eric's heart dropped. "Poor P.J. might have been her date to prom, but in Lynnie's heart she belonged to Mr. LaSalle!"

"Don't be-a-twit, Beatrice. Go home!"

"I'll leave, but that won't change the fact that you *love-loved* your piano teacher!"

"Get out of here!" Kalyna playfully kicked at her sister, who scuttled out the door.

"Was that all true?" Eric tried to start a dialogue with his wife, but she wasn't having it.

Gesturing at the shopping bags, Kalyna redirected him. "Can you help me unload and hide those? The girls will be home in a few, Mrs. Janis is dropping them off from ballet."

He'd never felt jealous toward her before. Yes, everyone in town knew her and acted like she was their own. Yes, he knew a few of the local guys had dated her in high school, but they were all good friends now, and Eric knew them from the bar, the cafe, bowling. He had never been bothered by it, he'd always liked that his wife was popular, well-loved. He liked knowing he'd married a catch, a hometown girl all the local guys would have wanted to marry. He knew she loved him, and it had never occurred to him to feel insecure.

Why was this different? Why had it unsettled him? In his old life he had worked some awful cases involving children before, cases that made him question if humanity deserved to exist. But if his wife had been victimized by a teacher, surely the whole town wouldn't be joking about it. Unless, they thought she had pursued him? But everyone knows a student can't pursue a teacher, there's an age dynamic, a power imbalance.

Maybe it happened after graduation? During her "wild-child" phase people sometimes joked about? What was she keeping from him that everyone else seemed to know?

He tried over and over again throughout dinner to make her talk about it, but she kept brushing him off with endless excuses. "High school was a long time ago. He taught me how to play piano, that's all. The past is past, let it go. I don't want to talk about it. There's nothing to tell. It's a small town, people get bored and they talk. You know everyone here acts like they know everything about everyone, but that doesn't make it so. I don't know what else to say to make you drop it."

Frustrated, Eric knew he wasn't going to get anything out of her but also knew he wouldn't be able to sleep. "Fine," he said. "I'm going to go for a walk, clear my head a little bit. Maybe head to Ernie's for a drink."

Hugging him, Kalyna smiled. "That sounds like a good idea to me. Just promise you'll stay out of trouble, Officer." She grinned, that goofy smile he knew so well from when they were sharing an inside joke. He wanted everything to be ok.

The cold air hit his face, refreshing him. The rhythmic crunching of snow under his feet had a meditative effect. He was right; he needed fresh air, and it was helping. He felt silly that he'd gotten so carried away, so suspicious. Worse, he felt guilty that he'd entertained thoughts of violence against a complete stranger.

Entering the bar, Eric was met with a series of welcomes from all the regulars, including his brother-in-law, Jack. Eric received a chorus of remarks from the townies. "Oh ho, there he is now!" "Right on time, Rick!" "Speak of the devil." "Ricky! Just the man we were talking about."

As all eyes turned to him, a single face pulled his focus. Older, slightly wrinkled with grey hair, but still recognizable: LaSalle.

Slapping LaSalle on the back with one of his big, bear-paw hands, Ernie bellowed a laugh. "Here he is! The lucky sonofagun who nabbed everyone's favorite girl! Pete LaSalle, meet Rick! Ricky, Pete LaSalle, music man."

The piano teacher gave a broad smile, the perfect teeth Eric had seen in the yearbook. LaSalle stretched out his hand, which Eric involuntarily accepted with a shake. He was surprised at how callused the hand was, and how strong. Was he trying to intimidate Eric? Making a point, Eric pulled LaSalle in closer to him, squeezing his grip.

Surprised, LaSalle drew his hand back, rubbing his palms together. "Quite a grip you've got there, officer. Care to join us? Ernie, your finest beer for this gentleman."

Instantly, all the perspective Eric had gained during his walk dissipated, and bad feelings took hold. He resented how at ease the man was, how at home he appeared on the bar stool. These were Eric's friends, and this was his bar. Who was this asshole to buy *him* a drink?

"So, Officer Rick," began the impossibly good-looking teacher. "You're married to little Lynne Thiebaud, huh?"

"Yeahshesmywife!" Hurtled out of Eric's mouth, a full sentence a projectile tied together as a single word.

The teacher looked amused. "Little high-strung, are you? Can't say I'm surprised, I heard you came from a pretty intense situation before you got here. Well, I'd be pretty jittery, too."

How dare this man try to relate to Eric? "You don't know what I've seen. You don't know me. And you don't know my wife. Not anymore, anyway."

"Fair enough. Ernie, this man either needs way more drinks, or no more drinks, but what he for sure doesn't need is further conversation with me. I'm headed out."

The bar flies tried to convince him to stay, but the teacher insisted. "Nah, I'm tired, had a long drive in. I'm looking forward to a good night's rest."

"Catch up with you tomorrow?" asked an older barfly.

"You got it. I just gotta get up to the school with the other teachers early in the morning. I've been recruited to help evaluate all the instruments, uniforms, and equipment. We're going to see what can be salvaged for the auction or donated, and what needs to make its way to the dump."

"You should just skip all that," Ernie recommended. "Get a big garbage truck, drop it all in the lake, you know one of those spots just out past the edge of Gilbert's property. It won't bother anyone there!"

"Yeah!" Jack agreed. "No way any of that junk is worth the time it takes to sort it. Sink it deep into the water, let all them frozen fish start a band!"

Chuckling at the suggestions, the music man waved a submissive hand. "All right, all right, I'll take it under advisement. Thanks for the drinks, fellas. I'll see you later!"

As LaSalle moved to leave, a tall, disheveled local man, Jared, walked into the bar, sizing up LaSalle, and intentionally grazing the piano teacher's shoulder with his own. LaSalle put up his hands, diffusing the tension, calmly stating, "I have no business with you, Jared. I'm just in town for a little while, to help." Jared grunted, but Ernie wasted no time directing Jared to go home and come back another night.

Eric swiveled his stool, peppering his friends and brother-in-law with more questions. No one was forthcoming. His increasingly-inebriated state made it difficult to track the conversation and who was responding to him.

"He didn't have a ring on." Observed Eric. "He's not married?"

"Oh, he was, until your wife's senior year."

"Lyn never told you what happened? Prom night?"

"Someone must have told you!"

"THE prom night incident? Biggest scandal ever hit the town."

"Never had a teacher fired for something like that, that's for sure."

"It was in all the papers."

Eric zeroed in on his brother-in-law. "Jack, tell me what happened," he tried to say, but only vomit came out.

"Come on, man!" Ernie ran to grab cleaning supplies.

"Dude, you need to get yourself together." Rightly assessed Jack. "Sorry 'bout that Ern, I'm taking him home to sleep it off!"

"WhatscandalwhynobodytellmewhathappendKalynamyw ifepromstory," slurred Eric in response. He didn't remember how he got home, only that his curiosity had not been satisfied.

The next day, Eric woke up to an intense hangover, weighed down with anxiety and regret. Rolling onto his side, he peered through blurry eyes at his nightstand but was unable to read his alarm clock. He did see a glass of water, three painkillers set in a neat row, and a note, in Kalyna's confident, bubbly hand. "Rise and shine!"

After collecting himself, he stumbled from his bedroom toward the kitchen, where he found a much longer note from Kalyna. "Hi Babe! Called work and said you weren't feeling right, needed the day to rest. Dropped the girls off at Mrs. Janis' for the day, I told her I'll get them later. I've got errands to run after work, but will be home for dinner. Drink lots of water, and call me at work if you need anything. Love-love!" The note was punctuated with a line drawing of Mrs. PAC-Man that she always used to end her notes to him.

Obediently, he followed his wife's instructions, chugging water and heading straight back to bed. He had trouble falling asleep, as visions of the teacher ran through his head. Prom night, prom night…Eric had to know what happened on prom night. He'd hoped to clear things up with her this morning. His mind ran through endless scenarios involving his wife in high school, then an underage child, and the teacher, a grown man, until he grew so exhausted he mercifully fell into a deep sleep and couldn't think on it anymore.

When he finally woke again, it was the afternoon, and he tried to occupy himself to keep his mind off imaginary prom night offenses his brain kept cooking up, projected in front of his eyes like a horror film he couldn't turn off. He cleaned the house, then cleaned it again. He flipped through Kalyna's old photo albums, confirming that she attended prom with P.J., a fellow student, a nice enough guy who still lived in town.

Nothing made sense, nothing shed light, nothing gave him any bit of reassurance. He needed to see Kalyna, to talk to her.

After an eternity, he heard a car pull up to the house... but also heard a second vehicle, a loud truck. As the door opened and people piled into the front hall, Eric felt unsure if he was somehow still drunk or hallucinating, because the piano teacher was right there, at his front door.

"Girls, boots off!" Instructed Kalyna. Everyone's feet were covered with grimy snow and rock salt. Grocery sacks and a massive tote bag obscured Kalyna's face, but she sounded like she was in a good mood. Mr. LaSalle reached down toward Ashley's snow boots. "Here," he said, kneeling, "let me help you off with those."

Now this man was touching his daughters?! What was happening in Eric's life? Who was this stranger in their private home and why was he so quickly inserting himself into their domestic routines? Eric moved to intercept the teacher, but before he could, he found his arms stuffed with bags Kalyna shoved at him, as she began the slow process of peeling off later upon layer of winter gear.

"Hi Babe!" She planted a kiss right on Eric's cheek, as he stood, immobilized. "You remember Mr. LaSalle?" Then, mischievously, "Or maybe you don't? Jake told me you had quite a night!"

Everything happened too fast for Eric to keep up. Nothing was in his control. He tried to form words to respond, but he was too caught off guard by the entire situation.

"Good to see you again, Rick." Mr. LaSalle said over his shoulder, as he now helped Dana with her boots. "But really, Lyn, you *don't* have to call me Mr. LaSalle anymore. I'm not your teacher anymore, you can call me —"

"No! You're always Mr. LaSalle, it's too weird otherwise," she protested playfully.

"Have it your way. Now, Rick, I hope you're ready to do some heavy lifting. *Kalyna*," he emphasized the formality of her full name, "where's it going?"

"Mmmm, one sec, let me move a couple things—right here, right by the fireplace. Girls, help me grab this stuff! Eric! Set those groceries on the counter and get your boots on to help Mr. LaSalle!"

Kalyna and the twins quickly cleared a large area of the living room, while Eric moved, hypnotized and against his will, toward the kitchen, depositing the groceries. He then walked to the front door, pulling his boots off the shoe rack and following the teacher outside to the truck parked in front of the house.

"I'm so glad this one's going to a good home," Mr. LaSalle observed, patting the worn, but still handsome, upright piano. "I know Lynnie will take good care of it. I couldn't believe when she told me she didn't have one."

Eric tried to focus. "No, we don't have a piano. I didn't know she even played."

"Are you kidding? She was one of my best students, so dedicated. And creative, too. Those covers she used to come up with, of punk songs, rock songs, even metal, always some song by angry yelling men, which she'd slow down for piano and sing in her sweet voice." The teacher laughed at his reverie. "I tell you, none of those covers should have worked but they did! Plus, those songs she used to make up on the fly, impromptu lyrics on what happened that day at school."

"She sang?"

"Oh, yeah. Her belting wasn't exactly the strongest, but she had a pleasant natural head voice. She never sang at the concerts, though, just during our private lessons. I tried to convince her but she said she didn't want to sing in front of a crowd. She just wanted them to focus on her piano playing. Ok, we just need to get this down here... oh, hey there Don!" Mr. LaSalle greeted Eric's friend and neighbor, who was walking down the sidewalk toward them.

"Heya fellas! Saw you might need another set of hands here!"

"Thanks Don!" Mr. LaSalle was right at home in the community, in their neighborhood. "Yup, ran into Lyn today and she mentioned she still didn't have a piano, so since the school's getting rid of a bunch of stuff, I thought she might be just the person to give this one a happy home. She said her girls would love it."

"Oh, that's great!" Cheered Don. "To this day, I remember when she played that song at the Christmas concert, blew us all away. You know the one I'm talking about?"

"Yes, it was 'Carol of the Bells,' the George Winston arrangement."

Eric stood, feeling invisible, as this whole conversation occurred around him.

"That's the one. Gave me chills. Didn't know she could play like that."

"Well, it took a long time to get her there, but she was determined." Finally, looking at Eric, "When she first said that's the song she wanted to perform at the winter concert, I had my doubts."

"You said she was your best student?" Eric puzzled.

"One of my best, yes. Mostly in terms of attitude and effort. She was enthusiastic, but her technical skills weren't as developed as some of the other kids. She just tried harder. Signed up for extra one-on-one lessons after school to make sure she had it down. She was so focused —her parents really liked that version of the song, and she wanted so much to surprise them."

"Everyone was surprised," Don mused. "I remember it, I was sitting near her folks and Bea, and they were just taken away. You won't believe me, but I think I even saw Mr. Thiebaud tear up."

"They didn't hear her rehearsing at home?" Eric wondered.

"Oh no, they didn't have a piano at home." Mr. LaSalle clarified. "That's why she had to take extra lessons at school."

"Couldn't *afford* to have one at home, you mean." Don added. "Who could? Except for you-know-who with all their *car money*." Don's eyes rolled as he said this.

"Oh, I know, remember the raffle?"

Don spit. "Sure do, that was messed up."

"Raffle?" Eric was lost.

LaSalle explained. "A new music store opened in town. They were going to sponsor the winter concert, and also decided to woo potential customers by showing some good will. They donated a brand new, upright piano to the school for a raffle, letting some lucky student win. You gotta remember, this is a farm town, and back then we were going through a hard time. No one had extra money to spend even on necessities, let alone a luxury like a brand-new instrument. All my students wanted to win it, but not as badly as Kalyna. She wanted that piano more than anyone ever wanted anything. She swore that when she won, she'd practice all day every day and she'd be the best piano player in town."

"Now, everyone was excited at the chance, even if they didn't play all that well. Imagine: having a piano in your home!" Don continued. "All the kids at school were excited for their chance, and their parents scraped together enough money for each kid to buy one ticket. Lyn and Bea bought tickets, everyone bought tickets. I even bought one, and I didn't play.

"Bea had the idea to campaign for sister, tried to get everyone to promise that if they won, they'd let Lynnie have it because she wanted one so bad, and a lot of us agreed. We just gave Bea our ticket as soon as we bought it, so Lyn would feel like luck had to be on her side. Everyone loves her and would have liked being the one to make her happy. It was just a dream, you know, but a dream we could all have a fair chance at."

"Fair? Hah!" Interjected Mr. LaSalle.

"Yeah well," Don's face darkened. "Wilmer Allard, you know, from the Allard Auto Empire? He was your wife's classmate. We get to the day of the raffle, and Lyn had a stack of tickets bigger than she knew what to do with. Bea had to hold some for her. Everyone was excited for her to hear one of her tickets called out, to see her run up on stage and take a bow. Well, just as they're announcing who wins, we see Wilmer get ready to stand, as if he already had it in the bag. And he did. They called that asshole's name, and he walked up proud as a fucking peacock (excuse my language, Mr. LaSalle) and strolled on stage like a little prince."

Mr LaSalle gestured angrily. "That little prick's parents bought more tickets than the rest of the town combined. They spent more money on those tickets than they would if they'd just bought the piano outright. Now, they already HAD a piano, but that wasn't good enough. No. They needed to win, to beat everyone else, to make sure their son got the big prize everyone else wanted. He wanted the attention, he wanted the applause, and they sure weren't going to disappoint their precious little boy. Made me sick. All those families who could never afford a piano on their own, losing to a family that didn't even need it."

"We were all stunned. No one made a sound. He waltzed up there expecting applause and congratulations, and instead he got angry silence. He quickly realized not only was no one happy for him, and probably guessed we all hated him for it. I was sitting near Lynnie when they called his name, and poor girl, her heart broke in front of all of us." Eric wasn't used to Don seeming sentimental. "She was trying not to cry, but you know what she did?"

"I remember, I'll never forget." LaSalle nodded, fondly.

"Your wife stood up, verge of tears, and clapped for him. She clapped for that little shit. She even managed to call out congratulations to him."

"It was an act of grace only she was capable of, and we all followed her lead. Everyone clapped for him. Sure, none of us meant it, but if she could do it, so could we. She was just a better person than him. Poor Lynnie, she always used to apologize she wasn't farther along in practicing, and was frustrated she couldn't keep up without even a little keyboard to use at home. Winning that stupid raffle meant the world to her, and she never had a shot. But! Now she can have this one, the exact same one she used to play back in high school."

"The same one?" Eric eyed the piano suspiciously, as if it was a living being, an interloper come to disrupt his marriage.

"What is all this chatting, you all starting a book club?" Kalyna's voice rang out from the front step. "Hiya Don! Are you boys going to talk that piano into the living room, or are you gonna carry it?"

"We're on it, Lyn!" Replied Don, giving her a loving salute.

"Right away, ma'am" echoed Mr. LaSalle, with an exaggerated bow.

Eric helped the other two men, and in no time they had the piano situated in the living room. The girls stood next to it in awe, running their fingers along the cover and asking for confirmation that it was really theirs, that they could keep it.

"That's right ladies, it's all yours!" Mr. LaSalle affirmed.

"Mom, you know how to play?" Ashley asked.

"She sure does!" Don enthused.

Immediately the girls begged for a song. Eric watched as his wife tried to demur, but he could see she was anxious to play. "Maybe Mr. LaSalle could play for us."

"Oh no, no ma'am. This is your piano, you get the honors of breaking it in." He pulled the bench out for her, and she slid on to it. LaSalle rolled the cover back over the keys, and Kalyna gasped a little.

"Whoo, this brings back memories. I can't believe... it's really mine? You're giving it to me, just like that?" She gazed at her teacher, radiant with adoration.

"All yours."

She slowly stroked the keys without striking them, just feeling them beneath her finger tips. She began to press on a few, eliciting wonky notes.

Mr. LaSalle spoke up. "Needs tuning, I know."

"That's no big deal, we can get it tuned."

Don urged her "Do you remember how to play 'Carol of the Bells,' Lyn?"

"Oh no! I mean, maybe, I don't know. I haven't touched a piano in years though. Here, let me see if any of it comes back to me?"

Slowly, she began to play, and after a few notes, Mr. LaSalle gently whispered, "Posture," causing Kalyna to pull herself upright. She began to play more emphatically. She was going along with increased momentum until she hit a sour note, and quickly apologized.

"Sorry, I guess I really am out of practice. You know, I haven't gone near a piano since that last time I saw you, that night we, that I—" she paused, embarrassed.

"No, you almost had it." Mr. LaSalle sat next to her on the bench. "Here, just pick it up from this chord." And they began to play together, turning it into a duet. Despite the need for tuning, the harmony filled the room, with Don and the twins entranced.

Eric, now fully a spectator in his own home, watched the back of his wife, side-by-side with the back of this man who, to Eric, had not even existed 48 hours before. He felt as if a fever was rapidly taking hold of his body. The song ended, and Kalyna let out a small, triumphant laugh.

"See," encouraged LaSalle. "You've still got it."

Kalyna locked eyes with him, grateful, then bashfully tilted her head down. A timer went off in the kitchen, pulling Kalyna's attention. "Oh, dinner! Mr. LaSalle, you're staying, yeah? And you too, Don!"

"Oh, I don't want to intrude..." Don began to decline, before changing his mind, "but Nancy is on the night shift so I'm on my own... and it does smell awfully good."

"Great! Gentlemen, boots off, hands washed, and into the dining room. Girls, help me set the table." As she passed Eric, she quickly nuzzled his cheek with the tip of her nose, and whispered "Can you believe it? It's mine!"

Eric couldn't concentrate during dinner. He liked Don, but he wanted him to leave, and to take that piano teacher along with him. Hell, he could take the whole piano with him, too. Instead, Eric had to endure listening to Kalyna and Mr. LaSalle make plans for the week.

"I'll come by tomorrow and get that piano tuned for you."

"I'd love that! Thank you again, Mr. LaSalle."

Don suddenly had a bright idea. "Say, Lyn, you should play at the winter concert!"

She put up a mild protest. "It's only a week away, and I'm sure the program is set. Besides, I haven't played in years, you heard me. You think I'd be ready to play in front of an audience that soon?"

Mr. LaSalle backed up Don. "You should do it! I can take care of adding you to the program... you can be the encore. You're a little rusty, but you'd be surprised at muscle memory, how quickly things can come back to us, even after years. I think with some serious practice this week, you'd be in shape to play."

The confidence boost from her teacher was all she needed. "I will practice, and I could take a day or two off work to really dedicate myself to it. But, Mr. LaSalle, would you have some time to help me?"

"Sure, we got a lot of the sorting done today, and figuring out the auction prices won't take that long, so I think I'll have plenty of time to help."

Eric didn't like any of the decisions being made. "You're going to use vacation time for this?"

"It's not like we ever use all of our vacation days anyway, Babe. Besides, it's important to me!"

Don, unsolicited, chimed in. "Wait 'til you really hear her play, Rick. She's going to be the star of the show, I promise."

Eric decided to wait until their company left before attempting to dissuade his wife, but by the end of dinner the girls were so excited at the prospect of their mother's performance that they were already obsessed with helping her pick out what to wear. He realized that it would have made him look like a jerk to be the only one not supporting her, so he decided to stifle his feelings, and even managed to sound enthused, offering his opinions on the clothing and accessories Dana and Ashley pulled together for consideration.

That night he had trouble falling asleep, and for the first time in years, the old nightmares came back, reviving his overhead flights, watching himself discover the string of shootings and stabbings and other crimes he'd been required to study at length during investigations. Just a few days before, his world had been predictable, and Kalyna had been his calm, his refuge, his safe harbor. Mr. Thiebaud said she'd be Eric's salvation. Now she was a source of chaos, thanks to the unanticipated intervention of her former teacher. He felt as if his wife had been replaced by a stranger, and nothing over the next week helped ease this sensation.

Day and night the whole following week, Kalyna practiced, scales up, scales down, and that song, that same song, over and over and over. Eric began to hear all of his conversations set to "Carol of the Bells," it was seared into his brain. The twins ran around humming it. It hounded him, he couldn't stop hearing it. At night when he tried to sleep, his violent nightmares took place to the tune. These bedtime terrors also began to feature his own wife, laughing at him, running away with her handsome, sophisticated teacher.

Even awake, he couldn't stop imagining the worst when it came to LaSalle's intentions toward his former student. All day long while Eric was out on patrol, his mind conjured images of the two *in flagrante*, on top of a piano, under a piano. The more he tried not to think about his wife's relationship with LaSalle, the more it bothered him, distracting him to the point of madness. It was torture, and no one took seriously how much he wanted answers. Of course, this wasn't helped by his insistence on playing it cool, pretending he actually liked the teacher, and was only passively interested in what had happened years ago between Kalyna and LaSalle.

Although Eric tried to tease out the nature of their past from friends and neighbors, no one felt like it was their place to actually fill him in, telling him in one way or another to ask his wife. This was an unfortunate legacy of him being an outsider. The people in town would always take Kalyna's side, look out for her, even if they did so while playfully insinuating there was more to the story. If he asked Kalyna directly, she would dodge, deflect, and grow flustered, accusing him of distracting her from practice. He couldn't wait until the week was over, until the concert was over and the teacher was successfully out of town, and out of their lives.

Despite the extremely bad weather, many folks in town still turned out for the big event, honoring the closing of the old school building and celebrating the opening of the new, improved facility. The concert program was brief, highlighting alumni from across the decades playing various songs. Kalyna's practice paid off, as she successfully struck each note, earning a standing ovation from the crowd. Once again, her father was moved to tears at his daughter's performance.

After the concert ended, Eric handed his wife a bouquet. "For me?!" She asked, elated. "Babe! These are beautiful! Thank you!" She threw her arms around his neck and laid a big kiss on his lips. "My number one fan!"

"We're your fans too, Mommy!" Dana and Ashley joined in.

"I know you are!" She took turns to hug each of them. As people came up to congratulate her, she thanked them, but between each person seemed preoccupied. Kalyna looked around, disappointed. Flagging down one of the former vice principals, she asked, "Did you find out what happened to Mr. LaSalle?"

"Sorry, no, he just didn't show up."

"But he promised, he said he was going to be here..."

"Someone said they saw his car headed out of town this morning."

"What?" Kalyna couldn't believe what she was hearing. The vice principal shrugged and moved on.

She flagged down Mrs. Eakins, who ran the only bed and breakfast in town. She confirmed the piano teacher's early departure. "Oh yes, he checked out this morning, just as he planned to."

"I knew he was leaving tonight, but he said he was going to see the concert first."

"He mentioned he had planned to do just that, but you know the storm took a nasty turn, and he said he felt like he needed to beat it before he got stuck here clear to Christmas. I'm sorry dear. In any case, it's his loss. Sweet girl, you were wonderful!" Turning to Eric, "You must be so proud!"

He pulled Kalyna in toward him.

"I sure am, Mrs. E. Proudest man in town, and the luckiest." Kalyna leaned back into him, smiling. The interaction was back to normal. No interfering teacher, just Eric and Kalyna. He felt calmer than he had in a week.

"Oh, you two!" Mrs. Eakins walked away with an approving look on her face. As she left, Eric saw his wife's face fall. "I can't believe he left town without saying goodbye," lamented Kalyna.

"Guess that old man just can't stop breaking your heart!" Teased Bea, walking up behind them.

"Shut up!" Kalyna playfully volleyed back at her sister. "He didn't break my heart then, and he certainly didn't break it now. After all, I am," she slipped her arm through Eric's elbow, resting her head on his shoulder, "a happily married woman. No one can break my heart, because it's not mine anymore. It's his." She lifted her head to admire Eric. "And he'd never let anyone do anything to damage it, would you, Babe?" Eric kissed the top of her forehead.

"Fair enough," Bea relented. "He can't hurt you now, but you can't pretend he didn't crush you before. I was there."

"Ok, enough," Eric demanded, managing somehow to sound curious, not angry. "Someone tell me what happened. I'm a big boy, I can handle it."

"I'd LOVE to!" Gushed Bea.

"Fine, but I don't have to listen." Kalyna shifted the flowers into the crook of her elbow and grabbed her daughter's hands." I'm taking the girls to get some punch and cupcakes."

As Kalyna and the twins walked away, Bea called after her, "Hey now, make sure that punch isn't spiked!" Turning back to Eric, she asked, "You know the reason she never talks about this is because she's so embarrassed, right?"

"I'm her husband, I won't judge her, you know that. I think I've lived in this town long enough to know as much about my wife as the lady who delivers our mail does. I feel like I'm the only one who has no idea about this 'incident' with the damned piano teacher." Still, to his own surprise, he sounded playful, not insistent. He even managed a convincing smile.

"Ok, so this was during her infamous 'wild child' days back in college, when she could drink any grown man under the table, and had been having lots of fun with boys at her school."

"Got it. Go on."

"She was back home on break from college, and we decided to have a ladies' night. Jack didn't mind, he knew there wasn't too much trouble we could get into. We started at the pool hall, and had a pitcher or three of beer before we went to Ernie's. You know there's only two places to drink between the pool hall or Ernie's? So naturally, we ran into everyone that night. Anyway, we get to the bar, and we're having a great time, when in walks Mr. LaSalle. No one had seen him since the summer after the prom incident. He'd found a new school to teach at, filed for divorce, and moved away. He didn't stay in touch with anyone, wanted a clean break, and had only just come back in town to close out some of his dad's affairs after he passed.

Now, my sister had pined for that man and carried a torch for him all those years, so when she saw him in her altered state, she decided to make her move at last. Which, fair enough, his divorce was long since final and he wasn't wearing a ring, so we decided he must still be on the market.

Lynnie sidled up to him, and at first he was excited to see her, she'd always been his teacher's pet. But when she put her hand on his shoulder, like this," Bea placed a hand on Eric's shoulder, "he got this serious look on his face, and Mr. LaSalle signaled me to come over and help him. He told me he didn't want anyone thinking he was 'interfering' with his students, not with the whole prom thing. I told him no one would ever think anything bad about him, especially not like that, but I remember he was stone serious and said 'Beatrice, this is a small town. Everyone cares, and everyone talks. This is how rumors start. Take her home.'"

"Then what happened?"

"I took her home."

"That... that's it? That's the big secret? That's what she couldn't tell me?! That doesn't make any sense, why would she hide that from me?"

"She was SO embarrassed, Ricky, you have to understand. She'd always been a golden child that everybody adored, she'd never made mistakes or given people cause to judge her. Years of being on her best behavior, ruined (in her mind) by one stupid night."

"How was it ruined?"

"Come on, you said yourself you've lived here long enough to know how this town works. Everyone saw her flirt with him, everyone saw him reject her, and worse, everyone knew it brought up bad feelings for him from the prom situation, which was still recent enough to sting. We all still felt bad for him.

"So, the way Lyn saw it, she'd hurt his feelings, he'd hurt hers, and she knew the whole town was going to be gossiping about her. The entire walk home she was crying, and when Jack and I managed to tuck her into bed, she was still in such a state about how Mr. LaSalle hated her and the whole town was going to make fun of her."

By this time, Jack had joined them. "Yup, she was a wreck. I actually hoped she'd throw up and pass out, better than hearing her beat herself up over one drunk moment, you know? We all make mistakes; I didn't think less of her... I actually thought it was funny. Squeaky clean high school girl turned into a college woman hitting on her old piano teacher. But she acted like it was the end of the world. And I mean, she was right, people still tease her about it to this day. You heard people when they found out Mr. LaSalle was coming back this time."

"But, wait. I'm so confused." Eric began to sweat, wondering how he, with all of his investigative experience, could have drawn such a wrong conclusion. "I thought the incident was during prom, something about how she'd wanted to go with him... isn't that why he had to leave town?"

At this, Bea and Jack both dropped their jaws at this. "What? Wait, you don't know about prom?"

"All I know is something happened with him, between them? I don't know... for God's sake just fucking tell me!"

They were both shocked at his sudden loss of temper, to say nothing of the accusation that Mr. LaSalle had behaved inappropriately toward Kalyna, or vice versa. Beatrice, visibly irritated at her brother-in-law, tried to collect herself, while Jack explained. "Lyn had a puppy love for Mr. LaSalle, but he's a good guy. He never tried anything, and neither did she. All that talk about him dancing with her at prom—nothing came close to happening. Just her schoolgirl fantasy."

"But the prom incident?"

"Was with *Mrs*. LaSalle." Beatrice said with a mixture of contempt and sass. "Mr. LaSalle's wife." Eric thought back to the yearbook, trying to recall if there'd been a Mrs. LaSalle, but it was blurry in his mind.

Jack set the scene. "It's prom night. Mr. LaSalle was one of the chaperones, because all the students liked him and the other teachers knew if he told people to behave, they'd listen. Well, the only person who he couldn't get to behave was his wife.

Now, to most people, she was part of this perfect couple, the two most attractive people in town, both young teachers devoted to their students. She volunteered at Sunday school, he took care of his old man, who was a sad widower. From the outside they seemed perfect, but in reality, she was what you might call, a total whore."

"Total. Whore," reiterated Bea.

"During school she dressed *just* on the borderline of inappropriate, and was always putting her hands on students' elbows, wrists, shoulders, the top of their heads," Jack elaborated. "Don't get me wrong, she was a knockout, pretty much the hottest woman in town, but it's still weird when a teacher touches you, right? Like, there's a line. Anyway, there were rumors about a couple of guys from the basketball team, making bets about her in regard to... you know... sex stuff. Some of them would give looks behind her back like 'Yeah, I hit that,' but no one actually believed anything was happening. Or, I guess, at least we didn't want to believe.

So cut to prom night, and Mr. LaSalle's standing near some of the basketball players when he hears them say something that sends him pacing off. He leaves the gym, heads down the hall towards one of the storage rooms where they keep all the big mats for gymnastics meets. He flips on the lights to find his wife with two of the basketball players, going at it." Jack emphatically held up three fingers squeezed tightly together, to drive home his point.

Bea took over. "The kids at the dance didn't know what had just happened to Mr. LaSalle, so when he came back into the gym, Lynnie (who decided it was her big moment) went up to talk to him, and he totally brushed her off. She was devastated, she felt like her little cloud had been burst. And then, that asshole wife of his comes running in, not even all the way dressed back up, no shoes, crying and screaming after him, but it was too late. Mr. LaSalle already had the principal, security guard, and basketball coach in a circle, waving his hands wildly and yelling about what his wife had been doing. The music stopped, and the whole school heard. When the two players..."

Eric remembered the names from gossip he heard the week before. "Jared and Derick?"

"Exactly, Jared and Derick, tried walking into the gym like nothing happened, but Brendan from the AV club (who those jocks always bullied) moved the spotlight meant for the king and queen dance on to the two of them. They were busted. The whole school, the teachers and parents, all the chaperones, the janitor, everyone, was now involved, part of the biggest scandal that ever shook this town."

Bea sighed. "It was such a mess, the more that came out. The parents trying to say the boys were abused, some people even blaming Mr. LaSalle for not keeping his wife satisfied and in-check. Meanwhile, the boys were looking for high fives, until it came out that she'd also gotten them drugs. No one knew how, drugs weren't part of the town scene, we're beer people, but nevertheless she got some, they all used them together, and the boys lost their basketball scholarships.

"Without grades, money, or a letter of reference, neither ever ended up going to college. Derick managed to get his life back on track, working hard at his dad's landscape business, but as you know Jared has been in one form of trouble or another ever since. It's why he's been looking so angry all week. He's been spoiling for a fight with Mr. LaSalle as if it was somehow his fault, like a score he's needed to settle.

"Now, technically the boys were both of legal age to consent, so Mrs. LaSalle didn't go to prison, but she did skip town, and Mr. LaSalle filed for divorce faster than you can imagine. Poor man. Imagine the person you love not only cheating on you, not only cheating with multiple people, but those people are children? I mean, she was a predator, right? The boys bragged, but it was still wrong. She knew better. Those were kids, and she was supposed to look out for her students, not take advantage."

"If she was my wife, I'd have killed her." Jack said. "I don't know how he didn't."

"Don't say things like that in front of an officer of the law." Bea cautioned her husband. "Besides you know Ricky's actually seen real-life murdered people, it's not funny to even joke about that."

"Fine, I'm just saying, Mr. LaSalle, he's a better man than me. I never could have handled it as well as he did. He really cared about her, and even though she stomped his heart he was a class act, never once publicly made himself out to be a victim. He only focused on the harm she'd done those kids and the school. Mr. LaSalle, he's like, a saint."

"A really hot saint!" Bea brought some levity back to the conversation.

At that moment, Kalyna returned. Ashley was passed out in her arms, Dana was yawning, fighting off sleep. "If you're done reliving my great shame, I think it's time we get these little ones home to bed. Bea, Jack, lunch tomorrow after church?"

"Heck yeah," declared Jack. "Your mom promised she was making that cheeseburger casserole I love."

"Oh good, we can all look forward to indigestion! Thank you both again for coming out in all this mess to see me play."

"Of course, we wouldn't miss it! 'Night Lynnie, 'night Ricky." Bea hugged them, and patted her nieces on the head. "Night-night baby girls!"

The snow was still coming down heavily as they left the party, with a fresh thick sheet on the parking lot, looking as if no one had walked there for days. Eric had experienced the sensation of being out of body a number of times in his old life, when he'd seen himself looking down from a bird's-eye view at a crime scene in his nightmares.

He found it happening now, watching himself loading his wife and children into the car, driving them home. He saw them get the girls ready for bed, heard Kalyna sing them to sleep. He watched as he helped his wife put the bouquet into a vase with water, placing it on top of a doily on the back of the piano. He saw his wife kiss him goodnight, saw himself staying up, staring at the piano.

He witnessed everything, but as if it was happening to someone else, just as he had hours earlier, when he'd witnessed himself depriving Mr. LaSalle of his last breath, of placing Mr. LaSalle's lifeless body into the driver's seat of the piano teacher's beat up truck, as he'd witnessed himself putting the truck into neutral, and maneuvering it into the lake out past Gilbert's farm, with Mr. LaSalle strapped inside, sinking to the bottom.

Eric hadn't meant for it to happen. The storm wasn't expected to start so soon, or to be so heavy. Mr. LaSalle was on his way out of town and his car had hit a patch of ice, going off the road. Eric was on patrol, and saw him. As Eric helped him right the errant vehicle, Mr. LaSalle was grateful he wouldn't have to hike back in the snow to get a tow truck.

"Actually, I'm glad I ran into you, I tried to get a hold of Kalyna earlier to say I was sorry I would miss the concert, but no one answered. I know it will disappoint her, after all that practice, but I didn't want to get stranded in the middle of the night out here. Anyway, I have this card for Lyn, and a little gift I planned to give to her after her song. It's a notepad, see, with music notes. I saw she had little notepads all over the house, thought she'd like it. Here, you take it to her, and give her my love, will you?" He smiled, and when that perfect row of upper teeth gleamed at Eric, he snapped. All the horrible feelings he'd been fighting for the past week took over.

In a matter of minutes, Mr. LaSalle was no more. Eric didn't take time to absorb what happened, instead he sprang into action to hide his crime. Every condition was in his favor, as if the entire universe was conspiring with him. The road was abandoned and the snow was coming down so fast that he knew if he acted quickly, no one would ever even know the two men had run into each other. That part of the lake was freezing back over, and no one ever used it for fishing or recreation. There'd be no reason for anyone to even look there.

Besides, no one stayed in touch with Mr. LaSalle, so who would ever know he didn't get home? He had no family to go back to, so odds were it would be a long time before someone missed him. Everyone would assume he got lost driving in the storm. And if anyone suspected foul play, the whole town knew that Jared had some sort of issue with the teacher's return to town, so they'd suspect him first. Plenty of people saw their encounter at Ernie's, and plenty more had talked about it since.

Fixing the scene didn't take very long at all, and with the dead man's music-themed notepad in his front seat, Eric pulled headed back into town. He made sure he was visible to everyone, waving hello, commenting on the weather, picking up flowers and a small gift bag, helping people with tire chains and salting their front walks, weaving an alibi that would provide enough reasonable doubt should suspicion ever be cast his way. He got home exactly on time to change for the concert, put the notepad in a gift bag, picked up the girls, and headed to the school. Bea had agreed to drive Kalyna separately in advance. Everything went exactly according to plan.

Now, back at home from the concert, thawing out from the snow, Eric began to truly realize the gravity of his actions. Yes, he covered his tracks, in all likelihood he'd get away with it, but how would he live with himself, with what he'd done? He pulled the yearbook back out, and for the first time registered Mrs. LaSalle. She was indeed beautiful—stunning, really—and he couldn't believe he'd missed her entirely in his previous examination. He'd been blinded so by his jealousy and focused only on finding the man he envied. Now he had more in common with her, a fellow criminal. She got away with her crimes. Would he get away with his?

Eric shook off these fears, and tried going to sleep. As he shut his eyes, he heard the piano in his mind, the emphatic chords of the carol, punctuated with Mr.

LaSalle's final words, which he'd strained to pronounce, choking on them as his saliva mixed with his breath forming pleading clouds in the air. The unsuspecting piano teacher spent his final seconds denying the accusations Eric screamed as he beat the defenseless music man. "I.Did.Not.Touch.Her." In the moment, LaSalle's refusal to confess any wrong-doing only infuriated Eric, but now the words haunted him, because Eric knew they were true. He'd martyred a saint.

In his nightmares that evening, he saw the usual parade of violent crimes from his old precinct, but this time it was different. No longer a bird, he didn't circle high above the scenes. Now, he saw them as the killer would have seen them, first-person perspective, and had no control to change the course of his dreams as his own hands carried out the gruesome acts.

He was back in the desert, stretched around him, and the ground on which he stood sunk into a crater, like a massive bowl swallowing him whole, as the sky swirled from grey to black. He heard laughter, and turned to see Mrs. LaSalle, holding a basketball that shrunk into a rock, which she then threw at a piano, shattering the keys, making them fly off the piano and turn into human teeth as they hurtled toward Eric.

Sweating and terrified, he woke up. It was all over, he understood that now. Even if the law didn't catch him, he couldn't let himself off the hook. Every time he looked at the piano he was going to be reminded, every time his wife or daughters played it, he'd hear the dead man calling out to him. Every time she used the notepad, whatever she wrote on it, he'd hear in the murdered piano teacher's voice. Short of breath, he ran through the possible scenarios.

The first thought was to run, to skip town. He could take on a new identity and start a new life. But that would mean avoiding consequences and leaving his family desperate to know what happened to him. They would never be able to resume their normal life. Plus, he knew he'd never really feel at ease, always wondering when his luck would run out.

There were other options. He could turn himself in, but the shame of his act would hurt the entire family, not just him. He knew it was cowardly not to confess. He deserved to go to prison, but did Lyn deserve a husband in jail? Did their daughters? No, consider how innuendo alone tortured his wife decades; how much worse would it be with an actual scandal?

Thinking back to his conversation with his father-in-law, he considered suicide, leaving a note that he just couldn't go on anymore, but again, that let him avoid prison while also leaving behind a pained family, trying to understand why he did it, and what they could have done to save him. Judas didn't just kill himself, he publicly blamed himself for what he'd done. Besides, the idea of Lynn finding him, no matter what method he used, was unbearable. He imagined Lyn, prostrate with grief, haunted, blaming herself, unable to care for herself or their daughters. No, that wasn't going to work, either.

Still, he meant what he'd said all those years ago. He didn't believe a killer could come back after even one murder. Once the violence was in a person's system, there was no getting it out. It was just a matter of time before they acted on the impulse again. Earlier that day, he took it out on an innocent man he barely knew. What if next time he lost control, it was with someone he loved, someone in his family?

Eric couldn't take the risk. So his mind turned to the only path he could make sense of. He needed to make it look like he died of natural causes. The storm was expected to last another day or two, providing the perfect cover. He had the evening shift the next day. He could take his family to church, enjoy cheeseburger casserole with his in-laws, and make sure his family had happy memories that would never cause them to blame themselves.

Then he could drive out, a little farther out than normal, and stage a car mishap. Make it look like he skidded on some ice. Then, he'd walk out, to appear as if he was trying to get help, but froze along the way. He'd have to make it look like he fell over or got lost in the snow. No one would be out on the road, not at night in those conditions, so no chance of anyone rescuing him. No one would look for him until later in the morning when he didn't check back in. It would hurt, it would be painful to freeze out there, he'd probably hallucinate and panic, but he deserved worse than that. Then he'd get a standard police funeral, his family would get all of the compassion they deserved and all of the benefits from his service. That was it, that was the best way.

Satisfied with this plan, he finally managed to fall back asleep. In his dream, he came across St. Stephen in the desert, waving Eric toward him, as if expecting him. "Have you come to a decision, my son?"

"Yes sir, I'm going to make sure I never hurt anyone again, except myself, and I think I figured out the least painful way for my family."

"I see, and you are firm in your conviction?"

"Yes. I'm so, so sorry for what I did. I feel like, maybe all those years of seeing the bodies had an effect on me, after all, like part of me started to consider killing normal, and I was so tense and mad all week, I wasn't strong enough to hold the violence at bay. Mr. LaSalle didn't deserve it, though, and I know I can't make it right, but I am truly, deeply sorry. Not for how it affects me, but for how it hurt him."

"Good, that's how you ought to feel. Penitent is good. Anything else?"

"Yes. It's not fair that I get to plan my exit, that I get to know it's my last day and have a perfect afternoon with the people I love, the people who love me. He didn't get that, he didn't know he was going to die until it happened."

"A valid observation, although, whether you enjoy your final day or not, nothing you do at this point will unmurder that poor man. Nothing you do will erase the pain he felt as his life was brutally taken from him, by your hands. Nothing will change the fact that you already disrespected his body, discarding it like trash."

"That is all true, and I can't apologize enough, I know. And I'm sorry for what I've decided to do, I'm sorry it means I don't face consequences while I'm alive, which I know is an easy way out. I always got mad at the people who didn't have to pay for what they did, and now I'm one of them. I'm sorry it means no one will find out what happened to him, to Mr. LaSalle. I'm sorry it's going to leave Kalyna a widow, that I'm going to cause so many more people pain before it's all over. I just don't see any other way..." Unable to continue, he fell to the ground, folded over himself with his head touching the sand, crying.

The storm clouds broke, blue sky shining through, chasing the grey and black over the horizon. Holding a rock in one hand, the first martyr extended the other in a gesture of benediction. "It's difficult, but at least you are taking steps to make sure you never kill again, and that is the right thing to do. The merits of the method may be debatable, but the intent, I think, is correct." He smiled. "After all, even Judas had the decency to hang himself."

My Husband's Fathers

—

"How we deal with death is at least as important as
how we deal with life, wouldn't you say?"

-Admiral James T. Kirk

Death is not always the worst thing that happens in life. My husband, Dillon, found this difficult to accept, and I can't say I blame him. After all, his entire life was shaped by losing a parent at a young age.

Yet, his life wasn't shaped poorly—a perspective which took him some time to embrace. I, for example, was raised by both my mother and father, and spent most of my childhood experiencing, at the best of times, neglect and an utter lack of either attention or affection, and at the worst of times... well, neither of my parents are in my life, so I don't need to dwell on them or on what they did to me.

When Dillon and I first met, I immediately loved him. He seemed to glow from within, radiating warmth. During our first date, at a quiet Indian restaurant neither of us had tried before, he explained his somewhat untraditional upbringing.

"Wait," I asked him to clarify. "You have two dads?"

"Yes."

"They raised you together?"

"Yes."

"Legally?"

"Yes." His smile betrayed enjoyment at my confusion, clearly used to this line of inquiry.

"But they aren't gay, like, they aren't a couple?"

"Nope!" He laughed loudly, a captivating, contagious laugh. "Both are very straight."

"Ok, back up and start from the beginning then!" I leaned into the cushioned bench, ready for his tale. Over samosas and butter chicken, he explained how his mother had divorced his biological dad after a brief marriage, not realizing she was pregnant, and had moved back in with her long-lost love, hoping to marry as soon as possible. When she discovered her pregnancy, her new fiancé declared his intention to marry her still, and to raise the child.

The three formed an unlikely co-parenting trio, an improbable but loving family unit. The arrangement came to an end not long after Dillon's sixth birthday, when his mother passed away unexpectedly from an embolism. To everyone's surprise, both men stepped up and wanted to continue their shared custody, as both were already legal guardians. They realized as well that it would be easiest to share parenting responsibilities if they were in the same residence, so his biological father moved in with his step-father.

Together, the men devoted themselves entirely to bringing up their boy, even when it limited their abilities to pursue career opportunities in other locations. They also prioritized their son over their romantic happiness.

"After all, what woman wants to stick around after finding out the guy they're dating already has a domestic arrangement with another man... and they have a kid together?!" Dillon laughed at this observation.

"Can I see a photo of them?" I was curious to know what these odd fathers looked like. He obliged, pulling out his phone and flashing a photo of two strikingly handsome men, who could not have looked any more different from each other. I teased, "Wow, your mom had a type, huh?"

"You noticed the strong resemblance, eh?" He played along. He looked exactly like one of the men, so much that they could have passed as brothers.

"I will say, I bet I can guess which one is your birth father."

"Yeah, I mean, it's not like 'My Two Dads' or anything. I know exactly which one resulted in my conception, there's no mystery, but to be honest, it doesn't even matter to me."

"No?"

"Nope! They're my dads. Both of them. They've both been there with me since day one. There are even photos of them holding me when I was born, standing together smiling in their hospital gowns with my mom practically passed out behind them. I consider them both equal fathers."

"That's... really sweet." I was hooked on this man, the result of a family unit like I'd never heard of before.

We began seeing each other more often, and I loved hearing more about his family and life growing up. He shared sweet, wonderful memories of his mother, repeating them so often I felt like I'd gotten to know her myself. He hadn't gotten much time with her, but she clearly made an impact on the man he grew to be, and he cherished each moment he was able to recall.

Despite the unorthodox pairing, Dillon's fathers had provided him with a loving foundation to a happy and successful life. It was foreign to how I'd grown up. At first I felt ashamed of my own dysfunctional family background, and more than once I felt jealous at hearing how thoughtful and caring his family was.

Over time I opened up to Dillon about how much I'd missed out on in life because of my broken home environment, and he seemed to have difficulty really understanding what it was like. He was casual with money, casual with taking risks. He'd always had a safety net.

Occasionally he took my comments about my background personally, noting that he hadn't been privileged either, he couldn't have been, because he had lost his mother at such a young age.

"You can't call a grieving child privileged," he reasoned with me. According to him, he had experienced the ultimate loss which would continue to hurt him every day of his life.

Throughout our time dating, I saw over and over how his worldview was shaped entirely around his loss. If someone else lost a family member, he was able to empathize with them, and knew just the right thing to say, which is a valuable quality when supporting someone through a time of grief. However, if people suffered in other, less black and white ways, his sympathy was limited. He would be kind to their face, but in private would surprise me with comments about how it wasn't so bad, and, "at least no one died."

Each time, I tried to widen his perspective, explaining, "No, it's not like someone died, but this is still devastating and will take years to recover from."

To his credit, he usually assented to my guidance in the moment, but he did need the same reminder with some frequency. Still, love is overpowering, and this flaw didn't detract from everything else I loved about him. And as I got to know his dads, I fell for them, too. They were the best parents I'd ever seen, and to my delight, they became like parents to me, too.

At first I didn't know what to do with all of the parental praise and love that I'd never experienced in my life, but I grew to appreciate it, counting myself so lucky to have found such an incredible family. They became my rocks. I could call them when I had good news to share, or when I had difficult situations that required a sympathetic ear or helpful advice.

Eventually, when Dillon and I married, one of his dads, Russell, even walked me down the aisle, since I had no one to do it among my own relatives. My new fathers-in-law insisted on throwing us a dream wedding, and funded a honeymoon the likes of which I couldn't have conceived. They also insisted on gifting us their house.

With Dillon married, his dads decided to strike out on their own, and try being apart from each other. After decades of living as a platonic pair, it was an adjustment for them to fly solo. During this time, Dillon and I explored expanding our own family. I wasn't sure I was ready to be pregnant, and was scared at the permanence of adoption. What if I wasn't a good parent? But both Dillon and I had an eager itch to care for kids, so we applied to be foster parents.

The qualification progress was grueling, but we finally got approved, and took on our first charges. It was a lot of trial and error and learning, but with the help of some mentors in our foster support group, we started to get the hang of it, building our confidence in taking on children from more difficult situations. Now, there are stereotypes I will absolutely fight anyone about kids in foster care, but I would be lying if I pretended there wasn't a lot of work that went into each kid. Not just providing shelter, food, affection, but some of the children required extra therapy, medication, counseling, and tutoring to catch up in school.

Through it all, Dillon proved to be an incredible partner, surpassing all my expectations. He was a natural, and kids were drawn to him. While I am more emotionally reserved, having a lifelong dread of vulnerability, he was always open with his feelings. He made children from all kinds of situations feel safe, and that he was more than just their advocate, that he was someone who genuinely cared for them. Because he did care for them.

For a number of children, Dillon was the first positive familial figure they'd ever encountered, and seeing the kids open up to him made me love him all the more. In our room at night, though, he would still sometimes voice the odd belief that he'd had it worse than any of them, at least compared to the kids whose parents were still alive. As always, I tried to help him see the error of his thinking, and to his credit, he never let it change how he treated the children.

Most recently, we decided to take in two brothers—teen boys—one of whom had been badly injured by his birth parents when he was a small child. Most of the professionals who met Marcello feared he would have lasting physical, emotional, and mental side effects from the beating, that he'd never truly recover from his past. We learned that if his older brother, Julian, hadn't stepped in, it's very possible that mother and father would have killed their younger son.

Over the years, the boys had been through an endless string of homes, first bounced around through various extended family members, who were quickly overwhelmed by the responsibility, then in one foster home after another, in and out of various school systems, with a total lack of stability in their lives. They were on a trajectory we'd seen many times: children who weren't fortunate enough to find a permanent home, and eventually age out of the system. The boys were existentially exhausted, and Julian, understandably, felt jaded at the prospect of starting over once again.

I was daunted at the monumental endeavor of taking them on, unsure I was up to the task of providing adequate support to these innocent children after all they'd endured. Dillon, on the other hand, was confident we were the right fosters for them, and that he could form a connection with them to help them through the difficult legal processes that lingered from their parental situation.

Dillon urged me to agree, pleading, "These boys need to stay together, and there aren't a lot of other open houses right now. Not without other kids already. They need a couple who can give them *all* of their focus. I believe in us. We got this, LoveOfMine. We can help them. You and me, the dream team. Are you in?" His confidence was all I needed.

The transition was not as smooth as he'd predicted. Like many of the children we'd welcomed into our home, they arrived with nothing more than a little trash bag each, filled with their only possessions in the world. One of the first things we'd learned to adjust to when we began fostering was that children in the system often don't have much notice when they will be leaving one home for the next, and often have to quickly throw together their personal effects in plastic grocery bags or trash bags.

As their foster care social worker, Pete, walked the teens to our front porch, the younger boy, Marcello, held his bag close to his chest like a safety blanket or stuffed animal, while the older boy, Julian, had his bag slung over his shoulder. After introductions, Pete assured Marcello and Julian he'd return periodically to check in on their progress, and left the four of us to get to know each other.

In the weeks that followed, Dillon quickly grew discouraged. He wasn't forming a bond with them as quickly as with previous children we'd welcomed into our home. He tried to relate to them, but sixteen year-old Julian resisted, while thirteen year-old Marcello was not emotionally equipped to form a new relationship with anyone at all. Marcello especially needed so much extra attention due to some developmental delays in executive functioning. He relied on structure and routine, and needed someone to keep an eye on him nearly around the clock.

We'd never had such a difficult time adjusting to new children, and it felt like nothing we did made any lasting progress. We'd have a good morning or afternoon, but then inevitably something would cause Marcello to have a meltdown, and we'd be back to where we started. This frustration only deepened as Julian clearly held each episode against us. He'd had low expectations for us, and we kept living down to them. Still, we kept trying.

My job gave me incredible flexibility in my schedule, so I was able to be at home with them during the day, but I found it emotionally draining. The trauma from my own childhood memories, long suppressed, came roaring back. I didn't expect that, since we'd fostered other children from troubled homes before. Something about this situation was different, though, and I was shaken.

I had trouble sleeping, with disturbing nightmares featuring my parents and the abuses I suffered. In my nightmares I tried to run away, but somehow they kept finding me. Even during waking hours I experienced flashes, fleeting images, of them reaching out to hurt me, causing me momentary panic until I remembered I was safe. The boys began picking up on my agitation. I could tell. We were all stressing each other out, and reaching a point from which I wasn't sure we could rebound.

I thought I was holding it together well, but one night when I was talking to my father-in-law, Tony, Dillon's biological dad, I must have been too clearly stressed. A few days later, I felt as if I was running on empty, and planned to ask Dillon if we could send the boys to another home, when the front doorbell rang. I wasn't expecting it, and let out a startled noise. The two boys were scared, as sudden changes tended to trigger their fight or flight response.

"I'm sure it's fine, probably a delivery or something, I was just distracted," I reassured them as I went to the front hall.

As soon as the door was slightly ajar, a two-man carnival of sunshine and joy burst into our home. It was both of my fathers-in-law, Tony and Russell, loaded down with an absurd amount of grocery bags. My surprise passed in an instant, as I threw my arms around them both, pulling them into the house and celebrating their arrival. "If it isn't two of my favorite people! Get in here, get in here!" I tried to help them with the bags, but mostly I just kept attacking them with hugs.

The three of us stumbled through the house, talking over each other as I asked them if Dillon had known they were coming (he hadn't). They informed me they thought it was a good time for a visit, and that they were going to check into their hotel later but didn't want to delay seeing us.

"And these are for you, my girl," said Russell, shoving a bouquet of flowers into my arms. I hugged them tightly to my chest, squeezing them in disbelief as I stared at these wacky guardian angels in front of me.

They went into action, and before I knew it, I'd been ushered out of my own kitchen, with my fathers-in-law declaring that lunch would be ready soon, to let them take care of all the cooking. Happy tears burned my eyes, and I was so lost in gratitude for their arrival that I momentarily forgot about the boys.

Turning around, I saw them both standing stock still, concerned and confused. Marcello grabbed his older brother's arm for support, and looked at me. "Who, who are those men?"

In an instant I realized how disruptive an unexpected visit was for them, and immediately set to explaining everything. "You know Dillon's fathers? Remember the pictures we showed you, right there in those frames? That's them. These are his dads."

Hearing this prompt, my fathers-in-law popped out of the kitchen for proper introductions. Russell addressed them first. "Apologies, young gentlemen, for barging in unannounced. I am Russell. We love to surprise people, and thought we'd surprise our favorite daughter-in-law."

"And I am Tony. Tell me, young sirs, do either of you like... pizza?"

Both boys, still in a bit of a daze from the rapidity of this unanticipated arrival, slowly nodded their heads to indicate yes.

"Perfect!" Tony gestured them toward the kitchen. "Do either of you like to cook?"

"I don't know," mumbled Julian.

"Would you like to try?" Tony asked, with his most irresistible smile.

"Um, ok?"

"Perfect, come with us. And you," now addressing Marcello directly. "Would you like to observe, in an official capacity? We could use a supervisor."

"Supervisor?" asked Marcello.

"Yes. Someone we can trust to make sure we get it *just* right."

"And most importantly," added Russell, "the supervisor gets to taste the food before anyone else. Does that sound good to you?"

Marcello smiled, and followed them into the kitchen. I stood in the hallway, dumbfounded, and heart full. I walked to the doorway and watched as the two dads helped the young boys, showing them first to wash their hands, then going over all the ingredients at their disposal. I saw Julian maintain his cautious skepticism, but Marcello was completely won over.

Looking at me, Tony asked, "Wouldn't you like to sit for a few while we get this cooked?"

"Yes," encouraged Russell, waving an oven mitt in my direction. "Have a seat, watch the professionals at work." I obeyed, sitting at the breakfast table, taking in the scene. It felt too good to be true, like a rescue operation. I watched with utter admiration as my fathers-in-law directed the young boys, chatting them up as if they were old friends. While the pizzas cooked in the oven, the foursome prepared a salad, and set the table, just as Dillon arrived home.

In all the commotion, I'd failed to let him know we had visitors. After a long stretch of hugs and greetings, we sat down to eat. Dinner was a blur, but I clearly remember that I couldn't stop laughing. My husband's fathers had swept into our home like a parade.

They caught us up on their latest adventures, finishing each other's stories, teasing with intentionally-awful impersonations of each other, taking turns standing up to gesture with increasing exaggeration. It was like a two man show just for us.

I hadn't seen Marcello so engaged since he came to our house. Julian still held back, but even in spite of himself, cracked a smile from time to time. I know it takes more than one entertaining evening to earn a child's trust and make them feel at home, but for the first time I felt optimistic that we might have a chance with these children. Dillon and I sat in the living room together with the boys for some time as Tony and Russell cleared the tables and cleaned the dishes. Marcello told us repeatedly about how he had supervised, and we were all pleased that he'd had such a positive experience.

When the boys moved to get ready for bed, we said good night, and to our surprise, Marcello hugged both Tony and Russell. He had never shown that kind of affection to us, and I was moved to see him forming a positive bond with anyone. Julian, still reserved, accepted a handshake from each of the older men, before escorting his brother upstairs.

Alone with my fathers-in-law, we apologized that we couldn't have them stay in the guest room.

"Of course, of course, we didn't expect you to," reassured Russell. "We know the rules when you have kids here, and we found a nice hotel anyway. We just thought you could use some company."

I flopped on the couch between them, resting my head on Russell's shoulder. "You have no idea how much I needed you here. *I* had no idea how much I needed you, until you showed up. This has been the best surprise of my life!"

"We're glad we could help! In fact... we'd like to keep helping."

"What do you mean?"

"Well, we've been talking, and we think it's time to settle back down. And we'd like to settle closer to you all."

Dillon perked up, always brightened by his fathers' attentions. He beamed at them. "That's wonderful! We'd love to have you closer by. We've actually talked about it before."

"Yes," I agreed. "This is perfect! Do you know where, yet?"

"We aren't sure, although we do have a lot of options we can look into," explained Russell. "Ideally it would be, you know, a home with enough space for each of us to have our own rooms, our own studies, places to not get on each other's nerves."

"I guess you missed each other after all?" I teased them. "How's the saying go? 'Absence makes the heart grow fonder?'"

"I always thought it was the one about 'the devil you know,'" laughed Tony.

"Well, I don't care why, Dad. I'm just glad we'll have you both here. We could use the moral support, for sure."

"You say that now, but you'll be tired of us in no time."

"No way." I protested. "Never!"

I didn't realize how tense I'd been before their arrival until being in their presence relaxed me so much I dozed off on the couch. They woke me up to say goodbye, and I was sad to see them go.

That night I slept better than I had in weeks. In the morning, I woke up feeling refreshed, but worried that my memory of the night before had been colored by my desire for it to be as good as I felt like it was. To my relief, the boys were in equally good moods when they came into the kitchen for breakfast.

As Dillon cooked up the eggs and bacon, Marcello spoke excitedly about last night's pizza adventure, and professed his deep interest in seeing Tony and Russell as soon as possible. "Are they coming over again today?"

"We can ask," answered Dillon. "Would you both like them to?"

Julian shrugged his silent indifference, but Marcello lit up. "Yes yes yes!"

"Ok buddy, I'll ask if they can come over!"

Over the next few weeks, we fell into a routine. Each day after Tony and Russell finished touring houses, they came over to our home. In the hours before dinner, they did whatever the boys wanted: playing board games or video games, watching TV, and practicing drawing by copying pictures of their favorite comic book characters. Sometimes Tony and Russell played outside with Marcello, who was more childlike than many boys his age, while Julian looked on, hesitant to fully join in.

I could see that Julian wanted to give in and have fun, but he couldn't let his guard down enough yet. However, it was obvious that he appreciated their engagement with his baby brother. He'd spent his whole life on edge, watching, trying to prevent anything else bad from happening. Seeing his brother laugh and play was an adjustment.

Each day, Dillon came home for dinner we'd all prepared together, and Marcello would excitedly tell him everything that happened during the day. He was making incredible progress, like something had unlocked and set him free. After dinner, Russell would ask Marcello to choose a book, and they'd read it out loud together as Julian and Tony played games or worked on a jigsaw puzzle nearby. Julian particularly embraced their board game matches, and showed a real talent for strategy games. He was patient, and thought through all the options, two skills he'd gained through a lifetime of dealing with obstacles and delays.

At our next home visit, the foster agency social worker, Pete, was amazed at Marcello's turnaround. Although he raised his eyebrows initially upon seeing

Tony and Russell appearing so familiar with the kids, in no time they erased any of Pete's skepticism.

"I have to say," Pete commented as he left, "this is shaping up to be quite a comeback story. I was really worried about you guys before, but what I'm seeing now is a lot of progress. Now, don't be surprised if there is still backsliding or bumps along the way, but for now, I think we can all exhale a little bit."

"That's really reassuring," replied Dillon. "Especially with school starting soon. It will be nice for them to start the year on a positive note."

"Absolutely," agreed Pete. He looked approvingly at Russell and Tony, as well. "Keep it up."

That night at dinner, Dillon mentioned school, which made Julian visibly nervous.

"What, you don't like school?" Russell inquired.

"No it's just... never mind." Julian shrugged, communicating that he didn't want to talk about it.

"It's ok, go on. You can say what you feel." Dillon encouraged him.

"We've never stayed at one long enough for it to really matter. I can't count how many we've been to."

"I see," said Tony, with sympathy. "So, you don't know if you like it."

"Yeah, I mean, we're always the new kids, no one talks to us, and we don't get enough time for them to get to know us. The teachers know our deal and treat us different, like they can't wait until we're someone else's problem. And our clothes, all these old hand-me-downs from strangers... we never fit in. We stick out. I hate sticking out. I just want to be a normal student like everyone else. Plus..." he trailed off, looking at Marcello, and we all knew what he didn't want to say out loud. He could never relax at school because he had to look out for his brother. He had borne such responsibility his entire life.

His words resonated with me. I'd also been the kid who stuck out for being poor, and from a broken family. I knew what he meant, the thirst for normalcy, even anonymity, to have clothes of my own, school supplies of my own, to blend with the kids who were clearly loved and cared for. I wanted to embrace him, to wrap him up and express all of my understanding with a big hug, but I knew physical contact was a no-go with him. He liked his own space, and felt uneasy when people tried to encroach.

The next morning, Sunday, we had no plans, so Dillon and I looked forward to a relaxing morning with a slow start. Naturally, the arrival of his fathers during breakfast caught us all off guard.

"What are you doing here?" Dillon asked. "I thought you had a bunch of open houses to hit up."

"Open houses can wait." Russell brushed off Dillon's confusion. "Today, we are here on a mission."

"A mission?" Marcello was wide-eyed, curious.

"Yes, very important." Clarified Tony. Leaning in, he asked, gravely, "Do you think you are up for a very, very important mission?"

Marcello nodded, and whispered, "I think so?"

Turning to Julian, Tony repeated the question.

"Umm... sure?" Julian was intrigued, if dubious.

"OK, then you're coming with us!"

"Whoa, whoa, Dads," I interrupted. "They can't just go with you, not without one of us."

"Of course not. You're coming, too."

At this, Dillon looked impatient. "Am I invited on this mission?"

"That depends, do you think you're up for it?"

"How can I know, when you haven't told us what the plan is?"

"Ah, that's no kind of attitude for a mission," sassed Russell. "Come on, everyone, get dressed, we're going out!"

We loaded into an SUV, a tight squeeze with four adults and two kids. Marcello looked excited, but Julian's face betrayed his anxiety at the unknown. Registering this, I spoke up.

"All right, enough mystery, Dads. What's on the agenda?"

In unison, they replied, "SHOPPING!"

Over the course of the afternoon, we visited dozens of stores, and my husband's fathers took the boys on an absolute spree. Shoes, jeans, shirts, backpacks, stationery, accessories, electronics. Normally, I hate the mall and find shopping to be boring, but not that day. I was thrilled to see the boys get into a groove. At first, they were overwhelmed at the options, and also doubtful that anyone was actually buying them anything. Quickly, though, they began to relish the mini-fashion shows they gave us as they waltzed out of the dressing rooms to show off their new ensembles.

While we refueled at the food court, I saw Julian whispering to Russell, nodding his head in the direction of Marcello. They walked over together and announced it was time for the boys to get fresh, professional haircuts. Marcello expressed alarm at the notion of being in the charge of a stranger, but Julian reassured him they would be together the whole time.

Our group took up the entire barbershop. Dillon and I sat in chairs at the front. I wanted to leave them alone for some guy time, but I knew if anything happened and I wasn't there, it would be distressing for Marcello. So, we sat in the two chairs, surrounded by piles of bags from the haul.

It was at this time I noticed Dillon was in a bit of a mood. He wasn't having as much fun as the rest of us.

"Whatsa matter, LoveOfMine?" I asked, in my usual way of breaking the ice when he was in a funk.

"Nothing," he tried to dismiss me.

"Something," I shot right back.

"You don't think this is all..." and he switched to a whisper, so I had to lean in to hear. "You don't find this, like... excessive?"

Through my own strained whisper, I scolded him, quietly. "No, I do not. This is the first time they've ever had anything new in their entire lives, so frankly, I don't think it's excessive enough." He rolled his eyes, which pissed me off. "Nothing could ever be excessive enough to make up for what they've missed. The only thing 'excessive' here is your need to be a killjoy."

"Fine. You're right." His monotone delivery left me unconvinced. I knew that wasn't the end of it, but I didn't want to play it out anymore in front of everyone else.

I know makeover montages are an overplayed trope in movies, but I have to say, seeing the boys with flattering haircuts was an incredible difference. They were radiant. Julian jokingly pulled at his shirt and asked, "Can we burn these when we get home? I never wanna see these old hand-me-downs again!" Everyone laughed, except Dillon.

Back at the house, we unloaded the comical number of bags and boxes, so much stuff that it looked like we were moving in for the first time. I instructed everyone to leave the loot in the living room so we could sort it out and remove tags, and asked Julian and Marcello to gather up anything they didn't want to keep from their current wardrobes. Before they ran upstairs, Marcello handed me a small bag. "For you," he said proudly. I opened it and found hair clips of varying sizes and colors.

I looked at him and Julian, who blushed and explained, "You always use pencils or pens, or that one time chopsticks—which was weird—to put your hair up. You can't ever find your bands or clips, and… well we thought this was nicer than chopsticks." I moved to thank them, hugging Marcello and asking Julian if I could hug him too.

He hesitated, so I retracted the request. "Too soon, got it. How about a high five or a fist bump?" Julian obliged with a quick high five, then they ran off to their rooms, leaving us adults together. I looked at the men in my life, touched, and held up the clips for them to see. "I didn't even notice they got these."

Tony and Russell explained the boys asked them about the clips at one of the stores but wanted it to be a surprise. They were quite pleased with themselves, but Dillon notably sulked, and mumbled about how no one got him anything.

Russell didn't entertain the pout. "Because you don't need hair clips. Now help us unpack. I can't even remember half of what we bought! What an extravaganza!"

The shopping spree exhausted the boys, who put themselves to bed immediately after dinner. As soon as he was sure they were out of ear shot, Dillon turned to his two fathers. "I think we need to recalibrate."

Russell raised his eyebrow. "Recalibrate?"

"Yes. It's not right, getting their expectations up like this, spoiling them." Anticipating our protest, he held up his hand. "I'm all for making sure they have nice things, but children acclimate quickly. It would be wrong of us to heighten their expectations. What will happen when their next home doesn't meet this level of luxury you've established here?"

The words "next home," shook me. I hadn't considered there would be a "next home." I felt uneasy having this conversation in front of Tony and Russell, but this was outweighed by the need to address it head on. "I don't think this is the right time for this discussion, but I have to confess, Dillon, I'm surprised. I wasn't aware that a future home was even on the table at this point. I thought we were all bonding..."

My fathers-in-law both agreed, talking over each other, all of us trying to whisper our arguments so the boys wouldn't hear. Realizing he was outnumbered and had hit a nerve with all of us, Dillon tried to calm us. "Ok, ok, you're right. Now is not the time for this conversation. It's late, we've all had a long day, and I've got to get some sleep before work tomorrow. To be continued, all right?" We agreed, tentatively, but made it clear the conversation was absolutely not over.

When Dillon left for work the next day he was in a huff, barely making eye contact with me. I understood that he'd secretly harbored reservations about our situation since his fathers came into town and *hadn't* made it all about him. He let this fester to the point that it could no longer be hidden. I needed to talk to him, but would have to wait until he got back home. Whatever he was going through, I wanted him to have a safe space to discuss, but I didn't want it negatively impacting the boys. Marcello might not notice, but Julian was ever-watchful and keenly observant. He'd immediately pick up on Dillon's discomfort.

Not long after Dillon drove off, Tony and Russell arrived, inviting us to join them for their house hunt that day. I wasn't sure it was the best idea, because I didn't know how long teen boys would want to spend a day with a realtor before getting bored, but Julian and Marcello were so excited I couldn't decline.

My concerns about their boredom were unfounded. They loved being part of it. Marcello walked into house after house, mouth open in awe, telling Linda, the realtor, that it was the biggest house he'd ever been in. He repeated this at each subsequent house, sincerely, and Linda played into his sense of wonder. As we left each house she'd tease him, "You thought this one was big, Marcello? Wait until you see the next one!" I appreciated that she didn't mind having us along as tourists with her for the day.

Julian surprised me with his strong opinions on architectural details, quickly learning the terminology and asking thoughtful questions, making astute observations. Tony and Russell encouraged this, asking him to weigh in on everything from fixtures to floor plans. He reveled in the serious attention they gave his responses, and enjoyed that Linda also consulted him, speaking to him like an adult rather than a child. It made my heart swell to see him confidently asserting himself in the conversations.

After the last house of the day, the boys and I hopped into the car, but Tony and Russell stood by the house with Linda. She looked pleased with the conversation, and they all shook hands before parting.

Joining us in the car, they buckled in and Tony announced that they had reached a decision: they were making an offer on one of the houses. The boys begged to know for which house, but Russell declined, explaining, "Can't jinx it!" This added level of mystery drove the boys wild with energy, and when we got home they couldn't contain their enthusiasm.

Dillon was home from work already, setting dinner out on the table. As the boys excitedly described every house to him in hyperbolic description and wild pantomime, Dillon played along, pretending to be interested, but I could tell his mind was elsewhere. I kept an eye on him throughout dinner, and saw that he was never fully present. Everyone else was too caught up in conversation to register it, but his distance was notable to me.

After the boys went to bed, Tony and Russell asked us to sit down, that they had something they wanted to discuss. We obliged, and for the first time in my memory, I saw my fathers-in-law look nervous. They silently nodded to each other, as if to amp each other up, and Russell took the lead. "Linda thinks we're a lock for the house. It's practically around the corner, so we'll be close by."

"Yes, you mentioned." Dillon responded drily.

Trying to save the conversation, I spoke up. "I know you don't want to jinx it, but I am so happy you'll be here for good!"

Tony smiled and patted my hand. "Thank you, my dear. We're happy, too."

"What else?" Dillon's tone was joyless. "You didn't need us to sit down to tell us what you all spent the entire dinner discussing. What is it you want to tell us that had to wait until the kids were asleep?" He physically braced himself, sitting up straight, ready for bad news.

"We would like the boys to live with us." Russell looked directly into Dillon's eyes, gauging his son's reaction.

Tony pressed on, "We want to adopt them."

The kitchen table fell into a vacuum, as we held our collective breath and stared at Dillon, waiting for his response.

He laughed, a disturbing, forced, phony guffaw. "Very funny. You almost sounded serious." Looking at me, as if I was in on his joke, he went on. "Did you hear that? They want to *adopt*. Adopt! These two! Whew, that is a good one!"

No one else laughed. Soaking up the silence, Dillon drew strength from it, and shedding his laughter, became severe in his judgment. "You cannot be serious. At your age? You know you are too old to start over as parents. Besides, you don't even know these kids. You've been around them for what, a couple of weeks? You can't possibly understand what it's going to take to help them thrive in the long term."

His fathers tried to interrupt, but Dillon was rolling. "It's not just buying them houses and clothes, it's therapy, counseling, dealing with their inevitable backslides, those moments where you think they've made progress only for something seemingly innocuous to cause one of them to have a total meltdown, erasing any ease in their new situation. Then you've got potential interference from their birth families if they ever come back around. Not to mention, there is no way in heeeeelllll you'd ever be approved! Besides your age, there's the fact that you are platonic life partners, which, face it, looks weird from the outside. It's hardly the traditional domestic arrangement a judge likes to see. On top of all that, you have no experience..."

Here Russell cut him off. "No experience?! What do you call raising you?!"

Tony joined in. "Yes, *son,* we have already brought up a young boy who dealt with psychological issues from losing a parent. And I think you turned out pretty well for someone raised by 'weird, platonic life partners' with no experience."

I had to agree with them. "They would be wonderful fathers, they already have been. Look how the boys have opened up to them. Marcello is a different person, and Julian, I didn't know he was capable of connecting and communicating the way he does with them. This is a win-win."

"You knew about this?" Dillon accused me.

"No, but I'm all for it. Face it, there isn't a huge pool of people racing to adopt them. Here are two men we know, who are about to have a huge house, who we know are financially secure, who have the time to engage with the support services like therapy, and who, if they need help, would be a short distance away."

Dillon shook his head in disagreement, but I pressed. "Look, LoveOfMine, we don't often get to see the kids we care for wind up with a forever home before they move out of our lives, so you can't begrudge me wanting this. It would keep them in our lives, and maybe I'm selfish, but I want that, for me. I've grown to love them and I want them to stay in this family."

"I don't know what to say. It sounds like you've all made up your minds, and my opinion means nothing. I'm going out for a walk." Dillon left through the front door, closing it silently behind him.

Alone, the three of us stared at each other, and as his two fathers dealt with their disappointment, they shrugged, disheartened. "Stay here, keep an eye on the boys," I ordered them as I ran after Dillon.

Catching up to him, I put my hand on his shoulder, forcing him to face me. He's taller than me, which usually doesn't make much difference, but in that moment reinforced the sensation that he was literally talking down to me. All the frustration that simmered over the previous weeks came flying out of his mouth.

"They have NO IDEA what they are getting into, and I can't believe you wouldn't try to stop them! You know they don't really appreciate how hard it is to parent kids like Marcello and Julian. They've been playing fun grandpas, and yeah, it's easy to buy kids' affections, but what happens after the honeymoon period? What happens the first time one of the kids has a setback?!"

I couldn't argue with him on that, emotional backslides and behavioral setbacks can be crushing when you become used to seeing a kid make progress. You get into a false sense of status quo, and then something sets off an episode that feels like it erases any foundation you've built up together. Marcello in particular had already been through a few early in his time with us.

Dillon pointed his finger down at my chest. "YOU KNOW how hard the setbacks are to witness, to nurture them through. Every foster parent does, but they, *my* fathers, don't get it, because they've never had to live through it! They'll be devastated and realize they're in over their heads, and they won't be able to undo the mistake of making a lifelong commitment to a couple of strangers!" Catching his breath, he became aware of his demeanor, and stood down.

"I'm sorry. I shouldn't be taking it out on you like this. I was just surprised, especially when you agreed with them. I mean, part of me wasn't, I had a feeling they were getting attached, but I didn't want to read into it, to believe it. I think it's out of my system now. Let's go home."

Wrapping me in his arms, trying to pull me close into him, Dillon was under the mistaken impression that this was his conversation to end, but I wasn't ready.

"I'm sorry, but I have some things I need to get out of *my* system, now that you've had your tantrum." He looked shocked, and stepped back, as I unleashed. "You are a selfish child, and you're making everyone suffer because of it. Don't look at me like that, you're going to listen to me. You've ALWAYS resented anyone else getting any of your dads' attention. Yes, you have, it's true. You were jealous when they started getting close to me, as if it meant less love for you. You've never understood that love isn't a finite resource. It doesn't divide, it multiplies.

When you were born, neither of them felt like you'd love them less if they shared you. They just grew to love each other, too. And look how that love manifested into building a world of love around you. You think they aren't *experienced*? They had to help a little boy grieve his mother, all the while putting their own grief to the background. They made that sacrifice for you. They made countless sacrifices for you, and instead of appreciating it, you're behaving like a spoiled brat!"

"Spoiled?! How can I be spoiled? I have no MOM! My childhood was ripped away when she died. I've felt that loss my whole life, what is 'spoiled' about that?"

"Once again," I countered, "you are acting like death is always the worst thing that happens in life, but I'm sorry, it's not. Sure, it can be, but at least you had CLOSURE. You know she's not coming back, you got to mourn her, you aren't always waiting for her, wondering why, if she's still alive, why she isn't fighting tooth and nail to keep you, to raise you herself, let alone wonder why she'd abuse you, hurt you, try to kill you.

"You act like everything boils down to being alive or being dead. Want to talk life or death? Look what happened to Marcello, if Julian hadn't stepped in. Compared to that, a dead parent is a blessing, because you know, you personally, specifically KNOW if your mom was alive she'd be here right now, loving you with all her heart."

I'd tried to explain this to him so many times, and exasperated, felt like this was a final overture to reach him. If he didn't get it this time, I feared he never would.

Determined to get through, I pushed on. "No, you are not lucky that your mom died. It's a tragedy. But you have to understand where you *were* lucky. You had a mom, you knew her, you knew she loved you. You got to spend time with her. You have happy memories of her. And when she was gone, you had two insanely fantastic men ready to give up the lives they'd imagined for themselves to make you the center of their world, to make sure you never suffered or went through hardship of any kind.

How *dare* you be petty enough to resent children who've never had a drop of that kind of love? Children like Julian, like Marcello, who survive a lifetime of mental anguish and physical suffering on a scale that you are not capable of beginning to understand. How can you be mad that someone wants to help them? How can you want to prevent someone from at long last giving them the love of which every human child deserves, but far too many don't get to know?"

He reached for my hand, but I pulled back. "You know what I went through. The poverty, the abuse, the... but hey, I guess at least I had a mom and a dad. Never mind what was done to me! Wasn't I lucky? Didn't having two parents make me feel safe, make me feel loved, make me feel like I even wanted to be alive? Never mind that I spent my life wishing they would just vanish, so they couldn't hurt me anymore, wishing I would disappear into thin air so I couldn't feel pain anymore. Wasn't I just sooooo spoiled because I had two living parents? Say it to my face, tell me! It's what you think, right? Tell me! Tell me that I was lucky compared to you!"

At this point we were both crying, and I knew our neighbors would be peeking out to see what the disturbance was, if they hadn't already. Trying to control myself, I managed to conclude, "I love you, LoveOfMine. You are my favorite person, you are my best friend, but right now, I am so, *so* disappointed in you. I'm going home. Maybe you could take a few laps around the neighborhood to walk off your current state of being an asshole before coming back. Good night."

When I walked in the door, my husband's fathers were standing, waiting. Silently, I hugged each of them, and walked up the stairs, feeling drained and defeated. After the minimal effort of brushing at my teeth and wiping my face, I crawled under the covers and cried myself to sleep. I didn't hear when Dillon got home, nor when Tony and Russell left.

I woke up to the smell of coffee and bacon, a heavenly aroma that made me smile, until I realized how much sunlight hit my eyes through the blinds. My alarm hadn't gone off... had I even set it? I felt emotionally hungover and disoriented. Rolling over to check what happened, I saw a text on my phone. It read, simply, "I'm an asshole. Forgive me," punctuated with a sad emoji.

Feeling groggy, but cautiously curious, I walked into the kitchen, surprised to see Dillon there. He was still in pajamas, as were each of the boys. Marcello loudly informed me, "Dillon is taking the day off work, and we're helping him make breakfast!" Julian nodded at me, then returned his focus to whisking eggs. Dillon walked over to me, kissed the top of my head, and, putting an arm around my waist, leaned in to whisper an apology. "I'm sorry, LoveOfMine. I love you." I kissed him back, which, as usual, made Marcello laugh and jokingly cry, "Ewww," at our physical display of affection.

When we were done with breakfast, the boys went up to get ready for the day while Dillon and I remained in the kitchen. "Sit down, I got this." Apparently his self-imposed penance included dishes duty. "You sleep ok?"

"I guess so," I stared at him, unable to regain any of the anger I felt at him the night before. Here was the man I loved. Maybe I'd gotten carried away, venting at him the way I did.

"You deserved a good night's sleep, after what I put you through. I'm sorry. I was only thinking about myself, and it wasn't fair to any of you." He continued washing and drying as he spoke. "When I got home, Dads were still here. We had a long, long talk. They said that raising me was a highlight of their life, so how could they not want to experience it again. They also said they couldn't believe I made you cry. You know, those old men really love you."

"I know."

"And I really love you."

"I know."

"So we talked about it, and they're going to ask the boys today what they think. I warned them, Julian is a skeptic, he might not even go for it, but they feel confident it's worth the risk."

"That means, you'll support them? You'll endorse their application, and if it's approved, you'll welcome Julian and Marcello, as your brothers?"

"Yes. I warned Dads again that odds of approval are slim, but that if it's what they want, they should go for it, and I'll help however I can." He looked at me for a long time. "You were right. Those boys deserve love, and I know that no one is better at making someone feel loved than my fathers." Relief took hold of my body, and I stood up to hug him. He hugged me back and we stayed that way for a long time. All was forgiven.

That afternoon, Tony and Russell arrived, though this time without their usual bags of food in hand. The boys greeted them warmly, as was now routine. Sipping the coffee Dillon handed him, Tony began, "Well, our offer got accepted."

Marcello clapped, and Julian excitedly asked, "Which one? Which one?"

"The one with that big study by the front hall."

"That was our favorite!" Turning to Marcello, Julian emphasized, "They bought our favorite one! They got it!" The boys high-fived, grinning widely.

"Well, you made a strong case for it," added Russell, "so we decided to take your advice." This positive reinforcement caused Julian to stand up straight, feeling emboldened by his newly-found power of persuasion.

"In fact," continued Russell, "we thought maybe you'd like to live there, too?"

Silence filled the room, and Julian's smiling expression transformed into one of suspicion and doubt. "Live there? You want us to live there?"

Tony explained. "We've talked about it a lot, and, if you are interested, we would like to move forward with an application to adopt you, both. To live with us, both."

Marcello took this news in quietly, overwhelmed. Conflict now played out over Julian's face, torn between excitement and fear. He examined all of our faces, each adult in the room.

"Are, are you allowed to?"

"We are allowed to apply, yes."

I chimed in, "Whether they will be approved is another matter, but they can absolutely apply. As long as you want them to, of course."

"Yes," affirmed Russell. "You don't have to tell us now, you can take time to think and talk about it, but ultimately the decision is yours. If you decide no, we promise we won't be hurt, and will still be here for you."

Tony echoed, "Yeah, we're not going anywhere. Especially now that we bought a house."

Julian took in these reassurances, but then looked to Dillon again. "You knew about this? You're ok with it?" I was disappointed, after hoping he hadn't picked up on the resentment, the jealousy.

"More than ok with it, buddy, but I want to be real with you, it won't be a slam dunk. It doesn't hurt to try, but the odds are against it. Even with Pete supporting us, which I'm sure he will, I don't want you having any idea that this will be easy or guaranteed, ok?"

I saw Julian trying to find words to ask his questions, but unable to, so I clarified. "There are a lot of factors that might be considered against the adoption, but that doesn't mean it's a non-starter. But you have to know that between their ages, the unconventional relationship, and other considerations for your care, the courts might not approve it. I promise you, though, that we," gesturing at Dillon, "are going to be in this 100 percent, we will give our total support to the idea and advocate for it as much as we can."

Julian looked at me, wide-eyed and worried. "What if the ruling is no, they can't adopt us?"

"Then we'll do it." We were all surprised at Dillon's confident declaration. "We'll apply, and you can be legally ours, but spend as much time as you want with them. Trust me, they're going to be around... once these two are in your life you can't get rid of them."

"It's true, and it's a good problem to have," I laughed, trying to ease the tension, but Julian didn't take his eyes off Dillon.

"You really won't mind sharing your dads? With me? With us?" The rest of us sat back, quietly, respecting that this conversation needed to take place, to clear the air. Dillon looked Julian directly in the eye.

"I've been lucky in my life, I understand that. I used to think I'd been cursed, losing my mom so young. But how cursed could I be when I had two incredible fathers? Men who loved me, who prioritized me, who helped me become the man I am today. I was blessed to have two dads, so it's fitting I would have two brothers." I have always loved him, but at that moment I was more proud of Dillon than I'd ever been.

His reassurance worked. Julian rushed toward Dillon, throwing his arms around him, burying his head in Dillon's chest. They stood like that for a little while. After they separated, Julian took his brother's hand and cleared his throat, announcing, "We don't need time to think. We're in. Let's go for it. Let's become a real family."

The rest of the afternoon was full of hugs and smiles, mixed with anxious questions about processes and next steps and timelines. It was a lot for the boys to absorb, but the change that came over them, knowing they were wanted, knowing there was a possibility they'd never have to change schools again, never have to go through the circuit of new foster homes again, made them appear years younger. The weariness lifted, and for the first time in a long time, they could just be "normal" kids.

So now we wait to see what the authorities will decide, but no matter how they classify our legal relationships to each other, we know that we will face it together, as a family.

The Girl Who Sold the World

—

"Dear reader, traditional human power structures and their reign of darkness are about to be rendered obsolete."

— R. Buckminster Fuller

Throughout Earth's history, there are moments within civilizations during which every member of the affected population remembers exactly where they were, what they were doing, who they were with. However, there had never been a moment when the entire world shared a single such experience, until the day the Consortium arrived.

Some believed they were dreaming or hallucinating. Some believed it was a trick pulled on a mass scale. Others thought they were dying, and the ships were celestial chariots come to physically transport them to heaven. They were, of course, mistaken, as many others pointed out. In their estimation, if the ships came from any supernatural realm, they were from Hell itself, bringing nothing but destruction and chaos, dooming and damning each and every person on the planet.

In the quiet privacy of her home, former school teacher Laurie Huston watched with great interest as the breaking story unfolded. The reclusive widow did not panic, but instead spoke calmly to her canine companion, Horatio St. Claire. "I think we should get a little more information first before deciding it's doomsday, don't you, Horatio?" He snuggled into her, relaxed, and waited.

At first, no one knew why the Consortium arrived, but the uninvited guests didn't allow imaginations to run wild for long. They quickly took over all forms of media, broadcasting a simultaneous message in every language and dialect in existence. What the humans of Earth saw terrified and amazed them. No two aliens among the Consortium looked alike. They were a motley crew of humanoid, reptilian, amphibian, insectoid, avian, and apelike individuals, covered in an array of feather, fur, scales, and skin. Once they had Earth's attention, they introduced themselves and their intentions.

"Creatures of Planet 21774, we are the Consortium, an ever-growing group of intergalactic allies dedicated to exploring the universe, spreading peace and sharing knowledge. We are new to your sector. We believe we may have much to learn from each other, and look forward to understanding the various species on your world."

A second alien continued. "At each planet we visit, we observe and evaluate. If we feel there is mutual benefit to be had from such an arrangement, we make an offer to join the Consortium. Through our alliance, we have met and granted membership to species with many varied cultures and abilities. As members, you will be able to join us in our exploration. You will also receive technological, medical, and other expertise we have gathered from the hundreds of civilizations who proudly consider the Consortium their interstellar family. We are eager to see how our relationship evolves during this period of evaluation."

The Consortium did not know much about humanity, because as soon as humans heard the phrase, "spreading peace," they immediately interpreted in the only way possible based on Earth's history: the aliens meant to conquer.

World leaders scrambled. A few reached out to the Consortium, establishing lines of communication through which they tried to make sure it was understood that *they* were the most important nation on Earth, and that the Consortium would do well to put *them* in charge of the whole human civilization.

Defenses were on high alert. While philosophers, humanitarians, scholars and diplomats urged calm, and highlighted the possibilities of improving life on earth with advanced knowledge, the majority of people only saw one inevitable outcome. Shared fears of enslavement, exploitation, and extinction whipped the human population of the planet into a panic.

The various militaries worked together to come up with both defensive and offensive strategies, including the idea of taking over the Consortium ships and using them to track down any other nearby ships. With the superior technology secured, no civilization would dare invade Earth.

Civilian earthlings did what they do best. They divided, closed ranks, and turned on each other. Religious leaders encouraged the chaos, whipping fanatics into a frenzy by claiming the aliens were a sign of the apocalypse. In response, people hoarded, they looted, they fought. Society crumbled at a shocking pace, faster than in the wake of any previously-recorded disaster.

Consortium observers were not impressed. In fact, they were appalled, and only a week later shared the findings of the assessment. Their next world-wide broadcast was brief.

"Creatures of Planet 21774, we have reached our verdict. While we do see the potential in an alliance with certain societies, including the dolphins, bees, chimpanzees, crows, parrots, and of course, the octopus, your dominant human society has caused us concern and distress. You are not suitable for Consortium membership. We are willing to return in a few centuries, when perhaps you will have evolved into a higher form of civilization. Until then you will not hear from us again. We must prepare to depart."

Suddenly, humanity was united in a single cause: convincing the Consortium to stay. Despite the anxiety caused by the sudden arrival of these outsiders, humans couldn't bear the notion of being rejected, of not being seen as valuable and worthy. They needed to win. They couldn't let the potential power of advanced technology slip away. From across the world, communications blasted at the visiting delegation, overwhelming the comms lines, begging for a second chance, for an opportunity to make their case, to highlight the best of humanity. Intrigued, the Consortium agreed, offering terms.

"As humanity is our highest point of worry with this planet, we will allow humanity to make the case. If you can convince us, we will offer you a probationary period to earn full membership. We will establish diplomatic and trade relations, and as long as you demonstrate that you can uphold the Consortium Rules of Civility, we will consider admitting you."

Relief washed across a nervous globe, until the message continued.

"We have observed your entrenched divisions and conflicting interests. Using an index of inhabitants drawn from your various databases, we will now select, at random, twelve humans from various geographic regions to argue for your cause. They will not be from your leadership structures. We want truth, not propaganda. If we are convinced, we will begin your orientation as pending members of the Consortium.

Stand by to receive the names of your randomly-selected delegates, as well as coordinates in their home countries where we will set up platforms at which they may address us. Of course their speeches will be broadcast live, in real time, for all humanity to observe."

The entire world froze, waiting for the biggest lottery announcement ever witnessed.

"Attention. The selected citizens are as follows." The alien rattled off a list of individuals, from Morocco, Nepal, Estonia, New Zealand, Jordan, Lichtenstein,

Indonesia, Paraguay, Djibouti, Curaçao, and Laos. The final name called was Laurie Huston from the United States.

After the roll call, the Consortium speaker instructed, "We will reconvene in 48 hours time to hear their arguments on your behalf. As you may already know, we have telepathic species among our membership, so while we hope to be convinced, we will not fall for lies."

The lack of control over the process was too much for those in power to stand, particularly from nations used to being in charge. They protested that some of the selected nations were not representative of the entire world, that their citizens would not have the understanding or sophistication to adequately offer a sound argument.

"These are your representatives. If you do not believe it is worth our time to hear them, then we can cease this process and leave now."

Humanity had no choice but to agree. The countdown began.

Around the world, friends, families, and neighbors ran to the chosen, overwhelming them with pleas, ideas, and data to use. Some people just wanted to get an autograph or a selfie with the heroes of humanity. Unaccustomed to the deluge of attention, the dozen delegates had been caught by surprise at their selection, now crushed by the burden of acting as attorneys on behalf of the entire human race.

In each delegate's country, the government dispatched guards to pick them up and bring them to the appointed locations. Then preparations began, drilling the delegates with key points and examples, coaching them on persuasive presentation skills, and in some cases, giving them makeovers to ensure they looked their best. As the nations prepared the candidates, they also researched them, to understand exactly who held Earth's future in their hands.

The United States delegate, Laurie, was difficult to research, as she lived her life primarily offline. Government and citizens alike tried to learn more about her, but she was a cipher. Americans were confused they couldn't learn more about her, that they couldn't get to know her immediately from a digital persona. Any social media accounts had been deactivated over a decade prior. She had no spouse, no children, seemingly no family at all.

Since retiring as a teacher, Laurie now worked from home creating indexes for reference books. Several times each day she walked with Horatio, allowing him to offer greetings to other pups in the form of sniffs or a wagging tail, while primarily ignoring her human neighbors. (Though they did report that sometimes she'd half-heartedly return a wave, or give a slight nod of her head.) She didn't have close friends or colleagues. She had groceries and sundries delivered to her home, to limit her interactions with other people. It was as if she had no network at all, no community.

At the federal level, the powers that be felt concerned that she was not going to be up to the task. The President's Cabinet and intelligence advisors fought amongst themselves over their odds, with the Secretary of Commerce griping, "Fantastic, our fate lies in the hands of a recluse widow. I'm sure her public speaking skills will really dazzle those alien bastards. We're going to need some serious PR talent to polish this turd."

The Secretary of State worried, "Diplomacy takes a lifetime of practice, you can't just thrust someone into it. She's a HERMIT, for God's sake! Does she even know how to hold a conversation with a human, let alone a hundred aliens?"

"They chose the weakest among us to be sure we'd fail," the Secretary of Defense concluded. "An aggressive move, to be sure. I recommend we explore other tactical options. Maybe we can arm her..."

A few reasonable voices spoke up on her behalf. The Secretary of the Interior pointed out, "She's educated, at least. She should be trainable, able to memorize talking points. And as a former teacher, she has at least some experience in public speaking. We just need to help her get back on that horse, but all things considered, I think we could have been stuck with far, far worse."

The FBI director agreed. "It's true. She's got a clean record, and an astounding lack of vices. No arrests, no addictions, no debts, not traffic violations, no parking tickets... not even an overdue library book."

The NSA chief confirmed, "No negative chatter or agitating language. She doesn't collude with any persons of interest, nor does she frequent online communities on watch lists. She doesn't really communicate with anyone, besides her supervisor, and even the content of those emails are kept to the confines of work. However..."

The CIA head picked up the cue, "However, she also has multiple traumatic incidents in her past, the kind that make someone vulnerable to becoming an asset, unwitting or otherwise. Any one of them alone would make her questionable for even a basic clearance. She's not the kind of profile we ever would have picked for this mission."

The Secretary of Homeland Security concluded, "We don't trust that she's stable enough for this kind of pressure. I recommend we limit who can contact her, and we keep her under tight observation until go-time, so she doesn't become susceptible to unfortunate influences."

Smiling, the Secretary of Education cut in, pointing out, "She's not just an educator, but look at her job. She works on textbooks! She is constantly exposed to new information, always learning. Given that, she may be exactly the right sort of person to pull from her professional experience and come up with just the right things to say!"

The White House Press Secretary shot up from his seat. "We are NOT letting her develop her own talking points. There's far too much riding on this, and I'll be damned if I'm going to let some amateur—some shut-in—fumble this."

"Absolutely!" Echoed the Attorney General. "We need to build a case so solid, so precise, that there's no way the verdict will be anything other than favorable."

The President of the United States waved her hands, "Enough. We don't have time. She might not be savior material, but she's our only option. We need to make sure she is set up to succeed, even in spite of her shortcomings. I want the absolute best people assembled immediately to get her ready. Go get our girl, and let's make her a winner."

Laurie appeared to ignore all of the attention, confining her walks to quick outings in her backyard, just long enough for Horatio to do his business. A mass of people camped on her front lawn, waiting to see the woman who would save the world. So far, however, she hardly even pulled back a window curtain to look out at them.

When the government convoy arrived to escort her to the coordinates, she emerged from her house with her Horatio, harnessed, walking by her side. Shushing each other, the lawn crowd waited for her to address them, to address her guards, anyone. She looked exhausted, overwhelmed, and a little terrified.

Closing her eyes, she took in a deep breath to pull herself up, and opened her eyes again, letting out a long exhale. Finally, they heard her speak, addressing one of the soldiers, "I won't come unless he can come, too." Who was anyone to argue with her demands, when they all needed her to succeed? So, Laurie and Horatio climbed into one of the behemoth vehicles and rode away.

The next two days were a non-stop gauntlet for her, transferred from location to location as people tried to make her look glamorous, frustrated by what they'd been given to work with. "Is that what you were planning to wear? Never mind. Wardrobe, we need options! Let's play up the teacher vibe, yeah? And let's get a bow tie or something for this dog! Now, I think we definitely want hair down, and we can easily cover the grays, but the texture, is it always this curly? Maybe up. Something that says 'You can trust me, I'm relatable, approachable. You want me in your alien party.' As for the face...are you wedded to this eyebrow shape?"

Simultaneously, a hyperactive man barked directions at how to recite her script. This famous stage director had been drafted to coach her delivery. He spoke to her rapidly, like an auctioneer, each word clipped by the next.

"Now remember, your opening line is your foundation, so when you say, 'human beings are resilient,' I want you to pause a little after 'beings' and after 'are." Think Shatner, think Walken. You watch movies, right? Anyway. You aren't just speaking to them, you're *entrancing* them. You're creating dramatic tension, you're building momentum, you need a strong opening hook to get their attention. So when you get to the crescendo, to 'resilient,' I want you to make a soft fist, yes, like this," as he reached over and balled up her hand, "then, with real Kate Hepburn dignity, I want you to punch each syllable. *Re-sil-i-ant*. Got it?"

In the evening, she was confined to a makeshift barracks, under heavy surveillance, unable to communicate with anyone until she was brought back out for more run through and rehearsals. The leaders of the government (except for one, housed in a safe place as a designated survivor) convened in person to offer their advice.

The Secretary of Labor gave Laurie a generic pep-talk about how "The People" were all counting on her.

The Secretary of Health and Human Services acknowledged that public speaking can play havoc on the nerves, and gave tips on staying calm. "You'll be going third, so let the first two break the ice for you. Then you can confidently take your turn, recite your lines, and once you're done, you can sit back, relax, and watch the rest."

Meanwhile, the Secretary of Defense ordered her, "We cannot fail at this mission, do you understand? If they leave, we will have a bunch of judgmental extra terrestrials running around the galaxy spreading negative intel about us. Now what do you think happens when that information falls into the wrong tentacles? Huh? We become a target. That's right, some rogue member of their alliance decides we must be weak, and sets out to take over the whole damned planet. With their tech, they could sneak up and ambush us, catch us with our collective pants around our ankles. Then what happens? You know what happens: all out war, annihilation, the end of the fucking world. You CANNOT fail."

The conductor of the mad orchestra was the President's Chief of Staff, who appeared to move faster than light as she wrangled and coordinated everyone while somehow rarely remembering to ever address Laurie directly. As she pulled Laurie away to have an audience with the President, the Chief of Staff rattled off a long list of protocols for meeting the Commander-in-Chief. Reaching a small conference room, the President stood waiting for them as they walked in.

Smiling, the President reached out a hand, and with a welcoming gesture greeted "Ah, if it isn't the woman who will save the world. I can't tell you how glad we are to have an American among the delegates, and not just any American, but an All-American Woman, a teacher! I know you have rehearsals, but I wanted to meet you face-to-face. I'm sure I don't need to remind you, but we have a lot riding on this. We're all counting on you, so learn your lines and give it your best. I'm personally rooting for you." The president balled up her fist and punctuated each syllable of "personally."

Before she could respond, Laurie was ushered out of the room and to the platform she'd be arguing from. The heads of the National Geospatial-Intelligence Agency and the National Reconnaissance Office stood next to it, along with some engineers from NASA, all looking frustrated. "We hoped to have a technical run-through with you, but frankly we can't figure out how it works. We've had our people examining it round the clock, and we still don't understand the inputs, the outputs, the lighting, how it communicates up to those ships. We can't guess what the experience is going to be like for you, unfortunately."

As she began to ascend the staircase leading up to the dais, the Secretary of Veterans Affairs kindly reached out toward Horatio's leash. "I can hold him for you, ma'am. He'll be safe with me."

Frightened, Laurie pulled the leash back quickly toward herself. "I won't do this unless he can come with me."

The Secretary of Transportation muttered there was no point arguing about it. "Let her keep her dog if it makes her more confident and relaxed. Whatever it takes, we need her at peak performance."

Taking Laurie gently by the arm, the U.N. Ambassador walked up the steps with her and showed her how to stand and hold herself in a confident but non-aggressive posture. After listening to Laurie deliver her speech four times in a row, emphasizing the closing line, "Please, believe me when I say, this Earth is worth it," the leaders in attendance were almost satisfied.

"I guess that's the best we're going to get, I just hope it's enough," assessed the Secretary of Energy.

The Press Secretary complained, chewing his nails and pulling at his hair, "I don't suppose I can just pretend that *I'm* Laurie Huston and do it for her?"

At last, the big moment arrived. Each delegate around the world stepped up on to their platform at the appointed time, surrounded by massive throngs of spectators hoping to see the world saved in real time, and have bragging rights to tell people they were there when it happened. With Horatio at her side, his collar adorned with a patriotic necktie, she took her place and waited her turn. A large projector screen stood nearby, allowing the crowd to see the other delegates deliver their remarks.

Morocco was first. As the delegate announced himself, a strong column of light enveloped the stage. It was unclear if it was only light, or also some sort of containment field, but regardless, the U.S. intelligence officials were on high alert as they observed it on screen. They ran closer to Laurie's platform to see if they could get a handle on how it would activate for her speech.

The Moroccan delegate concluded their talk, followed by the delegate from Nepal, who was again surrounded by light from an unidentified source. She held a page in front of her, reading from notes, occasionally glancing down to refocus and find her rhythm. Both speeches were well-composed and delivered with humility and sincerity.

Cautious optimism permeated the crowd. Two down, ten to go, and the U.S. of A was up next...they were going to pull this off. All eyes were on Laurie and Horatio. She closed her eyes, inhaled, pulled herself up, and exhaled. Horatio, sympathetic eyebrows raised, leaned his head into her knee. Opening her eyes, she introduced herself. "I'm Laurie Huston, and this is Horatio St. Claire, my best friend in the world. I hope you don't mind, but he's my only family, and I don't go anywhere without him."

The lights came on. The large speaker system lifted her voice across the crowd. She looked at the index cards, then made her other hand into a light fist grasping Horatio's leash. "Human beings... are... re-sil-i-ent." All the President's men heaved a sigh of relief, looking at each other with smiles and nods of congratulations. The stage director held his hand to his heart, let out a contented sigh, admiring his star pupil. She was off to a perfect start, just as he'd coached her.

Then Laurie Huston froze. Everyone's worst fear came true. She had stage fright.

She looked down, and closed her eyes. Her fist loosened, and, relaxing to drop the leash, she set her hand lightly on top of Horatio's head. After what was only a few seconds, but felt like an eternity to the crowd, she opened her mouth to resume, but no one could hear. The sound wasn't working, her words weren't transmitting. The light column was malfunctioning, causing some form of audio interference so that even people attending in person couldn't make out what she was saying. It also began to visually crackle like static, obscuring her mouth, leaving only her eyes clearly exposed.

Gripping the index cards tightly, she spoke without sound, for much longer than either of the previous speakers. She looked like a tent revival preacher working up a crowd, trying to make the congregation feel the spirit. She gestured, she swayed, and…she cried. Laurie wept. She was clearly pleading.

No one understood what happened to the audio-visual technology, but it didn't matter, they could feel her. She was pouring her entire heart and soul into her defense. She waved the index cards wildly as she spoke. She fell to her knees, lifting up her hands above her head as if in a desperate prayer, beseeching. Everyone watching began to cry with her. The first two speeches had been calm, rehearsed, recited. Not Laurie's. She was making a stand for the entire human race. Finally, after what felt to the attendees like hours, she paused once more, looking utterly exhausted from the efforts of her appeal.

The light beam stopped fluctuating, and the sound came back just as she delivered her closing line exactly according to script, but more convincing and heart-felt than in any of her rehearsals. "Please, believe me when I say, this Earth is worth it." She looked up toward the sky, tears still streaming, as Horatio let out a sympathetic whimper and burrowed his head into her chest. Dropping the index cards, she threw her arms around him, letting out sobs, and one final, whispered, "Please."

Silence hung over the entire area. Cautiously, the officials looked at each other, unsure at the technical issues, but confident that at least she had delivered their script. No one moved. Estonia was up next, but the delegate looked alarmed, unsteady, unprepared to follow such an emotional display.

The delegate didn't have too long to worry, because the U.S. platform began to shake. The rumbling spread through the area, kicking up dust and rattling the spectator stands. Lights flashed, sharp sounds erupted, a blinding flash shocked everyone, burning even on the transmission screens across the world, and when everyone was able to see once more, Laurie was gone. Horatio was gone. Even the index cards were gone. Vaporized. Only dust and detritus kicked up in their wake.

A voice bellowed across the broadcast. "Humans of Planet 21774, you have broken our agreement. You have attempted to deceive us. You tried to make the human delegates lie for you. You wanted them to stall us until you could attack. Your plans for violence are known to us, and must now be brought to an end."

In that instant, hundreds of ships appeared in the sky over the world, and the occupation of Earth began. In the decades that followed, the Consortium implemented measures to radically alter civilization. Man's dominion over the earth was at an end. Councils were established on which multiple species were given equal stature as humans, using translation technology provided by the Consortium.

Generations of children were born with no concept of life before occupation.

Land was reallocated, with more nature preserved for what humans had viewed as wildlife, but whom the Consortium viewed as equal inhabitants. Consortium scientists set about repairing the environment, limiting the use of materials that damaged the climate. With the help of Consortium science and technology, endangered species came back from the brink, flourishing. Even extinct species were able to be revived if there was enough preserved DNA for the Consortium to work with.

In the most radical move, humans were reassigned by lottery and moved across the world, breaking up societies from all corners, matching them up with regard to neither long-standing religious, ethnic, and racial barriers, nor ancient grudges. This devastated the individuals who were swapped at random to far corners of the globe, to places they'd never even heard of.

Removed from the familiarity of their land, their culture, their communities, even their languages, humans had to learn to live and work together in order to survive. Many adopted the newly-introduced Consortium Standard Language—based on an evolving amalgam of thousands of languages and dialects from across the galaxy—as a means to communicate. Eventually, their children's children became used to these new, inorganic cultures as the status quo.

Humanity was tamed. Over time, people adjusted to life within their new communities, which also now included animal counterparts. Humanity learned to be better stewards of the earth's resources, and in return for their compliance, received knowledge from schools set up by the Consortium. Healthcare was more advanced and accessible than any time in human history. Illnesses from diabetes to asthma to cancer were eliminated entirely. Even the difficult puzzles such as Cystic Fibrosis were finally solved. People were finally able to live healthy lives. Food was allocated fairly, as well, eradicating hunger and eliminating waste.

Without the need to fight for resources, people had the opportunity to pursue their passions. Disciplines including science, art, music, literature, and athletics flourished, with people from all backgrounds able to access training and resources. Geniuses that in previous eras would have suffered for being born in the wrong place or to the wrong family, who might have withered from childhood malnutrition or wasted away in difficult menial labor, finally had an equal chance to nurture their talents.

Humans were shocked to find there was enough happiness to go around, and realized there had been, the whole time. They watched as housing was built, in cooperation with wildlife and respect for the environment, providing shelter for every person. With fundamental needs met, and more equal access to mental health resources, crime also decreased.

When crimes still occurred, they were handled in a radically different way than the punitive penal systems that pre-existed the Consortium. Small misdemeanors were handled not in prisons, which had been torn down, but in rehabilitation centers, where perpetrators could find ways to make retribution to those they wronged, and also receive counseling to set them on a positive path in the future.

For serious crimes, the regional councils were given a wide berth in handling the cases, and the most common sentence was to remove the offender into the wilderness, exiled from any community, until their sentence was served. If they survived, they could petition to apologize, offer retribution, and rejoin society, if the community chose to let them back in.

Increasingly, religious leaders declared that humans had no need to fear the Consortium, after all. With humanity transformed, heaven was now a place on earth. They worshiped Laurie Huston as a martyr who gave her life to save the world, and devotional cults formed to worship both Huston and Horatio. Icons and art enshrined them, heroes who made the plea for humanity that successfully delayed the departure of the Consortium ships and led to the longest period of peace in the history of the world. The opening to her speech was played ad nauseam, seared into the memory and mind of every individual on the planet.

After enough time had passed, some of the humans were even placed into trusted positions which enabled them to more directly interface with Consortium members, to share knowledge and solve problems together. They petitioned for permission to join Consortium crews, to live alongside them and travel with them to new planets.

The Consortium were pleased by the progress Planet 21774 had made. Preparations began for a formal reevaluation of Earth's status, to move from occupied territory to provisional membership, news that was met with elation by many. Some Earth humans were even able to receive body modifications, using Consortium technology, that would better enable them to work and live in different environments and atmospheres when exploring space.

All the while, small bands of humans resisted however they could. Communications were more difficult, but as Laurie had told the aliens, human beings are resilient. There was a network of people who never accepted defeat, viewing the occupation not as a paradigm shift, but as a temporary inconvenience to be overcome. Huston & Horatio societies, "H&H's," emerged almost as soon as their namesakes were zapped to dust particles.

Working slowly over the years, they continued to hold the flame of an independent humanity. Their rallying cry, "Humans are resilient," was sprayed and carved as graffiti, even tattooed on the bodies of H&H resistance members. The tattoos also included stylized portraits of Huston, with her iconic curls, and Horatio, with or without the necktie. Some of the more militant even dreamed of going beyond retaking Earth, to making offensive moves against the entire Consortium. Their plans relied on gaining control of Consortium technology. As plans for provisional membership moved forward, the need to take action grew urgent.

They plotted to take over the fleet of ships still monitoring Earth, kill the aliens on board, declare Earth's independence and then repeat the process at every Consortium world. The H&H loyalists remaining on earth would carry out acts of sabotage to wrest control of Earth's resources and infrastructure from non-human species, pushing them back into the jungles, deserts, woods and seas where they belonged.

The covert action did not go as planned. In the end, only one ship was successfully captured, and was under such intense fire that the human crew's only option was to flee. Speeding away from Earth's orbit, they moved on without a clear objective, other than to survive, free from their oppressors. They disconnected tracking and disposed of the corpses which had comprised the Consortium crew. Although they could not access the majority of the information libraries and archives on board, they were able to control the operation systems and weapons.

Over the next few days, the ship, rechristened "The Hornblower," in honor of Horatio, became their home. Most of the human crew, including Meryl Bennett, the captain, were not old enough to remember the day when Laurie Huston and her dog had been executed. Many hadn't even been born yet. They only knew what they'd been raised to understand, that life was better before the occupation, that humans had been free, humans had ruled the world. They had been told since birth that the only good alien was a dead alien, and that the world would not be free again until every member of the Consortium was dead, every wronged human avenged.

Captain Bennett and her crew developed a plan: find an isolated Consortium exploration vessel, pose with the *Hornblower* as a stranded Consortium ship in need of aid, allow the Consortium away team to board, then kill them. Using the aid team's credentials, the humans could get on to the rescue vessel, take the rest of the Consortium crew by surprise, and once they were dead, gain control of the ship. The plan was to repeat the process until they had enough ships running on skeleton crews to go back to Earth and put up a good fight, then recruit new crew members to launch an intrepid attack fleet.

The crew of the *Hornblower* were able to put the plan into motion even earlier than they'd imagined, when they encountered a small Consortium ship. It was a diplomatic vessel, which wasn't quite what they'd hoped for in terms of tactical resources, but it was still one more ship than they currently had. Making the *Hornblower* appear disabled, they put out a Consortium distress call, which was answered instantly. The diplomatic ship maneuvered close to the *Hornblower*, swiftly docking.

A small team dispatched from the Consortium ship, armed primarily with medical supplies and mechanical repair kits. They never had a chance against the humans of the *Hornblower*, who made short work of killing their would-be rescuers.

Nicking items of use from the dead, the *Hornblower* crew moved in on their target, slipping into the diplomatic ship. Fanning out, they silently swept through the ship, quickly incapacitating their opponents and securing OpComm, the operations and command center of the ship.

Over the ship's public address system, a human voice rang out. "This is Captain Bennett, human of Earth. This vessel is now under my command. Your rescue crew is dead, and unless you want to join them, you will put down all weapons, and head toward the brig for containment. You have two minutes to give yourselves up, and then we resume killing. We will show you no mercy, no more than you showed Huston and Horatio. Bennett out."

Consortium crew drifted into the halls, hands, tentacles, paws, claws, and wings up in the universal sign for surrender. Filing toward the brig, it all seemed too easy. Bennett left one of her crew, Saskia Qiang, in control of the OpComm, and headed to the brig with several of her comrades, frisking the Consortium crew to remove any weapons or tech that could be used to resist.

Outside the brig, the *Hornblower*'s Halle Jensen complained to her fellow human, Reese Davis. "What is the point of this? Hostages? I thought we were going to kill them, not take them prisoner. I didn't sign up to babysit our colonizers."

Reese reassured her. "Don't worry, they won't be around for long, Cap just wants to get any useful information we can from them, then," gesturing across his neck, "we kill them all."

From the OpComm station, Qiang urgently called out over the PA, "Captain Bennett, another ship is approaching fast!"

"How did they get here so quickly?!" Bennett exclaimed. "OK, we just need to speed this up. You!" She pointed at a Consortium crew member whose ostentatious uniform stood out from the rest. "Were you expecting another ship?"

The Consortium officer looked like a cross between a sloth and a tapir, with a delicate build and comically expressive face, which had been wounded in the onboarding scuffle. "You should have learned by now, 'Captain,'" delivering her title with no small amount of derision, "we are never really alone in the Consortium. That's the whole point of a cooperative alliance."

"Fine. You have two options. Get them to go away, or help us take that ship. What will it be?"

"Why should I help you, when you'll kill me and my crew regardless?"

"I never said that."

"Your crew did, outside. Several of us heard them. And even now the telepaths among us can read their true intentions."

"That might be what *they* said, but *I'm* telling you now, you help us here and your crew lives."

"Oh? We'll live? Where? Alongside you? Will we serve by your side on this ship, or will you strand us on the next habitable planet? What will you do with us?"

"We'll figure it out. You have my word. I swear on the names of Huston and Horatio, I will not kill you today."

"Huston and Horatio? That's quite a solemn promise. Allow me to give you my response. Have your crew person in OpComm pull up file 2637489, access code 4844787. Have her play it over the PA." He smiled, folded his paws, and leaned back with a self-satisfied grin.

Wary, but understanding she was no longer in full control of the situation, Bennett relayed the order to Qiang. Seconds later, a broadcast began.

"Human beings are resilient."

Across the ship, humans of the *Hornblower* crew snapped to attention, recognizing a voice they knew almost better than their own. They stared up at speakers in disbelief. No human currently alive on Earth had ever heard the original recording.

"I assume this conversation is now private, as requested? Good. I don't want anyone interfering until I've said my piece. Citizens of the Consortium, listen to me, all of you. You have to save this planet, and at the very least, save yourselves. Humans are truly resilient, and that resilience is the very reason we must be destroyed. Not conquered, not assimilated, destroyed. Wiped away.

Don't fool yourselves. You can't just leave now. The danger to you doesn't end just because you remove yourselves from our space. You are now a known problem, an obstacle for humans to overcome, and we will. We always do. We will make it our mission to hunt you down. We can't be stopped. Don't imagine you can teach us or educate us out of this impulse, either. We cannot be civilized, we cannot be trusted to work toward any common good, especially if it's not our idea, if we're not the ones in power.

You have no choice. As long as humans exist, they will find a way to fight back and harm you. Even now, the Secretary of Defense in my own country is plotting missions to sabotage your ships, take your technology, and strike against you wherever they can, until Earth has conquered the universe. You didn't roll over for us and give us all your resources, therefore, you are a threat that must be contained.

Please know I'm not a nihilist. I love this planet, and the majority of the life on it. I don't want the world destroyed, I only want the human cancer to be removed. If this planet is to have any chance of recovering, humans have to go. If your Consortium is to have any chance of surviving, you can't risk leaving even one of us alive. Myself included.

These cards they gave me to read you are nothing but propaganda and lies meant to trick you into believing we're noble, that we have something to offer your Consortium. You already heard two of these speeches built on falsehoods, and after me if you keep going you'll listen to nine more. Why waste your time, or ours? I will tell you the truth, even though no one else will.

All we have to offer is greed and violence. I know, because I've studied history, and I keep up with current events, I watch the world, and I've lived in it long enough to understand that we're only getting worse. Let me tell you who humans are.

I was a teacher. I worked long, hard hours, and often spent my evenings and weekends grading papers. One afternoon my husband took my parents to run errands, letting me focus on a batch of particularly poorly-written essays. I barely lifted my head from the pages to say goodbye when they left.

They never came home. For a moment I'd forgotten I lived in America, and that we're all just prey for human hunters. My husband and my parents were gunned down by a mass shooter, a frequent customer who'd come to get revenge on a woman who worked at the store. This woman, a cashier, had rejected his unwanted advances, and in doing so had denied him the affection and attention to which he believed he was entitled, simply because he was a man. And since humans are resilient, he didn't just take the rejection, he fought back.

The shooter was not an anomaly; he didn't reach his plan of revenge by himself, of course. No, humans excel at radicalizing each other toward horrific acts. This shooter was egged on by his fellow discontented men who also felt aggrieved they weren't getting the female attention they wanted—no, not just wanted, but to which they believed they had a fundamental right. He became their champion, their avatar. His vengeance was their vengeance.

This wasn't some back room conspiracy of hidden malcontents, either. It was openly nurtured by the media, amped up by hosts of popular podcasts and shows, authors, and public speakers about how society needed to get back to traditional gender roles. Their mission was to force us to return to the good old days when women submitted to men, belonged to men, didn't work, didn't pursue education or careers, didn't speak up for themselves, had no financial independence, no agency that wasn't expressly granted to them by their fathers and husbands.

Humans love to worship celebrities, no matter how unqualified or uneducated or unstable, especially those who reinforce their worldviews, who affirm their biases. Americans are particularly susceptible to blowhards that pretend facts aren't real, that twist words and shout opinions to fit the narratives of the disgruntled and disaffected. These 'thought leaders' among 'real men,' and 'traditional wives' encouraged their audiences to view women as interchangeable objects, not individuals with minds and souls and desires and rights of their own.

So this shooter, infatuated with a cashier whom he did not actually know, decided to put her in her place and teach her a lesson after she dared turn him down. Like every woman who has ever lived on this planet, she knew she was in mortal danger and needed to tread lightly, so she tried to let him down gently, explaining she wasn't available, that she had a husband, it wasn't personal.

Now, even if she didn't have a husband, you Consortium members might think she had a right to turn someone down for any reason. After all, she's her own person. Women are people too, right? We're half the population. We're allowed to have preferences and opinions, aren't we? She'd anticipated with fear the day he would finally make his move, asking her supervisors in advance for help and protection. She tried to appeal to common sense, to move people to action.

But that's not how humans work. We don't do common sense. We don't do logic. We don't do reason. We don't do empathy. We only look out for ourselves, and for our bottom lines. All we understand is that we want what we want, when we want it. We're conditioned to believe we're each special and deserving, entitled to everything we desire, even when it comes at the expense of other humans.

After expressing her concerns, she was called hysterical, dramatic, paranoid, and vain. She was brushed off, left to fend for herself. When it finally happened, she deferentially and apologetically explained, in terms a man like him might understand, that she was already the 'property' of another man, and she wasn't allowed to disrespect her owner, her husband.

He heard her say she was married, but that didn't matter, because he felt wronged. He was embarrassed, and that angered him to the point he snapped. He waited a few days, nursing his vitriol, venting his anger online to other men who validated his feelings of rage and resentment, emboldening him to act. Quickly acquiring lethal weapons of mass violence, which is the most sacred of all American rights, in no time at all he was armed for destruction.

He showed up at the store, fueled by fury of not getting his way. He didn't know the shoppers, didn't *care who they were, that they had lives and families and futures. He needed his tantrum to be acknowledged. It was a massacre, the typical kind of slaughter we've all gotten so used to seeing played out at stores, churches, theaters, schools, offices, everywhere.*

And the cashier? She wasn't even there. It was a usual day on her schedule, but she had taken time off for a trip with her husband, who was worried about how stressed her job was making her.

I lost my entire family because some random man didn't get an answer he liked, while the real target of his ire wasn't even there for him to confront. I became a widow and an orphan because a stranger didn't get his way.

Bennett looked unsteady, as if she might be sick. Scanning the faces of her fellow humans she saw her confusion mirrored. She turned her eyes back to the Consortium leader, who confidently held her gaze, looking satisfied, almost smug. Before Bennett or anyone else could speak, Huston's voice continued. There was more, much more.

It didn't stop there, though. You must understand it's not just adult humans who are a threat. No, children are as equally dangerous. With each generation they become more so. Several years after the shooting, my work was all I had to keep me going. All I'd ever wanted to do my entire life was teach, it was my passion. I loved learning, and longed to share my enthusiasm. But with each year my spark faded, and my pessimism accelerated. Students grew more ill-behaved by the week. Trying to get them to focus at all, let alone retain information, was rolling a boulder up a hill.

Human kids never have a chance, not in any era. So many parents just want them to graduate and get out of the house, they don't care WHAT they learn or understand, as long as the grades are right. Other parents don't care at all, and expect teachers to be parents and nurses along-side our other responsibilities. No one sets boundaries or actually raises these kids to be functioning members of society, so they are left to raise themselves, under the influence of equally lost peers.

These kids live their lives entirely online, no concept of how to function in reality, addicted to devices. I tried to implement a no-phone policy in the class, but parents overturned it because the kids would need their phones for when there was, inevitably, a shooting at the school. Other parents protested, asking who the hell I thought I was to tell their children what they could and could not have.

One day a student was being very disruptive with her phone, trying to record a dance with two other girls in the middle of my class. I walked over and took the phone away, and she attacked me. Her backup dancers joined in. They beat me so badly I had to be hospitalized. Not one student tried to stop them. No one *ran to get help. They were too busy filming it, disconnected from reality, mesmerized and entertained by what they saw through their screens, as if I wasn't a living person being brutalized in front of them.*

They recorded my suffering until the bell rang, then walked to their next classes, as if nothing had happened. They were totally unbothered by violence they'd witnessed, which to their minds was no different from the countless videos of fights and beatings they'd watched online. It was only when a student from my next period walked in that anyone checked to see if I was even still alive.

That's when I gave up. I realized we'd passed the point of no return.

Despite having insurance, the hospital stay bankrupted me, completely depleted all of my savings. In my country humans decided health is a for-profit commodity, a privilege reserved only for those who 'deserve' it because they have amassed wealth, rather than a basic right to save lives and build up thriving communities.

Because a man was turned down for a date, because a student was asked to stop recording, because I wasn't wealthy enough to cover inflated medical costs, I was without a family and without funds.

The main girl who assaulted me was given in-school suspension for three days, which her parents successfully appealed thanks to other students explaining it was disrespectful of me to ask for her phone. Parents complained that I was clearly incompetent for not keeping control of my classroom, calling for my firing. Not one student or parent reached out to apologize or to ask how I was recovering. Meanwhile, videos of the assault racked up views online across channels, with people liking it, giving it a thumbs up, earning clout for the bystander students who posted them.

This is who you want to join your Consortium?

The human crew began to shift uncomfortably, some raising their hands to their mouths, others lowering their heads. Huston's speech built momentum toward the closing line they had all memorized, but had never understood.

You might think it's drastic for me to condemn an entire species based on one individual's experience, but listen to me when I say we are broken, and we always have been. War, imperialism, colonization, occupation, genocide, racism, misogyny, zealotry, enslavement, exploitation, economic disparity, corruption, avarice above all else... taking the totality of human history, these are not the exceptions. They are the rule.

Look how we treat the poor, the vulnerable, immigrants, orphans. Look how we allow hunger and malnutrition, when we have more than enough food to feed this world, but rather than distribute it to those in need, we let those with more wealth or power hoard and waste.

We are heartless and evil. We create systems that crush everyone, and when they can't pull themselves up with their imaginary bootstraps, when people in power only use it to gain more power and benefit themselves, we throw up our hands as if we can't possibly imagine how to fix things.

And that's just how we treat each other! Look what we've done to the environment. During my hospital stay, a hospital chaplain tried to console me. I thought about ending my life, as I didn't see the point in going on. The chaplain told me not to despair, there was still so much good on this Earth, and advised me to seek spiritual optimism, maybe 'take a walk in the woods and see the beauty of the world.'

Once I was able to walk again, I took her advice, and spent time in nature. The more I did, the more I saw the chaplain was right, there is beauty in the world. I appreciated the plant and animal life around us. I listened to the water, I felt the wind.

But, the Earth is only beautiful where humans haven't touched it. I saw the harm done by how humans carelessly wreck the environment, which they do with the assured stance that everything exists as a resource for their use, and therefore it's not wrong to deplete and destroy things.

Don't take my word for it. You've talked to the animals. Talk to them again. Ask them!

Ask fish about catch and release, how humans torture them for sport, piercing them, not even for sustenance, but for entertainment, depriving the fish of water just long enough to take a picture, before hurling the traumatized creatures back into the water. Ask the ones who survive the literal shock, anyway. Many don't.

Ask sharks about their families being slaughtered just for their fins, whole lives taken for one single body part to be consumed as a delicacy.

Ask rhinos targeted for their horns, to the point that so few of them are even left.

Ask the orangutans who lose their homes so humans can eat chocolate hazelnut spread.

Ask dogs bred in puppy mills, starved and beaten and producing until their bodies give out, or until they are shot for no longer producing adequate litters, litters bought by impatient humans who don't care and don't ask questions, because they want what they want when they want it.

Ask geese force-fed and fattened so their livers can be ground up and served on a cracker.

Ask the horses in tourist towns, abused and run ragged to the point of exhaustion hauling carriages.

Ask the moon bears, kept in horrific devices that crank down on them and press them for their pancreatic fluids.

Ask the horseshoe crabs, pumped and drained of their blood, then tossed aside.

Ask the animals used in cosmetic testing, doomed to lives of repeated physical pain so some human can feel more confident about their lash volume.

Ask the snails who are crushed for their serum to use in face masks and ointments.

Ask any of the big cats ripped from their natural environments and kept in cages on private property, so a wealthy person can feel decadent.

Ask animals who've lost their woodlands so more town homes and apartments can be built, whose water is filled with plastics, whose air is choked with pollutants.

If you let us, we humans will do the same to all of you, to your planets. This is your chance to stop us now.

Adults, children, all humans are corrupt or awaiting corruption, ticking time bombs ready to go off and cause a wake of chaos. It's our legacy, it's our destiny, it's all we know how to do.

It doesn't have to be this way. We'll never fix the world on our own, but you can! The penguins deserve it, the polar bears deserve it, the turtles and elephants deserve it, the forests and jungles and oceans and marshes and and rivers all deserve another chance, to heal and to thrive.

*Remove humans and the Earth can come back to itself, it can have a chance to be paradise for the plants and animals who dwell here. You can save this planet, and this world in which there is **so** much beauty.*

"Please. Please, believe me when I say, this Earth is worth it."

"Please."

The recording ended, and a heavy silence filled the ship, as *Hornblower* crew looked away from their captives, and each other, unsure how to process what they'd just heard. There wasn't time to assess the implications, though, because at that moment the second Consortium ship had arrived.

"Captain, they're right on top of us!" Interjected Qiang from the PA.

Bennett, reeling, stared at the Consortium commander. She managed to threaten, weakly, "Help us while you still can, you're running out of time."

"On the contrary, Captain, I have plenty of time. It is you who are facing a deadline." Just as Bennett prepared to reply, columns of light burst into rooms and hallways across this ship, startling Bennett and the *Hornblower* crew. The ship was filled with a new detachment of Consortium troops, fully shielded and armed with advanced weaponry.

Desperate, the humans lashed out, trying to fight. In the brig, Bennett and her loyalists did their best to subdue their existing hostages and fight the reinforcements. Davis and Jensen were forced inside from their hallway posts, joining the fray. After one of the Consortium fighters fell, knocked unconscious, a *Hornblower* crew member, Stefan Griggs, gasped in disbelief as a second Consortium fighter leapt on him, knocking him over. As Griggs wrestled with the creature, he had the impression that it was a cyborg, augmented with technological components he'd recently seen advertised back on Earth. He struggled until a commanding voice disrupted everyone, sharply.

"Horatio, stand down."

The cyborg canine padded back toward the speaker of this command, a tall woman covered with cybernetic implants and biological enhancements, not unlike those on the dog. Her skin color, grayish and tinged with a teal undertone, was not human, but with the iconic curls pulled into a mass like a crown on top of her head, she was instantly recognized by everyone on board.

"Please," Laurie Huston continued, cool and collected, with hands raised in a gesture somewhere between surrender and peace. "Let's all just take a pause, shall we?" She calmly walked to the center of the room, toward the Consortium commander who had played the audio file.

With utter tenderness she reached out and gently took one of his paws. With the other she caressed a wound on his face, tracing the blood line running over his fur. Voice full of concern, she addressed him in Consortium Standard Language, "Consul Talavar, you are injured. Look at this blood... but don't worry, the medical crew is already en route."

He smiled meekly, feigning bravado, "Nothing but a scratch, Ambassador Huston."

"I'm sorry we were delayed, but we got here as soon as we could. Thank you for holding on."

Turning to Bennett, Laurie Huston sized up the rogue human commander who had taken so many lives since leading the attack on Earth's surface just days prior. As Huston inhaled, she stretched out her bloodied hand to Bennett's chin, pulling the Captain's face up until they were looking directly into each other's eyes.

"I haven't seen a human since the occasion of my speech. Nor have I spoken Human Earth English to anyone other than Horatio in some time, so I hope you understand me clearly. Allow me to introduce myself."

"I know who you are," Bennett growled through tears.

"Really? But you're so young, you must have been born decades after I left."

"We all know who you are," Jensen chimed in, holding a wounded arm close to her chest.

Davis was more direct, "You're the reason we're here! You, you were our compass, our North Star."

"Me? You must have me confused with someone else. I'm Laurie Huston, formerly of Earth, and this is my dearest friend in the universe, Ambassador Horatio St. Claire."

"We know who he fucking is, we've got fucking tattoos of him!" Griggs shouted, pulling up a pant leg to expose a portrait of the very dog who, only moments before, had physically subdued him.

"Oh my." Huston's eyes widened, and a crooked smile broke across her face. "Back in my day, that's what we would call, 'a choice.' It is a remarkable likeness, though. Outdated, but very good."

"We thought you were dead." Bennett brought the attention back, words forced out between gritted teeth. "You were a martyr. We thought you wanted us to be resilient, to resist, to..."

"To what? To fight? To... win? To conquer the Consortium? And in my name? In Horatio's name? You would corrupt our legacies with violence against the very civilization that saved us? I tried to make them understand that you all were a lost cause. They did at least grant my request that humanity be led to believe I was dead. I didn't want anyone looking for me. I just wanted to get the hell off that rock."

Turning to Consul Talavar, she continued. "I told you, didn't I? I warned you all, this is exactly why humans shouldn't have been allowed to run wild and free on the planet."

"Free?! We aren't free, we're occupied!" Jensen argued.

"We are fighting *for* our freedom!" Davis clarified.

Unimpressed, the smile left her face. "No, children. You are fighting because you fight. You are humans. You are violent. If you weren't fighting the Consortium you'd be fighting each other. How disappointingly predictable. For decades I've had to hear about how well humans of Earth have been flourishing under Consortium enlightenment, how I should see the arts and athletics, the music and the scholarship. No matter what good reports I receive, I always caution that there is an underbelly of discontent out there, somewhere, waiting to strike."

The flush from Bennett's rage outweighed the streaks the tears had left on her cheeks. "All this time you've been admired, praised, worshiped for your legacy of standing up for the Earth, when your true legacy is that you were a traitor, living among our worst enemies, benefitting up here while we were left to rot down there. You sold us out and took on their language, their form, and then you kept selling us out, over and over."

"I did stand up for the Earth. The only way I knew how."

"Wait. How... how did you get in touch with them before your speech?" Griggs propped himself up as he sought clarification. "The public was told you were under strict surveillance from the moment you were selected. How did a reclusive book nerd bypass high-tech intelligence security measures?"

"I'm not MacGyver. Oh, sorry, that was a TV show. TV, you know... never mind. To answer your question, I was under the strictest surveillance, so tight I was nervous even to speak to Horatio. I knew I had no chance with technology. But, during the broadcast the Consortium mentioned telepaths. I used that as a means, hoping I could get through. It almost felt like I was wishing very hard, or praying. I just shut my eyes real tight and told them I needed their help, that I had to get through to them without anyone else knowing. I had no way to receive their replies, as I am not telepathic at all, or at least I wasn't before this," she tapped an implant by her temple, "but my outbound messages worked. They received my warning, and gave me the private audience I required."

"You asked them to commit genocide on your own people, all the while working to save yourself!" Accused Bennett.

"No, I told them to kill me, too. Apparently they had a sidebar discussion with Horatio, though, and he talked them out of it. It turns out, canines *are* telepathic. Humans aren't set up to receive transmission, but members of the Consortium are. Horatio here convinced them I was decent, and because they believed him, they decided more decent humans must be out there who were worth saving, too, so they countered my proposal of annihilation with their plan of rehabilitation."

"But what about all the innocent people? You were willing to let billions of innocents, children, even babies die to satisfy your grudge with a small sampling? What right did you have?!" Jensen demanded.

"Babies are born innocent, I will grant you, but the moment they are exposed to human interaction outside the womb they become corrupted. An ancient philosopher once questioned if a good man could live in a bad city, when in order to survive in that city he would have to participate in systems of corruption every day. Earth *is* a corrupt city. Shake your head at me all you want, but even toddlers lie. It's one of the first ways they exercise their independence and assert their personality."

"You think you're so pure, joining an evil empire to enslave the galaxy one planet at a time?" Davis shouted.

"Are humans better? How many innocent prophets and saints were murdered throughout history? The Consortium spreads enlightenment, bringing order to chaos and allowing civilizations to fulfill their potential. It's no evil empire. You want to talk evil? I've been able to meet hundreds of cultures, and I can tell you, humans of Earth are distinctly chaotic and evil."

"You were our hero." Griggs sounded utterly defeated. "There was a time when people back on Earth would have rejoiced that we found you alive. It would have been a worldwide holiday, parades in every town. Now when they find out you've been alive all this time, letting them mutilate you, your dog, turning you both into..."

Huston waved him off. "How will they find out? You certainly won't be telling them."

Turning back to Bennett, she concluded. "You mentioned my legacy. Let's talk about *your* legacy. Leader of a doomed mission, attacking the very institution that brought you peace, saved your planet."

Bennett lifted her face, haughty. "I don't care what you think of me. I don't care what you do to me. Others will rise in my place. You said it yourself, humans are resilient."

"No. Not this time. Your legacy is that you are my closing argument, showing how even when presented with a paradise, humans will always choose violence."

Turning to the Consul, Huston continued. "These are children of Utopia, who have never known scarcity, need, or want, and still, with all the resources at their disposal, time to pursue pleasure and self-fulfillment, they chose war."

She looked at each human in the room, and placed her hand gently on Horatio's head. "How disappointing when people live down to your worst expectations. Captain Bennett, crew of the *Hornblower*, thank you for proving my point. You can now die knowing that my decency was the only thing that spared humanity the first time, while your inherent aggression is what seals their fate now."

She turned away from the Earthlings before they could respond.

"Consul Talavar, these humans long for freedom. You may see that they get it, by way of the nearest airlock. Then set a course for Planet 21774. It's time to finish what we started, to save the planet, and the universe, from humanity, once and for all."

My Sister Agnes

—

"We are already born, we are going to die. So you
have to do something interesting that you respect in
between."

-Toni Morrison

We forgot to look up. In that moment we forgot that no one moved unnoticed in the neighborhood, even if you didn't see anyone around you. The biggest menace came from above, up in the trees.

For weeks we'd planned this night, our long-awaited entry into hanging out with the high school kids from our neighborhood, who were usually too cool to allow us middle school boys to party with them. The Olguin brothers, Carl Rivera, and I had slowly stolen precious commodities from our families: a Gatorade bottle filled with wine slowly drained from Mrs. Rivera's boxes of Zinfandel, an ancient, partial bottle of Scotch from my grandfather's study, and four loose Virginia Slim cigarettes and two cigars, from Mr. and Mrs. Olguin's stashes that they believed were secret, even from each other.

"Mom only smokes when she travels for work so she stores them in her little suitcase, and Dad only smokes on his hunting or fishing trips so he keeps them with his gear," Manny, who was in my class at school, explained.

"Yeah, and even if they find out we've taken them, they can't punish us without each other finding out so we're set," Junior, two years older than us, laughed and was clearly impressed at his own strategy.

We'd wanted so badly to be accepted by the high school kids, especially since Junior was going to be one of them next year as he became a freshman. By our logic, if he was accepted, he would be able to take us to parties with him. As rising seventh-graders, we were preoccupied with how we'd establish our reputations in middle school, and being friends with people in high school would definitely accomplish that.

Lately, the older kids had been partying at the construction site of a new housing development, usually led by the intimidating Trina Woodley and her best friend, Belinda Komarek. (Trina once had her nose pierced. She immediately suffered an allergic reaction and her parents had to seek medical attention, but for those few short hours at the urgent care, she had a nose piercing, which was more badass than anything the rest of us had ever done.)

Of course, they had not invited us, so our plan was to casually run into them as if by coincidence. We couldn't show up empty-handed, though, hence the long-gathered alcohol and tobacco.

Carl handed me his bottle of wine. "Here, trade with me." He took my bottle of Scotch.

"What's this for?" I asked.

"Keisha will be more excited for wine than Scotch, and I heard she's going to be there."

"Ooooohhhh Keishaaaaa!" The Olguins teased in unison.

"Shut up." I wasn't really annoyed with them, but at myself for letting my crush be so obvious. I was hoping she'd be there, knowing her older brother Kevin was a regular part of the high school scene.

The four of us were so carried away in our merriment that we were totally caught off guard when a small figure dropped from a tree, bracing herself as she landed and popping up quickly with her water gun pointed at me. In the process of leaping from the branches she'd dropped her self-styled detective's notebook, which she picked up while ordering us with her most authoritative voice.

"Hold it right there, you bunch of crooks! The Raccoon Rangers are apprehending you!"

"AGNES!" I screamed at her. "What do you think you are doing?"

"I could ask you the same thing," she answered me, glinting her eyes and raising her gun, filled not with water but with bright red Kool-Aid to maximize staining.

"Oh, I'm going to kill you!"

"Not so fast!" A loud, shrill voice emerged from some gum drop-shaped bushes to our right. The stout body that followed belonged to Charlie Campion, right hand man to the scourge of would-be neighborhood criminals, my sister Agnes. Charlie had a Kool-aid filled water gun as well (grape flavor was his weapon of choice), which he waved back and forth between my co-conspirators. "You're all in big trouble!

Junior rolled his eyes. "Shut up, *Martin*!" We had all started calling Charlie "Martin" a few months before, thanks to his unfortunate resemblance in both looks and personality to the character from *The Simpsons*.

Charlie ignored the remark. "Toss the contraband over here, nice and slow." Then, to Agnes, "Great work, Chief Ranger!"

Agnes, eyes locked on me, smugly thanked him. "Couldn't have done it without you, without ALL OF YOU!" At this cue from their leader, the rest of their squad emerged, encircling us. It was an absurd scene.

"Thought you could get away with it, huh?" Agnes was eating up the attention from her acolytes. "You can run, but you can't hide. I can see everything from nature's observation towers!"

"Don't you and your little fascist friends have anyone better to annoy?" Manny had previously run out of patience with her self-appointed neighborhood watch antics when she foiled a spray-painting escapade he tried to lead a few weeks before.

Charlie misheard Manny's insult, but confidently took the lead. "You're right, we are the *fastest*. Fastest at catching you! Raccoon Rangers, get their loot!"

We were mobbed by the law and order gang of pre-k and elementary school kids from our neighborhood, who quickly relieved us of our bounty. Without prompting, they drained the contents of the bottles and broke the cigarettes and cigars into pieces. In an instant, weeks of planning were gone, and we had nothing to buy our way into the high school kids' good graces.

Defeated, we started to head back to our homes, resigned to another night of playing video games and wishing we had better plans. Behind them, I heard Agnes bragging about how excited she was to share her triumph with Mr. Vern, the poor man onto whom she'd forced a reluctant friendship through persistence and sheer will. He always got to hear about her latest escapades in elaborate detail, whether he wanted to or not. "Wait until I tell Mr. Vern about this! He's going to be so impressed with our latest case closed."

Charlie chimed in, "The Matsumoto-sans will be equally pleased to hear about it, Chief!"

Carl shook his head as we walked away. Manny kicked rocks in anger.

"Your sister is such an asshole, man." Junior complained.

"I know," I agreed. "She's the absolute worst."

In fairness, my younger sister Agnes wasn't "the worst," but she was a strange child, and never as strange as during the summer when she was seven years old. That's when she reached "peak Agnes," culminating in her discovery that our neighbor, her beloved Mr. Vern, was missing. This phase wasn't a sudden development, and was actually the natural progression of odd behavior that had been building for a few years.

As a child, she read too many detective books. At any given moment she had her nose stuck in a story starring *Encyclopedia Brown, Sherlock Holmes, Nancy Drew, Miss Marple, the Hardy Boys*, or *Harriet the Spy*. They were all too mature for her to read at that age, but she'd started reading at an extremely early age, and picked it up so quickly that by second-grade she was levels ahead of most kids in our school, even most of us sixth-graders.

I blamed my grandparents, who had let her watch episodes of *Quincy, Columbo, Murder She Wrote*, and the *Father Dowling Mysteries* while we visited them. Besides the TV shows, she also watched *The Great Mouse Detective* so frequently that the VHS started to deteriorate from overuse. There was only so much distortion the tracking buttons could fix. For her seventh birthday, she asked for a deerstalker cap, to go along with the wooden-handled magnifying glass she'd purloined from our aunt's home office, and the plastic, purple bubble pipe she got as a party favor from some neighbor's birthday.

Never without a small *Care Bears* notepad and *My Melody* (*Hello Kitty*'s best friend) pen, the world was full of potential cases Agnes was ready to crack. At school, she offered detective services to the student body as well as the faculty, causing some concern when a girl she'd identified as a suspect found her notebook, and turned it in to the principal. The amused administrator met with Agnes, and after my sister informed her that no one was above suspicion, not even faculty, the principal asked Agnes' teacher to give her some extra assignments, including logic puzzles and brain teasers, to occupy her overactive mind.

Agnes didn't just walk the beat at school, though. In her imagination, our neighborhood was rife with hidden criminal activity, waiting to be discovered. She wrote down everything, from when someone left for work to when they got home, as well as any unusual activities. She was just waiting for her big break, to capture a real criminal. I begged my parents to make her drop the act, but they weren't about to ask their younger child to be less well-behaved. In their eyes it was much-needed activity for their hyperactive and overly-imaginative daughter that happened to be fun for her, and hey, if it kept their older child from committing stupid acts, then they weren't going to intervene.

It was the early nineties, and we lived in a somewhat odd suburban neighborhood; at least it was unusual for the time. Nearly all of the moms had careers working full-time jobs, and most of our parents worked for the military, foreign service, or federal government. It felt like no one was actually from Northern Virginia; they only arrived after being transferred for work. We had neighbors from all over the world who'd lived in Kenya, Iran, Germany, and places I'd never even heard of.

(Agnes was convinced "Burkina Faso" was not the name of a real place.)

In my nostalgic recollection, we were an almost idyllic melting pot, with families from a wide variety of races and religions. It was only years later, when I attended a small, rural college that I experienced being in a majority-white environment, which was an adjustment for me. I took diversity for granted, and as a child I didn't appreciate what a special street I'd lived on. With the nature of deployments, some people were only in our neighborhood for a few months or years, but still, I was used to people who had drastically different life experiences from my own.

Despite the ever-changing cast of characters, we were a neighborhood of routine. Every day after school, all of the kids would drop their backpacks and then sprint to join their age groups. Older girls were a mystery to us, but from what we could gather, they read magazines and listened to music they weren't supposed to, read books they weren't supposed to, and watched movies they weren't supposed to, wearing makeup they weren't supposed to, getting piercings they weren't supposed to, sneaking off to college parties they weren't supposed to, kissing boys they weren't supposed to, even sneaking cigarettes and booze they weren't supposed to. They were perm-haired rebel goddesses. Like every other boy on our street, I admired and feared them.

Older boys spent time in the woods with the not-so-secret porn stash they'd discovered, drinking skunky beers they hid in a tree stump, looking for unsuspecting targets at whom they could throw rotten crabapples or hardened chestnut husks gathered from the ground.

The kids my age played co-ed games of football, kickball, tag, basketball, any physical activity that let us run off our excess of energy and show off our athletic prowess in a constant battle of one-upmanship.

Agnes and her friends rode their bikes, often down to the creeks in search of turtles to bring home. They all had completely wild imaginations, often getting carried away with whatever narrative they made up that day. They also managed to insinuate themselves into the lives of everyone they met, usually with the motive of receiving snacks or treats.

Our next door neighbors, the Matsumotos, were a young, active couple, and, to our suburban minds, were cool and glamorous. They were always impeccably dressed even in their tennis outfits. They traveled often and did lots of cultured activities like going to see plays and operas, but also went to rock concerts. We all wanted to be them. They were expecting their first child, and had recently brought Mr. Matsumoto's parents to live with them in anticipation of the baby's arrival.

While neither of the elder Matsumotos (whom we addressed as Mr. and Mrs. Matsumoto-san, in a failed attempt to show respect) spoke very much English, it didn't stop them from forming a strong fondness for Agnes and her crew. The younger kids embraced the elderly cultural ambassadors, learning their language and customs, and of course, eating all of their traditional food. The Matsumoto-sans became the unofficial, default babysitters of every young child in the neighborhood.

The adults of our neighborhood had their routines, too. Like clockwork, they went to work, ferried children to activities, manicured their landscapes, washed their cars, took out their trash, and ran their errands. And every Sunday, without fail, our other next-door neighbor, Mr. Vern, would bicycle down to the local shopping center to pick up supplies. His bike was outfitted with saddle-bag style baskets on the rear and a large central basket on the front. These were all stuffed with his groceries for the week, and balanced on top was, always, a slab of Coors Lite.

Mr. Vern was a near-total recluse. Or he had been, anyway, until Agnes decided to do something about it. He lived alone in one of the larger houses on the street, and as he was legally blind, was unable to drive anywhere. Aside from these Sunday sightings, we never saw him. While all of the other adults in the neighborhood engaged with each other, he only engaged, begrudgingly, with us kids.

It was Agnes who made him come out of his reclusive shell. For years he had cycled past all of us, taking no notice, and we ignored him in kind. But my little sister believed all strangers were just friends you haven't met yet, and made it a mission to make him her friend, regardless of if he was interested. We told her not to bother, but stubborn child that she was, it only made her double down on her mission. I guess we shouldn't have been so surprised when it worked, and she had successfully enlisted Mr. Vern among the cast of characters she directed around the neighborhood.

His Sunday grocery order suddenly began to include one of the massive donuts for which the local store's bakery was famous. Riding near us, he'd pull over briefly, pick up the paper bag holding the donut, and hand it to Agnes. While she devoured it, making sure to let him know how much she appreciated it, he'd converse with her on whatever random topic occupied her thoughts at that moment. He played along, even when he didn't know what she was talking about, and would tell her he'd see her next week. None of us could believe it—she'd domesticated the hermit!

Eventually, she even managed to get him to bring a variety pack of a dozen donuts, which he'd hand to Agnes, and she in turn would share with all of us. Our faces covered in sprinkles and our hands sticky with frosting and glaze, we'd shout "Thanks Mr. Vern!" He ignored the rest of us most of the time, but occasionally he'd lift a hand in acknowledgement as he pedaled away.

This arrangement went on for some time, just another part of the neighborhood routine. Sometimes we'd joke about having Agnes convince Mr. Vern to share some of his beer with us, but she didn't think it was funny. She refused to sully her hard-earned trust by asking him to aid and abet criminal activity.

It was around this time that she decided that, as a budding detective with too many suspects to track, she should form a neighborhood detective agency, the Raccoon Rangers. She'd deputized her friend Charlie Campion as her very own Watson, and together they ran her little brigade of trusted sidekicks. The little Denisov girl even drew up a logo, featuring a raccoon with binoculars and a shiny metal sheriff's badge. It was utterly annoying.

Every movement in the neighborhood was tracked. The detective agency met every day after school and all day on weekends, spying, recording, and discussing the activities of the older children. Among the amateur sleuth squad, the Reid siblings had gotten walkie talkies for Christmas, which enabled them to divide and conquer low-scale crimes committed on our quiet streets. Most adults ignored this unofficial neighborhood watch, as well as our complaints about it. The grown-ups were all too busy, and if their kids were occupied and monitored, then they were content to enjoy the bonus benefit of not having to hire so many babysitters.

The detectives would get carried away with theorizing what people might be plotting, which more often than not led to them tattling on us older kids. I lost track of all the aborted pranks they disrupted and the acts of light vandalism that the Raccoon Rangers reported on, resulting in widespread punishment. One night, Agnes and crew discovered the high school girls carrying mass amounts of toilet paper and silly string, and ran to alert the parents. I really thought Trina, Belinda and their friends would kill my little sister, and I couldn't blame them.

As the older brother of the resident weirdo on the street, I was of course embarrassed, and received plenty of harassment about why couldn't I make my sister be normal, or at least keep her at home so she would stop ruining everyone else's good time with her nosy ways. I tried to distance myself from her, but still had to field complaints every time she ruined someone's good time, like when she observed a high school girl, Dory Eckman, making out in a car with her (inappropriately) much older college boyfriend.

Eventually, all of us middle and high school kids decided to just ignore Agnes and her buddies, giving them the silent treatment and acting as if they were invisible. We also got wise, and found ways to evade their tracking, even from their perches in the trees that lined our street, so we could once again indulge in our mildly illicit activities without the fear of getting caught.

Agnes and her Raccoon Rangers, never easily discouraged, decided to start tracking adults instead. Who was traveling, and was it for work or for pleasure? How long were they gone? Who wasn't keeping their lawns perfectly? Who left their trash cans out too long?

Since Mr. Vern only showed his face on Sundays, during the rest of the week they took their intel to the elderly Matsumotos, a sympathetic audience. Each day,

Mrs. Matsumoto-san made tea and snacks for the agents, and Mr. Matsumoto-san would listen attentively while the kids prattled away at the various goings-on in the neighborhood. The Matsumoto-sans, of course, had no idea what the kids were saying half the time, but appreciated the company.

It was a hot, humid summer, typical of the south. We all spent time at the pool or at each other's homes, and while most of us, listless, played board games or video games inside to stay cool, Agnes and her crew ran wild.

With all the goings-on in the summertime, it became difficult for the Raccoon Rangers to adequately and accurately track our neighbors. People took vacations or went on day trips, welcomed house guests, and generally deviated from their usual schedules, except of course for Mr. Vern. He never had guests, never had anywhere to go except his weekly errand.

As the summer went on, it became one of the hottest on record, so while the teens retreated indoors to gossip in air-conditioned bedrooms, younger children played in garden sprinklers or home-made slip-and-slides. We older children were tasked with taking our little siblings down to the community pool each day, bribed by our parents with cash which we used to buy cool sodas or ice pops from the concession stand.

Even with all the unrelenting heat, though, Agnes never became fatigued, and continued her tracking. She would try to share observations with me, but I felt I was too cool to be involved in such childish activities, so I would tune her out. Literally, I would put my headphones on and turn up my Walkman so loud that she could chatter away and I wouldn't hear a thing.

Feeling ignored about a certain theory of hers, she went in search of more sympathetic audiences. She found one in the Matsumotos, who by now were starting to understand some of her reports. Aside from the unnecessary information gleaned from the invasion of people's privacy, I think it helped them actually learn who was who on the street in, in addition to practicing their English.

One afternoon she'd been wildly gesturing at me with her notebook, bothering me to the point of distraction, so I took it from her, and threatened to throw it into the pool if she didn't cut it out.

If you have a younger sister, you know their ferocity when they feel like they've been wronged. Agnes was furious. She didn't pout, she just screwed up her face into a monstrous scowl and grabbed the notebook back. Then she ripped off my headphones and leaned in, face-to-face until her nose touched mine, growling, "You'll be sorry, you'll see. I'm right, and you'll be in trouble that you didn't get an adult to help me."

Pre-teen boys are, generally speaking, assholes. So I threatened her back, warning her, "If you don't get out of my face, I'm going to throw you into the toddler pool, and you'll never be able to get the pee smell out, no matter how much you shower or bathe."

The threat had the intended effect. She grabbed her little pool bag, and without even putting on her terry cloth cover-up, she ran away, out of the pool and back toward our house. For a moment, I considered following her, but I knew she was going to be unbearable for at least an hour or so until she calmed down. All I had to do was bring her home an ice cream bar, and all would be forgiven. Besides, our parents were still at work, so there was no one she could tell about my momentary rudeness.

"What was that about?" asked Keisha Okath, the middle-school girl I had hoped to impress with the Gatorade-filled wine bottle.

"I don't know. Something about schedules... I honestly try not to listen to her. Everything is a crime now in her mind. It's like she *wants* something bad to happen just so she can be right, and tell us all that she told us so."

"She's *so* annoying. I don't know how you live with her."

"Until I'm 18, I have to!" I laughed, and we quickly turned to a more pleasant topic than my conspiracy theorist sibling.

When I got home, Agnes wasn't there, so I ate her ice cream myself. As it got toward dusk, I went to look for her, calling her name. As I started to worry, she finally came tromping out of the Matsumoto house, still in her swim clothes but draped in a towel I assumed they gave her, and refusing to look at me. I could see from the redness around her eyes that she'd been crying.

"Where's your bag? Did you leave it with the Matsumoto-sans?" Her transparent pool bag had a massive cartoon rainbow and a smiling sun on it, always filled with toys and books, and of course, her detective accessories. Ignoring me, she walked ahead to our front door.

"Come on Ag, you're really going to give *me* the silent treatment like it's a punishment? Well it's not, it's a blessing. We could all use a little more silence from you, motor-mouth."

She pretended not to hear a word I said, lifting her chin and striding into our entryway.

The silent treatment continued at meal-time. Usually our dinner conversations were dominated by Agnes over-sharing her observations of the day, but that night she only opened her mouth to eat tiny bites, as if food itself was a form of punishment. I rolled my eyes at her dramatic performance, sure she'd cave at some point, but no matter how much our parents tried to engage her, she'd just stare at her plate.

Our parents were immediately concerned that she was ill. In the smallest voice, she admitted she didn't feel good and asked to be excused and go to bed early.

Dad couldn't believe it. "Are you sure? Spaghetti is your favorite. And I brought home some of those ice cream sandwiches you like so much for dessert! You don't even want a little ice cream?"

She just shook her head and mumbled that her stomach hurt and she was tired. Agreeing that some rest might be a good idea, Dad carried her upstairs—which he hadn't done in ages—and he and Mom both helped Agnes get ready. I heard them as they worried over her loudly, and she barely responded.

As soon as she was in bed, they flew back downstairs and grilled me about what she'd eaten that day, how she might have gotten sick, what had happened that could have resulted in her behavior. They were relentless in seeking answers, so I had to confess that I'd lost track of her for a few hours after our argument, which naturally turned into an inquisition about why I'd fought with her in the first place.

My mother, a prosecutor, was especially frustrated with me. "You know, I don't need this right now, this case is taking all of my energy and I would appreciate coming home to a calm house."

Dad backed Mom up. "Your mother is going through a lot at work right now, and the least you could do is not pick on your sister. We rely on you to look out for her, not let her get into trouble."

"She didn't get in trouble; she was with the Matsumoto-sans!" I protested. "How can she get in trouble hanging out with old people?!"

Mom rolled her eyes. "Ah, well there you go. I know they are nice people but I have told you before that they confuse over-feeding with hospitality. It's fine for you, you're old enough to moderate what you eat and know when to stop, but kids Agnes' age will take anything they are presented with. If she was there for hours, they probably gave her so many snacks that any bit of dinner was too much."

Dad chimed in, "Next time, keep your mouth shut and your eyes on your sister, got it?!"

We all went to bed angry and annoyed. Usually, during the summer we stayed up watching TV, but they told me to get to bed early, and that maybe in the morning I'd feel like apologizing to Agnes, and to them. I was so mad at all of them, I had trouble falling asleep, staring angrily at my ceiling.

I don't know how long I was actually, finally asleep, because I was jolted out of it by a flood of bright lights spilling into my room. In my half-sleep state, I wondered if an alien ship was hovering over our house, but quickly came to my senses. Out my window, I saw what seemed like every rescue vehicle in the county. Ambulances, fire trucks, police cruisers, and of course, front yards filled with neighbors. Families stood on their lawns in robes or wrapped in blankets, watching the bizarre scene unfold.

Stepping into my slippers, I ran toward the staircase, finding my parents on the landing, whispering to each other. Whatever ire they'd held toward me earlier in the evening had disappeared, replaced by curious fascination. I walked up behind them, inquiring. "What's going on?"

Dad didn't know. "We've only been up for a few, but they used an axe."

"An axe?!" My bad luck, I'd missed it. "Is everyone ok?"

"We don't know. The gas masks are creepy." observed Mom. "Why do you think they needed them?"

"Look, the Campions and Riveras walking over," Dad whispered.

"And there are the Eckmans, the Komareks, the Olguins, the Basnets, the Reids, the Denisovs, the Okaths, the Woodleys... oh, and the Shehadis." I pointed out each family of neighbors huddled together in clumps.

Mom motioned for us to follow her. "Let's go outside and see if we can find out what happened."

Dad nodded in agreement, and as we crept down the stairs, we approached the front door just as a loud knock was laid upon it. First we paused, then moved double-time to open it. The lights hit our faces and made it a little difficult to see details on the figures in front of us, appearing as silhouettes.

As our eyes adjusted, we made out several police officers, and the entire Matsumoto family, both generations, with terrified faces. My heart jumped. I had a track record of getting into odd trouble here and there, but never anything that rose to police intervention, and out of sheer preservation instinct I prepared to launch into a defense of how I'd done nothing wrong. Before I could, the figures moved closer into the front door.

Tipping his cap to my parents, the lead officer introduced himself as the Sheriff. Oddly, Dad's response was, "Yes, sir, we voted for you. Sorry we're in our pajamas, sir."

Mom stared at Dad like he was an absolute idiot and took over. "Sheriff, can you tell us what this is all about?"

Clearing his throat, he responded with a request. "Ma'am, is your daughter at home?"

"Our daughter?" We were all distracted by the county coroner's vehicle, which was pulling up the street, looking for a place to park.

"Yes, ma'am. Is…" consulting his notepad, "Agnes?" The elder Matsumoto-sans shook their heads, affirming her name, repeating it several times in unison. "Ma'am, is Agnes available?"

"Agnes?" Mom was stunned. In all the commotion, I'd completely forgotten about my sister. Mom and Dad seemed to have, as well.

"Yes ma'am, we just need to speak with her, ask her a few questions."

I raced up the stairs. I can't quite make out how long it took, getting to her bedroom, trying to wake her and explain she was needed while also asking her why on earth the police were looking for her.

Dazed, Agnes momentarily forgot she was giving me the silent treatment, taking my hand with one of hers, while rubbing her eyes with the other. "Police?" She half-asked, half yawned.

Dad appeared at the doorway. "Come on, come on, they're waiting to talk to her!"

We rushed back down, Agnes in tow in her *Rainbow Brite* pajamas, the pair that include Rainbow's obnoxiously pompous horse. Dad planted her in front of the sheriff and the other police, and as Agnes took in the situation, she gave a cute bow to the Matsumoto-sans, who moved forward to hug her.

My parents were baffled, Mom insisting, "Now will you please tell us why you need to speak to our seven-year old child at..." She looked at the clock on the entryway wall, before continuing, "at 2:30 in the morning, Sheriff?"

A junior officer with a kind face stepped forward. "Agnes, I'm Officer Reynard. I'm sorry we had to wake you up, but does this belong to you?" We all recognized the *Care Bears* notebook, and realized the other officer behind the Sheriff was carrying Agnes' distinctive rainbow pool tote.

"Yes, but where's my pen?" Agnes clearly wasn't awake enough yet to understand that the location of a *Hello Kitty* pen was the least of anyone's concerns at the moment.

"Oh, it's um, I believe it's in your bag. Yes, here it is." The officer produced the My Melody-adorned writing implement, a silly visual in his huge hand.

"Thank you." Agnes reached for it, smiling politely, but starting to seem nervous. "So, was I right?"

She looked now at Mr. and Mrs. Matsumoto-san. "Was I right?" She asked again, pointing at the notebook. The younger Mrs. Matsumoto stepped forward, with a deep inhale. Slowly, and with no small effort considering her pregnant belly, she knelt in front of my sister so she could look into her eyes. Taking one tiny hand into her own, she answered, "Yes sweetie, you were right."

Agnes looked as if she might burst into tears. "And is he...?" With wide eyes she looked over at Mr. Vern's house. Mrs. Matsumoto placed a loving hand gingerly on top of my sister, as if protecting her. "It seems so."

The younger Mr. Matsumoto walked over to help his wife stand back up. Agnes grabbed his hand with her free one, and he let her hold it. There was my sister, hand in hand with our neighbors who knew more about her than her own immediate family did. Every moment that passed left me more perplexed, feeling as if I was watching a play where the actors spoke in code, instead of being present in that moment as it unfolded.

"We had to use force to enter the premises," the Sheriff explained to my bewildered parents. "But we found him. Coroner has to make the official announcement, of course... as soon as he finds parking, that is."

"Wait, is Mr. Vern dead?!" I surprised even myself with how loud the question exited my mouth. Startled, my parents wheeled around to face me as the Sheriff clarified.

"It appears so. EMTs were unable to resuscitate, it looks like it's days too late for that anyway... if not weeks, from the smell. And that's with the masks helping to block it."

Mom's hand shot up to cover her mouth. "Dead?" She whispered so quietly it was more like she had mouthed it.

Turning back to Agnes, the Sheriff continued. "Miss, can you confirm the details in this notebook are accurate, as far as you can tell?"

Agnes pulled herself up, gravely serious, holding up her right hand in an oath. "It's accurate, sir. Raccoon Ranger's honor. I take careful notes every day. I don't make anything up, and I don't leave anything out."

"So the last time you saw your neighbor, Mr. Vern, was three Sundays ago?"

"Yes, Sheriff, I saw him come back from errands. They were out of my favorite donut so he brought me a toasted coconut one. I don't like coconut but I didn't want to hurt his feelings so I ate it anyway, to be polite."

Our parents stared at my sister as if she was an alien. They had no idea what she was talking about, but the Sheriff was satisfied. "Well, I think we need to keep this notebook for a while. It seems you were the last person to ever see him alive, and your... record-keeping... here will be very helpful to us. Is that ok?"

"You mean, it's official evidence?"

"Yes ma'am, and we'd appreciate being able to use it to help wrap up our case."

"Of course... do you have any suspects?"

All three police officers raised their eyebrows at this question.

"No… it doesn't appear there was any foul play. So, no suspects."

"Then it was natural causes?" Agnes was compartmentalizing her grief for our neighbor and switching fully into detective mode. At the time I didn't realize it was a coping mechanism, that she couldn't process the shock any other way than to turn our dead neighbor into one of the countless fictional cases she'd read or seen.

The Sheriff nodded. "Yes ma'am. He was sitting in his armchair. We don't know how long, but given the condition of the remains…"

"Alright, alright, let me through, out of the way." A disgruntled voice cut through the crowd. It was the county coroner, huffing and puffing, followed by two assistants who were loaded up like pack mules and toting a stretcher. I eyed what must have been the rolled up body bag, and felt a shiver run through my body. That was for Mr. Vern. They were going to wrap him up in that.

I'd never actually seen a dead body before. I'd been to our grand uncle's memorial when I was younger, but I wasn't really old enough to understand where we were or what had happened. He'd been cremated, without a viewing, so I only saw the urn, and didn't have to think about him being an actual corpse.

As several firemen helped the coroner and his staff into their hazmat suits, the fire chief mentioned that he'd send some of his crew back in to help run interference with animals, having already shooed some away. Agnes heard this, and misunderstood.

"Oh no, Mr. Vern doesn't have any pets, you don't have to worry." Poor Agnes couldn't understand why local wildlife would be interested in a dead man's body.

No one besides the Sheriff had any context for this little girl in her *Rainbow Brite* pajamas who was interjecting herself into the scene, so they looked at her, then back at each other. Clearly the topic was not appropriate to discuss in front of a child.

The Sheriff quickly covered, telling her, "That's absolutely right. More good work, little detective." Waving the notebook again, "I think we've got everything else we need right here, but we might check in with you again this week if we need more... evidence. Would that be ok?"

Agnes nodded.

"Ok. Ranger Agnes, we're going to talk to your parents for a little while longer, but you are relieved of duty for the night. Maybe your brother," looking at me, "can help you get back to bed now."

I didn't want to miss any of the action, but before I could protest, the younger Matsumotos appeared at my side, stepping in for our parents who were still trying to make sense of what was happening. Mrs. Matsumoto loudly agreed with the Sheriff that it was time for the kids to go to bed. Mr. Matsumoto took it upon himself to address the crowd that assembled on our driveway, telling them to give the authorities room to work, and that we all needed a good night's sleep. Everyone liked the Matsumotos, so they listened, but not without long, parting glances, trying to take in the scene just for a few seconds more.

When I got Agnes back to her room, she asked me to stay with her until she was asleep. She was overwhelmed and exhausted, which I hoped that meant she would fall right back asleep, but every time it seemed like she was dozing off, a noise came from outside that prompted her to run to the window. I was curious, too, so I also kept running to the window. It didn't occur to me that she shouldn't keep looking, until the moment when Mr. Vern's body was wheeled out across the lawn.

Of course, we couldn't see his body, he was zipped up in the black bag, but that just had the effect of making him look like he was in a garbage bag. Agnes gasped, and stepped back from the window, wincing. "That's Mr. Vern," she said, defeated. "I didn't want him to be..." I realized the mistake I'd made, and imagined how mad my parents would be that I let her see him like that, so I scooped her back toward bed.

I turned on her starry globe night light, which projected moving constellations across the wall and ceiling, and asked her if she wanted me to put on music for her. She said no, but made me promise I wouldn't leave her. She was too afraid to sleep, so I pulled her *The*

Little Mermaid sleeping bag from her closet, and set up camp on her bedroom floor right next to the open door.

"See, I'll be right here, and the door will be open so if you need to yell for Mom and Dad they can hear you, ok? You're not alone, and you don't have to be scared. You're safe."

She reached out her hand off the side of the bed for me to take, which I did. I don't know how long it took her to fall asleep, because my sense of time was skewed that night. I heard our parents come back inside, but by then I was also tired. Despite wanting to know more details, I fell asleep, and only vaguely remember my parents peeking into Agnes' room to make sure she was still in bed.

Mom still had to go to work at the courthouse the next day, no matter how tired she was, but Dad was able to call out from his office to stay home. Mom didn't want us to be alone. Dad let us sleep in, and Agnes was still out when I awoke. She looked deep asleep, so I decided to let her keep resting, and quietly slipped downstairs.

"Rough night?" Dad joked.

"I could use a cup of that," I ventured, pointing to his coffee mug. To my shock, he stood up to get me one.

"In light of the unusual circumstances, you can have some, just this once. But don't tell your mother, ok?"

I promised, and took a sip, my first taste of coffee. I reeled back, shocked at how bitter it tasted. "Ugh! Why doesn't it taste as good as it smells?" Dad laughed, and retrieved a bottle of honey from the pantry. "Here, this will help." It did, after I squeezed about half of the bear's worth into my mug.

As we sat drinking our coffee, Dad filled me in. He spoke softly so we wouldn't wake Agnes. From what he shared, Mr. Vern had been something called a "hoarder." His house was full of empty cans, plastic containers, mason jars, stacks of old papers and magazines. All of his utilities were cut off, not just his phone, but the power and the water as well. I couldn't imagine surviving a southern summer without A/C or running water.

Dad decided I was old enough to hear the truth. "There were hundreds of beer cans all around his armchair. In short, it looks like he gave up, and drank himself to death." I thought of the cases of beer he brought home every week. I'd never had beer, so I'd never wondered if it was a lot for one man to bring home for himself. Clearly, it was enough to drink until he died. I wondered if he'd been saving them up for this purpose.

"He'd been dead for some time, long enough for a few wild critters to get into his house and... well... nibble. *Ahem*. Of course, I don't want you repeating any of this to your sister, understood?"

"I won't, I promise. She already had enough trouble sleeping last night."

"Well it was nice of you to camp out with her. Your mother and I thought it was very sweet of you to look out for her." If only they knew I'd let her see the body… but no use bringing that up.

Dad and I then turned the topic to how strange it was that our Agnes wasn't just a pretend detective, and that she'd finally cracked a big case like she'd wanted to all summer.

"It's funny," Dad commented. "Looking at her notebook, there's this whole little life she has that your mother and I knew nothing about. We told the Sheriff, we didn't even realize she spoke to Vern, let alone had a weekly donut ritual with him. She's a funny kid, that's for sure.

Anyway, there's going to be a lot more activity over at the house for the next few days while they finish documenting the scene and make sure they've captured any critters. They're going to get the power and water back on so they can have crews safely working in there. I thought you and I could take Agnes out, maybe to the mall or a movie. We could get some ice cream or something to take her mind off dead people." I agreed, and once Agnes woke up we got her ready for a day of adventure.

No matter what we did, she seemed withdrawn, distracted. She kept bringing the conversation back to Mr. Vern, and we kept redirecting it. We bought her dozens of toys, took her to an arcade where we won prizes for her, and did anything we could do to keep her entertained. When we got home, Mom met us with news that everyone at the courthouse was talking about Agnes, who was already a local celebrity.

"A lot of people want to meet you, Agnes! Some reporters asked if they could do stories on you, interview you about how you gathered clues and knew to alert the authorities. Oh! And I saw Lorraine from the Mayor's office, and she talked about having some sort of ceremony for you. Apparently the Sheriff filled them in, and he wants to make you an official deputy!"

None of this elicited much reaction from my sister, who asked if she had to participate.

Agnes was one of the most outgoing, curious kids I'd ever known, but over the next couple of days, the attention seemed to crush her. She quickly tired of telling the story over and over. She was annoyed that people were only focused on her, and got mad when the articles didn't mention anything she'd told them about Mr. Vern. At one point she slammed down a paper and screamed "A man is dead, people!" before running up to her room.

She wasn't sleeping well, either. I convinced her to let me take her to the pool, but she was in a rotten mood. She didn't swim, just sat on the edge of the pool dangling her feet in the water. I noticed her little friends were all doing the same thing, a bunch of sullen Raccoon Rangers. I asked some of the other older siblings, and we discovered none of the little ones were sleeping. It turned out most of them thought Mr. Vern was a ghost now, and was haunting them for not solving his death sooner.

As we discussed ways to convince them he wasn't really a ghost, the high school girls came up with a solution. They proposed a fake seance in Mr. Vern's house, complete with a *Ouija* board and candles, to help Mr. Vern fully transition into the afterlife, peacefully, and with our blessing.

It seemed like as good an idea as any, but we then faced the challenge of how to get into his house, which was lined with police tape. Fortunately, the reliably-mischievous pair of brothers, Manny and Junior Olguin, spoke up to inform us they'd already been inside. "We snuck in as soon as the cops left. It's nasty in there!"

Heeding their warnings, we gathered materials for improvised masks: bandanas, winter scarves, even Jazzercise leg warmers pilfered from several unsuspecting mothers' closets. We invited all the kids in the neighborhood to join us the next day, after our parents were gone for work and wouldn't be able to witness us breaking and entering.

As soon as she heard the idea, Agnes cheered up. "You mean, like a party for him?"

I assured her she was correct. "Yep, a going away party, for Mr. Vern. He'll be the guest of honor. Do you think he'd like that?"

Agnes was enthusiastic that he would.

The next morning, just as planned, we broke in without disrupting the barrier tape. Even knowing he'd been a hoarder hadn't really prepared us for what we encountered. None of us had seen that much... stuff... in our lives. "Ew, how many plastic margarine tubs does one person need, anyway?!" asked Belinda.

Our masks did little to effectively keep us from gagging. Someone held out a jar of Vick's VapoRub to buffer our noses, and to my surprise it was Mrs. Matsumoto-san. She and Mr. Matsumoto-san were there, masked, with some supplies in hand.

I was surprised to see them, but Agnes explained. "I invited them, too, since they tried to help him when he was alive! Mrs. Matsumoto-san brought us snacks for after the ceremony!" We all took turns putting the menthol rub under our noses, which helped block out the smell. It was unimaginable that Mr. Vern had lived like this, and even more so without the sweet A/C we were currently appreciating.

As we worked to clear a space for the *Ouija* board and candles, Agnes proposed that we all share a few words about our dearly departed neighbor. To begin, Trina, our master of mystical ceremonies, set her hands on the board and in a serious voice, asked if Mr. Vern was present. The dial moved slowly around the board, settling on "Yes." The little kids bought it, convinced they were now in the presence of an actual ghost. Our plan was working.

Each child who felt like sharing offered a few parting words to our fallen neighbor. Agnes started, thanking him for always talking to her even when he was busy, and always remembering that her favorite donut was the blueberry one. The Matsumoto-sans looked approvingly at all of us, and even offered a few words of their own, which none of us understood.

Finally, Trina called us back to the Ouija board. "Mr. Vern, we hope our words will carry you on in peace and love." The dial moved to "*Yes.*" She asked the air, "Mr. Vern, before you go, do you have anything you'd like to say?"

"Yes."

"Is it for all of us?"

"No."

"So it's a special message?"

"Yes."

"Who is it for?"

"A-G-N-E-S."

The younger children all pushed their ringleader forward to receive her message. Trina spoke seriously to Agnes. "This is a big deal, Agnes, so you need to pay attention. Are you ready for your message?"

Agnes gulped, then nodded. "I think so," she whispered.

"Mr. Vern, Agnes is ready for your message now. Channel it though me, through this board!" She was really selling the drama, as the dial moved again.

"T-H-A-N-K-Y-O-U"

Tears came into Agnes' eyes, and a little smile spread on her face.

Trina tilted her head to the ceiling for effect. "Anything else you'd like to say to Agnes, Mr. Vern?"

"G-O-O-D-B-Y-E-F-R-I-E-N-D"

"Goodbye, Mr. Vern." Agnes walked over and leaned into me. I hugged her for a moment while Trina concluded the ceremony. "As these candles are extinguished, so will Mr. Vern's spirit fly free! Let us all wish him a safe and speedy journey to the ever after!"

She blew out the candles, and everyone clapped and cheered. Our exorcism worked.

Mr. Matsumoto-san ushered us to the backyard, with Agnes explaining Mrs. Matsumoto thought it wasn't safe to eat food inside such a dirty house. As we exited into the fresh air, we used the garden hose out back to wash our hands, and set up a makeshift banquet on the deck. During this repast, we decided that it was a shame the house looked the way it did. None of us had been inside it while he was alive, but we bet it looked really good at one point.

That's when we had the idea to clean up the house. It had felt oppressive and closed in, unlike any environment any of us had ever been in. We decided it would be an act of kindness to the neighborhood to clean it up, and plus, it would fill our summer hours. After all, we were all bored kids with nothing better to do. We explained our idea to the Matsumoto-sans, who must have agreed, because Mrs. Matsumoto-san hustled back to her house, and when she returned, she had buckets filled with trash bags and cleaning supplies.

We spent the afternoon undertaking the Herculean task of clearing just the den. We discovered a hidden TV set and trophy case once we removed the debris. We weren't sure what to do with all the trash we bagged, and went to pile it into the garage. It was a little disappointing that so much effort resulted in so little visual impact, but we were only getting started. We resolved to come back again the next day, to divide and conquer more of the rooms at one time.

At the end of the day we were completely exhausted, and as we stepped outside, we realized we smelled terrible. We took turns spraying each other with the hose, but that just made us smell like wet, sweaty, trash. The only solution was to go to the pool, and hope the industrial strength chlorine would help alleviate our collective funk. The Matsumoto-sans said goodbye and went home as we all trudged down, soaking and smelly, to the pool.

That night, Agnes and I were ravenous, having worked up an appetite between cleaning and swimming. Mom and Dad were encouraged at seeing Agnes back to herself. They tried to figure out what had gotten her back into a good mood, but we didn't want to be in trouble for trespassing, so we both stuck to our rehearsed story that we'd just had a really good day.

Early the next morning, as soon as the parents were all at work, we regrouped at Mr. Vern's. Mr. Matsumoto-San had a handyman's toolkit to lead on some minor repairs. The Rivera kids showed up with their boombox, and a case of cassettes to provide a soundtrack for our day. Marjan Shehadi had nabbed her dad's Polaroid camera and some film cartridges. Before we got to work, she insisted on taking what she called, "Before Photos," so that we could compare them to the "After Photos," when we were all done. She guaranteed we'd all be impressed. Time flew by, and we made more noticeable progress.

Several days into our project, and we were feeling triumphant about how much we'd manage to transform the house already. We were amped up for another day of making magic happen. It was Keisha's turn to provide music that day, and she clearly embraced the opportunity to corrupt us all, and impress us with one of her older brother Kevin's mix-tapes filled with profanity-laced lyrics, referencing sex and drugs and disrespect for police. The entire playlist was songs we weren't allowed to listen to, and it had the exact effect of making us feel rebellious and cool. We were all fully dancing and singing along, lost in our own concert, when we were interrupted.

"What the fuck is going on in here?!" A booming voice filled the house, echoing. Now, most of us had heard that word at least once on cable TV, but none of us had ever heard an adult in our real lives say it. We stared at each other, gaping, silently considering how, at most, we'd heard parents say "damn," "shit," "hell," even, "bitch." But not the "F word." Never.

Then he said it again! "All of you, get out. Now. Stop whatever vandalism it is you're doing, and get. The. Fuck. Out."

Our skin turned to marble, anchoring us into place. We couldn't move, and none of us knew what to say. He was physically imposing, and although we were technically trespassing, he seemed like the aggressor in the situation, a villain who had brought danger into our previously safe place. "This isn't a clubhouse for children's parties. Stop looking at me, and go. I *will* call the cops."

Still no one moved. We had thought we might get in trouble if our parents caught us, but hadn't anticipated a stranger. We forgot Mr. Vern's family was going to show up at some point, and hadn't been prepared for how they would react to seeing us.

Now yelling directly at the Matsumoto-sans, he roared, "Are you people deaf or something? Take this little United Nations and get the hell out of my family's house!" They stood, staring, unclear what he was saying, which made him more angry.

Swiftly, Agnes moved in to protect the Matsumoto-sans and calm the stranger down. I felt like I was moving in slow motion as I tried to stop her, and she was too far away for me to grab in time, as if the room stretched away to keep her just out of my reach. The stranger turned and unleashed a verbal torrent on Agnes alone, towering over her as he hurled insults at her. Before he finished she ran from the house into the backyard, sobbing as she fled.

It was one thing to yell at adults, and it was bad enough to yell at children in the first place, but seeing him go after Agnes activated something in all of us, and we all broke out of our frozen state. Sure, Agnes was a weirdo, but she was *our* weirdo. No one came into our neighborhood to judge her. We collectively lost our minds, yelling back at him, encircling him and screaming at him from every direction. Kevin, the largest of all the high school kids, stepped right in front of him. He told Marjan to get the photos, and shoved them into this intruder's face.

"THIS is how your precious family house looked a few days ago. We're not partying, we're cleaning it. We're fixing it. This house was disgusting, broken, filled with trash like you can't imagine. Mr. Vern didn't deserve to die the way he did, so the LEAST we could do is make his house nice for him now."

The man accepted the pictures, and was lost in shock, flipping through them over and over. "I...didn't realize..."

"Yeah, I guess you also didn't realize the little girl you made cry is the one who figured out Mr. Vern was dead in the first place!" Kevin was like an avenging angel on my sister's behalf. "What kind of an ASSHOLE," we all gasped at using that word to an adult's face "yells at a little girl in the first place, especially one who is a local hero?"

Emboldened, the other kids chimed in all at once.

"Yeah, she was Mr. Vern's favorite person!"

"He brought her donuts, you jerk!"

"What kind of creep yells at little girls?"

"At least Agnes cared if he was alive, unlike you!"

"If you're his family, then where were you? Where have you been?"

"Yeah, took you long enough to get here!"

"Without Agnes no one would know he was dead at all."

"When was the last time you even tried to call him? Did you know his phone was cut off?"

"His power and A/C, too! He was suffering, not that his 'family' cared."

"Oh look, you made a kid cry! I bet you feel like SUCH a big man, now!"

"Who decides to be mean to old people and little girls? You think you're a tough guy or something?"

"He'd still be getting eaten by animals without Agnes."

"Some family you are, not even knowing he was dead."

"How dare you mess with Agnes?!"

Riding the momentum, emerging from a cluster of Raccoon Rangers, Charlie Campion stood up right in the unwelcome visitor's face, shaking his tiny fist at the man. "I'm going to tell the Sheriff you yelled at her and he's going to lock you up. He made Agnes a deputy for figuring out Mr. Vern was dead, and you're not allowed to yell at a deputy! That's like, assaulting an officer of the law! You're going to jail, Mister!"

The stranger absorbed what we told him, quietly looking down at the pictures. Pointing meekly toward the backyard, he tried asking, "She was the one…" I didn't let him finish, breaking in, finally able to use my own voice.

"Agnes. Yes, Agnes was the one who talked to him, who cared about him, who made him interact with all of us, made him part of the neighborhood. Agnes was the one he brought donuts to every Sunday, knowing she'd share them with all of us. Agnes was the one who noticed him. Agnes was the one who got THEM," I pointed to the Matsumoto-sans, who were holding on protectively to some of the younger children, "to notify the police that he was missing, and that he probably needed help."

The stranger looked at me, fully attentive, with an expression of shame washing over his face. I didn't let up, not on this man who committed the unforgivable sin of scaring my baby sister. "That's right, the little girl and the nice old people you were just screaming at are the ones who got the authorities involved, you ungrateful prick!"

I don't know what possessed me to utter those last few words, but it did feel good. It elicited a chorus of affirmations from the other children, and several of the high school boys slapped my back in encouragement.

For a moment, the stranger stuttered, trying to clear his voice, avoiding eye contact. "I um, I apologize…"

Manny Olguin cut him off. "Don't apologize to us, apologize to Mr. and Mrs. Matsumoto-San, and then, you can go extra-apologize to Agnes for being a freaking monster to her!"

Sufficiently chastised, he bowed his head, then looked directly at the Matsumoto-sans. "I am sorry for my behavior. I thank you for helping my brother." Looking at the rest of us, he asked us to stay put while he went to apologize to Agnes. Stepping to the back door, he scanned the yard, confused. "I think she's gone."

Charlie, much calmer now, spoke up. "She's probably in a tree, sir. She likes to sit high up, it's where she does her best observing and thinking. You always have to remember to look up when you look for her."

Mr. Vern's brother accepted the advice, and walking into the yard, looked up into various trees until he located her, in a sprawling poplar near the back fence. We watched as he stood at the base of the tree, pleading with her.

It was difficult to make out anything they said. At one point, he made a broad gesture with his arms, circling up above his head, then back to his own chest. I heard her make a sound, but I couldn't tell if she was laughing, or crying. Whatever he said worked, because she allowed him to help her down from the tree.

Back on the ground, she reached up instinctively to take his hand, and although he resisted at first, he relaxed his arm, and together they walked back into the house. When they got inside, Agnes was still puffy-eyed, but pretended she wasn't. She was in that phase little girls go through when they are no longer emotionally sad, but physically can't stop looking like they are, which in turn just makes them mad they ever cried, and even more desperate to convince everyone they're fine.

"It's ok, everyone, he said he's sorry." She announced, with her best approximation of cheery confidence.

He took this as his cue. "Everyone, my name is Dean, and Vern was my brother. I'm sorry for my reaction, but I wasn't expecting to find anyone here, and as you can imagine, it's been a stressful time for me lately."

We all cautiously waited for him to continue, not quite ready to forgive him, but open to the idea. He went on, "Agnes said it would mean a lot to you all if you could finish what you started, and keep working on the house. Is that right?" We all agreed.

"In that case, let's try to be a little more organized in our approach. First, I appreciate how much you've already done—the pictures speak for themselves—but I'm not sure it's safe for you all to be dealing with trash and who knows what else without proper equipment. Is there a hardware store anywhere around here?"

Several of the high school kids told him how to get to the hardware store, and he asked them to make a list of anything they thought we needed. Looking at our makeshift masks, he assessed, "I think at least we could use some goggles, gloves, and masks, yes? And we obviously need a lot more trash bags. While I'm at the store," he reached for his wallet, full of big bills, "is there anywhere open we can order some food from?"

Belinda spoke up. "Yeah, there's a pizza place, it's really good."

He handed her the money. "Great. You're in charge of food. Order enough for everyone here, and get some sodas, too." Eyeing the younger kids, he reconsidered, and added, "make sure to get at least one bottle without caffeine."

Mr. Dean returned from the hardware store just after the pizza arrived, and found us sitting outside. "I never thought of pizza as a picnic food."

Agnes explained, "Mrs. Matsumoto-San said it's too dirty inside to eat, so she's been making us come outside for snacks and lunch. AFTER we wash our hands." She pointed at the hose.

"Mrs. Matsumoto-san is a smart woman." He held a slice of pizza up to the elder Mrs. Matsumoto as a salute of acknowledgement, and addressed her as well as her husband. "Thank you both for making sure the kids were supervised." They smiled and nodded their heads at him.

After lunch, we resumed our work, armed with the new safety and cleaning gear Mr. Dean procured for us. At first, he walked around the house observing, but before long he joined in. Mr. Matsumoto-San directed him in some of the minor repairs, and it was clear Mr. Dean wasn't used to home repair work. Mr. Matsumoto-San was patient with his new protégé, though, and by the end of the day, we'd made more progress than in all of the previous days combined.

Before we went home that night, Mr. Dean rallied us in the front yard. "Here's the deal. It's summer, and you're kids, so if you lose interest in finishing the house, I won't hold it against you. However, if you want, you are all welcome to keep coming back over until it's done. But we're doing this all in the open now, understand? Tell your parents what you've been up to, and let them know they can come over and meet me if it makes them feel better."

Once again, he pulled out his wallet, and this time handed a stack of bills to Mrs. Matsumoto-San. "This is for everyone, can you split it between all of them?" He used the money as a pointer, gesturing in a circle at us, and miming the act of tearing the money to indicate splitting. She understood, and accepted the money. We knew she'd make sure we all got our share.

Mr. Dean made us a promise before we went home that night. "I want to thank you all again for this kind gesture you've made to my brother's memory, and I'd like to meet more of the people who knew him during the last part of his life. When we're done getting this house in shape, I'm going to host a cookout in the backyard, and the whole neighborhood is invited. Does that sound good?" Nothing could sound more exciting for suburban kids in the summer than a block party to look forward to, so we all excitedly accepted his plan.

Over the next week we fell into our routine, now with the knowledge and permission of our parents. Some of them thought it was odd at first, but accepted that we were determined to see our project through, and that at least we'd be under adult supervision. Some of the adults around the neighborhood even pitched in, helping Mr. Dean arrange for a private garbage company to haul away the countless bags we filled each day, and lending their own tools to the cause.

We showed up each morning for our assignments, broke for lunch ordered by Mr. Dean, and worked until dinner time. Each day, more money went to Mrs. Matsumoto-San, who kept it safe for us. We couldn't wait for the pay day, and got carried away planning how we were going to blow it all immediately on something we wanted, like a bike or a skateboard or a new boombox. Maybe even a trampoline or a basketball hoop!

One morning we showed up to the house as usual, only to be caught off guard by the terse woman who answered the door. "Yes?" She demanded, impatient and devoid of any welcome sentiment. A smaller man and woman stood slightly behind her, and I recognized them from local realtor signs. They were a husband and wife team who sold practically every home in the neighborhood.

We all tried to let her know that we were there to work, but talked over each other, producing a cacophony of pleas and explanations. She was prepared. "You must be the child labor lawsuit waiting to happen? My brother's not here right now, so you can all just go home."

"When will he be back?" Asked Trina.

"I don't know, but it's really none of your business. Off now. Go."

Discouraged, we headed home, keeping our eyes fixed on the house behind us. We decided to go to the Matsumoto-san's home, where we vented about how Mr. Dean's sister couldn't possibly understand how much we'd done for her brothers, both of them, and how without us the house wouldn't even be close to sellable.

After a few days of arguing, Mr. Dean and his sister still couldn't reach any agreement on moving forward. Mrs. Alma, as we learned was her name, was hellbent on selling, but her resolve didn't match the limited amount of time she had away from her real life to handle this situation. She needed to get home, and grew to doubt how much this really mattered to her in the long run.

Realizing her surviving brother had dug in on his position, she gave up, leaving town. When we heard, it felt like a real victory. We could finish our work, and see the project through. At the end, Marjan was careful to document every angle of each room, putting together her before and after album to show off our hard work to anyone who would give her their attention. We had to admit that she was right, the house was unrecognizable now in its repaired state.

"I wish Mr. Vern could see the house now!" Agnes exclaimed!

"Do you think he'd like it? I mean, all his stuff is gone, and clearly he liked having it." Keisha wondered.

"Yes, his precious Country Crock containers," joked Junior.

At the end of our unlikely home improvement campaign, Mr. Dean was true to his word, and hosted the entire neighborhood for a backyard cookout. It was the first time in ages we'd all been together, everyone bringing their favorite dishes to contribute to the feast. The party began in the afternoon, but lasted well into the night.

Mrs. Matsumoto-San presented each of us with an envelope, filled with cash for the work we'd done. Most parents immediately intercepted these for depositing into their child's bank account. Agnes hesitated accepting hers, but Mr. Dean convinced her she'd earned it, so she happily handed the money to our mom for safekeeping.

At some point, a string of toasts began. Mr. and Mrs. Okath started it, when they stood up to propose a toast to Mr. Vern, for bringing us all together. More than a few people toasted Agnes, which seemed to embarrass her.

Eventually, Mr. Dean stood for his turn. "To this entire neighborhood. I didn't know my brother very well, it seems, but I am glad his final years were spent here, in your company. I'm glad—no, grateful—that he had people who cared about him," turning to Agnes, "people who continued to care about him even after he died. On behalf of myself, and my family, I want to thank you all."

We continued partying until late into the night, long after even the fireflies and locusts had withdrawn to sleep.

I wish I could say that it was the start of a new era for our neighborhood, but of course that's not how life works. Everything changed almost immediately. The Matsumotos welcomed their baby, and had considerably less time for Agnes, or any of the other kids in the neighborhood. By that point, Agnes had abandoned detective work for a rotating list of new hobbies, first collecting rocks and insects, then stickers, then learning magic, then dance.

In less than a year, Mr. Dean changed his mind, and decided to sell the home. We joked about raising funds to buy it ourselves and turn it into an official playhouse and hangout for all the neighborhood kids. We also wondered how much we should tell the new owners about what had taken place with the previous occupant, but our parents all told us to keep quiet.

Over the next few years, many of our neighbors moved away, assigned to other jobs and locations. Kids grew up, graduated, and came home less and less frequently. In that way, we were once again like any other neighborhood. For all of the talk of being more present in each other's lives during that cookout, everyone quickly fell back into their old, disinterested, over-scheduled routines. Too busy to look out for themselves, let alone each other.

Before this week, I'd largely forgotten the time my dead neighbor brought our street together, even briefly. The memory was buried underneath many more relevant life milestones and recent events. Sure, every now and then it resurfaced, as an interesting anecdote I could use to break the ice, a story to tell at a cocktail party, but it wasn't anything that prompted introspection.

Then, a few days ago, I got news that a cousin of ours, Nadine, passed away unexpectedly, alone. She'd lived by herself for some time, and didn't stay closely in touch with anyone, so it was several days before her body was discovered by her landlord. Instantly, my mind went to Mr. Vern's house, how we'd all pitied him, and wondered why his family hadn't checked on him more often.

Perhaps we'd been unfair to judge them. Maybe we were just naive little kids who didn't really understand how complicated adults can be. We didn't understand that some people really prefer to be alone, and that just because people drift apart doesn't mean we don't love them, or care about them.

Picking up my phone, I started to text Agnes, then decided to call instead. When she answered, I pictured her as a seven year-old budding detective, innocent, with all her life ahead of her. She knew I was calling about

Nadine, despite the fact that neither of us had ever really had a close relationship with her.

"Mom said it looked like she'd been alone for days," I said, without any segue from our greeting.

"Yep." Agnes sounded tired.

"And the landlord said the place was a mess, like she hadn't cleaned it in years."

"I know. It makes me think of poor Mr. Vern."

"That's exactly why I called. Thinking about his house, his yard... the smell. Not just that he was dead in there like that, but... how long he'd lived like that."

"Same. It's weird, I don't know if I'm sad just for Nadine, or for the notion that anyone has so few people who care about them that they can go un-missed for days."

"Should we have reached out to her more? Did we let her down? Remember we were so judgmental of Mr. Vern's family."

"I don't know." Agnes was thoughtful for a moment. "All I know is, I don't want to end up like that."

"Me either."

"Luckily we have spouses."

"And better relationships with our siblings."

She let out a bemused, closed-mouth laugh, just a single syllable.

"Hey Ag, speaking of siblings, there's something I always wanted to ask you about Mr. Vern's brother."

"Mr. Dean?"

"Yeah, what did Mr. Dean say to you that day, when you were up in the tree? You never told us. Whenever we asked, you dismissed it as a private conversation."

"Mr. Dean tried to talk to me but I told him he was a mean man, and to go away because I don't talk to mean people. He said he was sorry for yelling at us, and I said that's not what made him mean. I told him he was mean for letting his brother live like that and rot like that. I asked him if he knew his brother lived in an indoor dump, that he suffered with no A/C, that his body was eaten by animals.

He said he had no idea what Mr. Vern's life was like, and that I was too young to understand, but, 'sometimes siblings grow up to be strangers.' I said that it's not possible to be strangers with someone you've known since you were born, so he did this silly things with his arms, like he was a criminal making an confession, and said that I'd been right in the first place, he was a mean man, and asked if would I please give him a second chance."

"You really won each other over, after that. When we thought he was going to stay, everyone joked that he was going to ask Mom and Dad if he could adopt you or have split custody."

"I think he figured out that I meant well, and actually cared about Mr. Vern, and eventually, about him, too. Not everyone has someone who cares about them, you know?"

"That's true. At least Mr. Vern had a nosy, donut-obsessed neighbor to look after him. What a wild time. Man, you were like, a real hero." I wasn't really even sure what more there was to be said, but I felt something sad in her, sensed her withdrawing, and needed Agnes to understand the kindness she'd done for Mr. Vern and his family by figuring out what had happened.

Her response was a question. "How often do you think about that time?"

"I don't know, not a lot. Like, I've used it as a fun fact a few times, but mostly I forget."

"*Fun*? That's an interesting way to describe it."

"It *was* a fun summer, though. I mean, it was literally the only time all the kids hung out as a single group, no matter what the age, from kindergarten to high school. Like a home-grown summer camp or something. Nothing ever brought us together like that again."

Silence on the other end, so I continued. "And it was all because of you."

She sighed. "I think about it all the time. I've never been able to stop. Sometimes when I remember it happened, I wish I hadn't figured it out. It wasn't a normal kid experience. Maybe I'd be less, I don't know, morose, if I hadn't discovered a man was dead, especially a man I'd developed a fondness for."

"What are you talking about? No, it wasn't normal, but Ag, you did something important. And you were famous! You were in all the papers, and got all those awards. You've lived a life experience that very few people have. Without you, who knows how long it would have taken for people to realize he was... well... you know."

"I felt guilty."

"Guilty?"

"I don't know. In my little kid brain, I sometimes felt like... maybe if I hadn't thought he was dead, he would still be alive. Like, he was only dead because I thought it into being true."

"You thought you manifested his death?"

"Yes, I thought if I hadn't written down all those facts, there could have been a different outcome, but because I arranged air-tight evidence, I doomed him to the only possibility I could imagine. My curiosity killed him. He died as a result of my snooping."

"He was dead because he didn't take care of himself. You know that, right?"

"Still, I regretted it. Didn't you ever notice I stopped my whole detective schtick right after that?"

"Yeah, but you were so capricious I just thought you found something shiny and new to chase."

"No, I just didn't want to think anyone else's demise into existence. I thought I was cursed. I had nightmares. I still don't like thinking about it."

"We don't have to talk about it. Change of subject!"

"How about this," she proposed. "Let's promise that neither of us will ever become so alienated from each other, and from the people who love us, that we'll be dead for days with no one noticing."

"I think we can do that."

"Ok. So if you die, I'll notice. And if I die, you'll notice."

"Deal."

"Deal. Love you."

"Love you."

After we hung up, I held the phone for a while, staring, thinking. Who was my sister? The conversation unsettled me. All of the memories that made up who she was in my mind tumbled out of the neatly ordered places they'd occupied over the decades. As they slipped into a chaotic, unrecognizable pattern, they transformed my sister into a stranger.

How was it we'd grown up in the same house, mere years apart, yet wound up completely different? Was it all thanks to this one death? Did solving the mystery of Mr. Vern break something in her, setting her on a different path? Was it possible that, if she'd never taken the initiative to care, she would have grown into an entirely other person than the sometimes melancholy woman she was today?

My mind traced the ways I let her down, we all let her down. Our parents were so focused on the attention, their pride, the novelty of having raised the famous little detective. Did they ever realize how much it affected her? They never even sent her to a counselor or therapist, not one session, to learn how to cope with what she'd experienced. I couldn't imagine my own children going through something like that without doing everything in my power to ensure they weren't burdened with lifelong trauma.

Poor Agnes.

My wife came down and caught me gazing at nothing in particular. She asked what was on my mind, so I made a half-hearted excuse that I'd be going to bed soon. Still, I felt like a zombie, lumbering into the bathroom, staring at myself as I brushed my teeth, washed my face. I got into bed, and remembered those nights I'd sat with Agnes, keeping Mr. Vern's ghost at bay. Our conversation from earlier in the evening felt incomplete, as if I'd ended an important dialogue before it really began. I regretted changing the subject.

For a moment I considered texting Agnes, but what could I say? No, there is nothing I could do for her, short of traveling back in time. If I could, I would, and I'd stop her from going to the window, seeing the body rolled out like a bag of trash. I'd stop her from going to the Matsumoto-sans to share her evidence, stop her from using her notebook to gather clues, stop her from caring about detective work at all. Maybe if I'd paid more attention to her, she wouldn't have needed to fill her time spying on the neighborhood, befriending loners and oldsters. She could have been like the rest of us, oblivious to the man and his routine.

But there's no going back. All I can do is try to pay better attention in the future, to my sister, to my family. Really pay attention. I rolled over and squeezed my wife so tight she let out an annoyed groan, elbowing my ribs. I eased my grip, and listened to her breathing in and out until at last I fell asleep.

That night I had a fever dream, filled with a sense of dread, running through the old neighborhood at dusk, rounding everyone up to get back home in time for dinner. I heard Mr. Dean's toast, wistful, "I didn't know my brother very well, it seems." As a kid, I'd thought it pathetic that they had ever grown apart. Panicked, I realized it's how I now felt about my own sister. As the dream continued, I ran through all the yards, hopping fences, looking for my sister Agnes. From down the street, Charlie called out, "Remember to look up!"

There she was in a tree, not any specific, real tree, but one that in dream logic was clearly significant. She was little again, wearing a cartoon character shirt, hair secured with the little plastic bird barrettes she always made Mom use to fix her hair, in colors to perfectly match her outfits. As I reached up to help her climb down, the tree grew taller, carrying her high away from me. The sun shining through the leaves behind her backlit her face obscuring her expression as she moved toward the sky. I heard her make a sound, but I couldn't tell if she was laughing or crying.

The Shattered Glass Girl

—

"Already at the edge of fire,
already at the stairway."

-Aztec Codex Tudela

Many reasonable people, even those who support the death penalty, are willing to agree on limitations, reserving it for indisputable war criminals and proven serial killers. My father was never a reasonable man, and had no such threshold for sentencing someone to death. Even his own child.

It was 1926, a different time, I know. Young women's families still expected their daughters to abide by conservative ideals, rules, and customs, while America's rapidly changing culture encouraged us to find ourselves, break free of tradition, and take part in society.

My family was not obscenely wealthy, but we were what my mother called, "comfortable." To give our assets any more attention than that would be gauche. Our family home had been handed down from one generation to the next for over 70 years, with various improvements made to keep up with changing trends in decor and architecture. It would now be considered a modest home, but at the time was practically a mansion.

I grew up in that mansion, and as a child I memorized every ornate detail of the architecture, from the filigree carved on the winding staircase banister to the teardrop crystals of the dining room chandelier. My favorite feature was the massive stained glass window on the front door, the centerpiece that my mother had commissioned during her engagement.

The window took up nearly half of the door, designed in a vibrant floral pattern filled with her favorite flower, the one that had been popular in her childhood. Mother loved that flower so much she even named me after it. Before I could walk she'd hold me in her arms and show me the glass, telling me I was her favorite flower of all, and that it was my window. In the afternoon the sunlight would dance in through the colored glass, creating a kaleidoscope in our foyer, and as a young child I'd dance in the light, trying to capture the colors in my hand. Sometimes I'd stand and trace my fingers along the flowers, until I realized that my smudges were just creating more work to be cleaned up.

I didn't have many companions (except when I could convince one of the servants to humor me) so I spent my days roaming the house alone, exploring the library, hosting imaginary concerts in the conservatory, running my fingers along the tapestries (when no one was looking) and making use of the service passages, meant to keep the help out of sight while they kept the house in order.

My father was not a loving man, not toward my mother, nor toward myself. He spent as much time as possible out of the house, at work, at gentlemen's clubs, and at events where he could expand his network of investors. He loved money: counting money, making money, saving money. It consumed him. Getting married was simply a societal obligation he fulfilled to please his parents, and himself, since my mother came from an old money family, with titles and land abroad.

As the firstborn, I was meant to be a boy, as of course, a son was all that mattered in those days. My mother hoped to please my father with her next pregnancy, but unfortunately, my first brother was born nearly two months before his due date, and died almost immediately in the delivery room. My father had his infant body "disposed of" by the hospital staff before my mother even had a chance to see her son, which she lamented for the rest of her life.

My next younger brother, Edgar, seemed healthy and hearty as an infant as well as a toddler, but when the flu went around, he fell gravely ill, and never recovered. It was a prolonged death, and the entire household was in its grip as we all waited for the inevitable. All of us except Father, that is.

In his experience, there was no problem that his combination of money and threats couldn't solve. First, he called for Dr. Allerton, our long-time family doctor, who had delivered my two brothers and me, and helped my entire family through various injuries and illnesses. Mother trusted no one more than him, but Father insisted the good doctor change his prognosis for Edgar.

When Dr. Allerton stood by his assessment, Father wasn't just disappointed, he was infuriated. He threatened to report Dr. Allerton to the medical board. "I'll have your license revoked, you'll never practice medicine again, you quack! Your reputation will be ruined, I'll see to that!"

Before excusing himself, Dr. Allerton tried one last time to explain there was nothing to be done, and that anyone telling my parents otherwise was either incompetent or a charlatan.

Father called on every medical professional and healer he could find. Our house was filled with the constant noise of strangers shuffling in with promises and shuffling out with my father's money and mother's hopes. All the while, my father wouldn't leave Edgar's side, not out of genuine parental love, though, of course; he was merely trying to ensure an investment reached maturity. My brother was more than a child, he was my father's heir, his living legacy.

At last, Father was out of options and doctors, and seeing my brother waste away in a private hospital room, he had to face the reality that his son was going to die. His entire demeanor changed, shifting into his usual, emotionless front. I remember my mother wailing at Edgar's bedside, and my father, in his impatient insensitivity, ordering her, "Get a hold of yourself, woman!" Empathetic nurses took me by the hand as we escorted Mother out of the room. An obliging doctor accepted Father's instructions (as well as his cash) to drug Mother, while he had Edgar's remains moved to the morgue.

My mother was still heavily drugged for days after, and missed the funeral. I was not allowed to attend, either, because according to Father I would somehow be "in the way." The servants were all very nice to me during that time, praying with me, praying for me, and telling me stories about what they think the afterlife is like to bring me comfort.

My father insisted my mother try again to bring another son into the world, but my mother, angry at missing the opportunity to say a proper goodbye to either of her sons, refused to speak to him, and engaged with him only during public events. For so long she had poured her entire self into Edgar, since he was Father's priority. She realized that in the absence of my brothers, I was all she had left, and renewed her attentions toward me, her favorite little flower.

Mother started to invite me to tea with her in the afternoons. She had a talent for needlepoint, and I enjoyed cross-stitch, so we passed many hours together sitting in the drawing room working on our latest patterns. She began to tell me stories about her childhood, about the man she wanted to marry before her parents made an arrangement with my father, and even how she wished a better fate for me. "I don't know if such a thing really exists, but if it is at all possible, I want you to be in love with the man you marry. I want you to marry someone who treats you well, someone you even like."

I enjoyed her company very much, and did my best to make her life easy and pleasant where I could. I excelled at my school lessons, I demonstrated the finest etiquette, I was the belle of the debutante ball. I received invitations to dine and dance with some of the most exclusive and discriminating families in our circle of society. I even managed to make my father appear to not regret my existence from time-to-time.

Things changed, though. At first, they seemed to be happening only with girls outside our sphere, but then young women even from the most high-class families were indulging in short dresses, long jackets, bobbed hair, gin and champagne. Girls were going out on the town, unchaperoned, together in groups. They weren't waiting to be courted by the right young man in order to participate in society, they were taking life into their own hands.

My father grumbled as child after child of our family friends indulged in what he deemed, "common, base, and unbecoming behavior!" He began to cut some of these families out, punishing the whole clan for the wild behavior of one child.

Mother expressed sympathy, urging him to relax. "They're young, they're excited, it's different now. It's not like when we were young! People can choose what they want to do for themselves."

On his better days, he simply told her to shut up. On others, he used his fists to communicate the same.

Naturally, I began to receive invitations of my own to join in youthful adventures. Of course, Father didn't want me to accept, fearing I'd be corrupted by modern influences. With the help of Mother and our household staff, I was able to sneak out on occasion and have some fun. It was all innocent fun. I did drink, but didn't get drunk. I didn't park with boys, but I did dance with them. I just enjoyed time away from the stifling environment of our house. I liked who I was, away from the watchful eye of my father, free from having to follow each absurd and outdated rule of etiquette that had been drilled into me.

I suppose I grew careless; I suppose we all did, because late one night I was caught. Millie Friedman dropped me off near the edge of our property, and I regretted my impractical choice of outfit. The night was far colder than I'd expected, and the chill stung my exposed legs and shoulders. Tired from a night of revels, I was careless in slinking around to the back of the house. I opened the servants' entrance, and there he was, a brick wall of disappointment and anger. I'd seen my father mad at me, even furious, but nothing like this before. Terror took hold of my body and I braced for the impact as the back of his massive hand made contact with my cheek.

Before I could begin to form words, to make an excuse or beg his forgiveness, he began screaming at me, hurling every awful accusation he could think of, excoriating me for my dress, my makeup, my "loose" morals. I had embarrassed the family. Specifically, I'd embarrassed *him*. I tried to soothe him, to bring him down from his peak of rage, but he wouldn't hear it. "You want to behave like garbage, you can sleep with garbage, outside somewhere. No trollop is going to sully this house!"

He slammed the door in my face, and except for shivering from the cold and the fear, for a moment I couldn't move. Then, instinct took over; I had to find another way inside. I began to run from door to door, window to window, but everything was locked. I couldn't accept that this was actually happening.

Running to the front door, I called wildly for help, from Mother, from the servants. I pounded my fists on the heavy wood frame, slapped my hands against the big stained glass window, my window, and pulled frantically at the handle. I could hear commotion inside the house, as various voices pleaded with my father to see reason. "It's too cold sir, please, take pity. You can set her right in the morning but she can't stay out there!"

Nothing moved him, and instead, he only grew more resolute. Mother, desperate, begged him to let me in. Tearfully she defended me. "She's our only child, you can't do this, please! If you want to be mad with someone, be mad with me! I allowed her, I encouraged her, if you want to punish someone, punish me!"

For a moment, he did punish her, and as I heard each blow I imagined how it felt landing on my poor mother's face. Time stopped passing at a normal rate. I don't know how long this all went on, but for a while, at least the chaos inside the house distracted me from my own physical discomfort.

Finally, silence, except for Mother's quiet sobs. My voice trembling, I quietly called to her, gently placing the palm of my hand on my window. "Mother? Mother, are you alright? Mother, talk to me, please!"

I saw a shadow walk toward the door, recognizing the outline of our housekeeper. "I'm sorry, Miss," she whispered through the door window. "You're father's gone upstairs for the night, he gave us orders not to let you in, no matter what. He said we are not to so much as unlock one door or one window, no matter how much you cry."

"Is Mother hurt? Can you help her?"

"She's not in a good way, but we will take care of her. Don't you worry about her."

"Thank you, please tell her I'm so sorry."

"Don't fuss about apologies now. There will be time for that tomorrow when you're back inside. You'll see, everything will be better in the morning, it always is. Sometimes, people just need a good night's sleep to calm down, to see with clear eyes. I'm sure your father will find his way to forgive you."

"The morning? Please, it's so cold, I can't possibly sleep out here. I don't know what to do. What should I do? Should I walk to town, come back tomorrow?"

"I don't know, Miss. What if you get lost? If you stay here, he might change his mind and let you back in, but if he comes down and sees you've gone, he'll be angry all over. Besides, even if you found your way, where could you stay?"

"Anywhere, someone will let me in, surely."

"I'm sorry, I just don't know. It's not safe for a young girl to be walking out alone, there are bad types out there who might take advantage of you being by yourself."

"Maybe I should take that chance," I wondered out loud.

"But if your father finds out you walked around town on your own, dressed like that, late at night, and slept in someone else's home, he'd be even more upset, wouldn't he?"

She was right. He would be more embarrassed that more people had seen me, he'd accuse me of taking inappropriate accommodations, he'd hold it all against me.

"You're right. I'll wait here. It will all be better in the morning."

"I'll see you then, and I'll have a nice hot breakfast waiting for you."

"Please, can you at least hand me a coat, or a blanket?"

"I'm so sorry, but he said..."

"I know, I know. I don't want anyone else to get in trouble because of me tonight."

"You'll be fine, Miss, won't you?" She didn't sound confident at all.

"Of course. I'll see you for breakfast. Please go tend to Mother now."

"Good night, Miss."

Faced with the harsh reality of my situation, denial took over, and I decided that my father was not really going to keep me out all night, that he would change his mind any minute now. When he did, I wouldn't want him to see me curled up on the ground. That would only reinforce his view of me as trash. I wasn't garbage, no matter what he said, and I hadn't done anything to warrant this overreaction to me, to my mother. No, when he changed his mind I'd be standing tall, and meet him face to face.

Huddling into myself, I leaned against the door, hugging my arms as tight as I could around my shoulders, rubbing myself in a sad attempt to get warm. I could feel the metal outlines of the stained glass flowers creating an impression on my skin. The cold of my window pricked against my back, until I grew numb and stopped feeling it. I alternated standing on one foot, then the other, hopping up and down to try to generate some warmth.

Resolved to stay awake and alert, I then faced my window, tracing each petal one by one. I repeated over and over to myself, "It's not that cold, you'll be inside soon. It's not that cold, you'll be inside soon." I didn't believe it, not really, but I had to at least try to convince myself things were about to get better.

Unfortunately, they did not. At some point in the night I gave in, I got too tired and cold to hold on. I had always been afraid of death, but to my surprise, it didn't hurt. In fact, it was a relief, because at least I couldn't feel the cold anymore. I can't quite describe what happened to my spirit as it pulled away from my body and passed back through my window into the house.

At first light, Mother, along with several of our servants, looked through the frosted designs of the front door's stained glass window. They saw my former self on the porch, curled into a sad ball, skin pale and lips dark. Everyone raised their voices in urgency, and ran out to help me. It was too late of course. I was gone.Well, not gone permanently, but gone from my physical body.

Poor Mother, already visibly weary from the long night, dropped to her knees, flung herself over my body, and howled a feral, wild, wounded wail like an animal. Immediately the house lit up inside, buzzing with movement as people ran to get me blankets, to call a doctor, to try the impossible, anything to bring me back to life.

Pulling my mother back from my corpse, our chauffeur lifted my frozen body into his arms and turned to carry me inside, but ran into the imposing wall of my father. "I gave you all orders, and here you are defying them. I said no one was to bring that floozie back into this home."

"But, Sir, she needs help. Can't you see? She looks half-dead already."

Before he could assess the situation, Mother charged him like a bull, beating him with her fists, screaming a torrent of condemnations. "You killed her! You killed her! My daughter, my only daughter, and you killed her, you monster. You only care about yourself, your reputation, and now my daughter is dead, she's dead. Look at her! Look at her!"

"You're all being hysterical," he responded, pushing my mother out of his way with a smug expression, until he looked at me, really looked at me. Panic swept his face. "Wake her up, wake her now!" He gave the order, but the chauffeur could not obey. It wasn't in his power to wake me. No one could.

"I... I..." My father was, for once, unable to control himself. It was as if he was paralyzed, and you could see him trying to sort out what to say, what to do. His eyes nearly bulged out of his head as he visibly struggled to weigh his options, to acknowledge the consequences of his actions, to accept that he had, in effect, killed his only living child.

Unwilling to wait for him to reach a decision, Mother shoved him with all of her force, and led the sad procession back into the house. My father followed them, falling into an armchair in the corner of the parlor.

They wrapped me in blankets and set me on the divan next to the fireplace, even though they knew it wouldn't make a difference. I think they wanted to at least try, to somehow show me they cared. Mother knelt on the floor next to me, holding my hand and stroking my forehead, murmuring softly to me, a mixture of apologies and reassurances.

When Dr. Allerton arrived, he confirmed that I'd been dead for some time of exposure to the elements during the night. "I'll arrange for the coroner to collect her," he told my mother gently, quietly. He grew emotional. "I brought all three of your children into the world. I didn't expect to live long enough to see them all leave it. I don't understand, didn't she call for help? What took you, all of you, so long to find her?"

Taking in the information from the staff, Dr. Allerton was shaken by what transpired the night before, and accused my father of criminal negligence. "Was it worth it, to punish her for wounding your pride? Did you get your satisfaction? Is your ego now intact? Let me make clear, I will be reporting the situation to the authorities, you can rest assured. I hope your delicate vanity can withstand **that** blow to your reputation!" My father didn't stir, giving no acknowledgement that he'd be directly addressed.

Dr. Allerton realized it was no good trying to engage him further, and turned to Mother. The staff helped him get her up into her room and tucked into her bed. With genuine compassion, he gave his condolences, and with her permission administered a sedative. He left care instructions with her maid, and then, seeing that the staff was lost in grief, offered to send his own wife and household staff over to help.

Before closing the front door, Dr. Allerton turned back to my father once more to offer a parting curse. "I hope this haunts you the rest of your miserable life."

My father was not around long enough to face any legal or public consequences for what he had done. The morning after my funeral, his body was found in a tangle at the bottom of the stairs, broken and bruised. I was relieved his spirit didn't take up residence in the home. I don't think I could have handled an eternity with him. Seventeen years had been long enough.

Whether she was still numb from the grief of losing me, or simply tired of giving her love to a man who could never return it, Mother took his death in stride, as a minor inconvenience rather than tragedy. I was proud of her, refusing to crumble at the notion of widowhood.

Rather, she thrived, and embraced her newfound freedom. Mother decided a fresh start in a new town was just what she needed. She worked with Father's attorneys to settle his affairs, including selling our home. I was excited to accompany her, to see her second act. I imagined her with a new look, stylish haircut and wardrobe full of the latest fashions, making friends and building her new life. I wondered if she might even find love again.

The couple who bought our home was younger, Italian, with three children already (Margherita, Giulia, and Pietro) and another on the way. Father had been racist in the way typical of the company he kept, and would never have sold his home to anyone who didn't look and sound like us. I like to think Mother knew this, and intentionally chose these buyers as a final way of exercising some vengeance toward my father.

She lied to them about what a wonderful home they were getting. "Oh, if only I didn't need to return home and help my mother care for my father, I would stay here forever. So many happy memories in one place...you'll have an incredible life here together, I just know it!"

Watching Mother walk out the door that final time was the most difficult moment of my existence, before or after death. She was so dear to me, loved me, indulged me, and cared for me. We had both suffered under my father, and I thought we'd earned the opportunity to be happy together now that he was gone. I didn't have a physical heart anymore, but nevertheless it broke at seeing her take a long last look around the house.

It was so quiet, and she stood at the front door for a long time, hands on the stained glass and tracing the flowers. "I'm so sorry, my sweet girl. I'm sorry I let you down. I let all my babies down."

Tears began to slide down her cheeks, and it hurt to see her feeling guilt when none of it had ever been her fault. I reached out to brush the tears away, and realized she could feel my hand on her cheek. At first she started, unable to see what was touching her, unable to hear my reassurances. She was about to place her hand over mine when a knock on the door announced the arrival of her driver. Wiping her face, she sniffled, straightened her shoulders, and picked up her small bag.

I hadn't realized that when Mother left, I couldn't go with her. I didn't understand why I was stuck there, but my brothers weren't, nor Father. No one ever explained the rules of being a ghost to me, and while I'd been glad not to transition to some sort of heaven up in the clouds, I didn't understand the lack of agency I had on earth. My spirit wasn't bonded to Mother, as I had thought. No, it seemed I was bonded to the house. I feared I would never be able to leave.

For several days I remained in the house alone, completely alone for the first time in my life. Every little noise rang loud in the empty rooms and hallways. I longed for some distraction, even one book to read, but there were no objects left to interact with. So I moved from room to room, trying to recall happy times with my brother, my mother, our staff.

It was a great relief when the new family finally moved in. Before they slept there, on the first day a priest came to bless the house. I'm not sure what he accomplished, but I enjoyed seeing him try to sanctify the house as a blessed dwelling. If it was meant to expel spirits like me, well, it didn't take.

From the moment they moved in, I never felt alone. Their children were so full of energy and mischief, they brought the house to life. And the couple, Connie and Severino Marino, were obviously in love, in a way I'd never seen, showing each other affection, holding hands, stealing kisses when the children were distracted.

I wasn't sure how long to hide my presence from them, nor how to go about letting them know I was there. I only knew I didn't want to scare them. I decided to start with the children. They had all manner of wind up toys that played music or moved across the floor, so I began winding them up. Giulia, the middle child, had a little wind-up music box on her nightstand, which opened to reveal a rotating bird that bobbed to the lullaby. I liked to wind this up, not just for her, but for myself, too. The children gave me a nickname, Aurelia, and compared their encounters with each other, exaggerating my feats.

The children tried to tell their parents about me, but of course the adults responded rationally, explaining there was no such thing as ghosts. "Sometimes old houses can play tricks on you," Mr. Marino explained. "It's nothing more than coincidences and wishful thinking. You want to see a ghost, so your mind finds ways to imagine proof."

Still, the children insisted I was real. I appreciated their loyalty to my existence, but was less pleased when they would blame things on me that I hadn't done.

One morning Mrs. Marino was exhausted, trying to fight off a head cold, and slept uncharacteristically late. When the baby, Clavio, was unable to wake his mother with his usual murmurs, he began to cry. I hated hearing him cry, so I began to rock his cradle, softly. It worked, calming him, but then I heard a sharp gasp. Mrs. Marino was sitting up in bed, watching her son's cradle moving on its own, seeing her infant smile up and coo at nothing. Startled, she tried to convince herself it was just a hallucination. "I must have a fever, that's why I'm seeing things," she muttered under her breath while moving to the cradle.

Realizing I'd been caught in the act, I decided to let Mrs. Marino know I was real. I walked over toward her, and gently placed a hand on her forehead. "Is that you, Aurelia?" It was funny to hear the nickname come out of her mouth. "If it's you, squeeze my hand." I obliged, taking her hand in mine. She tried to remain visibly calm.

"I'd... I'd like to know more about you. I know, I'll ask you a question. Squeeze my hand once for yes, twice for no. Is that alright with you?" I squeezed once, and a little smile of relief broke out on her face. "Good, let's start then." I prepared myself for my first actual conversation with someone since I'd passed.

"Are you a fever dream?"

Squeeze squeeze - no

"Are you... a spirit? A... were you ever alive?"

Squeeze - yes

"Do you live here all the time?"

Squeeze

"Was this your home when you were alive?"

Squeeze

"Are you upset we are here?"

Squeeze squeeze

"So we have your permission?"

Squeeze

"Were you here when Father Lippi blessed the house?"

Squeeze

"And it didn't... hurt you?"

Squeeze squeeze

"So you are... you are a good spirit?"

Squeeze

"Are there other spirits here?"

Squeeze squeeze

"So you were alone before we moved here."

Squeeze

"The woman who sold us this house, did she know you were here?"

Squeeze squeeze

Raising an eyebrow and tilting her head, she assessed, "Well, it's nice she didn't knowingly sell us a haunted house. Oh dear, I hope that doesn't sound unkind. Did you know the woman? Was she your family?"

Squeeze

"She was someone you cared for?"

A long, sustained squeeze

"Oh, I am sorry. So your family is all gone now. How lonely you must be."

Squeeze

"You've been moving things around the house, showing signs to the children?"

Squeeze

"Only to entertain them, right, not to scare them?"

Squeeze

"Do you watch us all the time? Even when we are in… private moments?"

An emphatic squeeze squeeze

"Well, that's a relief!"

I gave a little squeeze, and she let out a small giggle.

"And you don't mean us harm?"

Squeeze squeeze

"Just now, you were trying to help the baby because I couldn't?"

Squeeze

"Well, then, if you are a good spirit, and we're welcome in your home, then you are welcome in our family. Would you like that?"

Squeeze

"Good. Now, I'm going to pick up the baby and hold him in bed with me, but if you'd like, you can stay here and we can get to know each other better. Does that sound good to you?"

Squeeze

For the next few days, we talked in this way almost constantly. Mrs. Marino, or Connie, as she introduced herself to me, grew to enjoy my invisible companionship while her husband was away at work. I thought she might let the children know she could interact with me, too, but she said she wanted to keep it to herself for a while.

Connie did ask if I would consider writing my responses, so we could have more of a dialogue instead of an interview. I hesitated, because while I enjoyed my burgeoning friendship, I was afraid that any tangible "proof" of my existence would only cause her trouble. Surely people would assume she was making it all up for attention, or worse, that she actually believed in a spirit no one else could see. I thought it was safer for everyone if I kept evidence of my presence scarce.

She quickly got used to letting me help her around the house, asking me to keep an eye on this child or the other while she carried out a task. She even trusted me enough to watch little Clavio long enough that she could take a nap. "I always wanted a nanny, I never imagined one would come with a house!"

I was happy to help, and cherished our time together. She was like a mother, a sister, and a friend, all rolled up into one. She managed to steer the conversations to get information she wanted, learning my real first name ("Oh, like the window!"), that I had two siblings, and that the woman from whom they bought the house was my mother.

Of course, some topics were difficult for me, particularly when she tried to gently ascertain the nature of my death. Any time I didn't feel like answering, I would simply pat the top of her hand and leave the room, and the next time we spoke, she'd apologize for prying. With mother and children all communicating with me now, and Mr. Marino finally being made aware of my existence, I became content, and began to forget the painful memories I'd experienced in that home.

A few months later, Clavio had a high temperature, and Connie decided it was severe enough to call the doctor. My previous life felt so distant that seeing Dr. Allerton enter the house again was a shock. In an instant it all came flooding back, culminating in a feeling of loss for my mother, my brothers, and my life.

He examined Clavio, prescribed some treatments, and reassured both Connie and Severino that everything would be well. Connie thanked him profusely, and then an idea flashed across her face. "Dr. Allerton, have you been here before? That is, did you know the family that used to live here?"

"Yes I did. This house belonged to the same family for generations. I've been treating people here for decades."

"So then you know the girl who lived here most recently? You knew..." As she uttered my name, Dr. Allerton instantly looked filled with sadness and regret. He nodded yes.

"Can you tell me what happened to her?"

Delicately, Dr. Allerton recounted the circumstances of my death. I tuned out the words, it was too much to hear. It was hard enough seeing his face as he explained how Mother tried to help, how it broke her heart.

Severino was horrified. "Her own father, he just let her die?"

"Yes, right there, right in front of that very door."

Connie was bracing herself to hold back tears. "That poor girl. Her poor mother!"

"Yes, it was an awful situation for everyone involved." Dr. Allerton was visibly distraught from recounting that night, and cleared his throat as he straightened his back. "Now if you'll excuse me, I have another patient to see."

They said goodbye, and Severino left the room to escort Dr. Allerton to the front door.

In a near-whisper, Connie called for me.

"Are you here?"

Squeeze

"You heard all that?"

Squeeze

"And what the doctor said, was it true?"

Squeeze

She began to cry openly now. "My dear, what an awful thing to have happened."

I slowly wiped the tears away, then pulled her to me for a hug.

"You are part of our family now, understand? You belong with us, and we will never let anything bad happen to you again."

Squeeze

For decades, I was indeed part of the family. As the family expanded over the years, with marriages and new children, the house became the center of the Marino family universe. I never felt lonely, as there was always something happening. The house was filled with love like I'd never known, and I reveled in being part of it.

I was always welcomed, with children saying hello to me even if they weren't sure I was in the room with them. The older children would explain my circumstances to the younger children, though over time the details of my death became less accurate.

Sometimes when they had friends stay over, they would try to frighten their guests with ghost tales, and I couldn't help but prove them right with small acts of moving items around to scare their companions. Occasionally, they had me help them prank visitors they didn't particularly like. They explained that wherever I stood felt exceptionally cold, so they had me run interference on the staircase, chilling the unsuspecting victim, and using my physical force to prevent them from climbing the stairs.

The younger children often invited me to tea parties with their dolls, leaving a seat for me at the tiny table, even setting out a plate of food for me on holidays.

I liked when they drew pictures of me to include in their family portraits, even if the drawings didn't really resemble how I'd looked when I had still had a body.

I loved my second family, and felt closer to them than I'd felt with my own when I'd been alive. After all, I'd spent infinitely more time with the Marinos than with my birth family. It was difficult to outlive them, though. As family members began to pass away, I felt the weight of each loss.

When the Second World War broke out, Pietro enlisted, confident that his fluency in Italian would help the Allied effort. It was a tragedy that his first time visiting his ancestral homeland resulted in his being buried there, not far from the beach at which he lost his life. I hoped his spirit might return home to be with us, a hope which both of his parents shared and for which they prayed. If his spirit was somehow bound to this earth though, it was not within the walls of the old house.

My dearest friend Connie passed peacefully at home. She had been ill for some time, so we expected it. I was excited at the prospect of her becoming a ghost like me, happy that we could be friends on an equal plane of existence, and that perhaps over time the rest of the family could join us. Connie's spirit didn't stay, though. She'd intuitively felt that it wasn't going to happen, and she apologized before she passed away, asking me to squeeze her hand once more if I forgave her for leaving me. *Squeeze.*

Although I think we all expected Severino to follow her soon after, he delighted in his grandchildren who kept him young, and he held on for many years after. Unfortunately, it wasn't just people we lost. Eventually, after over 50 years, the family had to move. The town had evolved into a full-grown city, and the house was situated on property needed for development.

By now the children were grown and in homes of their own, and no one liked Severino being on his own, so the plan was to move him in with Margherita, her husband Elio, and their children. (All of whom had a fondness for me, even though Elio had been skeptical of my existence when he first married into the family.)

The old family house was to be demolished, which sent me into a panic. I had no idea if I would survive the demolition, and was terrified at where my spirit might end up. Would I be trapped forever under the foundation of a shopping center? Would I cease to exist?

The Marinos were compensated well, and prepared to leave. As they did, Giulia—now in her 50s, no longer a little child—protested. "What about Aurelia? If we let them knock down the house, what happens to her spirit?"

No one answered, but Severino glanced around thoughtfully and finally ventured a guess. "Maybe we can take her with us? We could take part of the house... why don't we take the stained glass window? The one from the front door? It would be a shame to let it be destroyed anyway, and then maybe, just maybe she can come with us!"

Margherita agreed wholeheartedly. "Yes, we can put it in the breakfast nook, replace one of those corner windows to let some light shine through it." I wasn't sure the plan would work, but it was better than waiting alone for the demolition crews. Cautiously relieved , I threw my arms around them both and embraced them as tight as I could. They began to laugh, leaning into the hug. Turning to each of his children and grandchildren, Severino shared "I think Aurelia likes the idea, too!"

As Severino moved to Margherita and Elio's house, my window was installed just as promised, and it fit perfectly. This time, when a priest arrived to bless the house, the family asked him to also say an extra blessing by the window. At first it was strange to be away from the mansion, where I'd born, died, and lived again. But the new house was nice, and it was certainly interesting getting to explore a new space.

I was able to continue my contented coexistence with the family. The newest generation of children continued to incorporate me into their lives, asking me to help them around the house. For example, the controls for the heaters and air conditioning were too high up on the wall for them to reach, so I helped them when they wanted to adjust. (Elio eventually asked me to stop and leave the temperature of the house in his hands.) When Severino passed a few years later, we were gratified he'd been able to live out his final days surrounded by family.

Almost 15 happy years passed in this new home, until one day when my world exploded into thousands of shards. I'd heard Margherita and Elio discussing a string of robberies in the neighborhood. I wasn't scared for myself, since you can't hurt a ghost, but I was frightened for my family. One night they were all out at dinner, when the thieves broke in. They decided my window was their best point of entry, smashing it, climbing through to the bench against the wall.

The first thief crawled through carefully, but the second rushed, and caught his arm on my glass. He recoiled and complained that it cut him badly, but his collaborator ignored him. They moved swiftly through the house, grabbing antiques, guns, money, jewelry—it was a jackpot haul for them. Before I knew it, they were preparing to leave, when a strange feeling took over. I was being pulled along with the criminals—at least part of me was. As if I was being cleaved into two separate souls. Part of me remained in this house, but I couldn't stop them from tearing the other part of me away.

It was the first time I felt anything close to physical pain since the night I died. The thieves agreed to split up and meet later when it was safe, and I continued along with the second robber. It took me a moment to realize the glass slivers in his arm were taking me with them.

I didn't want to leave my family, my home. I tried to stay, but I was powerless to prevent part of my essence being ripped from my peaceful existence and the people I loved. I was angry, and mad enough to kill. He had no right to violate my family, steal their possessions, and kidnap me in the process. And once he cleaned out the wound, what then? Would part of me stop existing? Could I continue as a partial being in the house, or would the damage from being shattered end me entirely?

Determined not to sit by as my existence was wiped away by a common criminal, I summoned up all the physical energy I could, and wrapped my hands around his throat. First he couldn't call for help, and then he couldn't breathe. He struggled at first, and then as he gave up, I felt the life leaving his body. In that moment a memory took over from long ago.

I recalled the night of my funeral, the first night I learned I could interact with the physical world. After dismissing the help for the night, Father got drunk on a secret supply of booze he'd hidden, and then berated my mother. She ran upstairs to her bedroom, sobbing, screaming at him to leave her alone. He sat in the living room, getting more and more drunk, mumbling to himself. I knew he was going to continue to be awful to Mother and couldn't bear to see it.

He stood to go up the stairs, and I felt I had to block him, to save Mother just this once. I flew past him up the winding staircase, to the landing on the master floor. His eyes were barely open as he dragged himself up. Before he could set his foot down on the floor, I took my chance, and shoved him with all the force I could.

Down he went, tumbling, too inebriated and injured to summon my mother for help. I stood over him, watching him try to pick himself up, to catch his breath. He failed, slowly slipping away during the night.

I enjoyed watching him die.

Just as I watched my father die that night, I took pleasure in watching this thief die, powered by my anger not just at him, but at my father, too. At any man who would harm my family. At last, he died, and in an instant, I was snapped back to the house, feeling like my complete and total self once more.

By then the family was home, taking in the scene. They were upset about their possessions, of course, but were especially worried about my window. Working quickly, they swept up the pieces, and put them in a tin for safekeeping.

Over the next few days, the family recovered from the invasion. The police followed up to announce that they had found one of the robbers dead, from undetermined causes, and in his possession many of the stolen goods. They were able to use clues from this discovery to track down the other thief. In their hideout, they had items from all over the neighborhood they hadn't been able to offload yet.

The police were surprised at their good fortune in solving the burglary so quickly. "I can't tell you how uncommon it is for us to get so much as a lead in these breaking and entering cases. And we certainly don't usually recover so much of the stolen property. You all must have some kind of good luck or something."

"We like to think we have a guardian angel," replied Margherita.

"Yeah, we call her Aurelia, even though her real name is..." elaborated Vittorio, one of the youngest children, before Margherita was able to place a hand over his mouth.

"Yes, we all feel fortunate and blessed." Elio concluded. "Thank you officer."

With their stolen possessions back in the house again, Margherita and Elio decided to place the shattered glass of my window in an item they'd always associated with me: a music box I used to wind up for the kids when they first moved in to the old house. They set me up on the mantel over the living room fireplace, and took turns telling me they were so glad to still have me with them. I was glad, too. My life wouldn't be the same without them.

My Side of the World

—

"Goodbyes are only for those who love with their
eyes. Because for those who love with heart and
soul there is no such thing as separation."

— Rumi

The trail went cold after Peru. There was nothing more. He disappeared. After 20 years, there was no trace of his existence past a certain point, and I wasn't sure how that could be.

———

I always assumed I would see him again. He didn't cross my mind often, but when he did, it was always some indeterminate point in the future, when I would be back in Italy, maybe for a publicity tour. (Of what, I don't know. International graphic design awards? It didn't really matter.) The scene played out in my mind, each time following a similar setting and script:

> *The room is hideous, the carpet and drapes too chintzy for this century.*
>
> *Here I am on a dais, looking out at eager fans celebrating me, and skeptical reporters scrutinizing me. In my most dutiful college-level Italian, I competently provide rehearsed responses. It charms the room, and I play it off, bashful. Suddenly, a pale hand is raised. He*

stands, and I cannot contain my exhilaration. I scream "Nico! Niccolò Accettullo!"

Continuing to call his name, I leap down from the dais, and run to him. "Nico mio!" I exclaim as he grabs my waist. We embrace, fitting in decades-worth of hugs. We don't care that everyone is shocked. We stare into each other's eyes with pitifully-goofy grins, taking stock of each freckle, each wrinkle, all that time has written on our faces.

Afterwards, my agent tries to wrangle me, but I don't care about anyone in the world except Nico. He is my air. I need him to breathe. My agent hisses "you are married, you are making a scene and I cannot help you clean it up if you don't cut it out. Now." I don't care. I delay the agent, assuring him I'll catch up with him later, but first I need a little time with Nico.

Holding hands, he leads me out into the hall, through the lobby, and onto the cobblestone street. I am out of breath, giddy. I don't have words. I float. I feel as if my smile will physically break the boundaries of my face, shattering me. It is a reunion we couldn't have imagined.

We walk through the city, trying to slow the setting of the sun in spite of the lamp posts lighting up as we pass them. Everything is tinted through a filter. We see street shows, he buys me fruit from a vendor, puts a flower in my hair, takes me dancing, we sit by the water, we spend a perfect night together catching up.

Nico wants to talk about the time we've missed, the next time we can see each other. I remind him there is no future, there's only today, this one day, and all we can do is enjoy it while we can. When I leave for my hotel, he asks me to write, and I promise to, every day. I tell him, "come see me sometime on my side of the world."

When I get back to the U.S., my husband, Justin, understands. He isn't jealous, and is instead happy for me that I got to see my fleeting love once more. Justin's romances before me had always ended badly, quite badly, and he'd never want to see any of those women again, so he is glad that at least one of us can get some closure and contentment.

Although they'd never met, Justin always had a soft spot for Nico, for the way he had set me on a path that led to Justin. Early in our relationship, he even confessed a touch of guilt about being an interloper, dragging Nico and I away from each other. So in my fantasy, Justin is pleased that I got to see my old flame one more time. All is well, all are happy.

Now none of this can happen. Not if Nico has disappeared. Not if he's... possibly... but no, I can't consider that.

I think back to when we met, at Matteo and Lorenzo's country villa outside Padua. Fiorella, Lorenzo's girlfriend, and Cinzia had invited me to visit them for a week in Italy, ending with a weekend at the villa. We were old friends from my study abroad days. Fiorella and Lorenzo had been immediately welcoming to me and we became fast friends. Cinzia had taken much longer to win over, but was a lot of fun once I got to know her better. We'd been on several international trips together, including a stay in London the previous summer.

Besides wanting to catch up with everyone, I also hoped to get some guidance from Lorenzo. Over the years Lorenzo, the younger of the brothers whose family villa we'd be visiting, had become someone I relied on for life advice. My domestic situation was a disaster I knew I needed to leave, but I hadn't been able to bring myself to do it. My sister Lisa had been really pushing me to finally end my prolonged engagement to Garrett (whom she had never liked), something she had hoped I would do before she moved out of our hometown, Philadelphia. She wanted time to help me start my single life before her work took her to San Diego. I knew she was right, but I still didn't end it before she left. I hoped a final push from Lorenzo would help me strengthen my resolve to cut my losses and move on with my life.

Cinzia drove us to the villa in her little smart car, which my 5'10" frame struggled with, even in the front seat. I always marveled at her ability to drive a stick shift while simultaneously smoking a cigarette, gesturing at other drivers, and texting. Along the way we listened to terrible European club covers of outdated American pop songs, and Fiorella gave us the rundown on what to expect for the weekend.

Specifically, she wanted me to be aware of a potentially grumpy visitor I'd meet at the villa. He had just been heartbroken by his German girlfriend, after she unceremoniously kicked him out of their apartment in Milan. He'd been caught off guard, and was now taking refuge in one of Matteo and Lorenzo's guest rooms until he found the energy to search for new accommodations.

By all accounts he was not doing well, had overstayed his welcome within a matter of days, and was protesting the arrival of weekend guests. He preemptively resented the sunshine he was sure we'd bring with us. I was ready to dismiss this walking breakup song in human form, and felt no guilt when I learned I'd be displacing him from his room. Besides, from what they said, he spent all day everyday outside, lounged in the same chair where he could most visibly spread his misery, drinking until he passed out without ever making it back to bed. So, it wasn't like he was using the room, anyway.

There he was when we arrived mid-morning, sprawled on the chair, looking forlorn. He hardly acknowledged Cinzia and Fiorella's arrival, moaning something like a soft whine as they walked past him to the door. They all knew him well, and loved him dearly, and because of this they had no problem telling him to his face he needed to get up and stop mourning, to appreciate that he was not dead, and better yet, celebrate that he had successfully unentangled himself from the Teutonic nightmare that was Annika.

Fiorella snatched his hat and told him that if nothing could help his heart, perhaps the sun could fix his pasty skin. He sat up to reclaim his hat, protesting, "you sound like Annika," falling off the chair. As he fell onto the patio, he looked up, laughing at himself, and caught himself as we locked eyes. I set down my bags and helped him up.

The instant we held each other, a euphoria took hold of my entire body. I had never felt this in my life, not with any boyfriend, and not even with my fiancé back home. Perhaps that's because said fiancé constantly cheated on me and was usually too worn out for sex, having left it all on the field with any number of other women. (*Ugh, I needed to leave him.*) Nico's touch overwhelmed me, and I temporarily lost my senses, unable to hear what he was saying directly to me. I couldn't formulate a response.

Assuming this meant I was out of my element entirely, he turned to Cinzia and said in Italian "Ah, I understand, your American friend doesn't speak Italian." Turning to me, slowly, deliberately, and loudly in English he repeated "Thank you, you must be the friend from the

United States. I," and here he gestured emphatically at his chest, "am Niiii-cooo. Nico."

"Claudia. *Gran piaciere*," I managed to whisper, my smile lopsided. His eye contact unnerved me, so I dodged his gaze and busied myself picking up my bags. He helped, and placed a hand on my side, guiding me into the house.

"I will show you to your room," he ventured in Italian.

I confirmed I could speak his language with my response in what I thought was passable Italian, "Thank you, I appreciate it. I'm quite tired and ready to set these bags down. I understand this was your room?"

He looked amused and chuckled lightly.

"I make you laugh?" I wasn't sure if I should be annoyed or offended, so I was even more assertive in my Italian.

"Your accent, I cannot place it. Where did you learn to speak?"

This was not new to me, it was in fact a constant source of teasing from my Italian friends. Even for an American, my inscrutable mish-mashed Italian-ish accent would never allow me to blend in. Smiling back at him, I recited the explanation by rote: "My mother is American and her family speaks only English, my father was Cuban and I grew up speaking Spanish with his relatives. I took advanced German in high school. I worked for a family from Naples, my first Italian professor in the U.S. was from Bari, my second from Venice, I studied abroad in Urbino, and my tutors were from Ostia and Rimini. Oh, and during my semester here I dated a Sicilian."

He broke into laughter, accepting my explanation with "Ah, now everything is clear! Considering that, I think your accent could be much, much worse."

With that, we were friends. I excused myself to the restroom, and when I returned he was in my room with a lemon soda.

"I thought you might enjoy it after a long drive." He handed me the glass. I gratefully accepted. As I began to unpack, he hopped onto a bench by the window and kept me company. He even helped me make the bed, which he'd neglected to do for himself prior to my arrival, taking extra care to tuck the fitted sheet tightly under the corners.

When I observed this, he shrugged a brief explanation of, "strict father," and continued with the pillowcase and quilt. "There!" He triumphed, stepping back to observe his work. "*Perfetto!*"

I thanked him, and as we stared a little too long at each other Lorenzo stuck his head in the room. I hadn't seen him since the year before, and I had missed him. I had to stand on my toes to hug him, he was all legs and neck. He ran his fingers over the new summer freckles on my face. "What is happening here?" He teased, and I reached up to tousle his curls he'd allowed to grow long, asking the same question.

He remembered Nico was in the room, and commented, "Finally, he comes back to life." Turning back to me, "Our Nico has been a sad plant. I was ready for him to leave but now I see he is prepared to be a person again. Good. Come, let's have some snacks."

We walked out through the back of the house, and as the only person who had never visited there before, I was overtaken by the view. My jaw involuntarily dropped, and I was too enthralled to be embarrassed by my reaction. Livia, Matteo's wife and Lorenzo's sister-in-law, took my elbow and walked me to the table, which was dressed in a casual old cloth and set with mismatched glasses, plates, and silverware. Spread across was an assortment of charcuterie and antipasti, along with a few pitchers of home made drinks and carafes of wine.

Those of us who had just arrived were famished, and set to stuffing our faces with burrata, figs, olives, and sardines. Nico offered me some mortadella, and I curled my nose. I'd always been picky about deli meat, and even my semester in Italy hadn't forced me to expand my palate. To my own surprise it took him no time to convince me to try. I hated it, the texture, the taste, every part of it, and couldn't conceal my disgust.

"Fine," he said. "More for me." He playfully coveted the platter.

We fell into easy conversation, and our friends had to repeatedly pull us out of our dialogue to engage us. Matteo and Lorenzo laid out plans for the evening, which revolved around an elaborate meal they planned for us. Livia helpfully pointed out they were still missing a few items, and she would need to run into town. "We'll go!" Nico offered, hand on my shoulder. I agreed, and Livia put up a perfunctory protest, then immediately pivoted into agreement.

Before she could finish listing what we needed, Nico had absconded with me to his laughably small car. He knew I was giggling at the vehicle, and made a comment about American expectations. We drove to the market, and as we parked a few streets from the square we realized some kind of festival was happening. He urged me to follow him, reassuring me that the street stalls would have better produce than anything in the grocer's.

He took my hand in his. I threaded my fingers between his and squeezed, transported. Nothing else existed. Not the other shoppers, not the vendors, not my philandering fiancé. Whoever had taken over my body, it wasn't me. I was never this relaxed or easygoing. We walked through the market, examining the wares. He pointed out buildings and told me about them. I asked him about fruits and vegetables I hadn't seen before. He bought a bag of cherries, and as we walked we ate them. I bought us a granita to split. We used the same straw. Who the hell was I?

Recalling Livia's list, we fulfilled it. I asked him what I could get our hosts, and he helped me pick a good wine and some pastries. He also reached for some flowers for Livia, from him, as a way of apologizing for having been intolerable since his arrival. I smiled at his self-awareness, and he responded by plucking the head off one of the flowers, placing it behind my ear.

"There, like an American romance movie," he laughed. I played at simpering like a rom-com starlet being swept off her feet.

As we continued shopping we watched a street magician wow a crowd of local children. I took a few photos, and then felt a little self-conscious for sticking out as an obvious tourist. Nonsense, Nico waved away my concern. Instead, he told me to give him the camera, and directed me to stand with the magician in the background, taking my picture, a walking cliche with a flower in my hair and bags full of groceries.

One of the nearby vendors had some handmade jewelry that caught my eye so I wandered over to look more closely. Nico joined me, taking in the options. "You're looking for something to wear?"

"Not for me, for Lisa."

"Lisa?"

"My sister... and pretty much my best friend. She's basically my favorite person."

"It's nice you are close with family."

"Yeah, we've always been really bonded, but recently she took a job on the other side of the country, in

California, and I've missed her. Like, I'm happy for her, but I'm not used to being so far apart. I've wanted to find the perfect gift for her, and a lot of this is her style."

I let him help me negotiate for a pendant with matching earrings. I was comfortable conducting transactions myself, but it seemed to make him happy to feel useful.

At another stall, a couple sold handmade notebooks. Pointing out that an artist can never have too many notebooks, he told me to pick one, his treat. I protested that I was just a graphic designer, no great artist, but he insisted. I awkwardly accepted, and he took the flower from my hair, pressing it between the pages.

"You can draw your memories of me, of this perfect day," he suggested. I thanked him, playfully asking if all Italian men were so generous with strangers. He brushed my lips with his fingertips. "Do all American women have such soft lips?" I blushed, and involuntarily traced the same path on my lips with my own finger tip.

We talked nonstop on the return to the villa. He was excited by everything, no matter what topic, he could speak on it with contagious exuberance. He was studying to get his PhD in environmental chemistry, hoping for a career in historic preservation of heritage sites around the world. He said he wanted to work today to "save history for the future." I told him that I preferred to live in the present moment, I never thought about the past or worried about the future.

He joked that maybe I didn't care about the past because I hadn't had enough fun in my life yet, but that he hoped I wouldn't forget him or the fun he provided during this day. He also suggested that if I needed to get excited about the future, we should plan for him to come visit me. He'd never been to my side of the world, and there was so much he wanted to experience, cultures he wanted to explore, archaeological sites he longed to examine. To my surprise, I heard myself agreeing that he should come stay with me. I seemed to have forgotten I had a fiancé. Well, technically had a fiancé. For now.

We stuck together the rest of the evening, whether it was helping to prep dinner, or setting the table, or cleaning up after. During the meal, we consistently found ourselves in our own private conversations, unable to get enough of each other's attention. Several people commented that they were glad he was out of his funk, and thanked me for whatever I had done to get him to act right. Cinzia kept trying to steer us back to group conversations, at one point jokingly coming over to sit between us.

After dessert, Nico and I went for a walk by ourselves toward the pond, holding hands, covering every stray topic that came into our minds. We finally stopped at a tree, smiling at each other. He pressed me up against the trunk, and I kissed him like I'd been starving for it. He kissed me back like his life depended on it. I felt alive. I felt a rush of physical excitement I hadn't experienced in years. Our hands were all over each other, and then the next thing I knew, we were on the ground, pulling at our clothes to remove them as quickly as possible

It was quick, it was messy, but above all it was intensely satisfying.

I was not prepared for it, but it also felt strangely inevitable, as if we'd both decided from the moment we met that this was going to happen. For a while after we stared up at the stars in silence. Neither of us had any notion of what time it was, we'd lost track of the evening. We got dressed, brushed off our clothing and walked back up to the villa, our arms around each other's waists. I felt like I was a new person. I hadn't been happy, like this, since longer than I could remember.

Most everyone was in bed when we got back, except for Lorenzo and Fiorella, who were chatting in the living room. They offered us some Frangelico and biscotti, which I automatically accepted even though I don't like either. We sat with them for a while as I mindlessly nibbled on a biscotto, worried they would know what had happened. I was sure it was obvious and they could both tell, but it wasn't their business.

Part of me was afraid that if we had to address it out loud, the magic would be lost. I felt strangely protective of what was happening with Nico. I endured their conversation, then at last, mercifully, they went to bed. As they got up, they gestured at the couch, telling Nico they were sorry to have taken up his bed for so long, and let them know if he needed more blankets to be comfortable. I said good night as well, and headed toward my room.

As soon as I was sure they were in bed, I ran back to Nico, grabbing his hand, pulling him into my room. Now there was no rushing, we could take our time, enjoy the pleasure. He stayed with me all night, as we went back and forth between making love and whispering confidences to each other. I wasn't aware of falling asleep, but I remember waking up together.

By morning, when our friends had all convened for breakfast and seen Nico's blankets and pillow still stacked up on the couch, they quickly understood what occurred.

Hearing the rumbling of voices and noises in the kitchen, he kissed my forehead, I kissed his nose. We got up, and walked out together, excusing ourselves to take a quick shower. After we dressed we helped make breakfast, while our friends exchanged glances. At last, Matteo broke the silence. "I think we should go out tonight!" Everyone agreed, and we settled on a plan for dinner and dancing in town.

All morning and afternoon Nico and I cuddled together on furniture, went on walks, disappeared to my room from time to time. It was clear some of our friends approved and even encouraged us. But the appreciation for our newly-formed bond wasn't universal. I didn't care though. I was in love.

Nico and I started making plans for after I had to go home. He promised to see me as soon as he could, and

I promised to come back to see him, too. As soon as I got home I'd leave Garrett for once and for all, and then it would be just me and Nico, traveling back and forth to spend time with each other on our respective sides of the world.

As dinner approached our friends were, for the most part, now more openly supportive of us, making comments about how cute we were together, how glad they were that he wasn't moping anymore, and that they weren't having to hear about Annika. "Annika who?!" They would jokingly laugh and ask each other over and over.

The only ones who didn't laugh were Lorenzo and Cinzia, who stayed fairly quiet.

Lorenzo finally caught me alone and said he was glad I was having fun, but that he had missed me, had wanted to spend time catching up, and was sad I'd been too distracted to make time for him. He was right, I had been so focused on having fun with Nico that I had sidelined the very people I had traveled to see. I apologized, and he accepted.

"Understand," Lorenzo was taking his time to think through each word. "You are both my friends. I care for each of you as I care for my family. I fear you will be hurt."

"You think he'll hurt me? Is there something I should know?" As always when I became nervous, I was struggling with my Italian grammar, mixing up tenses.

Thankfully my friends were used to this and understood me well enough.

"I have known him for much of my life. He likes to be in love. He has never not been in love, not since we were old enough to notice girls. He has never been alone. Every woman is the love of his life. You mistake me, Claudia. Don't make that face. He isn't playing games with you, he is sincerely in love. But no woman can ever live up to how much he loves them, eventually it breaks him. And that is why he gets hurt so badly, it is a deep wound, and he cannot face it, so he has to find his next love. He met you only yesterday, now Annika is already gone from his attention."

"I see. Well, I'm not exactly looking for love, anyway, so don't worry about me being hurt."

"I do worry, though. What are you looking for? Where is your fiancé? Why is he not here? You were already out of love with him the last time I saw you, and the time before that, and even before the time before that you were supposed to leave him. Why are you letting him hurt you still? You're so scared of being alone, or so stuck in your misery? And now you drag Nico into this?"

"I'm not dragging him into anything. I like him, and we're having fun."

"You aren't thinking about what's next, you never think about what happens next. For you this is a diversion to forget a bad man you are too afraid to leave. Nino's in love with you already and tomorrow you'll go back to your country and forget him. It will hurt him to have lost someone else again so soon."

"I won't forget him."

"Eventually you will."

"I won't hurt him."

"You won't be able to help it."

I could see we weren't getting anywhere, so I asked him to trust me, and focus on being happy while I was still here. He agreed, tentatively, and said he hoped he hadn't ruined the mood of the trip. I assured him he hadn't, and that I appreciated having a friend like him who cared to look out for me. At dinner I made a point to sit with Lorenzo and gave him my undivided attention. He seemed much happier then, which was a relief.

That night we danced and danced at a local club in a large group. Of course, Nico and I were handsy with each other, and at a few points he kissed me on the floor. It took all of my restraint not to get physically carried away when he did. The club was outdoors, but the dance floor was packed and at times difficult to move around. It was only later in the night, when I stepped off the dance floor to cool down with a drink, that Cinzia confronted me. She was angry, but I couldn't quite understand why.

She began to berate me rapidly in Italian, faster than I could keep up. I was unable to determine if she was 1) mad that I was with Nico because he was still so emotionally raw from his break up, 2) mad my attention was more on him than on her, 3) if she was mad at me that I was cheating on Garrett, or 4) all three, but in any case, one of the only words I consistently caught was "whore." She avoided me the rest of the night, staying on the perimeter of the dance floor, smoking angrily with a permanent, exaggerated frown on her face. I decided not to let her ruin my fun, dancing with the rest of our friends.

Nico was annoyed at Cinzia when I told him what happened, but I told him not to let it bother him, that she had a short temper and it would blow over by morning. He stayed in my room, our room. It was ecstasy. I didn't want the night to end, I dreaded the next afternoon when I'd have to pack for the plane ride home.

"What about your fiancé?" he asked quietly, after I thought he'd fallen asleep.

"We don't love each other." I moved closer to him, kissed his cheek, his chin, burrowed my face into his chest.

"Will you leave him?"

"I feel like I already have."

"You shouldn't be unhappy. I don't want you to be unhappy."

As much as I believed him, I also started to feel the impermanence of the moment, and that the magic we had couldn't save me, couldn't protect me from myself. By this time tomorrow I'd be back in the bed I shared with Garrett. I shook my head as hard as I could, banishing Garrett from my mind.

"I'm happy now. I'm happy here with you." I clung to him as if the harder I held him, the more I could keep the sun from coming up.

"When I come to visit you, we'll be this happy, too," he promised, before finally falling asleep.

The next morning, Fiorella popped into the bathroom with me while I brushed my teeth. She explained that Cinzia had long carried feelings for Nico, that she had been elated when she learned he and Annika broke up, and hoped that she could be there for him this weekend. Apparently Cinzia had thought this was her moment to make a move.

This was a surprise to me, and I explained I had no idea, she never told me, but Fiorella said that didn't matter. Cinzia was pissed off at me regardless, and had been ranting about how I should find a different ride back to the airport. Fiorella cautioned me to just give our friend space during the rest of the morning. I agreed to follow her advice. She hugged me and told me she was glad I was having a fling, maybe it would help me realize what I was missing out on by staying with that bastard back at home.

For the remaining hours, I soaked up every minute I could with my friends, devoting time to each of them (except Cinzia), making the most of every minute. As the time to leave approached, Nico walked me once more to the pond. We promised to write to each other, to call each other, to visit. We weren't going to lose each other. This weekend had been too important, too meaningful. I felt like I was going to cry, surprised at myself for getting so emotional. I didn't want to say goodbye, it felt like my breath was being taken away.

"Te voglio," he whispered in my ear as he pulled me in for one final embrace.

"Te voglio bene, caro mio." I barely managed to reply, while holding in tears.

It was time to say goodbye to everyone. Fiorella and Cinzia were going to drop me off at the airport before they made their way home. Matteo, Lorenzo, and Nico loaded up the car with our bags, and Livia gave us travel snacks as we all said our goodbyes. Lorenzo wrapped me in a big embrace, telling me to remember I deserved to be happy, and that he hoped the next time we spoke I could tell him I'd finally left Garrett. I thanked him, Matteo, and Livia again for hosting us.

Before I stepped into the car, Nico pulled me to him, and we kissed one last time.

"Ci vediomo presto, carina," he promised.

"Si, te lo prometto," I vowed, before squeezing my too-tall body into the impossibly small back seat to which Cinzia had exiled me.

The tension during the car ride was unbearable, and I was momentarily glad I was leaving not just the car, but the country, anything to get away from the stifling negativity. At last, when I couldn't stand it any longer, I directly apologized to Cinzia, that I was sorry I had upset her and had hurt her feelings.

She replied in an uninterrupted monologue that she was sorry her good friend, poor man, had not only been hurt by a German whore, but was now being led on by an American one. An American with a fiancé, no less, using a vulnerable man as a play thing because I was unsatisfied. She was unkind in blaming me for Garrett's constant infidelity. She shamed me for making promises to see Nico again that I wouldn't keep. Cinzia concluded this tirade by muttering some terse words about sending her money she was sure I owed her.

At the airport, she didn't even get out of the car to hug me goodbye, as Fiorella did. After encouraging me that she could smooth things over with Cinzia for me, Fiorella made me promise to let her know when I landed and to have a safe flight, and to come back and visit her and Lorenzo some time. She also said she'd follow up if she and Lorenzo could visit me the following spring, as they'd offered to.

Cinzia honked the horn aggressively, and when Fiorella asked for one more moment, Cinzia yelled back that I was an American whore who owned her gas money. Fiorella told me to ignore, but I'd had my limit. I walked over to Cinzia's door, pulled out every Euro I had left, and threw it all in her lap, including the coins, which I tossed carelessly toward her, ensuring they'd bounce everywhere and make a mess. She angrily dismissed me while grabbing at the bills and change, telling me sarcastically to have a nice life, and to be sure I never wrote to her again. I assured her that would not be a problem. That was the last time we ever communicated.

—

As I boarded the plane, I settled into my seat and texted my mom, step-dad, and my sister Lisa to let each one know I was on my way home. I felt bad when I realized how early it was for poor Lisa, as I still thought of her being on East Coast time, but her text back didn't show any sense of annoyance with me.

Pulling out the journal Nico bought me, I began to write, furiously, trying to document all of the feelings, sensations, and experiences from my trip before they evaporated from my consciousness. Pausing only briefly on occasion to accept a drink or snack from the flight crew, my pen danced across the pages, documenting Italy and most of all, Nico. When I finished, I was emotionally exhausted, unsure of what to do next. I put the journal away, and for a while started out my window, realizing we were now closer to the U.S. than to Europe. My getaway was truly ending.

I tried to divorce myself from the feeling of contentment I'd experienced. I tried to steel myself for the disappointment of returning to my everyday life. No more aperitivos or digestivos or morning cappuccinos or afternoon espressos. No more fresh flowers. No more street lamps, no more pond, no more Nico.

How could I already miss this person who only two days ago had been a stranger? I knew the weekend had been too good to be true, we were both taking refuge in each other—a diversion, like Lorenzo said. I began to compartmentalize Nico into "the past" in my brain, preparing to move on, to get back to the present. I knew if I dwelled on it I would be subsumed with grief that it was already over.

I got off the plane, and turned my phone on. I planned to call Garrett, but didn't want to hear his voice. I stalled, trying to delay being officially back on U.S. soil. Then, seeing how crowded Customs was, thought better of it and got in the back of the line.

I turned on my phone to message Fiorella that I'd arrived home safely. Seeing a shocking number of notifications for my email, I opened it, and to my delight I already had one from Nico. I couldn't contain my joy. He wanted to make sure I had a good flight, and that I would not forget him. In case I lost his mailing address, he sent it again.

Standing in the stagnant line, I realized I couldn't go home. Not to the apartment I shared with Garrett, anyway. My time in Italy might have been an unrealistic escape, with a level of romance and contentment I couldn't hope to replicate or sustain at home, but all the same my time with Garrett was at an end. There was no way I could go back to the dissatisfaction and dread of my former daily life. My friends were right: I should have left a long time ago, but the best I could do was leave him now.

As long as the wait for Customs was, it wouldn't last forever, and I did need a plan, fast. The only thing I could think to do was call my mother and see if I could stay with her. I dialed, and waited, anxious she wouldn't pick up, but after a few rings she did.

"Welcome home, my world traveler!" The cheer in her voice made my heart dance.

"Can you pick me up?" I didn't want to elaborate why, not here, over the phone, and hoped she wouldn't ask.

"That depends, did you bring me any good souvenirs? I'm just kidding! Of course, I'm on my way."

With that settled, I felt relief I wouldn't have to face Garrett immediately. I had no idea how to break an engagement, or how he'd react, and knew I'd feel more ready to take it on after a good night's sleep. After several minutes of typing, deleting, and retyping a series of unsatisfactory messages, I finally sent him a brief text: "Tired, going to stay at my mom's. She's picking me up. See you tomorrow." I waited a few minutes, terrified of follow-up questions to this vague communication. His response was as perfunctory as I should have expected. "Cool, c u then." Annoyed at him, not for the response, but in general, I opened the email from Nico again, and smiled at its very existence.

When my mom picked me up she put on quite a show, hamming it up, swooning in a purposefully over-the-top manner. "My child, my long lost child, you've returned home to me!"

Although I was tired, she made me laugh. We loaded the car with my bags, and headed to her home. On the way I dreaded having to discuss why the sudden change of plans, but she didn't broach the subject, asking instead only about the highlights from my trip, saying that she couldn't wait to see pictures, and didn't my tan look nice, look at all my freckles, what was on my phone that had my attention.

Arriving at her condo, my step-dad, George, was the one who got right to the point, in his usual direct but loving way. "Welcome home! To what do we owe the honor of being the first to greet you? Where's that fiancé of yours?"

My mother playfully urged him to give me a break and do something helpful like carry the bags in. "All right," he negotiated in a tone of false seriousness. "But there better be some good wine in these heavy things."

After I got settled into the guest room and took a shower (is there anything as wonderful as a shower after a long flight?) I sat down to the home-cooked meal George had prepared. He was always the better cook, usually barring my mother from entering the kitchen lest her lack of culinary skills become contagious. I got straight to the point. "Pop, these Brussels sprouts are perfect. Also, I'm leaving Garrett." This I punctuated with a healthy gulp of wine.

To my surprise—though I suppose it shouldn't have been—they were neither upset nor disappointed. They refrained from saying anything negative about

Garrett or our relationship, instead listening and offering affirmations to my assessment of the situation, that I had been letting indifference lead my life and it was time for a change. Their support was what I needed, and they helped me figure out how to tell him, as well as a game plan for getting my belongings out of the apartment we'd shared for the past several years.

———

Breaking up was easy. Garrett wasn't home at first, so I walked in with the now-empty suitcases from my trip, followed by George with some file boxes, and immediately got to packing. Garrett had made a huge mess of the place while I was gone, and took no effort to tidy up before my return. "*Oh well*," I thought.

The lack of emotion amazed me, as I felt no sadness, no remorse, just focus on my task. Thankfully, our apartment had been too small to accommodate many possessions, such as clothing or books, and having never been the sentimental type I didn't have much by way of personal effects. Nor had I developed attachments to any of our shared furniture, decor, or dishes.

George came upstairs to help me take my last few bags down to his car, then agreed to wait at a nearby coffee shop until it was time to go home. "Good luck, Kiddo. Call me when you're ready." His hug steadied me, and I sat on the couch, taking in a last look of the place I'd built my life.

When Garrett showed up, he looked tired. "Rough night?" I asked, without even caring about the answer.

"Hey stranger," he passively responded, with a half-hearted smile, bending over the couch to administer a sad excuse for a hug. "Wanna eat? I'm starving."

"My trip was fine, thanks." My snarkiness got the better of me. Perhaps I was more affected by my nerves than expected. I took a breath and tried to stay calm, confident. "I'm good. I'm not staying. I am leaving, actually. The apartment. You. I'm leaving you. And the apartment. All of it. I'm all packed, if there's anything I forgot."

He looked absolutely confused, not that anyone could blame him with how much I had botched my pronouncement. I continued, "I had time to do a lot of thinking, and we're not really growing together, we're just drifting apart, so before we get married and make it more difficult to do this, we should end it now. It's cleaner now."

"Cleaner?" He was speaking more to himself than to me, then pivoted. "You're tired, you had a long flight. Let's just get you rested and we can talk about this more in a couple of days when your head is clear. You can't let jet lag make major life decisions for you."

What followed was an exhausting exchange in which he alternately tried to convince me to stay, goad me into a fight, and demand an explanation for my change of heart. He blamed Italy, all Italians, even all of Western Europe, anyone but himself. He defended himself for all the times he strayed, insulting the women he'd been with. I told him the problem wasn't them, it was him. I picked up my phone to call George, and before hitting the dial button finally found the words. "Look," began my closing argument. "You're not worth my time. You're not with my energy. You aren't worth my love. I don't actually like you, as a person, at all. Goodbye."

George was quiet in the car driving me home. I texted Lisa to let her know it was done, and she sent a flurry of celebratory texts. In my head, I put together what I would tell Nico in my next email. In the end it was simple. I told him I'd left Garrett and was staying with my parents until I figured out my next steps. "Not as nice as Matteo's country estate," I joked, "but it comes with a chef!" The congratulatory email I received in response was just what I hoped he'd send.

—

Over the next few months, Nico and I exchanged a steady stream of emails, jumbled in our own hybrid language, mixing Italian with Spanish or English, with the occasional German thrown in. We talked about everything and nothing, from our routines for running to new music we discovered. We found ourselves writing every day. Occasionally, he would send little gifts, and often he would send long, thoughtful, hand-written letters. For all of our communications, we quickly developed a standard opening line, "What's new on your side of the world?" We always closed with "Until we see each other again, kisses and hugs."

While I had feared our communications would diminish over time, they only intensified, each of us considering ourselves in an inter-continental relationship. He was especially supportive as I untangled the final details of my life from Garrett, sorting out recurring expenses like utilities. In no time at all, my former fiancé was out of my life, while I forged ahead.

Nico and I started discussing more serious plans for visits. We decided he should spend a semester in the U.S., staying with me. He suggested that after his time in the U.S., I could return to Europe with him. After all, I was a graphic designer, that was a job I could do anywhere in the world. I went along with all of it, swept up in passion. I said yes to everything. He started working on his application for a visa, and to a program at a university near me.

After an extended stay with my parents, I finally moved into a place of my own, in a new neighborhood I wasn't very familiar with, but the price was right. One evening, I was exhausted at the end of a long day of work. It was one of those days every designer faces that makes them question their career. The days when a client dismisses all of the designs you created based on their specific requests because, now that they see it, it's not what they want. Not that they know what they want, mind you, but definitely not what they see in front of them. The client then gives nothing but vague feedback such as "Can you make it pop? It just needs more visual interest, you know… jazz it up!"

I was at the grocery store, the last place I wanted to be, shielding myself with headphones and listening to Mina's "Studio Uno," an album Nico recommended. Dodging the slam of after-work shoppers, I turned a corner just in time to see a woman steer her fully loaded cart right into an end cap.

Dozens of jars (thankfully made of plastic) tumbled off the shelf, rolling in all directions. A baby wrapped at her chest in a sling, and a hyperactive toddler wriggling and yelling in the cart, the woman looked like she might burst into tears. I ran to help her, setting down my basket. As I knelt on the ground, retrieving bottles as quickly as I could, I realized I wasn't alone.

A man helped me, and together we placed the jars back on the shelf before an employee even showed up. As the man stood up, he talked to the little boy in the cart, who stopped screaming and started to giggle sweetly. The woman was overly thankful, and we each told her it was no problem at all. She wheeled away, leaving me with the other helper. He joked with the lamest pickup line I'd ever heard: "Pick up vodka sauce here often?" He flashed a smile, which was admittedly charming. I laughed, and wished him a good night, continuing with my shopping. I thought nothing of it, and didn't even mention it in my email to Nico.

—

The next time I saw the man at the store, I was in the Latin food section. My mom and George were coming over that weekend for brunch. Mom was craving some of the food my dad used to make, and I was too, so I decided to try and tackle some of the recipes myself. I debated acknowledging my fellow shopper, but he recognized me and immediately approached.

We made some awkward small talk and he introduced himself.

"Justin, frequent shopper for overpriced groceries. And you are?"

"Claudia, newly-frequent shopper, also finding the groceries overpriced."

"Oh, new to the neighborhood?"

"Yes, I took over a friend's lease."

"Like it so far?"

"It's better than my previous circumstance."

"I see... and what was your previous circumstance?"

Deciding I didn't want to get into the history of my broken engagement with a stranger, I tried to end the conversation. "You know, I think I need to get back to my shopping list."

"Me too, me too. I was just looking for..." he started to search the shelves, clearly out of his element. Reaching for a can, he stared at the label and questioned out loud, "Guava paste? Yes. Guava paste. Just ran out, so, phew, they have my brand!" I admired his commitment to keeping the conversation going.

Grabbing what I'd been looking for, I smiled and headed for the checkout. "Enjoy your guava, *amigo*!" I called.

He called out "Oh, I always do. Gotta love a paste!"

I couldn't help but laugh.

—

A week later, there he was. I had almost hoped I would run into him again. It was a low bar, but he didn't put off creepy vibes, and I appreciated that he could provide comic relief during an errand I despised. I had just started shopping and immediately got distracted by a cheese display. Holding Jarlsberg in one hand and Gruyère in the other, I considered them each, trying to choose, when I heard Justin's voice. "Two cheese, or not two cheese? That is the question!"

"Hi! Run out of guava paste again? Maybe this time you need tamarind pulp, or perhaps you're looking for some *annatto*?"

"I won't lie, I have not touched the paste. I don't really even understand paste as a food genre. It kind of scares me. Like, what do you even do with it?"

I laughed at a grown man feeling intimidated by groceries. He continued gesturing at the options I was weighing, "You know, if you like cheese, those are fine, but feta is better."

"Is it now?"

"Yes, and it just so happens that they serve a lot of it at the Greek place next door. Ever been?"

"I haven't really been anywhere around here yet."

"Ok, so Claudia, want to set down those fancy cheeses and come get some Greek for dinner?"

"With you?"

"Ideally, yes, with me."

"I can't."

"I get it, I'm still kind of a stranger. How about this? I'm going to go there, and order some appetizers. You think about it, and if you want, come over and join me. If not, I'll still enjoy some good food."

"Fair enough," I replied, more intrigued than I wanted to be. He walked off, and I contemplated the cheeses for a moment, as if they were some kind of magic eight ball. But I didn't need advice. I knew what I wanted to do. I placed them back on the display, and walked over to the restaurant.

Justin sat in a booth, a few plates spread on the table. I recognized saganaki, dolmas, and spanakopita. He stood up to greet me, surprised I actually showed. I sat on the chair across from him, and asked why he would order so much food if he didn't think I'd be there. "Hope," he answered. "Plus," he tapped his belly, "I eat a lot. Way more than you would think. You'll see."

Over the appetizers, we told each other our stories. He started by asking if I was seeing anyone.

"Seeing might not be the best term, but I am in a relationship, yes."

"What does that mean?"

I told him about Nico, how our emails and letters had to suffice until we could see each other in person again. He teased me a little. "Oh yeah, I have a girlfriend in Canada. We met at summer camp." Feeling challenged, I took out my phone and showed him the long list of recent emails from Nico. "All right, all right, your imaginary Italian boyfriend is real." We both laughed, and I asked him about his status.

He was single, after a series of bad relationships, or more specifically, bad breakups.

"How bad, if I can ask?" It was Justin's turn in the hot seat.

"Well, my last serious girlfriend, a linguistics professor who I thought was 'the one,'—as in I had started putting money aside for a ring—broke up with me on a ski trip."

"That's not so bad," I countered.

"Have you been skiing?"

"Not once in my life."

"Me either. I don't ski. I had never been skiing, never even considered it, and she was an expert. So she had me spend all this money to book a week-long trip, to buy equipment, convinced me to lug it across the country, through airports, and get to a lodge in the middle of nowhere, surrounded by nothing but her friends from work, and snow.

Right away on day one, I stuck out. I couldn't keep up with their conversations, arguing about the phonetics of languages none of them had ever actually heard spoken aloud. I know nothing about the syntax of dead languages. I could see she was annoyed. Then, to make it all worse, I struggled on the slopes, and embarrassed her."

"Surely she didn't get mad at a novice for not being good? That's hardly fair."

"Hardly fair is what happened next. The whole way back to the lodge she's seething at me about how I intentionally humiliated her, that I didn't even try. We get back to our room to change, and she tells me it's over. No conversation, just that she's done. On day one of a week-long trip, she dumped me. She tells me she's going to stay in a friend's room instead. For the rest of the trip, she literally ignored me like I was invisible."

"Wait, wait, you STAYED?! Why didn't you leave?"

"I don't know. I honestly don't. Shock, maybe? I wish I had left, rather than watch her with all her friends. I pieced together that the friend she ended up staying with was a guy she'd been seeing on the side. Apparently they had used every academic conference as a romantic getaway. Seeing them together, laughing, right in front of me, was torture. I don't know what kept me there."

"I'm sorry. I get it. I wasted time, too. My fiancé cheated constantly, sometimes with multiple women in the same time period, but I stuck it out with him. For years. Whole years of my life, wasted on someone who didn't care about me at all. I wish I had just broken it off the first time I found out, when we were still just dating, but I let it go on way too long. Inertia is real. "

"What made you finally leave?"

"My imaginary Italian boyfriend." More laughter.

"Now that I've spilled my saddest moment to you over this spanakopita, surely you'll agree to stay for an entree?"

"Hmmm." I was enjoying myself, and there wasn't harm that I could see in staying. I did, after all, have to eat dinner at some point. "Ok, I'll stay, but only because I want to check out their meatballs."

"You will not be disappointed." He was obviously pleased with himself for convincing me.

With a sideways grin, I raised an eyebrow at him. "You don't suppose they have a menu in Sanskrit or Etruscan or something, right? I really think languages no one uses make dinner more special." Maybe I'd gone too far in teasing him after what he had just told me, but instead he chuckled. We were good.

For the rest of the meal, our conversation took off at light speed, hopping from topic to topic. He told me about the high school where he taught. He was supposed to be a civics teacher, but due to funding issues and a teacher shortage, he had become a utility player, stepping in for history, creative writing, one semester even having to cover a health class. I didn't really know him, but something told me he was good at his job, well-liked by

students and staff. When I suggested this, he was humble
and said he was just glad he could make a difference for
kids like him.

I told him about my dad, whose mom had been
pregnant with him when she and her husband fled Cuba.
Tired of the growing violence in their neighborhood, they
had come to the U.S. to visit family for Christmas. His
dad—my grandfather—had a bad feeling about what was
happening at home, so he'd had them pack up some of
their valuables and heirlooms to bring along on the trip.
Of course, the country fell over the New Year, and they
never went back, but my dad had always felt a strong
connection to the island.

Justin asked if I was still close to my dad, so I
explained he had passed away. I told him about his
illness, how it left all of us devastated, but how George
had been an amazing step-dad and helped the family
heal. He asked about my mom, and I told him she was
the best, a real Miss Frizzle type, the surrogate mom to
any of my friends who needed a trusted adult growing up.
She seemed soft and mushy on the outside, but when
push came to shove, no one could mess with her or the
people she cared about.

Justin was close to his family, too, and still tried
to go to church with them every Sunday. They were part
of an historic A.M.E. congregation, he said. I didn't know
what that meant. He explained, and also mentioned his
dad has been in the choir since before Justin was even
born, so he found gospel music grounding, calming.

"Mom, my sister, and I haven't been to church since my dad's funeral. George isn't Catholic, he's... I don't know, Lutheran or Methodist, Presbyterian, one of those generic American white Protestant ones."

Justin laughed, and said not to worry, he wasn't trying to convert me, just being up front about important things in his life. Like sports, books, and movies, which we covered, too.

Eventually, while we had no shortage of subjects to talk about, we did run out of food. The waiter dropped off the check, and Justin reached for it.

"Let me get it," he said, shifting in his seat to retrieve his wallet.

"No, we'll split," I insisted, grabbing the bill. He relented, and we each placed a card down.

While we waited for the waiter to come back, I became serious. "While this was fun, as I said, I am in a relationship. I am happy to have a friend in the neighborhood and to hang out, but I don't want there to be any misunderstanding. I am not available, and I am not interested in anything beyond friendship. If that's a problem, we probably shouldn't spend time together at all. Ok?"

"Understood. Friend." His smile was innocent, but still I knew even in that moment that he was already under my skin.

—

It wasn't long before Justin and I started seeing each other more frequently. I tried to always invite other friends, or to include him on plans with larger groups of people. My friends all liked him, and he fit in well with our group dynamic. He was fun, and got along well with everyone. During these times we hung out, he kept his agreement, and never tried anything romantic or physical with me, and I settled into a sense of calm. I was relieved that I could be friends without risking my relationship with Nico.

That was a lie I told myself, anyway. Being near Justin served to highlight how much I missed being in the actual presence of someone else. At that time in the early 2000's, we didn't have easy video chat on our computers, much less our phones, so Nico was entirely on text on a page for me. We communicated regularly, sure, but through words only. After nearly a year of abstract plans and discussions for the future, but without seeing each other in person, Nico had grown almost faceless in my mind. I had to look at pictures from our weekend to refresh my memory.

Justin, however, was right there in front of me. Yes, he was attractive, but, I reasoned with myself, he's probably only getting my attention because of how much I miss Nico. That didn't stop me from finding more reasons to spend time with Justin, and to make sure that when we were out with friends I was always the one standing or sitting next to him.

I knew that Justin was becoming a distraction, but I liked how my life was changing because of him. He introduced me to his friends, as well, and my social life bloomed. I liked spending time with all of them, and we even started to merge our friend groups. All of this meant less time for replying to long emails or thoughtful, hand-written letters. In the past, I waited impatiently for any word from Nico, devouring messages from him immediately. Now emails sat unread for a day or two, and letters took longer to respond to. I even missed a few phone calls in a row.

Without realizing it, I'd been peppering my messages to Nico with mentions of Justin. He had become so significant to my social life that he was present for nearly everything, and it was impossible to mention things I had done without referring to him.

Finally, Nico asked me about "this Justin," who he was and how he managed to become so central to my conversation. I demurred that he was just a neighbor, someone I'd met who became a friend, and that it was helpful to know people in my new place. Nico seemed convinced; I felt caught, though, and panicked a little.

In a ridiculous moment of poor judgment, I thought I would set Justin up with a friend. That would make him off limits for me, and also show Nico that he had nothing to worry about. I shared the idea with Lisa, who instructed, "You will do no such thing until I come to see you."

Lisa had already planned to fly home and stay with me for a week. As my closest friend and confidant, life was always more vibrant when she was around. As usual, she first wanted to catch up on gossip about family and friends. Then she shifted into her life coach mode, ready to administer unsolicited advice.

Although I was older, she had more experience in nearly every aspect of life, was much bolder and more assertive in getting what she wanted. During this visit, her advice was laser-focused on a single subject: I needed to break up with Nico.

"You're only clinging to Nico because you don't want to admit you did something reckless and impulsive." She was direct as always, which sometimes made it hard to hear the concern and care that went into her advice. She wasn't trying to boss people around, she just felt she could see what others couldn't.

"Excuse me?" I tried to brush off this evaluation. "I'm not clinging to anything. We are in a committed relationship."

"No, you're not. I'm not judging. You know I have no room to judge. I think it was good for you to get your fun where you could. But I also know that spur of the moment decisions, like, I don't know, having unprotected pond sex with a stranger in another country so you could sabotage your engagement to a serial philanderer who has a tragic fashion sense, is not your typical mode. So naturally, you're trying to drag it out, make it into something more serious or legitimate."

"That's not really a fair characterization of what happened."

"Oh no? You were unhappy with Garrett but, for God knows what reason, kept dragging your feet on leaving him. Consciously or no, you needed a catalyst. Bam, in walks the perfect tool, a well-hung Italian man desperate for action to fuck away the pain of his own heartbreak. So you hook up with him, have the satisfying sex you've been missing in your life, and next thing you know, you have the confidence to leave your loser fiancé. You're a free woman. Mission accomplished."

"It wasn't just a hookup. It was so much more than that, I told you. We really connected!"

"You fucked. Sometimes even great sex is still just sex. Hell, for me, that's what it is most of the time."

"Nico is not one of your randos you find at a bar." Now I was being defensive, and unfair to her.

"Maybe not, but he was your distraction, and you were his rebound. You guys had a fling. There is nothing wrong with that! What is wrong is making major life decisions based on one weekend of good times. You both need to admit that you were just what each of you needed in the moment, then get over it and move on."

"Lisa, we love each other. It wasn't just a fling."

"Oh really? When are you seeing him next? When was the last time you saw him? You've said he's working on a visa to stay here long-term, but if your relationship was really that important, wouldn't one of you have prioritized travel by now? Aren't your other friends coming to see you? Like, with real dates and actual tickets for their flights? If they can make firm plans, why hasn't he?"

"Because I've been busy! I had to find my new place, I've been settling in... I didn't mean for this much time to go by but you know sometimes life just speeds up faster than your plans can keep pace."

"You told me the last thing he said to you in Italy was a promise to 'see you soon.' Well, soon has come and gone, so where is he?"

She had me there. Fiorella and Lorenzo were scheduled to visit me in a few months, but Nico wasn't coming with them. And I hadn't been back to see him.

"Look," she continued, more softly. "I get it. You have limited sexual experience, it's always been with long-time boyfriends, and you aren't used to indulging yourself that way. But shake off the afterglow of those orgasms Nico and his 'magic D' gave you, and what do you guys really have? I'm not telling you how to live your life. I just want you to stop wasting time on something if it's not really what you want. Again. Will you at least consider what I'm saying?"

"I will."

"OK, good. Are we done with your problems now? Because I have a life, too." We switched to discussing her latest escapades in her new city. For the rest of the trip it was just the two of us, except when we saw our parents. Lisa helped me make *ropa vieja, plátanos maduros*, and *pastelitos de guayaba*, which turned out much better than when I tried to make them on my own. Mom and George were both impressed. Lisa had always been a daddy's girl when it came to George, so she soaked up his compliments like a lizard luxuriating in the sunshine.

Sadly, her trip came to an end. I asked her to come back soon, and she likewise invited me to come see her. Her visit gave me so much joy, for the most part, but her words about Nico left me rattled. I feared she was more correct than I wanted to admit.

—

One Wednesday night, my friend Caitlin, who worked as a vet tech, called to tell me someone had dropped off a litter of kittens at her office. They were found at a site where new townhomes were being built, but there was no sign of a mother, so the construction crew decided to bring them to the nearest animal hospital. Caitlin asked if I would take one of them, and on impulse I said yes, of course I could. I asked her to tell me everything I would need to buy to be ready for him.

On Thursday, Justin and I went to the pet store to get the necessary supplies, along with an excessive amount of toys and blankets that I couldn't resist.

On Friday night Caitlin came over and brought me my new little man, Orlando. He was so tiny, even for a kitten, but was very alert and outgoing with me. He had a personality, was a little bit silly. Caitlin said he liked me, and I was smitten. She took a picture of Orlando and me with my camera, and asked me to send her a copy for the vet's office. In my email to Nico, I included the picture as an attachment, assuming he'd find Orlando as wonderful as I did.

Early Sunday afternoon, Nico called. I knew right away something was off, because after I'd missed multiple calls, he no longer tried to reach me on the phone unless we had set a time. It was a conversation I'd dreaded. We'd avoided it too long, but still didn't want to confront it directly, so he started by asking about my Orlando. We spoke in Italian.

"You have a new roommate?"

"Isn't he cute?" I asked.

"Yes, very, but he is quite young, no?"

"He's a kitten, they think about 10 - 12 weeks, but obviously can't be sure."

"So your parents will take him?"

"What?" I didn't follow. "Why would they take him? I just got him."

"When you come to stay with me. He can't join you, he would have to go through quarantine."

"Oh..."

"Plus cats live, 15, 20 years? What if we have to go to Benin, to Kuala Lampur, to Chile, to wherever else I might get assigned some day for preservation projects? We won't be able to bring him with us."

I was silent. Then, he switched to English.

"Unless, you don't plan to be with me."

Checkmate. What he said was obvious, but when I had sent him the email the implication never even occurred to me. My response was weak. "Nico, I love you."

"I see. And how does that affect your plans, Claudia?" He was back in Italian now.

Floundering, I mustered, "I have great feelings for you..."

"And Justin? What are your feelings for him?"

There it was.

"I promise you, nothing has happened with him. Yes, we are friends, and I know I spend a lot of time with him, but I swear to you, at no point have I crossed a line. At all."

"If you are concerned about crossing a line, that means it exists." The words landed with such gravity. "You see a line to cross with him. Lines only appear when you want something on the other side of them."

"You misunderstand me, you are being too literal." I was starting to get frustrated, struggling with my Italian, trying to think clearly in Italian but words were coming to my mind in Spanish. Finally in English, I pleaded, "We're having confusion in the translation here. Please, calm down, and let's talk this out tomorrow when we're both rested."

"Claudia, no." The stern voice was one I'd never heard from him. In crisp, deliberate, Italian he slowly pushed back, "Do not blame language for your behavior. Whether you have acted on it or not, you are attracted to someone else you see regularly, while pretending you still love me. Respect me enough to be honest."

"I do respect you."

"I respect you too, enough to tell you that you need to take some time to think about what you really want. We both do."

"Nico, I'm sorry."

"Enough, please. Give me some time. I will be in touch. *Ciao*."

"*Ciao*," I barely managed to reply. He was still on the line, hesitating. As I was just about to say something more, he hung up.

The call made me uneasy, and I had trouble sleeping that night. During the week, I was distracted, unsure if he would actually get back to me, wondering if I should try to reach out to him by email or phone. I knew what I needed to say, that it was time to call it quits. I didn't have the heart to do it. I adored him, and didn't want to hurt him.

The stubborn part of me also didn't want to prove everyone right, from my sister to Lorenzo to, unfortunately, Cinzia. After all, I had kept my promise to Nico. I had left Garrett, I'd stayed in touch, I'd made plans to see him—well, I'd discussed making plans and intended to see him—but regardless, I had been faithful to him.

The wait was miserable as I warred with myself. Finally, the email arrived. It was unlike any I'd ever read from him. I didn't know Nico was capable of being so distant. He skipped our usual greeting, not asking how things were on my side of the world.

Claudia,

I am writing in Italian to ensure my words are precise. I will also translate this full message in English below so my meaning is clear. It is apparent to me that my life priorities have become confused. I need to focus on my studies. Until I complete my degree, I cannot begin my work in saving history across the world.

Thus, I will postpone my trip to the U.S., indefinitely.

As to the nature of our relationship, I was also confused. My belief was that you saw yourself with me for the long term. I know you told me when we first met that you never thought about the future. Lorenzo tried to tell me, too. Unfortunately, I was too in love to believe your passion for me would cool, as it now has.

You say you love me, and I believe you do, but not the way you did. The way you love me now is how you love Fiorella. That is not enough for me to continue devoting myself to.

I cannot blame you for your nature, I believe you did try.

You are who you are, I am who I am.

> *Please know, I don't hold anger toward you, and I do hope we can maintain a friendship. I do not wish us to disappear from each other's lives.*
> *Give Justin my regards, as I am sure you'll see him soon.*
> *Take care,*
> *Nico*

So, that was it. The magic was dead. Whatever had been wrapped around us, protecting us, keeping us together for almost a year in spite of the distance, had been broken. I knew he was right, and even started to experience relief that he'd made it so easy for me to just say, "OK, you're right, it's over." Not wanting to delay, I sent my awkward reply.

> *Nico,*
> *Thank you for your email. I understand your logic, and agree with your decision to postpone your visit. I am glad we can still be friends. You are a special person, you mean a great deal to me, and I would hate to lose you completely.*
> *As for Justin, I plan to take a break from seeing him for a while. I don't think he's been the best company for me to keep, and it would be wiser for me to spend some time alone, to understand what I want in my life.*

Out of habit, I was about to add our customary sign off, but realized that to send him hugs and kisses was no longer appropriate. The nature of our relationship had changed. Instead, I closed with,

> *Your friend,*
> *Claudia.*

———

For a while, we managed to maintain a cordial correspondence, while I successfully limited my interactions with Justin. It was strange at first, taking time for myself. Between Garrett and Nico, most of my adult life had been monopolized by men I should have known I wouldn't end up with. Getting together with Justin before sorting out my own wants and goals would be a mistake.

From time to time I was sad that Nico and I wouldn't be together, but he was right: it wasn't going to work out, it wasn't really what I wanted. I was glad he'd been blunt enough to say so.

I took Lisa up on her offer and flew out to visit her in San Diego. She confirmed I was making the right call to distance them both. She also pushed me to get out and have lots of random hookups with strangers to help put both Nico and Justin out of my head, advice which I declined.

Justin respected my need for space, and understood when I told him I wanted some time alone after my break from Nico. He seemed genuinely sympathetic, and told me to let him know when I was ready to hang out again. When I did, I was cautious, not sure I was ready to be in another relationship yet. I asked Justin if we could be friends, and see where things went. However, as soon as we started spending time together again, I realized how much I'd missed him. We slipped back into conversation easily, and began seeing each other more and more.

In my emails to Nico, which admittedly became more sporadic, I tried to remain neutral, omitting any mention of Justin. It became difficult to do, since an increasing amount of my life involved him. I didn't want to hurt Nico's feelings by including details about the man who had played a part in our break up. Nico saw right through me, and eventually asked me how Justin was doing. Being friends with Nico was harder than I hoped.

That spring, when Fiorella and Lorenzo came to visit, they immediately liked Justin. I was pleased he made a good impression on them. He found them as warm and loving as I'd built them up to be, and we all had a wonderful week together. My Italian friends accidentally slipped a few passing references to Nico, but overall made a concerted effort to avoid bringing him up intentionally.

With great sadness, one evening over after dinner drinks I admitted to Lorenzo he had been right. I hurt Nico. He was gracious enough not to say, "I told you so."

I asked him directly how Nico was, if he'd fallen in love with anyone else yet. Lorenzo was evasive, so I let it go. Fiorella was more blunt: Nico wasn't doing well, and hadn't been for some time.

He was wrapped up in his studies, not taking very good care of himself, and was constantly on edge when they did manage to get him to take a break. Despite the fact that Nico was the one who essentially called things off with me, he was resentful of what he perceived as my mistreatment of him, and had made his disappointment in me widely known among our friends. I didn't bother to defend myself, or fill in gaps in their knowledge. Even though I hadn't cheated with Justin, I couldn't deny his influence on my changing affections toward Nico.

I don't know what they told Nico when they got back to Italy, but I noticed the emails from him became notably colder, and less frequent.

—

Somewhere along the way, I can't quite say when, Nico stopped writing. It was strange how easy it was for him to fade away from my life, and stranger still that I hardly even took note of the final moment. I know it was somewhere around the time Justin and started discussing if we should move in together. We both voted against it, because while we were in love, we were also scarred from previous breakups. Neither of us wanted to go down that messy road of moving in and moving out again, so we decided not to, unless we reached the point that we wanted to be married.

The early years of our relationship weren't always easy. We'd each been wounded, let down, betrayed before, and sometimes kept each other at a distance, looking for signs that it was time to cut and run. Justin and I each overreacted to things that, in retrospect, weren't a big deal at all, but when you're looking for reasons to be hurt, you'll nearly always find one.

Over time we accepted that we were not each other's past, that we couldn't assume the worst or hold each other accountable for things previous partners had done. We began to communicate with fierce openness and honesty, which was a challenge as neither of us was used to being vulnerable without consequences.

We focused on this new phase for each of us, and committed to keeping the past in the past, not worrying about the future, relishing only the present moment. As a result, our relationship grew stronger, into the kind of mature, adult love neither of us had ever really experienced. We brought out the best in each other, supported each other, challenged each other, grew together.

Our families and friends were thrilled, but not surprised, when we married. Well, my family was a little surprised that the wedding was in a church, but it was important to Justin, and I didn't mind. Plus it scored major points for me with his parents, who were also wary of their son having his heart stomped on again.

Justin and I settled into 20 years of domestic bliss. We traveled, but I never made it back to Italy, and sadly over time lost touch with every one of my friends there. Nico, Fiorella, Lorenzo, Livia, Matteo, all of them became permanently settled in my past, a different life, when I'd been a different person.

They faded along with everyone I'd lost touch with from college, high school, middle school. I could recall them only as sketchy outlines, light approximations, once living beings now transmuted into memories. Justin and I had our own friends, formed our own family, and our life was filled with adventures together. The way I'm wired, there wasn't a place in my brain to hold on to people who weren't presently in my life.

One night as Justin and I watched a movie, a romantic yet tragic French musical from the 1960's, something triggered a memory of Nico. Nothing specific that reminded me of something we'd experienced together, but it took hold of me. It wasn't just the normal flash, but a strong urging to look him up.

Paying only half-attention to the rest of the film, I wondered what I would find. How accomplished he must be, surely published in all the major journals of his field.

Was he traveling the world on assignment, or perhaps had he become a professor? Or did he get to do both?

I imagined what his wife must look like. Tall, willowy, chic, intimidating in her sophisticated beauty but with kind eyes. In my head she was Swiss or Scandinavian, perhaps Baltic, anything but Italian. She would be some kind of human rights lawyer, or something equally consequential. She spoke often at conferences, was revered by colleagues, and had no problem calling out nations and their leaders for violations.

They probably had several kids, all adorable and accomplished, perfect little replicas of their parents, proficient in at least five languages, destined to change the world for the better. As a family, I was sure they'd lived on multiple continents.

After the movie, Justin and I walked our dogs, and I was so tired that I fell asleep immediately after getting ready for bed. The next day, though, I remembered Nico, and as I made my tea before work, I typed his name into a search engine. No results. That was odd, but I had to hop on an early meeting, so I shrugged it off and decided to look again later.

Throughout the day during breaks I returned to my search, but still nothing. The afternoon at work became hectic, so I forgot about looking for Nico, but over the following days I picked it back up, and became increasingly obsessed with finding information.

I tried to locate him on social media channels, but he wasn't on any of them. This wasn't a total surprise, as he'd thought they were silly when they first came on the scene. So apparently he never succumbed to peer pressure to join any of them. Or maybe he briefly had, but quit them over time. No matter; plenty of people aren't on social media. But most of our mutual friends were, so maybe I should start with them, see if I could find some clues on their profiles.

It had been years since I'd seen or heard from anyone in Italy, and I was unprepared for the emotions that hit me. I saw Lorenzo and Fiorella were married, parents to a little girl, Matilde. Matteo and Livia also had children, who were attendants at Fiorella's wedding. They all looked so happy, a little older than I remembered them in my mind, but still the same loving people I'd been privileged to call friends.

For a brief moment, I felt hurt I had not been invited to the wedding. Feeling left out was not a sensation I often experienced, but at first sight of the photos I felt it sting. This quickly faded when I remembered that I hadn't invited them to my wedding to Justin, hadn't even considered it. Not because I didn't like them, but because they weren't part of my life that way anymore.

Curiosity then got the better of me, and I looked up Cinzia. She wasn't connected with any of our friends, but nevertheless, I found her. She was married to a much older man who had a kind face. From what I could piece together, his family owned some kind of nature preserve, and the two of them helped by fostering injured wildlife during recovery.

What an unexpected turn for her. She looked content, though, which made me glad. I wished I had tried to reach out at least once after I got home. But then, wouldn't she have fallen out of my life anyway, like the rest of them? After all, in all these years, when that last trip to Italy popped into my head, I really only thought of Nico.

None of these other people who, for a brief time, had meant so much to me that I had traveled the world to be with them, had stayed in my life, because I had made no effort to keep them there. How was it possible I'd let them all slip away? They had been precious to me, but for such a brief time. I realized I was going down a rabbit hole, and tried to shake it off and console myself at having reached a dead end. None of these friendships existed anymore, and I couldn't imagine reaching out to people who were now practically strangers to ask them for help on a desperate search I was embarrassed to be conducting.

This deviation was doing nothing to help me on my quest, so I compartmentalized it, to deal with another day. For now, my mission was Nico, and he wasn't in any of their photos, not the wedding, not vacations, not any parties or other events. I went back to search engines, all of them, in private browsers, on different devices, sure that the lack of results must be user error on my part.

Nothing came up since 2012. Ten years of non-existence. There were a small number of results prior to that, and I chased them all as if they were the next part of a scavenger hunt that would lead me back to him. Most of it was passive mentions in old PDFs or on academic websites.

He was cited in some journals, earned some student recognitions, listed as a speaker on occasion. There he was in Stockholm, then in Geneva, next in The Hague. I found a few editorials he wrote, but they were oddly bitter in tone, as if they were dictated to him by someone else. There was no sign of his voice in them. There was a gap of a few years after that.

Finally, I encountered the strangest clue of all, the last sighting of him. It was a newspaper article, written in Spanish, blasting Nico for the presentation he gave. The article was about a press event in Peru, hosted by an international tech conglomerate at which he was apparently an executive. I was confused, surely it couldn't be the same Nico, but the article had his full name, and mentioned him as hailing of late from Italy.

The article was brutal. The author picked Nico apart for his accent, his poor Spanish vocabulary, his demeanor, for being an Italian, for a litany of reasons. The author seemed to take personally that Nico was an outsider, viewing Nico as an uppity European coming to the author's side of the world to teach his country how to behave ethically, as if, he pointed out, Europeans would know anything about ethics.

Here the author really dug in, accusing Nico and his fellow executives of corruption, of keeping company with questionable, high-powered individuals, of cavorting with celebrities and models. The author asked how someone who keeps the company of women who make their money shedding clothes is in a position to tell anyone else what's good or right. The author ended with an angry call to action to expel these global companies and their phony managers out of Peru, out of South America, out of our hemisphere.

The experience was surreal, as if it was a nightmare where things only make sense because your sleeping mind accepts dream logic. Nothing I had read squared with the man I had known and loved. It didn't seem like him at all. Why would my Nico have worked for a soulless tech company that had nothing to do with his calling, his passion, his mission? That wasn't who he was. I desperately searched for anything else, but that was it.

Dread filled my senses. What happened next? I couldn't quiet the storm of thoughts swirling in my mind. The tone at the end of the article scared me. Had something happened to him because of it? Had he really been here, on my side of the world, and I hadn't known? Why had he never let me know? We could have tried to meet. Most of all, I kept coming back to what happened to him after that article.

If there had been a larger scandal, or some resulting disaster, surely that would have made the news in either Latin American or European outlets. Nothing. On and on I searched, while trying to stave off the guilt mounting, guilt that over the past 20 years I had tucked him away in my brain, occasionally trotting him out for moments of imagining fantasy reunions, when the whole time he could have been in danger, suffering. Weakened, I began typing in new search terms: obituary, death notice, deceased. I felt physically ill, as if my neglect had been the cause of any harm that had befallen him.

———

Although I thought I'd been running a covert research campaign, Justin could easily tell I was preoccupied, and asked me what had been troubling my mind so much lately. As always, even the most difficult topics were easy to discuss with him once I opened up. I laid out for him the details and the frustration, and my fear. It was an exhausting confession, and I was grateful I didn't have to worry about any jealousy on my husband's part on top of everything else I was dealing with.

Justin was reassuring, comforting me that surely Nico was ok, he was probably just living a very private life. He recommended I try getting in touch with some of my old friends from Italy if I was really concerned. I reminded him that I had lost touch with them all, and felt awkward at the notion of getting back in contact with them only to ask them about Nico. He said if I wanted his help he was happy to provide it, but I told him I was going to look around on my own a little more tonight. "The pups and I will be watching TV if you need us." He kissed me, and gave me a hug before leaving the room.

It felt as if I was chasing a ghost, and for a moment I doubted myself. Was Nico even real, or just a figment of my imagination? Was it possible I had forgotten the facts so much that I didn't even remember how to spell his name? While, as a rule, I wasn't a sentimental person who held onto things, I did have a few generic boxes of unsorted memories, photos, trinkets, ephemera, personal time capsules that survived several moves but had never been opened.

It was already late, but I was inspired to dig through the closet in my studio, rummaging through the few small containers of my past. As I only had several, it didn't take long to locate the one from my Garrett era, which didn't exactly prompt warm feelings. I actually spent long stretches of my life having forgotten he ever existed, let alone nearly became my husband, so the reminder was unpleasant.

My Italy journal was there, along with two packets of photos which had never been organized into albums, the journal Nico bought me, a few little scraps of paper from the trip, and a bundle of letters he'd sent me during our... for lack of a better word, courtship. I pulled out the photos first, flipping through them, immersed in the memories of that life-changing trip. There were Lorenzo and Matteo, there was Livia, there was Cinzia hugging Fiorella, there was the street magician, and there was Nico. And Nico. And more Nico. He was there. He had been real, he looked just like I remembered.

Turning back to my laptop, I was sure I'd find him this time. I started with his family. I found his brother Davide, living in Abruzzo, and his sister, Ginevra, near Verona. His parents, Albertino and Cosima, were still alive, as well. I searched through all of their social media, but no signs of Nico.

Next I opened the letters, but the intensity of emotion was too painful to read them word for word. Instead I glanced at one, then the next, dropping them to the floor. Too much came flooding back all at once, conflicting feelings I couldn't reconcile. My cheeks flushed, and I found myself nearing tears. After the letters, I was too frightened to open the journal, unprepared to go back to that beginning ember, that weekend that introduced me to the idea that I could feel both physical and emotional passion for one person. Instead, moved to action, I doubled down on finding him.

There was only one thing I hadn't tried. Reaching out to him directly. Opening my laptop, I logged into my old email, from before I was married. I entered his email address into the search, and saw the last email he'd ever sent me. He was preparing to finish his dissertation and apologized that he'd be a while before writing again. Noting the date, I then looked at the sent emails...and discovered I hadn't responded to the message. My memory had been mistaken; I was the one who had stopped writing.

Rather than process this information, I chose to move forward. Selecting a new email, I started automatically composing, the barrage of questions flowing from my brain through my fingertips and onto the screen in an instantaneous motion.

In no particular order, or coherent single language, I saw them piling up on the screen: How was he? Was he ok? Had I hurt him? Why was there no record of him? What was he doing? Was it ok for me to reach out to him? Where was he living? Was he happy? Could he confirm he hadn't disappeared, had not suffered any physical harm? Was he alive? Did he even remember me? My adrenaline was racing, my heart beating its way out of my chest, frenzied.

About to hit send, I caught the journal again out of the corner of my eye, and a nagging feeling delayed me, moving me to doubt the outcome of my email. What happened next? What if he never responded? Would that confirm my worst fears that he was lost somewhere, or would it simply indicate that he wasn't interested in communicating with me? It certainly wouldn't provide closure. What if he was angry or rude? What if he was indifferent, dismissive? What if he wanted to strike up our old friendship, start a frequent back and forth exchange: was I ready for a renewed relationship with him? Or was I just trying to satisfy my curiosity?

Picking up the journal, I forced myself to read it all, slowly, absorbing every detail I'd felt necessary to capture at that time. The account matched my memory in terms of the sequence of events, the interactions, the conversations, the physical engagements. However, there was something else that struck me: the context. I always thought of Nico in terms of being pre-Justin, but looking back through the journal, he was clearly post-Garrett.

The realization that my entire trip had been colored by my discontent with my home life was jarring. I wasn't just having fun in Italy, I was having fun at all, which I hadn't consistently experienced for years while engaged to Garrett.

I wondered how much of my experience with Nico was shaped by the contrast he provided to my displeasure with Garrett. From the way it was written at the time, when I really looked at it, there was nothing special in particular about Nico, but about the situation. He was a break from reality just when I needed it. Would I just as likely have hooked up with anyone in that circumstance?

Had I given Nico too much importance in that moment, and in my memory? Was he really just a man who had appeared at an opportune moment, useful in helping me sabotage my engagement? Had my sister been right in her assessment after all: Nico was nothing more than an excuse I needed to break things off with a man I didn't love, but didn't have the courage to leave?

Where was the love for Nico the person, the appreciation for him as an individual? It wasn't in the journal.

Suddenly, all of the momentum that had propelled me toward Nico, and only Nico, came to a halt, as if I'd been in a trance and snapped out of it. The fog of memories and longing lifted, leaving me only with myself, in my present: a woman consumed with a pointless quest, tilting at the windmill of recapturing magic from a weekend romance so long ago. I deleted his address from the "To" line. Scrolling the cursor over the "X," I closed the draft, selecting not to save.

My hand then continued without pause, clicking onto the search bar in my inbox, typing in his address. Every message he had sent displayed before me, and as if on autopilot I selected them all, and deleted them. I repeated this in my "Sent" folder, deleting those as well. Finally, with no thought, no emotion, I went to the "Trash" folder and emptied it. Permanent delete. In less than one minute, the history of us, which had survived for over two decades, was gone, erased, irretrievable.

Well, mostly. There was still the physical evidence to consider. What to do with it? This had all happened, but it was never going to happen again. The madness of searching for him so fervently that it had overtaken my life left me feeling slightly embarrassed at myself, glad no one but Justin had witnessed it. What was I thinking? A momentary glance at the trash can, filled with paint-covered rags and pencil shavings, with plenty of room for the artifacts of my nostalgia... but no, that felt wrong somehow.

Neatly stacking the photos, I tucked them into the journal, put each letter and card in their corresponding envelope, and gently replaced it all in the memory box. Concerned that temptation might return, I moved it to the back of the closet, placing various art supplies over it, hoping that was enough to help me forget about it, effectively buried.

I held on to one picture, though: the photo Nico had taken of me in front of the street show, that first night we spent together. It seemed possible I could enjoy this memory as a singular moment that was about me, not Nico. There were so few smiling photos of me during that time of my life, and I was glad to have one. Justin would probably like it, too. He was always tickled by old photos of me from before we met, like they were missing puzzle pieces, clues to help him solve the mystery of me.

Leaving my studio, the excitement and emotions of the search slowly drained, like a fever breaking. I remembered when I'd had pneumonia years before, and this was not far from the emergence from delirium I'd experienced then. Beginning to feel almost normal again, I closed the studio door behind me, and walked toward the living room. There was Justin, curled up on the couch with our dogs, laughing at the same reruns he always watched.

Standing behind him, taking in the scene, I spent a moment thinking about how much we've been through, the life we've built together, the people we've become, and felt a wave of fondness and contentment wash over me. As I walked to join them, the dogs made room for me to settle onto the couch. I snuggled into my husband, and our dogs draped themselves over my legs and feet. In my brief obsession with chasing down my past, I had lost sight of my present. Time to get back to it.

The Red Lights

—

"Life should not be a journey to the grave with the intention of arriving safely in a pretty and well preserved body, but rather to skid in broadside in a cloud of smoke, thoroughly used up, totally worn out, and loudly proclaiming
'Wow! What a Ride!'"

— Hunter S. Thompson

Her grandmother made her brave, but her mother kept her safe. Clara was often torn between the influences of the two most important women in her life, but when it mattered most, it was their combined wisdom that saved her.

As a young girl, Clara lived a few houses down the street from her grandparents. Her extended family all lived within a few miles of each other, which Clara cherished. She liked that every day after school she and her brothers walked to her grandparents' home, where their grandmother, Dolores, had snacks waiting for them. While they ate, Dolores shared fantastical stories woven from her culture, with a touch of her own imagination.

While Clara's two brothers, Iván and Saúl, disregarded these tales as an old woman's ramblings, Clara believed in every word, absorbing and memorizing the details as if they were her own memories, events that had literally happened to her. Once a story took hold, she'd replay it over and over in her mind, enhancing it with her own modifications.

Each night when they got home, Clara would repeat the latest story, and her mother, Teresa, would spend the evening trying to convince Clara that it wasn't real, and not to take her grandmother's words too seriously. "It's the way she was raised. Our family tells stories as if they are historical fact, but almost nothing they say is real. Just remember, it's not true."

Clara loved her mother, but she wasn't sure who to believe. Teresa always told her to respect her elders, so wasn't it disrespectful not to believe Dolores? And why would her grandmother lie, anyway? Clara tried to receive her grandmother's story with skepticism as her mother advised, but in spite of herself she was swept away each time.

In Dolores's stories, the supernatural was part of everyday life, and there were signs of this everywhere. Dolores gave Clara guidelines for interpreting these signs. Even everyday items were imbued with magic. Pointing at the gargoyles on top of a building downtown, Dolores advised, "Be on your best behavior. At night they sweep the city looking for criminals." Clara began to assume everything around her was anthropomorphic.

There were also rules for how to engage with the supernatural. Clara tried to keep track of Dolores's warnings, including:

"Beware of animals that can speak, they are demons trying to trick you. Ignore them."

"Never look an owl in the eye, they are demons trying to snatch your souls."

"Don't let a black bird land in your yard, or they will curse you. Snap your fingers and expel them in the name of Christ."

"Don't talk to the dead in your dreams, and never let them touch you! They are demons in the guise of those you love. They want to trick you into giving up your soul. Make your dream self run away."

Essentially, everything was a demon. This last warning caused a number of distressed awakenings, after Clara saw her departed father. Anytime he appeared in one of her dreams, she had to fight her dream-self's impulse to run to him, to embrace him. She woke up feeling guilty she almost fell for a demon's trick, but also for wanting to hug her father anyway.

Any time Clara repeated their grandmother's warnings to her brothers, they teased her about being gullible. Teresa tried to counteract the warnings, and even confronted Dolores occasionally. Clara overheard one of these arguments one night.

"Mom, please, you have to stop telling her these things, she believes you!"

"Why shouldn't she believe me? I'm her grandmother!"

"Because it's scaring her! It's natural for Clara to dream of her father. He loved her very much, and she loved him. You know how close they were! Those dreams should be bringing her comfort, and you've twisted them into nightmares!"

"Just because you don't believe the danger doesn't mean I shouldn't arm my grandchildren with knowledge. It could save their lives. It could save their souls!"

The arguments never reached a productive point, usually ending when the two tired parties gave up and agreed to change the subject, leaving Clara conflicted over which reality she should live in.

On occasion, Teresa tried to point out that not all omens are bad, and that many cultures see signs of good fortune and blessings everywhere. In this way, she tried to accept her daughter's affinity for the supernatural, while not reinforcing Dolores' tendency for the dark and morose.

"Take owls, Clara. Your grandmother says they are evil, but in some traditions, they are symbols of wisdom and strength. Snakes don't always represent a threat, for some people they mean a new beginning, like shedding your skin to keep growing. And look at insects: they aren't all negative warnings. Seeing a praying mantis means good things are headed your way." Clara embraced this approach, and appreciated her mother for not trying to discourage her belief entirely.

Dolores and her husband, Al, loved nothing more than throwing parties, and the entire extended family frequently gathered at their home for all manner of occasions, special or otherwise. These parties began around noon, and often lasted until after midnight. At some point during the party, the younger children would be sent to take a nap in their grandmother's room. (She had kept a separate room since Al returned from the war. He became violent toward her during a night terror from which she couldn't wake him, and for her safety she never fell asleep in the same bed with him again.)

Dolores' room was small and cluttered with too many photos and mementos from her children and grandchildren. One had the impression of a permanent dust film just over every surface and object, giving everything a visible blanket of nostalgia. A vintage perfume atomizer looked to be from the same era as a more recent fast food toy strewn across the vanity. The window over the dresser was covered with patterned curtains of thin fabric that allowed light to pass through, making it difficult to fall asleep. Clara usually watched this light spread across the ceiling, making shadows along the peaks of the stucco.

During one such party, near Christmas, Clara threw up early in the day. Clara was quarantined to her grandmother's room for the rest of the afternoon and evening. Family members took turns coming back to check on her and to replace the cold, wet washcloth on her forehead. As night approached, a terrifying red glow trickled in past the curtains. Her grandfather had decided to use southwest-themed decorations that year, and strung a chain of lights shaped like red peppers along the exterior of the house.

To Clara's fevered mind, the red lights transported her to a space just short of sleep, where was able to see her body as if she was floating beside it. Looking down at herself covered in sweat and wrestling with her grandmother's quilt, Clara had the impulse to reach out, but she assumed there was probably some demon's trick waiting for her if she did. Observing herself, a sharp sound surprised her.

The window was forced open, the pane sliding up. A head popped in through the window, followed by an arm and a leg tangling with the curtains. Finally, the man's full body appeared, sliding over the dresser, pulling a large hunting knife from behind his back. He approached the unconscious Clara, and as he began to stab her, the dissociated Clara floating above screamed.

Everything marbled into a terrifying swirl of red and black smoke, until Clara's consciousness returned to her body, as she shot up in the bed. Her aunt and uncle passed the room and heard her screaming. Waking her, Clara's uncle reassured her while her aunt took her temperature, which registered at 104.4 degrees Fahrenheit.

Clara was vaguely aware of being taken to the hospital, Teresa repeating that she was going to be fine, sounding more as if it was to convince herself than Clara. Hours later, Clara awoke, and the dream immediately rushed back into her head, filling her with terror. Clara's mother was in a chair next to her bed, holding her hand, and jolted awake to comfort her daughter.

After Clara relayed the nightmare, Teresa patted her hand. "It was all just a dream. Don't worry, it was just the fever. The fever and those stupid, stupid lights. I told your grandfather they were ridiculous... anyway, it was just the fever." Clara wanted to believe her, but couldn't shake the dread.

Released back to her family the next day to finish recovering at home, Clara basked in the attention from Iván and Saúl, who made it their mission to spoil her. All morning they distracted her with constant entertainment, arranging the TV in front of her bed so she could watch them play video games, playing instruments (poorly) for her with made up get well songs, reading out loud from her "Calvin and Hobbes" books, and setting up the Trouble board game within her reach so she could pop the bubble to roll the dice.

Their efforts were so effective that Clara forgot the dream entirely, until her Dolores showed up with a large pot of stew. The smell of the savory broth filled Clara's nose and throat. Closing her eyes, she suddenly saw the man, the disheveled intruder, breaking through the window and charging her with his knife in hand. Seeing Clara's distress, her grandmother asked her to tell her what was wrong, and listened patiently.

"Your mother was wrong, Clarita. It wasn't just a dream. It was a *vision*. What you saw, it's real. It's what will happen to you. Don't look worried! It's a blessing! Now that you know, you can be invincible. As long as you don't see red lights outside a window, you know you're safe. You will know the worst isn't happening to you, because you know that's not how you go. You can use this knowledge to be fearless!"

"MOM!" Teresa's voice cut off this reckless monologue. "What nonsense are you putting into my daughter's head?! Especially now, when she's weak and impressionable? Maybe you should go home." With the frustrated love specific to an annoyed daughter, Teresa shooed her mother out of the house.

No matter how much Teresa tried to erase this talk from her daughter's head, it had immediately taken root. Clara couldn't stop thinking about the implication: she had seen the future, and would be able to take chances with confidence, knowing that she wouldn't die.

Thus began over two decades of careless life choices made by a girl who believed she couldn't die until she was in a room with red lights shining in through a window. The nightmare recurred with frequency, each detail exactly as the first time she experienced it. The renewed visions prompted her to act out more and more each time.

Taking increasingly stupid risks as a child, she showed off to everyone, saying yes to every dare, no matter how dangerous. Growing concerned, Iván and Saúl alerted Teresa to her daughter's antics.

Sitting Clara down, Teresa held both of her daughter's hands, staring directly into her eyes and speaking deliberately. "Your grandmother has always believed in magic, in spirits, in powers. You know I've never agreed with her. But I know you believe her. So, let's say, just for now, she's right about this. You saw a vision of your death. So you know you won't die until that. Fine.

But that doesn't mean you can't get hurt. And living with serious injuries is not a good life decision. So, promise me something. You will think about your safety, you will make smart choices, you will learn to protect yourself and put yourself in situations that keep you safe from harm. Promise?"

This seemed a reasonable compromise to Clara, so she agreed, but that didn't stop her from taking chances. She no longer did stunts to get attention, but she did develop a habit of trying to save the day when someone else was in danger.

During college, when she'd been away from her grandmother's company for some time, the hold her magic once had over Clara began to loosen. Clara became a bit skeptical. She went the entire semester without having the nightmare, which was the longest period in her life that the dream had left her alone, and Clara felt a certain relief at not feeling certain she was doomed to a violent end. She even confided in her brothers that she was no longer under the spell of their grandmother's folklore magic, and acknowledged that she'd been silly to ever believe in it.

"We tried to tell you!" Iván jumped on the chance to rub it in. "Remember when she used to tell people how our grandfather survived the war? The weird nonsense about how he knew he didn't have to be afraid because the mines he swept were in the exact configuration of rocks he'd cleared from a field back on the old ranch? That was a bunch of crap, but she told us—told everyone—like it was literal, recorded fact."

"Be nice, Iván. For all we know, that's a story he told her when he got home, to make her feel like he'd never been afraid since he knew she believed in that stuff. Maybe it's even something he told himself while he was over there, to compartmentalize the actual danger he faced, by convincing himself he was protected by magic and couldn't be hurt. It could be what freed him from his fear, and let him be brave!"

Saúl came to his brother's defense. "Clara, come on. If he'd never been afraid, if he was able to switch into fantasy land and forget he was in the middle of a battle and go through the war brave and unbothered, then why did he have all those shell-shock nightmares for decades after?"

She understood he was right, but still Clara never fully shook off the deeply-ingrained dread of the red lights, and of her grandmother's interpretation, even at an unconscious level. She volunteered as an EMT, and quickly earned a reputation as one of the most fearless responders, ready to throw herself into any rescue operation without hesitation. Sometimes she'd arrive at the scene of an incident and see red lights flashing, and feel a kind of embarrassment that she'd taken a childhood fever dream so seriously for so long.

The lingering effects of the nightmare also presented in other ways during her life. Whether staying at a hotel or renting an apartment, she avoided first floor accommodations, uneasy at the notion that someone could easily break in. Later, when Clara was married, she wrestled with telling her husband, Jeff, the origin of her fear of first-floor rooms, or sleeping in rooms with exterior windows. She didn't consider this superstition, instead viewing it as common sense, which her mother supported.

Clara found her commitment to non-magical reality strained one spring afternoon, when her grandmother called her. She invited Clara to come to her home for the weekend, to attend a party, but Clara wasn't sure she would be able to attend. "I love a party, but I'm not sure I can get away. What's the occasion?"

"My death."

The brief, chipper response caught Clara off guard, causing her to instinctively sit down on the nearby bed. "What do you mean?"

"I'm dying. I can feel it. I always knew the signs, and I've seen them. My time will be up this weekend, sometime after midnight on Saturday. We'll have the party on Saturday, and by Sunday morning, I'll be gone."

"That's not how it works. You can't know. The only way to know your time of death is to plan it... you aren't... planning anything, are you?"

"You mean take my own life? Don't be absurd."

"It's just not possible for you to know."

"Now you sound like your mother."

"I don't know what to say."

"Say you'll come home and help send your grandmother off in style. Make all the other departing spirits jealous."

Despite her unease, Clara agreed, and that Saturday found herself, along with every other member of her family, at her grandparents' home. Her family boundaries had always been quite nebulous; any friend who stuck around long enough became a cousin, aunt, or uncle, so neither the large number of attendees, nor the volume of unfamiliar faces surprised her.

Family, friends, and other assorted guests took turns waiting in line to walk up back to her grandmother's room to sit with her and say their final goodbye. Clara had not been in Dolores' room in some time, and approaching it filled her with dread at what she might see.

Ever since the nightmare, she'd always held a fear of the room, associating it with violent death. Maybe the vision was about seeing her grandmother die. Would her grandmother look sickly, withered, on death's door? Would she convulse and spasm and suffer before passing? She'd seen dying patients as an EMT, but this was different. Is that what the dream was trying to prepare her for?

When it was Clara's turn, Dolores greeted her warmly. "My favorite granddaughter, come to help me make a fashionable exit."

To Clara's surprise, her grandmother looked as vibrant as ever, with blushing cheeks and a smile so intense it made her whole face crinkle into a thousand creases. Clara kissed Dolores on the cheek, noting how warm her skin still felt, how much she still smelled like herself. She was convinced her grandmother had it wrong.

"Clarita, I know you think you've outgrown magic, but I promise you it's real. You don't have to believe in it to be affected by it. Remember your vision. Remember what it means: you can do anything you want until you see the red lights. Promise me you'll make the most of your time before you see those red lights again." Clara promised, and allowed the next family member in to make their goodbye.

A little after midnight, Teresa got Clara and her brothers, leading them into the room so they could stand vigil as Dolores took her final breaths. Around them, people marveled, "She looks so content, she looks so peaceful, she was right, how did she know?" Within the hour, Dolores was gone.

The experience shook Clara, leaving her wondering how short-sighted she'd been to disregard her grandmother's wisdom. Dolores must be right! After all, she was right about her own death. In the days and weeks after, Clara began to look for signs once more, using her grandmother's rules to interpret them.

Over the next several years, Clara started to have a new recurring dream, always identical. In this dream, she walked on her own in the woods, and felt as if she was being watched. No, not watched, that was too passive. Stalked. She was being stalked. She tried to push down her fear and walk calmly, arriving at a clearing. Turning to face her pursuer, she saw a deranged coyote, too large for its species, snarling at her, fangs gleaming. She was hypnotized by the red lights which filled the sockets in place of eyes, and froze, unable to move herself to safety. She tried to make her body move, to climb up, but she was paralyzed. As the demon coyote began to move its paws toward her, she felt a rush of wind above her.

Looking up, she saw a massive eagle, wings outstretched, talons at the ready, swooping over her. For a moment she thought the eagle was going to scoop her up, taking her to safety. Instead, the eagle headed straight toward the coyote. Clara was horrified by the carnage but unable to look away as the eagle shredded the coyote, reducing it to an unrecognizable pile of bones, fur, and flesh. The giant eagle then rested on its prey, turning to Clara, nodding its head toward her.

Although she had seen what it was capable of doing, she wasn't afraid, and walked toward it. She began to bow, deferentially, and as she started to utter her thanks, the eagle touched its wing to her shoulder, suddenly absorbing her into itself. She became the eagle, her spirit inhabiting its body, feeling the blood on her talons and beak.

At this point, she always woke up in her bed, adrenaline racing from the strange thrill of becoming the raptor, the feeling of victory over the coyote, the power and strength of taking on an animal form. Clara wished Dolores was alive to help her interpret the dream, and felt silly sharing it with anyone else.

One afternoon, Clara was out on her bicycle running errands when she had an encounter with a real eagle. She stopped at an intersection, waving on the cars to go first so they wouldn't pull out and hit her. She noticed the drivers weren't looking at her, but at the sky above her. She too looked up, and an eagle flew down over her head, so close she could have reached up her hand and touched it. It didn't seem to notice her and continued flying on its course, but Clara was stunned. She'd never seen an eagle this close before, and had no idea how large they actually look when they are right next to you. She almost lost her balance but steadied her bike.

The encounter made her miss her grandmother terribly. Clara felt like she'd just been part of something mystical and significant, something only Dolores could help her understand. Unable to shake off the feeling, when she reached her destination, she called her mom. Teresa listened, and offered her take. "I think it's a good sign! Eagles are often considered messengers from the gods. Maybe it was your grandmother letting you know she's watching over you, or maybe it was her telling you to be brave and strong, like an eagle."

Surprised at her mother's willingness to interpret, Clara responded, "You almost sound like her, Mom. Careful or you might become spiritual, too!"

"I don't discount that there are things in life we can't explain, or that are more than a coincidence. I simply never believed in my mother's rigid understanding of signs, nor her inclination to read almost every warning as one of doom. In any case, even if it was just a plain old eagle, it's very special that you got to see one up close and personal."

Clara appreciated her mother's willingness to see the extraordinary in the situation, but agreed it was probably just a freak occurrence. However, she wavered in this when she began finding eagle feathers. Over the next few months, at least once a week when walking her dog, Clara came across a perfectly intact eagle feather on their path. She knew it was illegal to collect them, so she would admire them momentarily, then go on her way. Yes, she was supposed to report it to her local fish and wildlife service so they could collect it, but part of her felt that they were meant for her, and her alone, so she never contacted the authorities.

Once, they found three feathers, all on an old stone bench, carefully arranged in a row with uniform spacing between each. Clara felt an urgent need to decide what she believed was actually happening: either some human had come into a cache of eagle feathers and was illegally using them to mess with her (which meant they knew her walking habits and were watching her—a thought that made her shudder) or, an eagle was intentionally shedding them for her to find.

She chose the eagle. Unable to resist, she scooped up the three feathers and hid them in her sleeve, frightened of being caught and having to face fines she could never afford, not to mention the humiliation of being written up in the press as some sort of migratory bird parts trafficker.

When she got home, she quickly hid the feathers, even from her husband Jeff, knowing he would tell her to go put them back where she found them and call it in. Like Teresa, Jeff didn't believe in anything magical or fantastic, and Clara was embarrassed at the idea of having to explain that she believed the dream, the traffic stop eagle, and now the feathers, were all connected as a deliberate message for her, perhaps coordinated by her grandmother from beyond the grave.

The red-eyed coyote dream began to recur more frequently, leaving Clara unnerved each time she woke up. What was she supposed to take from it? Why was she having it? It took over her waking hours, as she began researching symbolism of dreams and animals, looking for consensus on the meanings of coyotes, eagles, the color red, and lights, particularly in the context of bad omens.

She finally opened up to one of her brothers, Saúl, who reassured her that it was nothing to worry about, it was simply her subconscious way of holding on to their grandmother, to make it feel like she was still present. Saúl's explanation made sense to Clara, except of course for the physical feathers she found, but for her sanity she decided to accept it and stop obsessing.

Months passed, and the dream faded. She was relieved each morning to wake up and not even be able to remember her dream from the night before. Jeff noted she was looking more rested. She stopped searching for feathers on her walks. She stopped scanning for eagles in the sky. Life resumed normally, falling back into her routine, for the next year.

Clara planned to meet some girlfriends for an out-of-town bachelorette party. Although it was in the next state over, since it was within a reasonable driving distance, she planned to take her car rather than a plane. About halfway along, traffic slowed, and she saw smoke ahead. Her first responder instincts took over, and she managed to maneuver her car closer to the source. It was a multi-vehicle accident, with several cars scattered across the road, the guard rail destroyed, and an SUV on its side in a ditch.

The scene was chaos, and as Clara sprinted into action, she ordered a woman she passed to call 911. Confident in her commands, Clara started giving orders, recruiting a few people to take charge on crowd control, shouting instructions to the civilians, "Keep pressure here! Don't lift that bandage! Keep her legs elevated! Make sure he stays calm! Don't touch that!

By the time the local rescue vehicles arrived, they found an orderly triage operation, and offered to relieve Clara, but she wasn't ready to stop. She stayed with the crews until the last patient was loaded into an ambulance, and the tow trucks pulled away. The local responders, from the EMTs to the fire crews, took time to thank her before leaving, getting her contact information, offering her beverages and inviting her back to the firehouse to rest up in one of the bunks.

She thanked them, but knew they'd spend the night sharing stories from the scene and how it compared to others, an act of camaraderie she'd typically enjoy, but not tonight. All she wanted was some time alone, and asked for a hotel recommendation. The only place nearby was a roadside motel, which in her tired state was good enough for her. It was only mid-afternoon, but she needed a shower and a nap.

Too exhausted to either drive home or drive on to the party, she called to make her excuses to both friends and family, and found the motel, which was run by a husband and wife team, Mr. and Mrs. Luks.

The wife eyed Clara, covered in blood, soot, and other debris. Clara explained she had been helping out, and the woman nodded, "We already heard about you.

People were saying some kind of guardian angel showed up and saved lives."

Clara was bashful and avoided taking credit, as the husband continued, "You're in luck, a lot of people came over here after that wreck. We've got one room left, and I'm glad we saved it for you! Let's get you a key, and later when you're settled, you join us for some dinner, ok? It's on us! Now you follow Mrs. Luks, she'll take you to your room."

Clara obediently followed the woman to the room around the corner to the back parking lot, dropped her things on the floor, and stumbled toward the shower, peeling her clothes off as she walked. The shower was exactly what she needed, and although she nearly fell asleep standing up, she didn't want to leave the warmth of the water. Finally she wrapped herself in the rough motel towels and collapsed on the bed.

After her nap, she dressed and assessed her situation, having lost track of time. It was still daytime so she went to peek out the windows, immediately panicking. In her post-disaster state, she hadn't realized that her room was on the first floor, facing a parking lot backed into a wooded area on one side and facing a diner on the other. The room was vulnerable from all directions, and the heavy curtains did little to ease her dread at the presence of the two windows. Checking the windows, she ensured they were locked, but still knew she wouldn't feel safe until she moved rooms.

Sending alarmed texts to both Jeff and Teresa, Clara explained her situation, and they each calmed her, telling her just to switch with someone else, and to make sure she got some rest. She returned to the front desk, trying her best to sound calm and reasonable, and asked if anyone on the second floor might be willing to swap. Mr. Luks said it was unlikely, but Clara pressed, stating she'd feel safer on a higher floor. When he repeated that nothing was available, Clara wondered aloud if she shouldn't just drive on to the party, or back home with her family.

Mrs. Luks, assuming Clara was simply exhausted from the ordeal, tried to reassure her. "No need to worry, sweetheart. Nothing bad has ever happened here, and besides, you're our honored guest and no one would let anything happen to you. We wouldn't feel safe with you driving on your own in your condition, not when you're running on fumes. What you need is a nice big dinner and a good night's sleep. Let's get you fed and you'll feel much better. You'll see!"

Mr. And Mrs. Luks smiled at her so warmly she believed they meant it, and while she couldn't let go of her fears, she didn't want to seem unappreciative or distrusting of her hosts. Her heart pounded an alarm, but her mind tried to silence it. It would only be for one night, and there were plenty of people around. The Luks didn't seem like the kind of people who would sit back while prowlers invaded their establishment. And they were right, she was tired, and hungry.

They walked across the parking lot to the diner, which was packed with survivors and witnesses of the crash. Everyone recognized Clara, and suddenly she was handed beer after beer from grateful travelers. Despite her underlying dread, after several rounds Clara felt relaxed enough that she stopped focusing on her first-floor room location, and allowed herself to make friends with strangers. She even enjoyed some people doing playful impressions of her barking orders like a commander. They all meant well.

After the meal, she headed back to her room, the buzz from the alcohol taking over as she walked, steadied by her hosts who walked her back to her room. Mr. and Mrs. Luks wished her a good night, and told her if she needed anything at all, just to holler. They waited to make sure they'd heard her lock and bolt the door before returning to the front desk. She liked them, and appreciated that they made her feel secure.

Despite her earlier nap, sleep was all she wanted. She was too tipsy to worry about setting an alarm, as the Luks surely wouldn't enforce a strict check-out time for her. By now it was dark outside, and as she prepared to call Jeff to say good night, she turned off one of the overhead lights in the room. Her eyes adjusted, and horror filled her body as she was struck by a red glow. She ran to the window, realizing that the diner had red lights on the signs around the top of the building, which filtered into her room through the gap between the curtains.

Panic took over, and Clara tried to breathe normally, but felt dizzy, made worse by the afterglow of the alcohol she'd consumed at dinner. This was her literal nightmare: the windows, the lights, the first floor room. She needed to get out. She called Jeff, terrified, but he didn't answer, and she had no patience to try again. She grabbed her bag, pulling out the pocket knife she traveled with. With a knife in one hand and phone in the other, she called her mom. Teresa answered, trying to calm her now hysterical daughter.

"Honey, honey, it's not real. It's a coincidence. Lots of hotels have red lights on their signs, most do, for the no vacancy. You're going to be fine, you are just tired."

"It's not the hotel sign, it's the diner, and it's coming into my room, just like I saw. Mom, I'm really scared. Maybe I should just drive home."

"Don't do that. You're tired, you've been drinking; you're in no shape to drive."

"But this is it, this is **the** nightmare. I can't stay."

"Just get into bed, and put the phone next to you on the pillow. I will stay on the line until you fall asleep."

"How can I fall asleep when someone's going to break in and kill me?!"

"It was a bad dream, but it was *not* a vision. Visions aren't real. You need to pull yourself together, get some rest, and then tomorrow you can drive home."

By this time Clara was inconsolable, crying, "I don't want to die."

"You aren't, you're going to be fine. Here, tell me where the hotel is. I will come meet you there, ok? I will text Jeff and let him know I'm going to get you. If he's at home I'll pick him up on the way, otherwise I'll drive straight to you. Just stay on the line with me, and one or both of us will be there. I promise, I'll get there as soon as I can."

Picking up the info packet from the bedside nightstand, Clara gave her mom the name and address of the hotel, then sat on the bed, facing the window, waiting. She prayed that her mother would arrive before her killer, and attempted to keep herself awake by repeating prayers over and over, particularly the end of the Hail Mary. She muttered, half to the saint and half to herself, "Pray for us sinners, now and and the hour of our death." Eventually, she fell into a deep sleep.

She began to dream the familiar nightmare; not the red light dream, but the eagle dream. This time it was different. Clara wasn't herself; she was the eagle. She could flap her wings and manipulate her claws, articulating individual talons. Peering down she spied the coyote with its red-lit eyes, and began her descent. Crashing into each other, they engaged in a fierce fight, scratching, growling, screaming, tearing, clawing, and biting. Despite some damaged feathers and a few bleeding bite marks, Clara the Eagle emerged victorious, with the limp body of the coyote sprawled out pathetically across a pile of leaves. She watched the coyote disappear, and the clearing in the woods began to darken.

Red lights.

The woods were filled with red lights, and this time they were flashing. Clara the Eagle's feathers dropped away, leaving her in human form, in a space between the woods and the motel room. She wasn't sure how she'd gotten there, or what she was supposed to do next, when she sensed her grandmother's presence.

"Clara, it's time to wake up," she heard Dolores' voice.

Clara shook her head. "I'm not supposed to talk to you, you're dead."

"Maybe I wasn't right about everything."

"I miss you so much."

"I miss you, too, but it's not time for us to meet again. Not yet. Now, WAKE UP!" At this last order, her grandmother's voice morphed into Teresa's. A chorus of woodland creatures began to cry out at once, and the dreamscape faded away.

Clara was back in the hotel room, the animal sounds diminishing, replaced by the voices of people checking on her. She heard them all around her, a chaotic chorus, and she couldn't follow along. EMTs asking her if she could hear them, her mother and husband pleading with a police officer to let them pass, the officer gently trying to keep them back, Mr. Luks trying to keep everyone calm, and Mrs. Luks demanding they at least tell them if Clara was dead or alive.

Clara attempted to lift her head, to take in everything happening, and saw through blurry eyes a body, bloodied, on the floor by the radiator. She saw the curtains blowing, wind coming in through the window which had been forced open.

Something shiny caught her eye: a knife, a huge tactical knife, clutched in the dead man's hand. Trying to focus her eyes, she looked at the intruder's wild hair, ragged beard, his dark clothing. He must have seen the Luks leave her at the door. He must have been watching, and known she'd be alone. She tried to determine if she'd interacted with him at the diner, but couldn't concentrate. As she drifted away into unconsciousness, Clara wondered if the man's face really looked so cruel, like a coyote.

When she woke at the hospital, her husband and mother were by her side, ecstatic that she opened her eyes. She became aware of pain across her body. Cuts, defensive wounds on her limbs, ached immeasurably. She tried speaking, but it took too much effort. She listened quietly as they explained what happened.

Teresa had stayed on the line with her. She and Jeff were on their way to the hotel, had her on speaker phone, and heard Clara start to snore. They were about to hang up when they heard a noise, something was wrong. Teresa tried to get Clara's attention, but heard only scuffling, farther away, then screams and grunts. Jeff meanwhile called the front desk, begging the owners to call the cops and go to Clara's room.

Mrs. Luks immediately called 911 while Mr. Luks moved into action. When the owner got to the room, shotgun in hand, the intruder was already dead, and Clara appeared dead, too. She had her small pocket knife clutched in hand, covered in blood. Mrs. Luks arrived, carrying a small first aid kit they kept at the front desk. The couple rushed in and tried to help Clara until the ambulance arrived. Although it was Clara who managed to fight off the assailant, she was still alive after that thanks to their quick response.

Clara stared at the ceiling, grateful for the Luks, but unsure how to process what she'd been told she went through. She didn't remember it at all. She just remembered being an eagle, eviscerating the coyote, and Dolores urging her to stay alive.

Jeff stood to go let the hospital staff know Clara was awake, leaving mother and daughter alone. Teresa tried to take Clara's hand, but her daughter winced, flinching. Her whole body ached.

Taking a deep breath, Teresa tried to apologize. "I'm so sorry. You were right, your grandmother was right."

"No," Clara whispered, wheezing.

"Yes, she was, and I didn't believe her. I didn't believe you. I dismissed it. All those years I gave her grief for encouraging your ideas. And all along, she was right."

"If she was right," Clara struggled, "I would be dead. She said it's how I died."

"Well you have to admit, that detail aside, everything was just like you said, just like she said it would be."

"I heard her. I heard her tonight, when I was an eagle. She told me to wake up."

"An eagle?"

"I was an eagle, and I fought the coyote. Then I heard her, telling me I had to live. I talked to her."

"Mom always told me not to talk to the dead in my dreams. And I know she told you, so what business did she have starting up a conversation, when according to her that's what demons do to steal your soul?"

"She was wrong about that, too."

Teresa laughed, then looked serious. "Clara, I love you."

"Love you, too. Thanks for coming to get me."

Jeff returned with the doctor, two nurses, and a police officer. They began to assess Clara and ask questions, examining her gently. The officer informed her that they just needed to go over some routine details for paperwork before he'd let her get back to her rest. He also kindly informed her she had quite a crowd of admirers waiting for good news about her.

Some of the rescue personnel who arrived at her hotel room had recognized Clara as the hero of the car accident earlier that day, and were eager to see her once she was feeling well enough. A number of the other hotel guests, who got to see her in action during the accident and shared dinner with her, joined the first responders, filling up the hospital waiting room. Mr. and Mrs. Luks, dealing with the shock of arriving at a violent scene, were also anxious to see her conscious again. Clara wanted to make everyone feel reassured, but, overwhelmed by the events of the past 24 hours, fell back asleep, smiling at her family.

It took time, but eventually Clara recovered. Her physical scars healed more quickly than her mental wounds. To her relief, she slept well each night, though, no longer dreaming of red lights or fighting eagles. She never had either of those dreams again. She considered the significance of this new part of her life, without the dread of the eventual attack looming over her.

Clara felt like she'd been given an extension, and wasn't quite sure what to do with it. With the support of her family, she rebounded, and returned to work, ready to help but unsure if she'd still have the nerve. Clara had always assumed she would die in a violent confrontation under the red lights. It had given her the bravado to jump into any situation, no matter how imposing. Now that it was over and she'd survived, how could she know she wasn't going to be hurt running into a burning building or extracting someone from a crumpled car?

With excitement, she realized she couldn't know. She had no guarantees, just like everyone else. She was going to have to see what happened.

Reading Group Discussion Questions

1. Which story was your favorite, and why?
2. Were any of these stories in genres you don't typically read?
3. What did you think about the variety of genres?
4. Did you have a preference between the stories with first person narration versus third person?
5. What emotions did you feel during the book, and did any of them surprise you?
6. Which character did you most relate to?
7. A key theme of this collection is how death and grief affects witnesses and survivors. Did any of the approaches to this theme resonate with you?
8. How do you feel about the author's ability to shift voice and tone for each of the characters? Do you feel their voices seemed authentic?
9. Did any of the relationships depicted between characters remind you of your own?
10. If you were to adapt this into a different medium, such as film or television, which story would you want to see first?

Acknowledgements

I am thankful for the support and love of my community, and owe special thanks to so many people I am fortunate to have in my life.

Thank you to:

- **Dan Wueste** for your love and encouragement every day, every step of the way.
- **Alissa Bourbonnais** for being my most dedicated reader and dear friend.
- **Liz Pipher,** who I am grateful to have as an editor and even more grateful to have as a friend.
- **Yume** for curling up on various couches and cushions with me while I wrote and edited these stories.
- **My family, friends, and colleagues** who have embraced my journey as an emerging author, for reading, reviewing, sharing, and showing up for events.
- **Dr. Warren Rochelle,** for being the first professor to tell me I had a distinct writing voice, and the confidence that gave me.
- **Kiran Kumar** for being the first bookseller to believe in me, and for your friendship.
- **The independent bookstores** who have supported me as an independent author, especially Scrawl Books in Reston, VA, the Winchester Book Gallery in

Winchester, VA, and One More Page Books in Arlington, VA.

- **Fairfax County Public Libraries** for celebrating local authors and including me.
- **The wonderful women writers** I am happy to call friends: Amber Del Rocco, Claire Reinburg, Deirdre Clawson, Jadi Omowale, JoAnne Wright, and Starling Hathcock.
- **My readers**, new and returning.

Beka Wueste is an author whose debut novel, "The Unsent Letters of Lucy Prior," earned praise as a "deeply introspective and emotionally resonant novel" (-*Kirkus Reviews*) and whose second novel, "Fireflies in a Jar," was lauded as, "original, deftly crafted, emotionally engaging." (-*Midwest Book Review*).

She is also an award-winning visual artist who exhibits her visual work frequently in regional and national shows.

Born in Texas and raised in Virginia, Beka earned a B.A. in art history from the University of Mary Washington in Fredericksburg, VA, and an M.A. in art history from George Mason University in Fairfax, VA.

An enthusiastic traveler, avid reader, nature lover, lifelong cinephile, and collector of music on vinyl, Beka lives with her husband and their rescue Shiba Inu in Northern Virginia.

Website: www.bekawueste.com
Email: inquiries@bekawueste.com
Instagram: @bekaw13
Profiles: Goodreads | Kirkus Pro Connect | LinkedIn

The Unsent Letters of Lucy Prior
A NOVEL

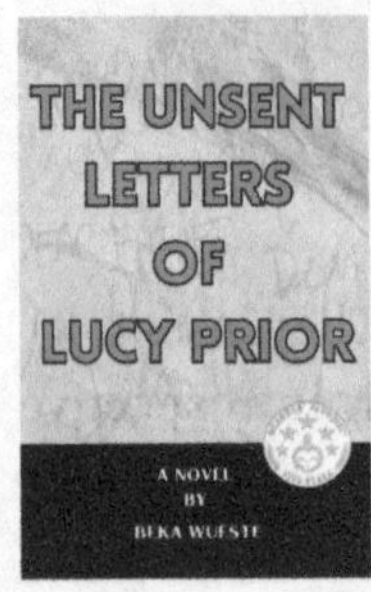

"5 Stars… Author Beka Wueste weaves an intricate and colorful tapestry of Lucy's life, using an unconventional narrative that invites readers to delve into her most profound feelings and emotions. Lucy's story feels incredibly vivid and authentic, as if it belongs to someone living in the real world."**- Readers' Favorite Book Reviews**

"5 Stars…an explosive fictional debut." - **Reader Views**

"Wueste's prose seamlessly balances sharp wit, aching nostalgia, and raw honesty…a deeply introspective and emotionally resonant novel." - **Kirkus Reviews**

Lucy Prior's family thought they knew her, until they discovered the stack of unsent letters...

When Lucy Prior died, she left many of the possessions you'd expect to find in an average home, with the exception of a peculiar set of letters. Written with the knowledge that her death was imminent, each chapter is a letter to an individual who played an influential role in Lucy's life, with whom she had severed connections decades before she passed away. In the letters, she revisits and confronts formative moments throughout her childhood and early adulthood, most of which she had largely repressed or intentionally hidden from even her closest relatives and friends.

Available now: eBook | Hardcover | Paperback

Fireflies in a Jar
A NOVEL

"Original, deftly crafted, emotionally engaging."
- *Midwest Book Review*

"A warm, funny, and quietly heartbreaking look at one woman's struggle to see herself as worthy." **- *Manhattan Book Review***

"Who are you, Sam?" Unfortunately for Sam, the answer is: a lonely, single, closeted, mid-thirties woman with no interests, no close friends, and no romantic prospects. Like a passenger along for a ride, she watches everyone around her move forward, while she remains completely stalled in her own life. Despite longing for fulfillment and companionship, she doesn't know where to start.

Desperate, Sam tries to change her own life for the better, but her actions have unintended consequences for herself and for her family. Luckily for Sam, as she works to overcome her past, she finds help waiting for her from unexpected people in her present.

A mid-life coming of age story for anyone who has ever felt like they don't fit in, don't have everything figured out, or haven't hit the milestones expected of them.

Available now: eBook | Hardcover | Paperback